SERENDIPITY with CONSEQUENCES

SERENDIPITY with CONSEQUENCES

M.E. Fischer

ISBN: 978-0-9994058-1-9

To
M and S
flip sides of my good luck penny

And to
Whitney and Theresa
who made me believe my scribbles were beautiful

PROLOGUE

I don't remember what you were wearing, what I was wearing, the weather, the day of the week but yet there you were standing in a doorway and when you turned your face toward me I distinctly remember the way everything hurt deep inside. Like the Big Bang in reverse, the whole universe sucked down into a tiny pinpoint and in the middle of that aperture was your face.

I stared at my feet as you walked closer because I was afraid to look up. When I stole a sideways glance, a blasé neutral hello I suddenly saw it. I saw you. And I saw you see me too, so I hid. I pulled the shutters down, yanked the curtains closed and you did the same, I think.

I shook your hand politely and it stung. A flash and something was conceived instantly, violently. Bloody and undefined, it scared me so I killed it. I pushed it deep inside and smothered it. Slamming my hands down, I sucked the air out of every thought of what could be might be but would never be. I dug a hole and buried that flame running into the darkness leaving behind no marker.

You clenched my hand in yours and I thought desperately *pull, pull me away.* Tell me there's a car outside and I'll go with you. I'll leave right now with you, damn the consequences. If you'd simply tugged right then, I'd have fallen. Backward, I saw us falling backward onto a bed and I'd be right there, right there with you, inside you, your hands in multiple places simultaneously and your mouth moving slowly up my thigh.

But you let go and I looked away, everything isosceles. Time went one frame click too far where everyone remains frozen in half-life. When you moved, I watched from the corner of my eye and when you laughed I wanted to know the joke and when you moved your lips I had a flash of dark nights and sweat and I felt ill.

You turned away and I wanted to follow. Where were you going and do you want me? Want me with you on your journey? I will carry your pencils to the desk next door. I will hold your lunch while we wait for the bus. I will wait patiently in the hall while you do whatever it is you are doing without me. I wanted to tip up on my toes and fly to you, with you, away from here.

Far away to a dark corner where you would try to stand too close and I would let you.

I cannot forget that first time and when it comes unbidden to my mind I pray to forget you and I hate myself. I abhor my sinful weakness and despise you with a strength beyond all reason, with a power that feels like only God himself could stay my hand from striking your memory down. Desperately I try to rip you from my mind. Grind you up, away on the wind scattering you discarding you as I run, as I run away.

Please…please just be gone from me because I alone must have you but I can't. I cannot have you but I cannot stop. I am in limbo falling forever falling.

At night I lay in my bed and burn. I burn for you.

ONE

I heard you that autumn afternoon with them lined up by your side shooting down that dark runway like lightning. Straight up on a blue flame you flew with them, flew with him next to you up up toward the heavens. Face up in God's arms you rose, spinning slowly through Alaska's autumn skies. *Here is where I belong* you said *where I feel free,* power losing out to science tipping you over sliding drifting twisting back toward Earth. Five brief days a month you appeared above those Cook Inlet clouds a glistening brilliant creation.

How long will you be out, I typed, *because I'll stalk you long time, baby.* Stalk you long time on my laptop live streaming base airfield operations. *Two v. eight today,* you'd sent back. *Then I think the two of us are hitting a tanker and doing some BFM. Rage safely,* I'd replied. *Raging safely* your standard reply *stepping now…love love.*

Thirty minutes later your voice talking to the tower, me folding socks in the salon of our boat. Demon 1, Demon 1 asking Tower for permission to leave, to take off, to head out into bleak wilderness to rage. Your voice streaming a velvet ribbon down to me, wake from Kenmore's float planes slowly shifting the great vessel side to side, those words pulling you out of range as Tower let you go.

Smiling, I knew you were smiling as you pushed it up, nose up you pushed it always too far, you pushed it too far.

Vertical into the September sunlight rolling out above the earth I saw you out there doing fighter things shooting things dropping bombs on things. Far above the horizon in a swirling slicing cloud of black you shot your brothers, laughed, and began again.

Your war calls rang in my head, your wings scraping past shooting the gap through Star Wars Canyon playing your wicked games of tag up there in distant peaks. Mute Denali bright as a copper penny always watching, sitting calmly each time you screamed by as the earth buckled beneath your thundering flock.

Past that mountain's blank face like a bullet, you were already gone from there and on to the next thing. Always headed to the next big thing, breaking things, breaking things like it was your job. He was on your wing that day because you called him friend, called him brother. And so it was him, it had to be him that saw you blazing at the speed of sound from a half-mile away when that light came on when that tiny light flickered on.

Bad luck penny blinding now, Denali turned its cruel face abandoning you as your canopy came off. Ripping, straight up it ripped and off it came with you behind. He blinked, your seat on a yellow flame; that bitch bird going down, your scald-crow drifting slamming into that green ever so slowly.

His voice screaming out *Demon 1 Demon 1* as the forest spread its arms wide consuming swallowing your wreckage in a single snapping bite. Stunned, he ripped off his mask with a sweating trembling hand, a bright flash of light off your helmet visor catching his eye.

Flipping sharply, he shot back around and around frantically dogging your slow descent until a warning buzzer rang out fuel low. And so straight home he sprinted marking that scar of black smoke rising, your parachute falling silently into endless desolation.

Marking a red X on paper tucked beneath strapping wrapped tight around his thigh he came back.

He came back alone.

TWO

When my phone rang an Anchorage extension five hours later and you hadn't yet sent that good-to-go text you send every time, just a simple GTG when you landed, when you returned full of yourself, when you had returned every time before this time with that GTG, I knew.

I knew.

I knew the takeoffs hadn't equaled the landings. And he knew I knew because it was him on that phone. It was him that called. Calling to say nothing while we sat there in suffocating silence. I didn't ask what he wanted because he couldn't say it and I couldn't think straight. There was nothing to say, the words fell out all jumbled up and backward.

"We couldn't find you they couldn't find you. There's nothing at the address you're not at that address Jesus Christ why aren't you at the address he has listed…where are you, where are you," he sucked in a deep breath. Stiffly I informed him it's a PO Box because the post office won't bring the mail to the boat, that the address is a lovely Korean deli down the street from our Westlake marina selling prepackaged tuna sandwiches and ice cream. Heard him crying as if from a great distance, "This isn't the way it's supposed to happen, not like this I'm sorry I'm so sorry."

I could hear Tower talking. Such a stupid thing to make all this available to the public. I leaned ever closer, tuning the phone out shutting him out cranking up the sound, a faceless voice releasing jet after jet into the sun, those birds taking off to be with you. To look for you. To bring back Demon 1.

Your Hellions snapped at Satan's heels, Dicemen laid down all their cards in force because the house always wins. Today of all days the house must win. Unruly Dogs of war now flooded into dusky skies racing, tumbling, clawing from the kennels as I heard the shrill APUs screaming in my head blowing out engines in hard start. Shivering, gripping cold hands over my ears, I tried to drown out the howling, that horrible howling of Tower's soft voice spitting them out in ones and twos.

Cable is up Tower said because safety first. Safety first as they raced toward that bad luck penny.

A tanker preceded angry vultures fuming silently in the hot pits waiting for their shift, for their time. Deep shadows lurking with coiled readiness knowing there was nothing at their destination because that is what you do for family. You go, you go and you keep going until there isn't any more gas. Until there isn't any more time. You go until someone else stops the madness because you can't do it, can't pull it, can't bring yourself to finish it.

Then…his voice said something about arranging something. He would call back or something and a dial tone marked where he had been as it was all stop. It was all stop up there where you were. Where what used to be you would be forever.

The tower began bringing them back reeling those lines one by one. I could see that inky cloud seeping through gray skies gently beginning the slow hungry roll home to the slots, ground control telling them to cross here, hold there, stop on the ramp to the right. That voice, that voice in the sky crying out as they identified themselves in roll call rounding the last point on final.

But your voice was never there. Tower never brought you in. Your brothers flowed in great waves toward base in careful sequence looking for home desperate for home and Tower answered. Tower answered every one as they all came back. Every one of them came back. In the smothering night they all came back but you.

Radio silence. A split second of static and Tower was gone. Everyone instantly gone. Someone had finally pulled the plug on the public feed severing the voices mid-flight. I stood, packed a duffel with two pairs of pants and started the dishwasher. I put your folded socks neatly in our top drawer then stepped off our boat into the soft Seattle rain and stumbled coatless out to Westlake Avenue, my flip flops hard against the dock leaving my boots jumbled up in the closet next to your running shoes and boarded the number 40 bus headed downtown.

THREE

Can you get to the airport? There's a ticket there I bought for you. I bought you a ticket, it's waiting at the Alaska Airlines counter. Can you get there, will you go there? His texts kept zinging in as I sat alone on the Link down to SeaTac clutching my bag tightly. Once there, I TSA PreCheck'd my way silently through security, boarded ten minutes before departure and sat stiffly in a worn leather middle seat during that three-and-a-half-hour flight he put me on.

Thirty-three thousand feet in the air I sat there eating a fruit and cheese plate.

In Anchorage there were three of them in wrinkled olive flight suits waiting in baggage. I saw the marks from the harnesses on their bodies as if they'd only fallen from their jets but I only looked at one of them.

I only looked at him.

Blankly I stepped toward the door out of the airport and they all fell in formation with him at my side. "No bags," I whispered numbly when he reached out, quietly taking that duffel from my hand. We all moved in silence, like they thought I would break if they said hello, how was the flight? How's the family?

Out front I climbed into an anonymous gray government car while he drove, the others sitting behind. At the base's front gate he walked me to a shack where they give out the credentials for people who don't belong. He was the one that answered when the sergeant asked the reason for my visit. I turned and stared at his profile when he answered *personal business* while they stamped my pass and told me I needed an escort at all times.

At some point, I found myself alone in the squadron bar staring blankly at the solitary names hung upside down along the wall. Would you be tacked onto the end? Is it chronological? I stood there silently counting as the owners of the upright patches headed back out into the night to keep vigil over where you turned into dust. There was a hot batch of jalapeño popcorn in the bin, a lieutenant's Snacko duty fulfilled even in the most desperate moments, those random Bullpups slipping in silently with cases of water, their heads slung low. I stepped back unseen into the shadows watching the unspoken hand offs while fuel trucks frantically shot gas into bird after bird rolling through. I imagined you flowing through them, into their intakes, over and around their wings, skipping across canopies as they blew holes through the sky that stole you.

If I could just get up there and see it for myself, see where the heavens tripped you, see where you disappeared into vapor…maybe if I touched the leading edge, the soft skin of the bird that saw it all. The one with you at the end that came home alone, that carried someone that wasn't you back home. He snuck me out to meet her. Pulled over a ladder and shoved me up so I could peer through the same canopy where he watched you depart but it was all curves and angles and sharp points. I couldn't get my head far enough into the cockpit to see it. I couldn't see you at all in there.

Hours passed as I wandered the hallways, waiting. Waiting. Eventually the Eagle showed up, sat me down on a dubious couch and said what I knew was true since I saw that area code pop up. Since I listened to him screaming silently on the line, the tower spinning up the boys for battle, those helicopters out for recovery now it was a recovery mission now.

Where was I staying? Did I have anyone here in town? Was I hungry? I stood up. I just stood up and left.

He fell in behind, coasting in my wake as I went out the door because I needed an escort. Because I didn't belong. I wasn't a spouse but not a stranger. I wasn't legit, just halfway acceptable. A partial person. I couldn't even check into base lodging on my own merits so he signed the ledger for me taking an anonymous key from the desk clerk's bored hand and delivered me gently to a dark room with atrocious curtains, a worn recliner hovering in the corner. He gave me my shoeless bag and silently walked away when I shut the door in his face.

FOUR

"I'm over here, there's a will here at the legal office. There's a problem, I have a problem," I said the next morning into an ancient pushbutton phone strangling my fingers with the cord while the Airman behind the desk pretended not to listen. "They won't let me have the will even though I'm his executor," I said. "I have no proof of rights," I said.

You're not his spouse. You're not in our system, they said.

"They said they don't even know if he's dead," I whispered, shivering in my thin sweater, toes wet from walking in new snow, stammering out I have to wait for them to declare you dead and gone.

Ten minutes later, he ghosted in with the Eagle who stood stiffly upright by the desk and ordered the airman to get that will right now get it right now that's an order and then suddenly there it was, an open manila envelope because someone had come before me pawing at your private things. *I've been co-opted* I thought and pinched it open, pulling out a cover sheet.

There was a name scrawled there in your handwriting. I realized it was his name and the line next to it was dated two years prior. It said if something happened that you wanted him to be the one to call, you would send him to do the dirty job, that he would take one for the team.

I suddenly remembered you turning to me on our car rides home like you did every time saying, "You like him, don't you." I always rolled my eyes and pretended I didn't know what you meant, "Like who? I like all your friends." Every time, you turned your face away from mine and softly said, "You know who."

You know who.

And then I would lie. Boldfaced, I would lie, over and over I lied. *Don't be ridiculous*, that falsehood slipping out so easily even as I couldn't keep it straight in my head always realizing too late you were still talking, as if you hadn't said enough you would just keep on talking. Every time you dug it in, always grinding it down. I couldn't figure out what was happening on those car rides, in that goddamn car every time we drove back to lodging from those dinners when you were right there asking what I would do if you died and me telling you I would be devastated knowing it was the truth.

We'd shared a toothbrush one of those nights wedged into lodging's dark bathroom. "If I packed it in you'd probably end up with one of my friends," you'd snickered, bumping me with your shoulder, "You're a fighter hag. Just admit it." All elbows and awkwardness, I remembered bending over to spit telling you I'd rather poke around in the engines than fly around in those deathtraps like my ass was on fire. Nonchalantly I said our conversation was weird and morbid but I still asked.

Asked what you thought when you saw a future without you, a future where I was with someone else as I stared at the water circling down the drain, "Come on. Be serious. Who do you think I could possibly end up with?"

I remembered you stilled, standing frozen staring deep into wherever it was you went sometimes, softly telling me I should go to him. That I would go to him.

Go straight to him if things went to shit, you'd said. That I would probably end up with him, whispering *you whore* your mouth hot across my breast, your hand pulling me down in that dark room, down together into our bed.

FIVE

I wavered and drew in a gasping breath, my hand crushing your envelope. I glanced at the side of his blank face then across at the Eagle and realized this was just a duty to them, that handwritten name on the line. I was an obligation to them all and I wanted to run but instead I just stood there silently gripping that fucking envelope. I stood there like the single sock you hold onto because that's what you do, you hold onto the other halves of things that are gone because you're gone now and I came here carrying a bag with no shoes.

There was an SUV with its door open outside when I left so I got in it. It went out the gate toward the other side of town, the nice side of town, the drinks at dusk after steak dinners side of town. A house with a door was there but the door was closed so I stood next to it while he put the key in the lock and then I was in. I was in and he was in and pushing me gently to a chair in the kitchen.

Then only silence. There was just silence because I had nothing to say there was nothing to say we had nothing to say to each other. Eventually he got up stiffly and I heard my bag softly drop, a cabinet opening, a blanket coming down over my shoulders. Who went into my room and touched all my stuff, gathered all my things? Who touched all my things. He grasped me under my arms and up I went down to a room in his basement he'd made up for me. A room with boxes stacked against one wall because I wasn't supposed to be there on that bed in that house on the nicer side of Anchorage.

He sat me down and then my shoes were off. I told him to be careful, they were the only ones I had. "I can fix that," he whispered. He gave me a towel and pointed out the bathroom. I used his toothbrush without asking. He told me I was welcome to it when I brushed past him back to the bedroom.

I closed the door then and heard him just inches away holding himself very still before gently sliding down to the floor. Standing there I listened to him sitting motionless on the other side with his back against the wall, waiting. In case I needed him to fetch me a pair of socks.

I choked back the tears realizing it wasn't just duty and honor and obligation anymore. We were family now and he was trying his best to hold on so I could let go. So I could fall down while he came behind picking things up, picking me up, wading through the broken pieces, keeping track of my shoes and opening envelopes even though no one comes behind him. No one is there to catch him when he falls because this is what you asked of him. This is what you wanted. This is what you set in motion two years ago when you put his name on that line, when you chose him over all the others.

I pressed my face against that wall, closed my eyes and I listened as your best friend sat outside my door and cried.

SIX

I woke up to the creaking of the floor above my head. At some point I'd crawled up into the bed and he'd gone away to wherever it was that people go at three o'clock in the morning. Probably to pass out although the fact that I smelled coffee at noon made me suspect he didn't sleep very much either. I put on the sweatpants that had been left folded neatly outside the door and, self-conscious about not wearing a bra, I slung that blanket over my shoulders clutching it to my t-shirt before padding up the steps to the kitchen.

He looked like shit. The creases across the side of his face suspiciously resembled the stitching on the leather couch I spotted in his living room. I peered around his back and saw him standing in front of a fancy gas stove with a spatula in one hand and two eggs in the other. I watched as he twisted his hand to the side, cracking both eggs open sliding them smoothly into the smoking pan.

"What the hell was that?"

"What was what? The eggs? I worked as a breakfast cook my second year at the Academy," he smiled over his shoulder, "Early morning egg-cracker, that was me." Looking quite pleased with himself, he set down the spatula and picked up another two eggs in each hand. He looked back at me and held them over the stove. "Watch this," he said, smacking them against the counter in a single move as he squeezed his fists and suddenly there were four more eggs in the pan lickety split.

"Well, shit."

I laughed silently watching him realize he'd literally put all his eggs in one basket. I made the lame joke and he rolled his eyes, lifting an arm up to a cabinet bringing two plates soaring over my head onto the kitchen island. It was so surreally normal. Two people in a kitchen making eggs. Two people and eggs and plates on a table and you were dead. I swallowed silently, my throat tight.

"You can sit anywhere you want, if you want to sit down. Or not. You can stand, too, that's fine. Whatever you want…is fine," he swallowed and shifted his feet. I realized I was making him uncomfortable lurking in the doorway so I sat. I sat at his black marble island and ate two and a half eggs with a piece of slightly burnt bread while he propped a hip against the counter holding the other plate, fork tines down mopping up his yolks with toast. Who eats toast with no crust? Who eats crustless toast with a fork? With a fork that's backwards? Who does that?

He cleared his throat and I looked up from my toast-with-crust. "What?" My heart sank.

"There's some stuff we should probably take care of today." He slowly placed his plate in the sink and dropped the fork in the dishwasher.

"Why did you do that? Why the fork and not the plate?"

"What the hell are you talking about?" He turned toward me slightly.

"The fork. You put the fork in the dishwasher and the plate in the sink. And you eat crustless toast. Who does that?"

"I do that," he acted offended. "The fork gets all sticky if I let the egg dry on it but the plate doesn't because I clean it up with the toast."

"But the fork just sits there drying in the dishwasher," I said patiently, "You're making no sense. The egg is still drying on that fork, it's just doing it in a different location!"

He leaned forward and stared me in the face, slowly reached under the kitchen sink and pulled out a bottle. Leaning to the side, he reopened the washer door and very deliberately poured a thin stream of soap into a small tray. He clicked it shut, flipped the door up with his foot and threw the latch. I snickered, "What are you doing?"

He stretched out a finger and jabbed a button. "I'm cleaning my sticky fork, you ditzy broad."

"It's a waste of water," I flung a hand up, "That fork is the only goddamn thing in there!" He shook his head. "No, it's not. My bread knife is in there, too."

"You have a bread knife?" Incredulous, I just couldn't even wrap my mind around what was happening. It was just too much with crustless toast and sticky forks and then, suddenly, a bread knife.

"Your goddamn bread came pre-sliced, you dingbat." He blushed and turned away, "Someone gave me that knife. So you can suck it."

He scrubbed industriously at his plate with a fancy sponge and I slid off the stool taking my plate and fork over to the sink holding the blanket carefully shut across my front, "You wish I would." I turned away, I almost got away when he paused for a split second. Just a split second and then softly, "Can you be ready to leave in an hour?"

"Sure," I said, "Where are we going?" choking suddenly on those simple words.

"Medical." He shut off the tap and leaned his arms on the edge of the sink, his back to me, head and shoulders sagging. "There's something there you might want to see."

SEVEN

And there it was. A piece of it, anyway. I leaned in closer and tilted my head from side to side peering down from all angles. Searching, examining intently the tiny part of your face staring back at me from a slip of charred plastic. Your military ID, right there on a metal desk in the Med Group commander's office next to a green plastic letter opener shaped like an alligator.

Your face. Right there.

"Where did this come from?" I glanced up.

The Med Group commander cleared his throat. "We located the ejection seat a few miles from the impact site."

"And?"

"We were able to recover some…items. From the wreckage."

"How many items? How much is left?" I stared at his face but he didn't answer.

I bent over and rested my elbows on the table on either side of that twisted shard staring downward with my forehead in my hands. I didn't know what to say. What do you even say? Look, there's the guy that told me he loved me on our second date and pretended not to notice when I started shoving all my clothes into the back of his dresser drawers, who said nothing when I slept over every single night for months and gave me flowers on a Tuesday for no reason. Hey look, it's that guy, only now half his face is missing.

Actually, I realized, all of him is missing.

I snorted and slapped a hand over my mouth, suddenly appalled. Jesus Christ, what the fuck was wrong with me? I stared across the table at the Med Group commander who gave me that stiff not-smile smile you show the gossipy people after church when you're trying to get out the door to KFC. I turned swiftly and saw him leaning against the wall in the corner of the office staring me straight in the face. He slowly raised an eyebrow and tilted his chin telling me silently to pull it together, you moron as I clapped both hands tight over my mouth and bent over.

I bent over laughing in that office in front of the table holding half of your face.

EIGHT

"That was incredibly humiliating. I don't know what's wrong with me." I felt sick but like I might start laughing again with no warning, the sort of laughter that swells up in the back of your throat with an itchy tinge of hysteria, where once you start you can't stop and it's suddenly all hyenas and great apes and then you're bending over sucking in air like you're drowning. I clutched the side of the front car seat with a sweaty palm. He clicked his seatbelt shut, jingling the keys in one hand.

"He's seen it all, I wouldn't worry about it. Everyone reacts differently. One time I saw a guy throw up in the lobby." He blanched. "Sorry. That was bad. That was a bad thing to say." I looked away, looking down around anywhere but at his side of the car and spied a bag at my feet.

"What's this? I didn't know you were a closeted Macy's shopper." I picked it up and felt something shift inside, "Can I open it?"

"It's for you," he said, "I figured since you only had those silly flip flop things and September is pretty cold here I thought you might need something else maybe…might want something different maybe…" I could see him wondering if he'd picked wrong, made the wrong choice, if he'd done another bad thing. If what was in the bag was a bad thing.

It was shoes. A shiny pair of brand new silver sequined slip-on Top-siders in my exact size were in the bottom of that brown paper sack.

"When did you buy these?"

"This morning before you woke up. I went out and I thought maybe they would have something in your size that you would like because it's a nice store, the nicest store we have here, and I remembered you had really small feet. Like, bird-size feet."

"You asked the salesperson for bird shoes?"

"Yeah. Pretty much," a tiny smile peeked through as he turned his head, checking his side mirror before merging onto the highway. "We can take them back if you want something different or they don't fit. They have all sorts of stuff there. It's overwhelming, actually."

"No, I like them, they're pretty." I turned my hand, watching them sparkle in the afternoon sunshine. "Why'd you pick these? I figured a guy without adult supervision in a shoe store would probably come back with 6-inch red leather heels or something equally ridiculous."

"I remembered when you were up here last summer for the change of command you mentioned you'd always wanted a pair of wizard shoes—"

"Wizard shoes? What the hell are wizard shoes?" I looked at him from the corner of my eye and saw him shift awkwardly in his seat.

"You know, the ones from the movie with the witch that gets crushed by the flying house and all the dancing orange midget people…" His voice trailed off uncertainly.

I stuck out my chin and gave him some serious side-eye, "You mean Dorothy shoes? But those were red! These are silver." He stuck out his tongue and told me that I could have ended up with tacky leopard thigh high vinyl boots just as easily, that the hooker boots were cheaper and he wasn't made of money, to shut my smart mouth and put on the damn shoes. I stacked my old ones on the seat between us and slipped on the

Topsiders. They fit perfectly. I dipped my head to the side and tapped the heels together making a dull smacking sound.

"Sorry, pal. These are busted. That Macy's shyster sold you some broke-ass wizard shoes."

He laughed, whacked me on the head with his hand and tossed my flip flops over his shoulder into the backseat, "Whatever. Nobody up here wants to see your creepy finger toes so broke-ass or not, keep those fuckers firmly on, please. For all our sakes."

The miles passed silently as I admired my shiny wizard shoes while he listened to some crappy country station sing about a dog with a gun. We were turning into his neighborhood when I asked quietly what would happen to your ID. Could I have it back? Does it go to your mom, maybe? Everything went suddenly gray like I was staring down a tube at a brilliant light bulb.

"Has anyone told his mother?"

He sighed, "I called her when I was waiting for your plane to land. Her number was in Andy's paperwork when we got it from the legal office."

I heard your name come out of his mouth and it was just too much. Too much. He said your name and suddenly I wanted out, out of that car, back home without those wizard shoes, back home where you had your whole face. I couldn't breathe I couldn't see anything, just blackness. Everything was thick black and then nothing. There was nothing but your name hanging out there like a huge bell ringing and ringing louder and louder.

His fingers gripped my shoulder, shaking. I could hear him shaking me, his hand hard on the back of my neck pushing my head down between my knees shaking shaking me *what's wrong, what's wrong, are you ok, just breathe, talk to me, please talk to me.*

"I'm ok, I'm fine, I'm ok now," I choked, "I'm ok, I'm ok," as I lied and lied and lied.

NINE

"There isn't anything left to see, June," I said on the phone the next morning while your mother talked right over me. "You can come here and look all you want but there isn't anything to see."

"What do you mean, nothing to see? How can there be nothing to see, nothing to see—"

"There. Is. Nothing. Left."

For the first time in all the years I'd known her she was silent. For a millisecond she considered what that statement meant. I drew in a deep breath, "It was a high speed ejection, June. He was going over Mach 1 when it happened and it's just not…no one survives. No one survives that kind of thing. He's just…there's nothing left." I could hear her grinding her teeth all the way down there in Tampa sitting ramrod straight in a stiff horsehair chair next to her perfect doily collection.

"You're not sad," she snipped. "You get life insurance, right? Andy left you everything. He didn't marry you but you get everything," carelessly she tossed those words out like daggers. "After you move in he didn't care about us, about his family, but you know that already. That boy who called instead of you, he said you go and get his will and now you move on. You just move on."

Homicide. Carnage. I clenched the edge of the counter and glared at the mist dripping down the kitchen window. A red haze and visions of me driving a large steak knife into her eye socket, braining her with a hammer, holding her head under freezing water until she turned blue suddenly flooded my mind.

"Listen, you old bat, I loved Andy," I spit the words out, "he loved me and you know that full well. Eight years, June. Andy and I were together for eight years so I don't know what your fucking problem is with me being here taking care of things. You're perfectly capable of getting on an airplane yourself, you know." Your mother screeched, "My son is dead! I'm his mother and you talk to me like this right now? You treat me this way when my son is dead?"

She slammed the phone down and it clicked loudly in my ear. I set my phone lightly on the counter and stepped back.

"Is everything ok?" He was leaning against the refrigerator behind me and I wondered how much he'd overheard. "Was that Andy's mother on the phone?"

"Yes. It was." I met his quiet gaze, "It was Andy's mother who apparently thinks I'm a gold digging whore who's going to steal Andy's life insurance and run off with the lawn boy." He said *wow* in a low voice, "That's…I'm sorry. When I called her I guess I didn't realize I wasn't supposed to be telling her about the will and stuff. People always wanted to know the details before when…" He glanced away.

"How many times have you done this?" I couldn't comprehend the horribleness of having to do this once, much less doing it more than once.

"Three times."

Three times. Three times. I couldn't wrap my head around it, "Three times? What are you, the squadron's default choice? How often does this kind of thing happen?"

He shrugged, "I don't like to talk about it, ok? I don't want to talk about it anymore. Let's get out of here. Do you want to get out of here for a while?"

"I have to sign some papers first," I rubbed my eyes with the back of my wrist, "Can you take me over to the Med Group? I can't get on base by myself." He hung his head, "I can get you on base, sure. I can do that." He knew what papers I was talking about. He took my elbow gently, "I'll take you over there and then we'll go out, ok? We'll just get out of town for a while, you and me, maybe do some fishing if the weather looks ok. Come on, let's go over there and then we'll disappear, just for a few hours."

When we went through the gate the guard leaned in, "I'm sorry for your loss, ma'am." Quietly I said, "Thank you," and turned my head away.

"How does he know who I am? How does he know why I'm here?"

He shifted uncomfortably and told me the base newspaper had published a photo of you and me the day before that had been taken at last summer's squadron awards ceremony where you had gotten some big fancy plaque and then jumped down off the stage, grabbing me and bending me backward, kissing me with way too much enthusiasm while all the guys egged you on. They'd put it on the front page next to the official Air Force picture of you standing in front of your jet, in front of that jet, jauntily holding your helmet against your hip.

"Can they do that?" I felt violated, "How can they do that? Is that even legal?" "Technically," he whispered sickly, "They only had to wait 24 hours after notification before they released Andy's name."

Suddenly it seemed like everyone was staring as we drove by, people turning their collective heads whispering *there she is, his…what is she? Not his widow because he never married her…his girlfriend maybe? How sad. How sad.* Instantly, a crushing guilt set in as I realized I was thinking about me, how people saw me, instead of thinking about you. You were the one that was dead. You were dead and I was worried about what people called me, labeled me. I felt like a horrible person.

No, I was a horrible person. I was the person June thought I was, realizing the sick truth. You were dead and I was here. I was here in a new coat wearing a pair of sequin shoes on my way to Med Group where I would sign the papers allowing them to cremate what little remained of you. It was me sending you off to Dover accompanied by a crisply folded flag that would lay next to a uniformed escort who would pass the time eating lunch out of a cardboard box. Where they would eradicate what was left, sliding you on a metal tray into a giant furnace.

On that military flight they were sending you alone to burn and I was the one signing the papers.

"Stop the car. Stop the car. Stop the car right now," I gasped.

He slammed on the brakes and swerved toward the side of the road next to the flight line as I flung open the door and threw up onto the gravel. Shaking, I stood next to his car with my hands on my knees and heaved at the end of your runway.

TEN

"Do you feel like going out for a while?" he asked politely when we left Med Group a few hours later. "I can take you back to the house if you need to rest, if that's what you want..." "No," I held up a shaking hand and shielded my eyes from the glaring sun, "Getting out of here, away from here would be good, I think. Fishing sounds good, I think."

He paused, "How far away do you want to go?"

"As far as I can get," I replied.

"Well, the weather's ok now and we can get pretty far out of town if we go down to the lake and..." he stopped when he realized what he was saying. What he was saying to me. "I'm ok, I'll be ok, it's ok," I said. "Andy always said you were the safest of all the guys...and you were the one that came back. You came back, so..." I stared out the window as we wound down toward where his float plane was docked.

When we pulled into the parking lot I saw it sitting there just metal and paint and thin fabric and I froze. "I can't, I can't," I gasped and turned my face to the side but he moved so fast, snapping out his hand and turning my face to his he told me it was ok.

"Hey, look at me, we don't have to go if you're not ok," he pinched my jawbone with his fingers, "It's ok. Stay with me, look at me, it's ok."

I suddenly remembered your words telling me I should go to him, run to him, call him if things went down. If you went down. That he would help, that you trusted him to fix what might be broken, if I were broken. If you left me, when you broke me and suddenly I couldn't breathe, I couldn't go on. I reached out a hand and grabbed his arm, fingers trembling.

"I'm ok, I'm alright," I sucked in a quick breath, "I'm good. I'm good. Let's just go. I'm good."

He nodded and shoved me gently up onto the floats wedging me into what seemed to be an impossibly small space. The headset wouldn't stay on and I could see out all the windows at the same time. I started to panic, shaking my head back and forth faster and faster no no I can't I can't do this while he peered at my face. Quietly he reached across my arms to grab the harness, his hand pressing awkwardly on my thigh for balance. He pulled the straps over my shoulders, snapped them tight across my waist and pushed the front seat back. It hit the tops of my knees and then I was stuck. I stared straight ahead as he climbed in and clicked shut the door. A door that sounded like it was made of paper.

How could he do this, shove me back here like this, like cargo. My hands quivered and I wanted desperately to jump out, to be out, be away from there.

When the engine started the whole goddamn thing shook. I shivered there in that tiny tin can on that lake and realized I'd made a horrid miscalculation. We pushed back from the shore and it was so loud, it was too much and I couldn't hear anything. His mouth was moving but I couldn't tell what he was saying because the headset kept slipping forward. Oh Jesus, does anyone know where we're going? If we break down? What will happen if we go down?

If he goes down who will fix all the broken things?

Across the water we sped, going faster and faster until up we went leaping smoothly into the afternoon sky drifting along the plains those striped wings flashing brightly against the patchy green stretched endlessly below, my fists gripping that harness tightly. Along the cuts we soared like a giant butterfly floating up and down. So small, I felt so small.

I leaned forward to peer out the window and caught the edge of his smile as he slowly angled down toward a long stretch of glistening water. I watched his face in the reflection of the windshield and sucked in a deep breath because the ground was coming up it was right there because the water was right there and then we were racing across the surface kicking up great plumes in our wake.

He slowed and turned toward shore sliding the floats up onto the muddy bank before he jumped out and tied down the plane with a long line. When he opened the door I fell out like poorly folded origami and he laughed.

He pushed me back up onto the floats with a grunt. "What about my shoes," I realized I had no boots. No waders. No fishing pole. No nothing. I had nothing. I just stood there in a blue TJ Maxx coat with a fur lined hood, a pair of skinny jeans and wizard shoes.

"No worries," he reached past me into the cargo area and pulled out a large canvas bag, "I came prepared."

My throat tight, I saw him pull out a set of heavy waders. I stared down from the floats at his hands on the zipper as he pulled it up to his chest. Watched while he strapped a pistol in a brown leather holster over a vest that had scissors pinched off a pocket edge, the ones he used to pull out the fishhooks. He strapped a long knife to his forearm and held out another set of waders.

"Seriously?" I gripped the wing supports tightly, "I don't know how to put those on!"

"Well, you're certainly not going to get them on perched up there like a stork," he put his hands around my waist and slung me up over his shoulder. "Ugh," the air went out of me as I bounced upside down, him sloshing through the water and up onto the shoreline toward the grass with me hanging halfway to his waist.

"Put me down! I'm not a side of beef!" I said indignantly, my voice disappearing into the back of his jacket. "Hang on, you heifer," he whacked me on the ass then slid me carefully down to the ground. "Jesus," I choked out, dizzy from the blood rushing back to my head, "This isn't fishing, it's assault and battery!"

"You call your lawyer," he shouted over his shoulder and headed back toward the water. Bending down at the edge, he threw the canvas bag over one arm and carefully picked his way back up the hill.

"Ok, take off one shoe at a time and step on in, cow lady," he ordered and set down a pair of boots holding out the waders. They looked way too big and I glanced up at him squinting my eyes in the sunlight, "Cow lady? That's so…special of you."

"Come on, it's simple. Just stick one leg in at a time. I'll make sure you don't fall down." He reached out his hand and tightly grabbed my upper arm. *Ok, I can totally do this. Totally do this, no problem. No problem, this is not going to be a problem.* I bent one knee up and took off my shoe. Balancing carefully, I propped my hand on his opposite shoulder and pushed my leg into the waders down into the boot. *It's not a problem. Nope. No problem. No problem here.*

Nothing to see folks, move along folks, nothing to see here.

I jammed my other leg in. He loosened his grip and bent down to put my wizard shoes on top of the canvas bag as I reached for my zipper. I shifted slightly to the side and then I was pitching forward into his pistol slamming my head against the hard metal.

"Ouch! God, I didn't realize this was a fucking full contact sport," I laughed and put a hand up to my forehead. "Shit!" he held my cheek in his palm, angling my face sideways, peering closely. "I'm sorry! Man, I'm really making a mess of this, aren't I," he whispered and suddenly we were howling with laughter, him resting his forehead on mine, his hand on my waist and me leaning into him.

"Get off me, you tool," I wiped my eyes, "You're a hazard. You should wear a warning label." He tilted his face up toward the sun then looked down. Slowly he reached up his index finger and pointed at my head.

"What is this," he leaned toward me, "Uh oh, what is this?"

"What? What is what? Is there something on my face? Is there something on me?" I reached up, ready to frantically brush off whatever it was when he flicked his middle finger right into my nose and crowed triumphantly, "Smith and Wesson!"

"You're a fucking moron," I held a hand over my nose, "and that hurt. You hurt me!" He leaned forward and palmed the back of my head pulling me in as he smacked his lips against my forehead.

"Buck up, buttercup. It's time to murder some fish."

ELEVEN

We slid on our heels down the bank and he dug two fly rods out from a waterproof duffel lifted from the plane. With quick fingers he snapped them together, pulled out two reels and strung up the lines. After opening a small clear box of tiny flies he tied a bit of what looked like feathers onto the end of each line with precise movements before handing me a rod. It was absolutely silent. Emerald trees staggered downward, their dusty lines pitching head-on toward the rushing water.

This was peace, with nothing here but all these big things, those tiny bird shadows tipping off the edges of the riverbank into nothing. I bent over and looked at my toes in the water.

"What the hell are you doing?"

I thumbed a thick line through flaky mud and felt scales squish beneath my fingers. "Looking at the colors."

"Why?"

"Because they're pretty, the way they shine silvery blue and red in the sun."

"Well, just make sure you wash your hands." He wrinkled his nose and winked at me, "Personally, I like the red ones the best."

"I prefer blue."

"That's because you have poor taste." He placed a soft hand on my head and stepped sideways over and away across a sandbar.

I stared at my feet. There's more reds than blues here so reds are cliché. Yes, reds are common and blues uncommon with bad taste mass produced polyester, gold rubber soles under white laced cotton. Common is poor taste which is red. Red all over but not hardly any blue here mixed in with grays and blacks and mossy greens.

No, blue is better and less. *Yes, less is more* I thought as I held up this and that one round and limply lumpy with their sharply jutting curv'd wet edges. So less is best taste, poking around now for two. Two, to myself softly, two more because I like them in threes.

Yes, threes or fives even sevens sometimes, those whispering silver slivers slipping in darkly distant waters stirred up and about by legions of trashy reds all straining to make it upstream.

I heard a small humming noise and turned to see him carelessly flipping the rod over one shoulder, his line flowing in a glistening s-curve over his head. Quick as an arrow, a tiny bit of feather and metal shot out into the water resting just downstream from a large rock. It floated there for a split second before he snapped it back out with a single smooth movement.

I stood mesmerized as he placed that fly in the same spot over and over. "You're really good at this," I said softly. "I come out here a lot," he replied, tugging on the line with his free hand and whipped the rod forward again, "Just to be alone." Embarrassed, I told him I didn't know how to fly fish. That you and I never went. It seemed like there just wasn't any time not enough time, our visits were so short and it wasn't fishing season whenever I was here anyway. That I only came up here with you a few times because your trips were always last minute, always scheduled around all the other things.

Deep in thought he looked up at the clouds drifting by and said, "Time is the most precious commodity, isn't it? There just never seems to be enough time." I swallowed and nodded mutely, my nose turning red, staring at my boots as tears rolled down my face off my chin into that crisp clear river.

"Hey, it's ok," he splashed over, rod in hand. "I'll teach you. I'll show you how to do it. Please don't cry. I'm sorry. I'll help you. Here, let me help you." He set his rod off to the side so it didn't get busted up by my clumsy too-big feet and stood behind me, his hands on mine, "Relax. That's the key. Just relax." He pressed his chest against my back and twisted my arms to the side, the rod swinging at a stiff angle.

"Relax! Jesus," he laughed, "Loosen up a little." He jostled me a step or two and then our hands snapped the rod forward. I looked up. Slowly, so slowly, a thin line of sunshine zinged over us sailing out into the water landing skipping sinking a tiny fly into the shadow of his rock. I could hear him smiling. Tilting my head, just a tiny movement backward I saw him squint his eyes as he lifted our arms smoothly, the fly drifting upward, rebounding back. "It's like dancing," he told me, "like dancing. You should be good at this."

"What do you mean?"

He glanced sideways at the side of my face and softly answered, "You're the only person I know that manages to dance and stand still simultaneously."

I swallowed lightly, "So you come out here and dance by yourself a lot, huh."

"Yeah, I do. I always come out here by myself." He seemed sad for a minute and lonely. He pulled the tip of the rod briskly backward, "So relax."

"Just relax and let it happen," he whispered as the line swung past us with a blinding brilliance.

TWELVE

I flew back to Seattle two days later wearing my new coat and those sequin wizard shoes lugging two giant olive mobility bags full of the things you'd kept stored at the squadron. On final, we passed over the city center and I saw the Space Needle shooting up through the great rolling fog coming in off the Sound while the muted lights of the city blurred below.

It was cold and wet so I took a cab home, sat there on I5 in traffic with one of your bags jammed up onto the seat next to me and wondered what I was going to say to all of our friends. At the marina I dug my keys out of the bottom of my duffel and walked slowly down the dock pushing an overloaded cart toward our boat, dragging those bags toward that floating piece of furniture we called home. I couldn't bear to pick up the phone so I just sat there in our living room with the shades pulled shut. I stared over at your things and couldn't bring myself to make those calls. Huddled in the darkness I listened as the rain pummeled Lake Union and beat it into submission outside our windows.

The next morning I sent email after email telling the same story, repeating the common refrain read in every newspaper, every tweet, every Facebook post of every family who has ever lost anyone to anything—I need privacy please, don't call me right now, I understand everyone is upset, I'll contact you as soon as I have any details for the service, I love you all but I just need to be alone.

I always wondered why the families bothered to make those statements, always thought it was ridiculous to ask people not to call. Of course they would call. They would want to know want happened, to say something, to show support. Confirm the gossip. But I really did want to be alone so I sat there in dark silence with the phone face down in sleep mode and spent a restless night in that big bed where I always slept on the right-hand side, an arm and one leg poking out of the covers because I always got overheated.

Shivering even with the heater on high with dampness below the waterline seeping through I huddled under the blanket unable to stop my mind from thinking about the last time you were here, when I rolled over and saw your face, when I said to you *don't trip over the laundry* as you got up quietly in order not to wake me. I thought about you standing in our tiny kitchen cooking eggs on that gas stove, making coffee in a pot that always blew the electrical outlet because you forgot the toaster wouldn't run at the same time. Every time you'd laughed and yelled out to me *hey baby, go flip the goddamn breaker*.

He called a few days after I arrived home telling me that arrangements needed to be made, that he could handle them if I needed him to. I said no. I knew what you wanted because we'd talked about it. "We talked about this," I told him in a tired voice because every pilot talks about this, it's always there. Every time you left, every time I heard your voice on the radio, every time. "I'll take care of it," I whispered, "I just need to know who to call. I'm sure there are papers. There's always papers."

"Will they even listen to me?" I asked in a soft voice and firmly he said, "Yes, I'll make them. I'll make them listen to you."

THIRTEEN

I told your mother you wanted to be buried at the Air Force Academy, that we had talked about it and you had written it specifically into your will. "But he's from Tampa," she explained, as if I were five years old, "He was born here. He should be here. In Tampa. With me."

I said no. I told your mother no for the second time in her life, that you wanted to be at the Academy and by god I was going to follow your wishes.

I always thought it odd you wanted to be buried there. You had always laughed and said it was the worst four years of your life, like being in hell. As if they'd shoved bamboo shoots under your fingernails every day with you hating the routine, being forced to stand up against the wall in the hallways as a new cadet when upperclassmen strolled by. The sheer ridiculousness of it. You said the food was shitty and those polyester pants itched in the summer.

"It was horrible. I would never go there if I could make the choice again," you would always say, throwing your hands up in the air, "It was awful," finishing with a full-bodied shudder worthy of a Hollywood horror movie.

You and I had gone back to the Academy just a year ago to attend a funeral of a friend who had also gone down and left behind a family.

You had bowed your head and told me how proud you were of his widow. Proud that she was so calm and kept it together as she and the children stood there in a row at the front of the Academy chapel amidst long lines of brothers and sisters who had traveled halfway across the world to remember someone who was in a box like you would be in a box. Who is right now in the ground at the Academy like you will soon be in the ground only a few short rows away.

I remember standing there and hearing you breathing hard, listening to all the pilots around us fight back the tears as people spoke, that service live streamed across the world for those who couldn't make it, those far away family members who had crammed into bland government conference rooms to watch the calm widow speak words of comfort in an even voice. Chin up, she'd walked briskly down the aisle under the soaring chapel roof out the door passing through a sea of patches striding out of the building next to her children without stopping because the box was already at the cemetery underneath a cover sitting quietly on the grass next to a hole dug by a careful groundskeeper.

When we arrived at the graveyard that day I remember being surprised at the sheer number of people, the enumerable chairs lined up for the family and close friends, for the leadership who always came. That row of scruffy bikers wearing leather vests emblazoned with American flags who lined the cemetery access road, bikers who had no connection to our friend but were there every time because they're always there silently watching. I knew they would be there for you, too.

I recalled flags set up in the sunlit grass waiting for the honor guard that would march in measured steps trailed behind by boys carrying guns. Those rifle shots snapping into the air, the crack rebounding off the mountains around us. I remember flinching at the sound when the boys from the Academy moved in perfect unison placing the rifles to their shoulders pulling the triggers before uniformly slamming those rifles back down in perfect synchronicity. I thought about standing in a silent cold river as I pictured those rifles in my mind shooting and shooting and shooting knowing the honor guard and the gun salute would be there because it's tradition.

You going down was tradition.

I stared out the window of our transom at the lake and remembered the shells our friend's squadron had fired from the remaining jets out over the Atlantic Ocean. The brothers shooting out those live rounds while the casings stayed inside the jets, shells launched a jet that had carried your friend gently down while yours had just spit you out. Those shells lined in precise rows upended on a table some filled with apple juice for those who didn't drink, for the children. Others steeped in tradition of pilots gone before were filled to the brim with Jeremiah Weed, that horrid concoction of alcohol so beloved and hated simultaneously by fighter pilots the world over.

Each shell stood stiffly at attention ready to make the final toasts, the final personal toasts they would all give after choking that poison down, tossing the brass down around the hole where our friend was headed. Shells those shells of war and destruction raining down on piles of nickels spread amongst the grass.

I remembered thinking to myself that the groundskeepers must hate this, coming through with metal detectors picking up all the metal left behind before they can mow.

What happens to all the shells and nickels, each carrying the finger-prints of the friends still alive, I wondered They couldn't all go in the hole, which was deep but not that deep. Where would they go, where do all those things go? I swallowed the questions down as a great and terrible rumble sounded from the horizon and everyone snapped to attention except civilians like me.

I had craned my neck overhead as a flight of black objects coming from the south shot low and slow in perfect formation over us. A terrible bone shaking roar rang out as one split away, straight up toward the sun peeling off incredibly high before turning over slowly against the cerulean sky. Righting itself, it blasted on a blue flame toward the horizon as the other jets carried on. Carried on alone without their missing man until they disappeared over the mountains.

I remember you said, "I don't know why I stood at attention, we all wanted to look but I guess it's ingrained to stand there at attention. I wanted to look. I wanted to see but I forgot to look."

I promised myself I'd make sure when those jets came over, came over your hole, came over that box where you would be, that hole where you'll be forever that everyone looks up. That no one stands with eyes straight ahead. That everyone sees that missing man soaring up into the sunlight, that jet flying toward the horizon, flying toward the horizon alone.

After the service we had walked through the graveyard while you silently looked down at the plaques lined up in the grass. I remember you stopped at one for a long time. You looked down, stiffly took your hand and scrubbed it across those brass letters until they shone and softly told me a story about your classmate whose jet had burned him down to cinders and how his widow married his best friend two years later.

I remember you looked up at me and smiled, "And they're deliriously happy from everything I've heard. They've got kids and everything."

I had answered, "That must've been weird for everyone," puzzled at how you go from losing your soulmate to marrying your soulmate's best friend? Isn't that soulmate always there between you, isn't he always there? How uncomfortable to be in a relationship of three. You stared face up toward the sun and squinted, "You'd be surprised at how often it happens. A guy dies and his widow ends up with somebody else from the same squadron. Makes sense in a way because we're all family. All the same personality. We're all the same, all the same. Replaceable, I guess."

"That's a little incestuous," I cringed.

"It's just the way it is," you replied, lost in thought as you threw a nickel down next to your buddy's name. Moving along those rows I noticed that not a single blade of grass was out of place, each plaque lovingly maintained by the groundskeepers and the cadets on the volunteer honor guard who stood watch over the alumni who had already departed.

I remember seeing statements and phrases, words of love and sorrow, of hope burned into those brass markers, remembered seeing other names written underneath the titles of the fallen. Underneath those names was the word *spouse* always the word *spouse, wife, beloved wife,* and I suddenly realized you would be alone forever because I wasn't allowed to be there with you. I wasn't allowed because I was half-family but not fully in the circle. Those jets streaking away toward the horizon, away from the fallen man were leaving me behind, not you. It was me that would be missing, that would be gone forever, it was me that would disappear into nothing as everyone else stared straight ahead.

I sat in Seattle remembering that funeral with a thick stack of papers in my lap making plans to fly across the country to Dover Air Force Base where I would sit on a plane with your mother on a long slow return trip with you back to Colorado Springs. Where at the end of the trip I would be the one walking down the middle of the chapel trying to keep it together, trying not to embarrass you.

Where I would be the one standing in the front row staring at your picture on an easel, striding down that aisle by myself in the middle of a uniformed group of people who didn't know me. Alone in a group of people who knew you, of people that were strangers to me but family still the same, would be family until those jets screamed by and the grass went back to sleep.

We scheduled the memorial for a month after you died to give everyone time to make their plans, to get on those flights from Japan, from the sandbox, traveling through Guam, streaming in via the sunny islands of Hawaii. From across the world they would all be heading back to stand in that chapel again, in those long rows at attention as I would walk by in a new black dress.

Deep in thought I wondered if maybe I should wear heels because you liked the way I looked in them even though you had always said I resembled a drunk giraffe hobbling along tipping from side to side unfamiliar with that raised center of balance with you gripping my arm. Maybe I would give it a try, telling myself I'd have to practice walking down the sidewalk in front of our marina. I knew I couldn't practice on the dock because I'd fall and bust my face like the last time when the car keys had sailed off into the water next to slip 109.

Time inched toward the day I would have to make that long trip, when I would have to leave our home carrying a bag again down to SeaTac. Every morning as that day grew closer I brushed my teeth in our bathroom putting my toothbrush carefully back in the jar next to yours, put my deodorant back in the cabinet next to yours, your towel hanging on the rack above mine and your razor in the drawer.

Your running shoes sat jumbled in the closet as every day I got up, made eggs on our stove and blew that outlet when I ran the toaster and coffee machine simultaneously.

I went out and bought an outfit at Macy's two weeks before the service on a cold afternoon in the rain and tried it on with those wizard shoes.

FOURTEEN

That day finally came and I took the Link back to the airport pulling a roller bag holding a pair of red leather high heels tucked in next to a tissue-paper wrapped black crepe three-quarter length sleeve dress. When I walked through security and arrived at my gate I saw him standing there in civilian clothes ready to get on the flight with me. Ready to sit there next to me, ready to pay for that fruit and cheese plate as we lifted off the ground in that big Boeing jet humming softly toward our Minneapolis connection.

In Delaware, I got off the plane and walked silently out of baggage and got into another government car that took us to a hotel outside the Dover gates. I saw your mother there in the lobby but she turned away. She turned her back and I watched her walk down to the elevator, step inside and let the doors slide shut in my face.

We went to the base the next day, him in service dress prepared to badge us through the gate as I sat in the backseat, your mother in the front chattering about the insufficiency of the hotel's continental breakfast. In front of a nondescript building we met the escort who would accompany us as we brought you back to the Academy.

The same escort that stood solemnly at attention on the tarmac that next morning as you rolled up the baggage slide into the bottom of the plane like luggage.

Everyone on your side sat quietly looking down from their tiny windows watching as you were being loaded on like postal mail while the other side chatted about jobs, kids, vacations, seemingly oblivious to the fact that he was sitting there in full uniform next to me dressed in all black while your mother reclined twenty-six rows ahead in first class drinking a mimosa.

I watched that honor guard standing ramrod straight disappear into the distance, the airport firetrucks shooting great sheets of water over our plane as we headed for the taxiway. Our flight was late departing, the inevitable weather over the Midwest causing trouble, always trouble in the air. Taking off swiftly at a steep pitch it was bumpy and I white-knuckled the armrest. He glanced over to me and asked if I was ok. "I'm a nervous flyer," I said, "I always have been. Andy used to tell me what all the noises were so that I wouldn't be afraid."

I smiled uncomfortably, "I always used to say what's that, what's that, is that bad, what's that and Andy would laugh and tell me it was normal to see the ends of the wings bending, that what doesn't bend breaks. That breaking up here would be bad." My upper lip started to sweat. He looked straight ahead and told me he'd tell me if something went wrong. I glanced over at his profile and whispered, "I know," as we flew on through the storms toward Minneapolis.

It soon became clear we were going to miss our connection, that last connection, that last flight out to Colorado. We were going to miss it because I knew we would never be able to get off the plane in time, off that crowded plane from row thirty-two. Your mother would make it but we would not. I would be stuck in an airport terminal my face smashed against the window staring at an empty gate while your mother flew onward with you in the belly of that plane, her hand clutching another mimosa. I would be left there waiting.

Waiting to hear whether you had landed safely, waiting for that GTG.

As we descended down toward the airport he stood up stepping across me into the aisle and walked toward the front of the plane. He paused and laid a hand on the shoulder of our official Air Force escort sitting ahead in row twelve bending over him briefly before continuing on toward the front where he stood with his back to the cabin and had a hushed conversation with the flight attendant in first class who glanced back at me over his shoulder.

When he returned to his seat, he whispered, "We need to be ready to move quickly once we land, we might be able to make it." I saw the flight attendant pick up the telephone, turn away and say something to someone else, maybe to the pilots who were controlling this giant lumbering hearse. As we circled down on final approach the standard announcements filled air about seats and tray tables. Seatbelts fastened for safety, safety first.

Then the flight attendant took a deep breath, and continued, "We'd like you all to remain seated when we arrive at the gate. We are carrying precious cargo today, a service member headed to his final resting place. His family is on board and they have a very tight connection, a tight connection they need to make. We are asking that you allow the family to exit before standing up and moving about the cabin when we stop at the gate." She stopped, opening her mouth like she was going to say something else before she turned and hung up the phone. There wasn't anything else to say, nothing to stop the assholes that would get up anyway, to the people shifting uncomfortably thinking about their own connections to sunny beaches, to the people frozen in their seats seeing their own loved ones long gone flashing before their eyes.

The attendant sat down in the jumpseat and snapped herself into a harness pulling it tight across her chest and stared down that empty aisle directly at my face.

When we landed, I stood up and he stood up, gently shoving me out into the aisle pushing me toward the exit. No one moved. We walked down the long length of that plane, everyone seated on your side staring out the windows. An old man stood as we approached Economy

Comfort and raised a trembling hand in salute when we passed and I saw the veteran's baseball cap from a Navy ship gone long ago in tropical waters where a single drop of oil still rose and rose and rose sending out its missing men into the sea.

Your best friend paused and saluted back then softly took my arm carrying us on out and away through the door up into the terminal.

Those people all watched as you were unloaded from the belly of that plane into the waiting hands of the uniformed escort who had slipped down the outside stairs joining the Minneapolis honor guard waiting at the end of the baggage roller.

That honor guard standing ready, waiting to whisk you over to the connecting flight hovering three gates over; the connecting flight that had waited for us for thirty minutes. Not one passenger on the connection complained or met our eyes as we walked down the aisle to row twenty-two where I sat in a middle seat next to a silent salesman from Poughkeepsie and white-knuckled it through stormy skies all the way to Denver.

When we landed they whisked you off somewhere for that drive to the Academy under the watchful gaze of your escort because it's tradition, that escort going with you making sure that you were carried carefully towards your final resting place in a brilliant black hearse under gray November skies. I followed in the backseat of yet another government car while he drove, your mother chattering in the front the entire way. After checking into a standard Holiday Inn, I clicked open the lock, closed the door, placed my back against the wall and cried.

I sat on the floor and cried for you.

FIFTEEN

I spent the night under the covers in that hard bed with my face pressed into the down pillows sniffling because I was allergic to feathers and didn't think to ask the front desk to switch them out. You always did that. That was your job, making sure those pillows weren't down because I would keep you up all night sneezing before you finally threw up your hands in frustration and stomped down to the front desk to make sure everything was fixed and correct.

That was your job.

The next morning a knock sounded at the door and he was standing there in a flight suit looking haggard, lines sharp across his forehead, eyes red holding two cups of coffee in his hands. "Are you ready?" he handed me a soy latte. I nodded, throat tight, and asked him how he'd slept. He turned away and in a strangled voice answered, "I didn't sleep. I sat with Andy last night. The escort would have stayed with him but I wanted to do it."

I collapsed and bent over, digging both hands into my face and broke down picturing him sitting in some empty room with you, with you in that burnished wood box, sitting beside you so you wouldn't be alone. Not sleeping, he sat next to you all night as you rested in silence.

He pushed me back into the room and shoved the coffee onto the counter ledge grabbing me in his arms as we laid our heads side by side and wept, my tears leaving dark spots on the front of his flight suit. A few minutes passed before he lifted a hand and stroked the back of my hair. "It's time to go," he stepped back with a quavering breath, "You look like a deranged raccoon. Go fix your face and let's blow this joint."

SIXTEEN

The next few hours passed in a blur of chaplains and solemn *I'm sorry for your losses* from people with stars on their shoulders, from colonels, from airmen, from an endless line of brothers in green and the Academy cadets from your squadron who stood at attention in the back ten rows of the chapel. He stood guard outside the door as I sat in a room waiting to walk down that aisle. Waiting to walk down toward your picture resting on an easel at the front. Alone I would walk down that aisle with him following behind me, picking up all the broken pieces.

I would walk down the aisle with your mother preceding as she simpered on the arm of a three-star general gripping him tightly with her perfectly manicured fingers.

I don't remember the service. I don't remember the statement your mother gave or what I'd said in a quavering voice, my sweating fingers gripping those paper notes. I don't remember the long walk out wearing those high heels I'd worn for you, the shoes I'd managed to walk in without falling on my face, down face first in that long aisle. I stepped carefully down the long rows of stairs outside the chapel, climbed into another government car and changed into leopard print flats so that I would be able to trudge through the grass toward your hole. I held a hand to my eyes shielding them from the sun that glared through the car window and thought about the long walk. The gap in the grass where you would be placed down into the earth, a coin emblazoned with a flag on one side with the image of a pitchfork-wielding devil on the other gently laid on the shining wood. I got out of the car nodding a silent thank you to the driver and started toward a long line of chairs where I would stand next to your mother in the shadow of a rustling flag.

I remember someone walking across the grass and handing your mother one of those flags. I looked up and saw the eyes of a stranger handing me the second flag they had unfurled over you and refolded with precise movements. I remember a moment of silence before those shots rang out, as the cadets from your squadron stood at attention pushing a crisply snapping standard firm against the wind while scruffy bikers in leather jackets held back the edges of the access road.

I stood there watching everyone stare straight ahead as your flock crossed overhead and opened up that gap, sending a lone pirate upward toward the sky. One solitary jet rolling over before raging out and away toward the mountains leaving everyone else behind.

I saw your mother take a shell filled with Jeremiah Weed from the hand of an olive-suited pilot, look down at it and pinch it with her fingertips. I gripped one in my sweaty palm, saying *thank you* quietly to your squadron commander, his hand briefly gripping my shoulder before he turned away. I remember your mother lifting that shell to her lips and tilting it back and as she dropped her hand back toward the ground I saw a thin stream of amber liquid pour into the grass before she flung the shell toward your hole.

I remember smelling that atrocious liquor, choking back the vomit in my throat before I swallowed it down. I held the brass for a minute, caressing it with a trembling thumb before moving forward. Bending gently, I placed it upright next to your box feeling the grass brush against the back of my fingers before stepping away. It was my thumbprint there on the shell next to you, that would go in the hole with you. My thumbprint would be the only part of me with you here where you would be forever. I wavered and felt the chair hit the back of my knees then myself falling before his hand shot forward firmly gripping my elbow.

Your brothers moved abruptly in a great wave of green, each standing silently in front of your box individually bowing their heads, silently raising their hands up toward the sun as they tossed back that hideous Weed, launching their shells in smooth flipping motions sending them soaring end over end through the air down onto the grass where they plinked off the nickels.

Landing, bouncing, those shells piled up next to where they were packing you in.

As the boys trickled slowly away into the distance I could see them grouping together, saying hello to old friends, a peal of laughter ringing out here and there. I sat there on that seat alone staring at your box for a long time before slowly rising and walking away past the flags, past those cadets, past your brothers.

I walked down the rows glancing down reading *beloved wife beloved spouse beloved beloved*, bent over placing a nickel from our shared boat piggybank on your friend's name before climbing back into yet another anonymous government car.

He shut the door softly behind me and stepped to the side watching as I drove away alone.

SEVENTEEN

That evening I put on a pair of dark jeans and boots and slung a coat over my heavy wool sweater gripping it tightly to my chin while I shivered in the crisp fall air. I stood outside the hotel waiting outside for an anonymous officer who ushered me into a car, badged me through the Academy gate and drove me down to the flight line. When I arrived, I saw two dilapidated pianos propped against a pile of plywood outside an open garage, the gliders the Academy students flew lined up inside in long white rows.

A giant table of barbecue and what seemed like a million kegs were strategically arranged around long tables. Pictures of your face, your childhood, pilot training, photographs of you with him, of you with your brothers before you met me, then pictures of us in Hawaii, us eating crazy street food in South Korea, us out on the deck of our boat in the middle of Lake Washington on a brilliant Seattle summer day with your hand pulling at the string of my bathing suit top flashed across a screen. Those pictures looped endlessly as I stood there and talked to strangers who told me stories about you I'd never heard as pictures of you I'd never seen shot past.

I remember walking over and sitting at a table in the corner alone tucking my chin down into my coat collar, your brothers wandering by uttering condolences. People I didn't know wished me the best, reaching down to touch my gloved hands *I'm sorry I'm sorry* while those pianos hovered silently outside the open door next to a box holding thrift store dishware. Chipped plates and coffee cups shattered in the background as the boys gleefully launched them at a large poster of Putin stapled inside a makeshift plywood booth.

I rose a few hours in and slipped around the side of the building and stood there with my back to the metal looking out as the sun slipped down over the mountains. Just stood and stared out at that long runway stretching off into the distance toward the chapel. He came around the corner gripping a beer can in a gloved hand wearing a heavy green coat, a black watch cap pulled down low. He propped himself up next to me against that building and silently stretched out an arm pulling me into his side and looked at the tears running down my face. "You don't have to stay, everyone will understand if you leave, it's okay if you need to go," he leaned his cheek on the top of my head.

"No, I'll stay," I wiped my face with my coat collar, "I'll stay until they burn the pianos."

I looked at him from the corner of my eye, "Where did you get those pianos, anyway?" He shifted uncomfortably and looked rather guilty, "Some of the guys looked in the papers and went out and bought them from a nice old lady downtown." I pushed a finger into his cheek suspiciously, "I find it hard to believe someone would sell you a piano knowing you're just going to burn it, tradition or not."

He bit his lip and snorted. For a minute he had a distinct resemblance to Dennis the Menace. He squeezed my shoulder and leaned in, "You think we told her what we were going to do with the pianos? Yeah, right. As far as she knows they're going to a lovely family with 2.5 children who will happily bang away at them in the formal living room for a solid hour a day because it's good for their minds." He gave me a full toothed grin and I laughed at the deception feeling slightly bad that some old lady's heirloom piece-of-shit out-of-tune pianos would be sacrificed to the God of tradition. "Note to self," I tilted my chin, "Never sell a musical instrument of any kind to a fighter pilot."

That night the brotherhood stood and launched long streams of lighter fluid across the parking lot into the bonfire, howling with laughter and shoving each other playfully toward the embers as piano strings snapped discordantly in the heat. Running across the concrete they heaved big pieces of wood on top of the conflagration along with that banged up poster of Putin, all of them completely trashed weaving with arms wrapped around each other's necks, drinks in the air singing those songs, those hilariously inappropriate fighter songs.

I stood to the side and watched those pianos burn, sparks shooting up into the air fading and blowing away around the building. Up up into the darkness the sparks flew, the cinders below seething an angry red. The jet, the bitch who spit you out? She was cinders now too. A black gash in the forest floor with trees snapped and shattered around a pool of darkness lurking in the Alaska wilderness was all that was left of her and I was glad for it. I hoped it hurt, when she saw the light come on, that tiny light come on. When the canopy ripped off I hoped she screamed in agony as she turned and fell from the sky, that she saw the ground coming and felt the impotent rage I felt, that maybe you felt at the end. I hoped with a desperate futility that you were gone, long gone the instant after she abandoned you, that she was the only one to see the imminent destruction because you had gone before, because you were already gone from there on to the next big thing.

I stared blankly at those pianos melting down to their separate parts and disintegrating piece by piece remembering the way the sunlight shattered across your face on a warm Seattle summer day. He turned and saw me hiding in the shadows, handed his drink to a stranger and walked past me to the parking lot. I drove off with him in his rental car a few minutes later looking behind me in the side mirror at those flames visible even from the highway. Giant sinuous ribbons of orange shot up into the sky as your brothers burned it down, always grinding it down, they burned it down at the end of that runway.

EIGHTEEN

Back at the hotel he walked me to my third-floor room and stopped when I put my key in the lock. I cracked open the door, he cocked a hip and leaned in, an arm slung across the opening. I turned, "Are you going back?" He nodded, "Yep. We'll be there all night probably and into most of tomorrow morning, too." "Well, we have those vans," I patted his cheek gently with my palm, "to chaperone all your drunk asses home so nobody gets a DUI. You know those Academy cops are lurking out there just waiting to bust you."

He laughed. "Yeah. I made sure we took everyone's keys as they came in. Also," he sniffed self-righteously, "we have a bunch of sober responsible people standing by in the parking lot making sure no one does anything stupid." I smiled, "A bunch of highly intoxicated middle-age men torching musical instruments next to a runway of dry grass doesn't qualify as stupid?" He stood up tall, propped his hands on his hips and replied, "That's tradition, madam." I raised my eyebrows, "Well, enjoy your traditions. I'm sure tomorrow morning you won't quite so enthused about your night of revelry."

He looked down his nose at me, "Killing massive amounts of brain cells with adult beverages is also tradition. Now, unless you need something else, Miss High-And-Mighty, I'm going to go back, get dangerously drunk and burn a bunch of shit." He put a finger to the side of his nose and gave me a naughty grin, "I'll call you when I resurrect myself tomorrow morning. Maybe we can go get breakfast at this great little diner down the street Andy and I used to go to all the time when we managed to sneak off school grounds to party with the local girls."

I rolled my eyes, "Yeah, I'll see you when I see you." He knocked his knuckles against the door, "All right, I'm off to do irresponsible things," and sauntered away.

I didn't hear from him by breakfast. Or lunch. The phone finally rang at two-o'clock in the afternoon and it was him sounding like death warmed over croaking that maybe we could do the diner some other day, that he had somehow lost his pants and his shoes and ended up in a buddy's bathtub, that he wasn't quite sure where his buddy's hotel was located and probably wouldn't be back for at least a few more hours.

"I'm pretty sure there's Macy's somewhere in this town where I can buy you a pair of replacement wizard shoes," I said and laughed when he told me to speak more softly then suddenly said he had to go, had to go right that second. As he hung up the phone I could hear him gagging and smiled at the thought of him paying the price, all your brothers undoubtedly paying the price of pushing it up, pushing too far, they always pushed it too far.

NINETEEN

That evening I was wedged into an armchair, chin on my knees staring out the window at the mountains when a soft knock sounded at the door. I pulled myself slowly upright, walked over to the door and rose up on my toes peeking through the peephole. It was him in the hallway wearing faded jeans and a t-shirt carrying a paper bag in one hand. I opened the door as he tilted his head to look through the crack at my face.

"You look horrible," he said, leaning one hand on the outside wall. "Like, really awful. Terrible awful. Horror movie awful." I pinched my lips together and I gave him a tiny smile, "So glad to know you care. You're looking a little rough around the edges yourself, you ingrate." He grinned and held up his bag like trophy. I closed the door and flipped off the safety latch.

"Greeks bearing gifts, huh," I tugged the door open just enough to let him slip through.

"Well, Alaskans bearing Big Macs at least," he announced and slid by me pulling out a stack of wrapped hamburgers. "Jesus! How many did you buy?" my eyebrows raised in disbelief at the huge bundle of yellow wrappers cascading over the surface of the coffee table. "I bought one of everything except the nuggets," he leaned forward and shoved a French fry in my mouth. "I don't trust those nuggets. Chicken isn't supposed to have edges like that."

"Ha! Cows aren't circular, you know," I took a giant chomp out of the steaming burger he gripped in his hand, "Oh man is that good." "I know! I know," he said around a mouthful as sauce dripped down the side of his hand. "I was so hungry and figured you probably hadn't eaten much today either so I thought maybe you wouldn't mind a big greasy McDonald's-fest." He lifted his wrist, licked ketchup off his fingers and crumpled up the wrapper before hitting a perfect three-point shot into the trashcan across the room.

"Nicely done, sir. Nicely done."

"I slay," he said modestly, leaned over my arm and ate the rest of my Big Mac in a single bite before flopping down on the bed. He kicked off his sneakers, rolled over and reached out his hand for the remote on the nightstand, "Take a load off. And bring me another burger."

"You're a tool, you know that?"

"Yeah, well, I'm a tool who needs a burger so get on it, toots." I tossed him a wrapped sandwich overhand and laughed as he yelped, putting up an arm to protect his face. "Hey! Watch it! My eyes are my livelihood." He winked at me then ripped the paper off the burger he'd neatly snatched out of the air and flipped a pillow up against the headboard, "Seriously, sit down. You're exhausting me just standing there. Relax and put your bird feet up."

Two hours later as we sprawled across the bed in a complete Jerry Springer-induced fast food coma I heard him softly ask, "How are you doing, really?" I told him I was ok and he said stop fucking lying to me. I turned my head and stared at the wall. "I know you better than you think I do," he leaned over me on one elbow. "Andy couldn't keep his trap shut about you, you know."

I looked over at him.

"You were practically all he talked about. It was sad," he put the back of his hand to his forehead as he fell into the pillows. "So sad to see him whipped and pathetic, mooning over you constantly. I miss her so much, Isn't she beautiful, Look at this picture, Look at that picture blah blah blah," he made puking noises over the edge of the bed. "Sickening. Just sickening."

I flung out a hand and gave his back a hefty shove. He put out his arm and braced himself on the nightstand, laughing. "Seriously, he talked about you all the time," he glanced down at my face, "He really loved you. He really did. I hope you know that."

My throat tightened as I laid there next to him, tears pooling in the corner of my eyes and dripping down toward my hairline. He continued in a soft voice, "I remember when we were at the Academy he used to talk about his dream girl when we were supposed to be studying. He always said he wanted someone smart and beautiful. Andy always liked the smart girls." I sucked in a quivering breath and he inched closer, sliding an arm under my shoulders slowly tucking me into his side.

"And voila! He found you." He took a deep breath and turned his face gently resting his cheek against my head, "We were all jealous of him. Everyone wants to be happy but he actually really was happy. Like, for reals happy. Legit happy." I rolled toward him curling my arms into my chest, mashed my face into his shoulder and started to sob as his arm tightened against my back.

"It's ok," he whispered, choking back tears of his own, "I have another t-shirt." A few minutes later I sucked in a deep breath and wiped my nose on his sleeve. I said, "Well, Andy always talked about you too." "Yeah?" he cleared his throat and raised his eyebrows, "What'd he say about me? Lies. All lies, I'll have you know."

I stuck out my tongue at him. "I've heard some crazy stories about you two raging through entire countries on the prowl trailing broken hearts in your wake." He waved an arm with high drama above his head and sighed nostalgically, "Ah, the good old days. Lady killers we were. Nonstop broads just falling all over themselves to get in our pants."

"Uh huh," I lifted a palm and pressed it over his face pushing it away from me stifling his laughter, "which is why you're alone."

My stomach sank when I felt him go very still. He turned his head away from me and silently slid his hand lightly down the arm I'd thrown across his waist. "I'm sorry," I choked out, "I wasn't trying to be mean. I didn't think before I said that. If I hurt your feelings I'm sorry." He let out an ironic laugh, "It's ok. I know I'm the lone wolf. El lobo solo. Class Bachelor. Class B for life." He held up his hand and wiggled his fingers, "I'm allergic to rings, you know."

"Haven't you ever been in love?" I asked. "Andy said you were always going out with a million different girls when you guys first graduated from pilot training. How come you never got married or anything?" He shrugged and told me he never found the right one; that they were all either beautiful but dumb or brilliant and looked like a donkey's butt. He snickered and told me a story about a girl in Alabama who used to follow you two around from bar to bar until he was the one who finally broke down and took one for the team.

"Was she smart?" I teased. "Nope," he replied with a wicked grin. "But wow did she have great tits," he held his hands three feet from his chest. "I still can't believe Andy passed up that fine piece of ass." I whacked him on the chest and he lifted a hand to deflect it. I rolled away onto my back. Side by side we stared up at the ceiling as I told him he was a cad.

"I slay," he whispered softly into the fading light and reached down rubbing his thumb across the back of my hand, "I slay."

TWENTY

The next morning, I schlepped my luggage down to the lobby where I checked out at the front desk and hopped in his rental car. We sat in that tawdry diner as he waxed poetic telling me story after story of the absolutely asinine things you guys did at the Academy while we laughed over truly atrocious plates of greasy hash browns. He consumed with great relish a giant plate of food that could only charitably be described as horrid; I surreptitiously hid my slimy eggs under toast-with-crust.

He sucked down the rest of his coffee on the drive up to Denver and said, "I have some things to take care of here and then I'll be going through Seattle on my way back home. How about I give you a call and we can go out and grab dinner, if you're feeling up to it?" I said that would be nice, gave him a hug and turned away pulling my rolling bag behind me carrying a black dress I would hang in our closet next to the custom suit you bought in Hong Kong, those red leather shoes back to Seattle where I would unpack my toothbrush and place it next to yours in the mason jar that sat on our bathroom counter.

He came through two days later and I took him to a small Mexican restaurant in Wallingford where I had street tacos and he inhaled a giant chicken burrito dripping with cheese. I smiled at him and said you had ordered the same thing last time we had eaten there when we'd been lazy and didn't want to cook. "Birds of a feather," he replied and crammed another fistful of chips into his facehole.

I softly asked if there was any news on the safety board and he shook his head. "Not yet. They're only supposed to take thirty days to release a report but sometimes these things can take a lot of time. So far it looks like it's mechanical so we're all grounded until the other jets can be inspected." He raised his beer bottle, and paused, "It was an accident. You know that, right? Just an accident." I nodded and fidgeted with the chip basket.

"Well," I replied, "when they come out with the report please let me know. I don't want to read about it in the newspaper if for some reason they blame Andy. If for some reason Andy's at fault." He gave me a stern look, his hand shooting out across the table and grabbing my wrist. "Hey," he said firmly, "it wasn't his fault. It was just bad luck. Just bad luck. It could have been any of us."

I spent the next week washing and folding our dirty laundry and putting away your t-shirts in our drawer. I pulled our sheets off the bed and rolled them into a small cylinder before shoving them into a Ziploc bag because they still smelled like you. I walked aimlessly around South Lake Union in the dead of night for days avoiding unpacking your things until I finally got tired of your mother leaving messages, messages I only returned when I knew she was at bridge. Messages, constant nagging messages until I finally boxed up and mailed her the things she would want of yours, things she had given you, things I was happy to let go.

Things that would finally stop the goddamn telephone calls.

I set aside some of your clothes and repacked the rest in those green mobility bags I had taken from the squadron storage room when I left Alaska. The bags where you kept your shoes and toiletries and your favorite sweaters so that you never had to take a suitcase up there. You just picked up and went. I stacked those bags in the corner and stared at them every night from my side while I reached across to where you used to be.

Text messages came from him every week like clockwork asking was I okay, how was I, was I okay did I need help, was I okay and I would answer back I'm okay while I watched your bags lurking in our room. I finally started taking your things off the boat a month later, those things you hadn't liked. The shoes that pinched, a shirt with a grease stain from when you dropped a can of oil all over the engine room floor yelling out God fucking dammit as you kicked the side of the manifold and stubbed your toe. The jacket you never wore because it was too tight across your shoulders *cause I'm such a buff hamster* you'd said, preening in the mirror while I laughed at you from under the sheets. I started with those things, driving slowly up to Goodwill and taking a receipt from the hand of a man who casually swung the bags up into a giant dumpster as he looked past me saying, "Next!"

As I drove away I glanced in the rearview mirror and felt like a lonely sock seeing your things go down into that hole.

TWENTY-ONE

It rained every day that January and I didn't see the sun once. I checked the mail on the fourth day of February and saw a note saying I had a package.

I peered through stacks of boxes haphazardly thrown in the back corner of the deli and saw an Amazon one with my name scrawled across the top so I grabbed it under my arm and tossed it behind the driver's seat next to the orange juice. I drove back to our boat, loaded it in the dock cart with the canvas Fred Meyer bags and pushed the heavy load down to the transom where I set the box on the back table. After I put the ice cream in our freezer I used my car key to slit the tape across the top opening it to find a gray cashmere sweater with a card that said *Something to keep you warm on your birthday so you won't be so frigid. I love you, Andy.*

I sucked in a sharp breath dropping the box to the floor and clutched that sweater to my chest realizing you had set up an automatic shipment before you went up there that September day. I slipped your sweater off over my head and pulled the gray one on brushing the sleeve up against my face as I stared blankly out at the sailboats slowly passing by.

The phone rang later that day but I didn't answer. I checked the message at dinnertime and it was him wishing me happy birthday in a soft voice as he told me about the annual first of summer camping trip the squadron was planning. That everyone would love to see me if I wanted to come up. He volunteered to pick me up, "You can stay here at the house and maybe we could do some fishing, if you feel like it." I bent over, opened my phone and marked the calendar with a question mark as I pushed up the gray sweater's sleeves and made myself a turkey sandwich with no crusts.

He called on February thirteenth leaving a quick message saying I should make sure to check the mail the next day. So I slowly rambled down to the Korean deli in a light mist holding my hands to my eyes looking skyward at where clear skies used to be. Where they undoubtedly were above that blanket of gray or so said the unbearably chipper KIRO weather team.

In the deli sitting next to the tuna sandwiches was a vase of sunflowers with my name on it. With my hair plastered against my cheek, I clutched that vase in my arms the six blocks back to the marina and put it in the kitchen next to the toaster. I pulled out one of the bulky stems and saw a small white card tucked inside the bunch. *Stand tall* it said in neat precise writing with his initials scrawled below. Deep in thought I snipped off the smallest of the giant yellow blooms and wedged it into a drinking glass that I placed in the bathroom next to the toothbrushes.

I paused with my hand on that glass, reached out and took your toothbrush from where it was resting next to mine. I turned on the tap clutching the brush tightly before spreading toothpaste across the bristles. One hand on the counter, I bent over and closed my eyes scrubbing your toothbrush across my teeth for a long minute before leaning over and spitting into the sink. I rinsed the toothbrush and watched the water circling down the drain. Standing straight up, I turned and gently placed the toothbrush into the can screwed into the wall of our bathroom and softly closed the lid.

Silently, I put your toothbrush into the trash and walked out.

TWENTY-TWO

"Sorry I'm late, we had some issues leaving Seattle," I said hurriedly a few months later as I rushed out of Anchorage airport's secure section into baggage. "It's fine it's fine it's perfectly ok and fine it's ok," he said, waving his hand in a jittery motion. "What the hell's wrong with you?" I peered at his face noticing that his eyes were completely bloodshot. "I had six cups of coffee while I was waiting because I was bored and there's a Starbucks here downstairs do you need coffee I can get you some if you want some just let me know I'll totally go down there right now here let me take that bag for you," he said in a rush finishing breathlessly as he snatched the bag from my hand and race-walked toward the exit.

"Holy shit, dude," I ran after him, my boots slipping on the tile floor, "You need to slow your roll before we get in a wreck or something." He gave me a manic smile as I reached out and pinched the keys from his jacket pocket saying very deliberately, "You're a fucking menace and I'm driving." He turned and sprinted into the parking garage shouting SHOTGUN abandoning my suitcase in the middle of the road.

"I'd ask if you want lunch but I don't think you should be out in public in your current state," I laughed as he wiggled around in the passenger seat on the drive home jamming all the radio buttons in quick succession. "I'm good, I'm good," he said, rubbing his eyes. "I'm coming down off it now. Man, that Starbucks is tasty. Like crack in a cup." "My hometown coffee shop," I smiled, "Welcome to Seattle's little addicted family." "Well, make sure you bring some of that coffee when we go camping tomorrow," he said, his hands shaking, "because I do believe I might have developed a wee bit of a dependency."

Two hours later he was still sleeping on the couch in the living room, a single bare foot tossed off the side as I puttered around in the kitchen. I closed the refrigerator door and was surprised to see him propping up the doorway, his hair flying in all directions as he pulled his shirt up on one side to wipe his forehead. "I feel like death," he whined, "I need a sandwich. Make me a sandwich, kitchen wench."

"How about a cup of coffee," I said straight-faced. "How about I put you outside in the mud," he leaned forward, grabbed my forearm and dragged my stockinged feet across the tile toward the back door. "No no I'm sorry no no," I screeched as he opened the screen and started to shove me outside, "I'll make you a damn sandwich! Let go of me, you asshole!" "That's better," he said, "I'm glad we've clearly established our roles."

He sauntered over to the island shuffling his bare feet and I opened the refrigerator with a huff, throwing out roast beef and cheese onto the counter clanging the mayonnaise and mustard jars down hard onto the marble as I glared at him narrow-eyed over the door. "Allow me to help," he said loftily, getting up and pulling a loaf of bread from a cabinet. "As a token of goodwill," he turned around to face me and held up a victorious arm, "I'll let you use my bread knife."

I looked at him with his post-electrocution hair and crumpled shirt holding that knife in one hand and a loaf of sliced bread in the other and I lost my shit. Leaning into the refrigerator I laughed so hard snot came shooting out of my nose as he huffed and puffed in the corner of the kitchen indignantly muttering it was a privilege to use that knife, that it was German and did a really nice job. "I just cannot even with you and that bread knife," I sighed and slammed the refrigerator door.

He shrugged his shoulders, "Your loss," and reached around snatching a piece of lunch meat off the counter as he walked by. Over his shoulder he told me, "I have something for you. Keep making those sandwiches, wench. I'll be right back."

I rolled my eyes while I slathered mustard across the bread and stacked up the thinly sliced roast beef folding it carefully so it reached all the way to the edges where he'd neatly trimmed off all the crusts. I turned when I saw him walk back into the kitchen wearing a clean t-shirt, his hair damp from where he'd tried to fix the damage from his coffee crash carrying a file box in his arms with a series of numbers written across the front in thick black marker.

"What's that?" I asked, and set a plate on the counter. He gently lifted the box up onto a stool. "It's the stuff from Andy's locker. The safety investigation board was done with it so I asked them if I could have it."

I paused. "What's in there? I thought I had everything when I took Andy's bags home from the squadron."

"The board always comes in and takes all the stuff out of the lockers when there's an incident," he looked away from my face. "Just to see if there's anything in there that may have…contributed."

"So they were looking for something that they could use to blame the accident on Andy," I said, getting angry. "That's fucking bullshit. Everyone knows that fucking canopy was faulty. Their own report said that canopy latch was broken and Andy didn't do a damn thing. He didn't do a damn thing wrong and they're just now giving the rest of his shit back?"

I turned away, and took a deep breath. "Thank you," I told him softly, "It's not you. I'm just upset. I thought I already had everything."

"I know," He placed his hand on the top of the box. "I'll leave this with you and you can look inside whenever you're ready." He gently lifted it onto the counter.

We sat there and ate those sandwiches in silence as that box hovered on the corner until I couldn't take it any longer. "Fine," I snapped, "I'll open the goddamn box." He grabbed the sleeve of my sweater with a hand, "No, you can wait. It's ok." I pulled my arm away and picked up the bread knife, running it along the official sealing tape holding the box shut and flipped the lid onto the floor.

Inside was a pair of jeans and a green t-shirt neatly folded on top of a pair of Vans sneakers. Ray Bans sunglasses. A black iPhone in a red case. A tube of spearmint Chapstick.

"There's no wallet. We never got his wallet back," I looked up. "They only found his ID, remember?" He put his hand on his chin and peered over the edge of box. "We always take our wallets in case we have to divert for some reason. Nothing sucks worse than ending up in Fairbanks or King Salmon with no money. It was in his pocket probably, that's why no one found a wallet in his stuff."

"But you have this, at least," he tugged the phone out from in between the shoes.

I froze and looked at that phone. "Andy's phone isn't black, it's silver." He swallowed, pulled the phone away and got up from the island. "Must be a mistake, must be someone else's. I'll just take it back to the squadron and find out whose phone this is." He backed away from the kitchen island babbling some nonsense about a misplaced phone, stupid lieutenants and careless investigators as I slowly stood up and advanced toward him.

"Andy had his phone with him in his pocket," I gritted my teeth. "He texted me while they were sitting on the ramp waiting for someone to go to a backup jet. Someone broke their jet and they all had to wait and he texted me from the ramp."

"He had his goddamn phone with him in that fucking jet so what the hell is this phone and what is it doing in his locker," I snapped out my hand and tried to snatch that phone from his grasp. He shrugged his shoulders as he pinched the phone tightly with his fingers in a tug-of-war with me in the middle of that kitchen. I reached over my free hand, grabbed his index finger and bent it backwards until he gasped and let go. He backed away turning toward the wall placing his forehead on the plaster as he held his fingers tightly to his chest. I looked down at the phone in my hand. I pressed the power button and saw that familiar Apple icon as the phone began to boot. I glanced up and saw him with his face propped on his forearm against the wall, his back to me as he slowly shook his head.

I realized the safety board had charged the phone, presumably to keep the information on it from being lost and closed my eyes as a password screen came up. Thinking back, I typed in the four-digit password you had used on your phone. The silver one that had gone down with you into the Alaskan forest.

Rejected.

I tried our bank account PIN number. Rejected.

I tried my birthday and your birthday. Rejected. Rejected.

I knew I had one more chance before I exceeded the allowable phone password attempts and paused with my finger over the screen. I desperately wanted to type in a random number and erase what was on that phone.

What I suddenly suspected was on your phone.

Slowly I reached down and with a cold index finger typed every fighter pilot's default passcode 6-9-6-9 and saw the familiar home screen icons flash onto the screen. From the corner of my eye I saw him turn his back to the wall, hands braced behind him as he stared blankly over my head out the kitchen window.

I sank down onto the stool, pushed my sandwich plate away and placed the phone face-up on the marble counter. Saw there were unread text messages and emails then glanced at the Photos icon. I sat back as his hand suddenly came into view and slapped down on the screen pinning the phone to the counter. "I'm asking you to let me have this," he said in an even tone, "Please, let me just take this."

"Remove your goddamn fingers from this phone before I cut them off with your fucking bread knife," I answered calmly and stared down at the back of his hand. I saw his knuckles whiten as he withdrew his hand and stepped back. I reached toward the screen and clicked on the text message icon.

I miss you.

I miss you too.

When do you fly in the morning? Want to come over tonight?

Sure, I don't have to brief until 7am.

Plenty of time.

Never enough time when I'm inside you.

LOL. See you soon.

I gasped and dropped the phone on the counter. What the fuck was this, what the shit, what the fuck was this! I flipped up through the text history and saw pictures of a stunningly beautiful dark haired olive-skinned girl baring her breasts for the camera, you and your whore wrapped up together in a bed, your fingers sliding beneath the sheets as she threw her head back, eyes closed.

Noticed there was a video.

I couldn't breathe, couldn't get the air in. Room spinning, I put my face in my hands in stunned silence before I spun around frantically. I saw him standing motionless in the corner of the kitchen. Did he know about this?

I screamed at him, "Did you know about this?" He looked down. I suddenly realized I was the squadron joke. They all knew. They all fucking knew and no one told me, they just stood there and said hello and nice to see you and gave me hugs every time I came up with you to visit and all along they knew, they knew, they knew you were fucking this girl right under my nose.

They stood there in the squadron and told me it was a recovery mission straight faced. Stiff at attention they watched me walking alone down that goddamn chapel aisle and stared at me placing a shell next to you on the grass knowing your dick had been in some other girl the day before you died. The day before you packed it in. You'd been in her bed the morning you told me from your jet that you loved me on the phone you carried in your pocket as this blackness hid like a serpent in your locker.

I felt so stupid. I jammed my hands on top of my head as I stood and turned around in circles thinking about all the times you had gone to bed early in order to get sleep before a mission. All the times you had said you'd gone out with him and laughed the next morning about passing out on his couch. I remembered ribbing you about your profligate ways as we FaceTimed while you zipped on your uniform, the dull wallpaper of billeting visible in the background.

I spun around and looked at him in the corner of that kitchen and asked, "Did you know? Did you know about this?" He slowly lowered his head and nodded. "Oh my god," I said, louder and louder until I could hear screaming and realized it was me. It was me making that horrible noise as I bent over in his kitchen feeling the vomit rise in the back of my throat. I felt a hand touch my shoulder and sprang up, pushing him back. "Don't you fucking touch me you bastard," I gasped but he kept coming until I was backed into the corner where the sink counter joined the stove. He reached out his arms and grabbed me tightly as I hit him with my fists over and over finally breaking out in great gasping sobs, knees collapsing as he held me up. He whispered into my hair, "I'm sorry I didn't know he was still seeing her. Andy told me it was over, he said it was over, I'm sorry, I'm sorry."

"Did he love her?" I choked out, "Did he love her? Where did he meet her? How long has this been going on?

"I found out last year," he started to say and I threw my head back, sickened. "A year, it's been going on for a fucking year?" I put my hand over my eyes. "Jesus Christ, I'm so stupid. How could I not know? How could you not tell me?"

"I threatened to tell you and Andy said he'd stop, that he'd broken it off." His hand landed on the back of my head and pulled my cheek into his shoulder as tears poured from my eyes. "I didn't know. I didn't know it was still happening," he whispered.

"Did he love her?" I pressed those small words into his arm. "No," came the answer instantly, "He loved you. She was just available, I guess." I shook my head. "What a joke, she was just available. No one sleeps around behind their girlfriend's back for over a year with the same person if they're just available," I scoffed.

"People do crazy things sometimes," he said over me into the darkness. "We do crazy things for no reason. Sometimes it's better to just not ask a question when you don't really want to know the answer, I guess. And I didn't ask the question. I didn't ask him and I'm sorry."

"I'm sorry," tears dripped down the end of his nose onto my cheek.

I closed my eyes and choked out, "I guess I shouldn't judge." I pressed my fingers to my lips and shook my head. "If this is our big fucking confession night we might as well get all the secrets on the table, right? I'm no better than Andy. I just never fucked anyone. Never held hands with anyone, never kissed anyone, never did anything. Not even once."

"What are you talking about," he sounded confused. "None of this is your fault. You did nothing wrong. Andy's the one who fucked up, not you. We all thought he was an idiot. All of us. He was the fucking idiot because any of us would kill to be with someone like you." He grabbed me by the shoulders and stared down at my red face, "Andy was a fucking moron shithead to cheat on you."

"Everyone fucks up, yeah he fucked up but I've fucked up too," I muttered and shook my head, "I'm hardly one to talk about questions and answers and all that other bullshit." My hands reached up and shoved my hair away from my wet face.

He stepped back. "You're making no sense."

"I'm not making sense? You're the one talking about unasked questions. You didn't ask questions? You're afraid of the answers? I didn't do anything wrong? What a joke, you're joking, right?" I turned away. "How about the goddamn fucking truth about the day I met you? Think you can handle that? Andy fucked around and no one told me anything so how about I educate you about some of the shit about which you are ignorant and see how you like it." I shot those words out and threw my napkin in the air, fed up with this goddamn ridiculousness.

"Here's some truth for you! I'm a hypocrite. How about that? The day I met you, I saw you, I shook your fucking hand and then I went to the bathroom and texted my mother. My mother! I told her He's here He's right here and she said Who's here and I said Him. He's here. THE Guy. He's right here. And it's not Andy."

I couldn't stand it anymore, couldn't think straight standing here by the sink, my hands clasped around the back of my neck as I stared out the window at the lawn. "She said you have two choices: you can humiliate Andy in front of all his friends, in front of his new squadron for a maybe," I turned back toward him, "…for a maybe because you don't know if 'THE Guy' even feels the same way!" He looked at his feet and said nothing. Those words just came out, they poured out, my mouth kept talking and talking as they kept pouring out, "Or, she said I could let it ride. I could let it ride."

"And I did! I fucking did! I let it ride! I said nothing and every day I've regretted it!" So angry I was suddenly so angry as I charged across the kitchen and grabbed him by the front of his stupid t-shirt and shook him a little, trying to shake him up just a little. "I let it ride! Goddamn it!"

I pushed away. "Do you know it used to take me weeks to get over seeing you every time I came up here?" I felt like the oxygen was getting sucked out of the room. I flung my arms out wide and swung around to face him, "And every time Andy came up to fly I would tell him to tell you I said hi and he would tell me after every one of your fucking dinners together that you said hi back."

"Andy would tell me on the telephone, he always asks about you, you know, in that snarky tone because he knew," I jabbed my hand into his face, pinching my index finger and thumb close together in front of his nose, "He knew I liked you a little too much. He knew I liked you way too much but he enjoyed twisting that knife deeper and deeper, didn't he. Didn't he. He told me that and then went out and fucked someone else while I went to bed alone and wondered what you were doing!" The whole room tilted on a crazy angle, why was I even saying this to him? I'm in hell, I thought, this is hell I'm in hell I'm burning in hell. Stop talking just stop fucking talking.

But I didn't.

"I'm hardly better, am I," I clasped my hand to my throat. "I don't have any room to judge him, do I? Do I? This whole time, practically the whole time I was with Andy I've been thinking about you when I should have been thinking about the guy I was actually living with!" I shook my head and turned away from him and said quietly, "The women of Anchorage are absolutely insane to leave you out here unsupervised. Ignoring you. Just letting you wander through this town single and unattached. I just don't get it. I just do not understand the level of stupidity that must take." He angled his head away from me and smiled.

I sucked in a deep breath, "Yeah, Andy fucked some other girl. Maybe a lot of other girls while I just kept it all inside, kept it hidden inside my mind but I'm just as bad. I'm just as guilty as he is but at least I didn't rub it in."

Breathing faster, I gripped the side of the counter. "Women show dominance with possessions, this bag, my big ring, new car car blah blah blah. Men do it with people." I looked up as tears filled my eyes. "I always felt like Andy had me by the back of the neck up here, just shaking me, holding me up saying look at this, look what I got, look who loves me when all along you were all standing there knowing! All of you, all the guys every single goddamn one of you knew he was fucking some other girl and you just sat there at those dinners with us. You just fucking sat there and said nothing!"

"You know what Andy said to me once?" I said, on the knife edge of complete hysteria, "Andy said to me I think he has a crush on you. Who the fuck says things like that? Who? Who says that? Why would Andy say that to me? Andy, of all people! After all this, knowing he was going out and… Why? Why would he say that?"

He glanced up.

"And I always said I didn't see it, that you had a crush on me. I said I don't see it," I lurched around to face him, "and I didn't. I never saw anything but polite indifference but I always left out that all along I may not have seen it but I've damn sure been looking for it—I've been looking for it all along, every single time I looked for it! And every time we went out you wouldn't even look at me. You acted like I wasn't even there, like I was invisible. I just can't even…why would you…Was it pity? Did you just pity me? Was that it? You all must have thought I was a fucking moron to not see what was going on and you just let it happen." I turned away, I couldn't get it out.

That silence just got bigger and bigger and so I filled it up with things I didn't want to say, didn't want him to know. I didn't know why I was telling him these things. I couldn't think straight, the words came out in the wrong order. I felt like I was losing my mind.

"My god, I'm losing my mind," I put my fingers up to the side of my head.

He just stood there and looked at me as if I had horns coming out of my face, like I was a crazy person. "You don't have anything to say to me? Nothing? You're just going to stand there and say nothing?"

He shrugged a little, avoiding my eyes until I got right up in his face. Goddamn it, if I was going to jump in front of this fucking train he could at least give me the courtesy of watching. "Look at me," I grabbed his face, "What the fuck is wrong with you? You seriously have nothing to say to me? After all this, after everything, you have nothing to say?"

I backed away and shoved my hands against his chest, "Maybe we're not even right for each other, maybe we'd be terrible together, you and me," my voice cracked. "Maybe it's all in my head and kissing you would be like smashing my face into a rock." I threw my arms up in frustration.

He let out a tiny smile, "Or licking a light socket." Jesus Christ on a cracker I wanted to put my fist through his face, that beautiful face.

"Or maybe you're gay! Please god be gay because that would be so much easier for me," I slapped my hands on my knees, bent over and shook my head in disbelief. "You've never had a serious girlfriend as long as I've known you, for years now you haven't—and I know because I hang on every word anyone says about you and your fucking relationship status. Maybe you are gay. God, please god, if you were gay we could just laugh about this and you could help me pick out curtains or some shit like that."

"I'm not gay," he said very quietly.

"Oh god," I looked up, sickened, "are you a Republican?"

He cringed.

"Jesus Christ!" I dragged it out, I really drew that Jesus Christ way out. "I'm in love with a fucking Republican." I couldn't even believe it. My blood pressure was so high I felt like I was having a stroke, like my brain was dissolving and falling out of my head.

A Republican.

"How could this be any worse? My god, I'm in the twilight zone. I'm in the motherfucking twilight zone." Dazed, I didn't know which way to go, so I just turned in random circles in the center of his kitchen, hands flailing. Now I knew what it was like when people have nervous breakdowns. I was stunned that this epic humiliation was actually occurring right now in my reality. It was infinitely worse than a naked-in-front-of-a-crowd dream because here I was, awake, running my mouth while he was just standing there like…like something.

"A light socket?" I was so mad now, oh man, it was on. It was on like Donkey Kong. "You think kissing you would be like licking a light socket? Oh, please. Look at you!" I flicked my fingers toward his chest. "You look like Peter fucking Pan. Your shirt is hideous. You look like an accountant! Nobody fucks accountants!"

He rolled his eyes and I put both palms on his chest and shoved. I put my hands on that t-shirt where it stretched across his broad shoulders and shoved him as hard as I could sending that black iPhone crashing to the tile floor as he leaned back, elbows propped on the counter, and cocked his head insolently to the side.

"Fucking you would be like fucking a paper towel," I taunted him, "Flat and limp." His eyes narrowed. I saw that crack and pounced, "You'd probably just lay there like a starfish. Like a fifties housewife, you'd just lay there and take it like a bitch." I laughed right in his face.

"I bet you can't even get it up!"

Yikes. That was a bit much, even I knew that. Eyes wide, I clapped my hand over my mouth. I knew the instant those words escaped that things were about to get downright nasty. "Oh, you think so? You think I can't get it up?" His hand shot out grabbing my face pulling me forward until our noses touched, "Well, allow me to educate you, sweetheart. You couldn't handle me on my worst day." His mouth slid along the side of my face, his voice dark and silky. "If you could ever even be so lucky."

Slowly, very slowly his arm slipped around my waist pulling me tight up against his hips as he ground into me, one hand grabbing my ass as the other wrapped itself in my hair. He turned my head sharply to the side and licked a hot wet trail up my neck. Teeth biting, tugging at my earlobe, he kicked that iPhone across the kitchen sending it shattering into the far wall and whispered, "Welcome to the major leagues, bitch."

TWENTY-THREE

I spent a sleepless night hiding down in that basement room fighting the urge to sneak out of the house in the middle of the night and run. Because that's what I do, I realized. I run. I'd run from the kitchen just hours before when he'd touched me, when he'd whispered those words in my ear because it's what I do.

I run. And I keep running until I'm right back where I started. It never ends, does it, it just never ends and I'm so tired. All I wanted was a dreamless sleep but instead I curled up in that bed tangled in sweaty sheets with a terrible throbbing headache trying to get the image of her breasts, of her face out of my mind as I drowned in a guilt-ridden agony.

I jumped out of the bed at two a.m. and rushed to the small bathroom, retching. I turned on the shower and huddled in the bottom of the bathtub with water beating down onto my back in complete darkness as my head pounded with a nearly unbearable pain. A small knock tapped on the door.

"Are you ok?" he whispered through the crack.

I answered, "I just have a migraine, I'll be ok, I just need to lay here for a while. I'll be fine in the morning, I promise."

The door slowly shut, reopening a few minutes later with a soft click. The corner of the curtain slipped a millimeter to the side as his hand placed a can of ice cold Coke on the edge of the tub. "Google, Source of All Truth and Knowledge, said this is supposed to be good for migraines," he whispered, closing the curtain slowly. "Thank you," I answered, crying softly in the bottom of the tub as the snap of the can opening filled the tiny room.

I crawled out of the shower around three a.m. and snuck up into the kitchen for some ice. I saw he had swept up the pieces of the shattered iPhone and moved the box into a corner next to the back door. I stood in the middle of the kitchen in my t-shirt and wondered where that phone went. My fist clutched a bottle of Advil as I decided that what I had seen was enough, that some things were better left unknown.

I turned away and left that kitchen with its unasked questions because I no longer cared about the fucking answers.

TWENTY-FOUR

Early the next morning we threw the tents, sleeping bags, coolers and what appeared to a giant traveling moonshine distillery into the back of his SUV and took off into the backwoods. When we pulled up to a clearing I saw what looked like the entire squadron, wives and kids included, milling about smartly next to a giant stack of firewood.

I got out and slammed the door shifting nervously next to the SUV as he dropped down the tailgate and started throwing stuff onto the ground. "Hey," he peered around the bumper, "Lazy ass! You feel like contributing today or what?" I shoveled random objects off the ground into my arms and trudged past the group of your friends burying my face in a rolled up sleeping bag as I nodded a quick hello to the guys as I walked by. Suddenly I felt like I wasn't supposed to be there. I didn't belong anymore, that my invitation was the recreational equivalent of a mercy screw and everyone was wondering when I'd get my fill and leave.

"I don't think I should have come here. Everyone knows. I know they do and they're all staring at me. I shouldn't be here," I whispered as he upended a long bag on the ground, sliding my tent out with a quick jerk. "It's ok," he replied as he handed me a set of stakes. "They're happy to see you, really. Sure, it'll be a little weird but only until everybody starts drinking and then you'll blend right in."

"So you're saying they have to be drunk to tolerate my presence," I snipped. He whipped a long groundsheet right in my face with a snap.

"Yep, pretty much."

TWENTY-FIVE

"You almost don't need the moon these stars are so bright," I said softly the next evening as we walked away into the darkness toward the edge of the river while a chorus of drunken pilots clustered around the bonfire singing about eye-poking sticks in a horrendously off-key tone. A soft breeze wafted through the close-set trees pushing a stray piece of hair past my cheek.

Such tall trees, up and up and up. Who owns these trees?

God…unless we've had them so long adverse possession's kicked in.

Maybe, then, trees own themselves considering since the beginning there'd just been them here for millions of years, that statute running out eons ago with the Good Book inadmissible for lack of specificity. Certainly not determinative, a conspicuous lack of dates a serious impediment to proof of ownership. Or proof of anything else.

The Omnipotent Almighty should have had that document reviewed by outside counsel.

Self-representation means he's got an idiot for a lawyer.

But we'd run out the statute too, our trampling feet given tacit permission to remain. So…we own the trees again. Yet they'd remained and run the statute and back and forth and back and forth and back and forth maybe we're just renting, my face stared up at the sky.

"It's even more beautiful up north where you can see the auroras," he whispered. "Why are we whispering," my voice muffled when his finger smushed up against my lips. "Because there's bears out here," he told me in a solemn voice. I stepped closer. "Are you serious?" I felt like an idiot. Surely there weren't bears this close to camp and even if there were I'm pretty sure they'd smell us whether we were whispering or not.

He told me I did stink like a dog's behind and shied away as I pinched him. "Pffft, I haven't had a shower in two days," I tugged my jacket tight to my chest. "Are you cold?" he pulled me by my ear toward him and slung his arm around my shoulder, "Get over here, cow lady." He swung his other arm around front squeezing me tightly.

"I can't breathe," I gasped. He kept squeezing and squeezing harder and harder, laughing.

"Can you breathe now? How about now?"

He pushed his hand over my face pinching my nose shut with his thumb and forefinger and I started to flail around.

"How about now? Huh? Can you breathe now?"

"Stop it you twat," I smacked his hand away from my face and sucked in a deep lungful of cold night air. He leaned his chin on top of my head and we stood there looking across the water listening to the trees shift softly in the wind. "I love it here," he said wistfully.

"It's so peaceful this far outside of the city, isn't it?"

"Well, you know what they say about Anchorage," he shifted a little to the side, "You're only fifteen minutes away from Alaska."

"I have heard that, actually," I smiled, "I've just never been any further than Seward before you took me fishing and that was by highway."

"When did you go down to Seward?"

"Last summer, I think. We only drove down for the day. It was such a pretty trip through the mountains. I didn't see any sheep, though. That was kinda disappointing."

"Dall sheep?"

"Yeah, those things. With the horns. Andy said they jump around on the cliffs right next to the road but I never saw any of them."

He told me the sheep weren't there all year long but I should keep looking. We could drive back down to Seward if I wanted or take the float plane. That there was a landing area right there in the harbor.

"I've always wanted to buy a sailboat and rage around Alaska," I reached up to brush my hair away from my face again. "Middle-age rage? How exciting," he rolled his eyes. He pulled my ponytail to the side and tucked it under the edge of my scarf. "I don't know who you're calling middle age, buddy," I reminded him he was a good five years older than me. At least. "Near death," I said. He made crotchety old person noises.

I shushed him, leaning back reaching up and pinching his lips shut with my free hand. He lifted his arm and grabbed my fingers off his face turning my hand palm down as he gently kissed the back of my hand. I swallowed and tried to pull my hand away but he flipped it over and pressed his mouth to the underside of my wrist before cupping my fingers around his cheekbone, his hand holding mine against his face. "Hey," he turned me slightly and pushed my waist away with his free arm, "Dance with me."

He laced his fingers through mine, wrapped his other arm around my midsection and swung me gently in a circle a few inches off the ground making grunting noises like I weighed three hundred pounds. "Whoa!" I protested, "This isn't PT Barnum and Bailey!" He gave me a full-on leer and leaned in toward my face, "Every day with you is a circus." He moved closer and closer. I took a step back when he tightened his grip on my hand.

"You should be careful walking around in the woods with strangers," his mouth moved toward mine. I felt a tree brush up against my back. "There's more than just bears out here, you know," he whispered, the moonlight glinting off his hair. I turned my face away when he set his hand on the tree above my shoulder and pressed his body up against me. I couldn't breathe. Everything suddenly seemed like it was made of molasses dripping swirling sticking together. The air was so thick I could hardly suck any of it into my lungs. Twigs snapped under his feet as he pulled my lower body in tight and slipped a leg in between mine, pressing his hips forward.

He angled his face toward mine, gripped my shoulder and trailed his knuckles across the back of my neck. Gently pulling me in to him, our lips brushed feather-light against each other and I closed my eyes. It was like touching a hot stove and eating ice cream at the same time, everything pressed against him burned while the rest of me shivered ice cold. I opened my mouth slightly and his tongue slipped along the edges before we pushed into each other. Like someone hit the sharpen button on a camera one too many times everything just crystallized as he kissed me, his hand gripping the jacket between my shoulder blades, crushing me into him as his tongue swept hard inside my mouth over and over. I heard him let out a happy sigh when suddenly the sound of a crinkling beer can rang out into the night. I squinted into the darkness over his shoulder and saw three of your squadron mates standing frozen in a silent row.

I jammed my eyes shut and pressed my face into his neck. "I think we have company," I whispered sickly. His hand tightened briefly on the back of my neck as he stepped away. I heard him curse under his breath before he turned around to face the boys keeping one arm wrapped around my waist.

"Gentlemen," he solemnly nodded at them and stepped past towing me behind him like a suitcase. I stared desperately at my feet, two of the boys moving slightly to one side, the other merely rotating to face us as we passed through their silent gauntlet. I tried to choke back the vomit as he hauled me up under his arm shoving me back down the path toward camp. As we walked away he glanced over his shoulder at your buddies and I saw one of them grin and raise his beer in a silent salute before we disappeared around the corner.

TWENTY-SIX

"I think I should probably head back soon," I said awkwardly the next evening, shifting from side to side in his narrow hallway. "I have to plan some stuff and I need to do things, you know, there's things I should probably be doing now…back home and stuff…" my voice trailed off into an awkward pause.

He brushed closely past me, sliding past, full up pressing against me bumping me gently against the wall, before whispering, "Of course you have things to do. I'm surprised you stayed this long, actually." Uncomfortable, I felt like I had missed signs that I'd overstayed my welcome. That he was ready for me to leave long ago, that last night had been too much and he wanted me gone.

Maybe he regretted touching me, wanted to pull back those words he'd whispered in a dark corner of his kitchen, that kiss in the woods witnessed by all your friends, my stiff goodbyes with the boys staring and smirking at one another, giving him a high five as he sauntered to the pickup truck and drove off with me in the passenger seat with a hand shielding the side of my face, red with embarrassment.

"Ok, well, I'll look at tickets and let you know. I'll let you know today when I'm going and maybe you can take me to the airport?"

He pulled his finger lightly across my collarbone as he sidestepped by, "Sure thing, sweetheart." He glided away toward his bedroom at the end of the hall then poked his head around the door and said suggestively, "I'll be in here if you need something. Anything. Anything at all you might need…just come right in if you decide you need something." I shrugged a shoulder and told him I thought I was good. He puckered up his lips and blew me a kiss, "I'm sure you are, baby. I'm sure you are." He turned away and closed the door. I stood mutely next to a fancy Asian end table holding some weird twisty sculpture made of iridescent green glass.

Ok then. I marched over to the top of the basement stairs and tramped down to the room to pack my suitcase. In went my winter pants and high-topped boots, a few pairs of socks I'd pick up at TJ Maxx while he poked around in the sports gear section and the fingerless wool gloves he'd bought me on a whim at the base Exchange. A rolled up t-shirt went in next alongside the gray birthday sweater and the blue one I'd set aside when I packed up your things. Your things laying inside those olive bags still stacked in the corner of our bedroom in Seattle.

That blue sweater. Your sweater. The one I'd worn under my lightweight coat when I came back to Anchorage.

I laid my hands on the dark wool slowly running my fingertips over the weave as I bowed my head. I'm sorry, I apologized desperately. I'm sorry. I sent those words out to wherever you were, into the air where I knew you were watching me kiss your best friend in the dark. Where you saw him kissing me back and knew that I liked it.

I'm sorry, I'm so sorry my mind whispered into the ether as I stood there clutching your favorite sweater to my nose searching for the smell of a perfume that wasn't mine.

TWENTY-SEVEN

I should have told you but I didn't know how the text said a week later. *He did love you. He did. He did. I swear it.*

I didn't reply. Down in the bathroom I started our shower and sat in the stall with my head on my knees. Perfectly still I sat frozen on our boat in the darkness of a hot June afternoon. I sat there in silence and steamed.

I know I replied back the next day. *Shit happens. Let's just move on, let's just not talk about it anymore please.*

There was no answer.

That night I tossed all your shit in a giant garbage bag and threw it up the stairs into the living room. I ripped your shirts off the hangars, kicked your running shoes from the bottom of the closet into the hallway and pulled down the photos of us I'd taped up on the bathroom mirror and the wall next to my side of the bed.

I tore open that Ziploc and threw our sheets into the washer with a cup of bleach and set it on the extra heavy scrub cycle. Then I sat on the couch in the living room staring at those green bags, my hands clutching the edges of a fur throw you'd given me the winter before because I was always cold. So frigid, you'd joked, covering me up with blanket after blanket until everything but my nose was buried. Was I frigid? I looked at those bags and ran the fur between my fingers.

Was that the reason you went to her?

Was I really that bad? I wondered as I sat there in the living room with your stuff strewn about on the floor, a ripped photo of your face smiling up at me from the coffee table. Could I have done better, been better, looked better, remembering her perfect face and long dark hair. Her giant tits pushing half out of the camera frame as you bent in close snapping that picture. I ran a hand across the top of my head and thought about your fingers under that sheet and the look on her face.

Questioning…What did my face look like when your hands were on me?

I cringed, remembering those times you would tell me you wanted more, needed more, to do more adventurous things and me answering *ok* in an awkward voice. If I'd put out every night would you have colored inside the lines? I thought back to a long ago vacation where you asked me quietly on a dark balcony what I would say if you told me you had cheated on me and me telling you I'd be so disappointed because you're better than that.

I felt sick. The tears wanted to come but they got stuck somewhere in the back of my throat as I thought about unasked questions in an Anchorage kitchen. I never asked you the question when you softly said those words but even then I knew. I knew, I told the air silently as I ran that fur over my cheek. I knew but I didn't ask because I couldn't bear to hear the answer. I knew.

I knew.

I knew but I stayed because I loved you. I sat there crying on our salon couch telling the silence that I loved you, that she didn't matter, that the others didn't matter because I loved you I loved you. I thought back to me telling you I love you as I stared at your gorgeous face while you sat with your head in your hands, as you blamed me years ago for it happening again some other place, some other time but never apologized, never admitted it while I stood in a dark kitchen in my work suit and heels, sobbing. Me telling you it didn't matter, I loved you anyway that I couldn't live without you, that even if it was true I didn't care I didn't care as you sprang across the room taking me in your arms, covering my face with kisses. How we just ignored it, plastering over the cracks with passionate caresses in the night.

Cracks that kept widening beneath our feet as I just moved on, I moved on like I always did. I just moved on through like I always have. Chin up, I balanced and took one for the team. I didn't ask questions, our silence the great equalizer as I craved you desperately with the part of my heart that didn't belong to him while you texted me *love love* before walking out of your hotel room on your way to her.

I put those bags in the back of my car and took them to Goodwill and didn't look in the rearview mirror once as I drove away. I crumpled up the receipt and threw it out of the window as I passed by our favorite Italian restaurant.

Let me know next time you're in town the text said as I hit Send.

Will do he replied late into the night as I rolled away toward the middle of the bed and turned my back on that empty corner.

TWENTY-EIGHT

The phone rang around two o'clock on a random Tuesday three weeks later and it was him on the line. "Hey, guess what!" he shouted out, "I'm in Seattle! Surprise!" I sat up on the couch, pushed the quilt off to the side and hit mute on the remote. "What do you mean? How are you in Seattle?" I flipped on a light as he told me that on his way down to California they'd had to stop because something went wrong with the plane, that he wouldn't make crew rest and was being forced to stay over.

"But what about all the widgets? What will people do without their ice skates and frozen fish and laundered money?" I teased him. "Luckily, we were just moving an empty plane from one location to another," he explained, "It's not carrying anything otherwise we'd have to move all that shit all over to a new jet which is a total pain in the ass."

"So…since I'm stuck here I was wondering if you'd like to get a drink or something. If you're not busy. On a Tuesday," he mocked my hermit ways in a snooty voice. "I'm sure your social schedule is totally full. So full. Out every night, you're so popular. Veritably packed, your Tuesdays are."

I retaliated by telling him there was a great place on Capitol Hill that only served food made of tofu. "Tofu beef, tofu chicken, tofu shrimp," I said innocently, "They have it all! You'll love it." Politely he told me he'd rather lick dog shit than choke down beef flavored tofu and announced that we would be eating at Metropolitan Grill and I would be buying.

"Hey," I protested, "I don't have that kind of money." I put on a nice pair of leather pants and some eyeliner anyway, holding my heels in my hand as I padded barefoot down the dock a few hours later. He was waiting in the parking lot leaning against the side of a cab wearing a pair of dress pants and a polo shirt. I walked out of the gate as he strolled forward and gave me a hug, escorting me back to the car and opening my door. "It's good to see you," he smiled, "You look good. You look nice…great pants." "Thanks," I said, sliding across the seat bending down to put on my shoes awkwardly, not meeting his eyes.

"This place is really nice," I warned him as we headed south on Westlake Avenue, "so you need to be on your best behavior, you back-woods heathen." Quirking his mouth to one side, he sighed dramatically, "I'll do my very best not to wipe my mouth on my sleeve, mom."

At the restaurant a maître de in a tuxedo asked us if we had a reservation. When we said no, he announced in a haughty tone that he could not accommodate us at this time. "We can sit at the bar," I said, "I don't mind sitting at the bar." He shrugged, "I don't care where we sit, as long as I get a drink ASAP and you pay for it." I pointed out two empty seats which he quickly poached.

"Are you in town long?" I perched atop a leather stool and a waiter promptly handed me a drink menu which apparently doubled as the greater King County telephone book. "Depends on how long it takes to get this disaster fixed," he said. "They're putting me up over at the Fairmont Olympic tonight for sure. Don't know anything more than that right now."

"Wow. The Fairmont. That's pretty swanky," I whistled under my breath, "I'd love to have that expense account." I stopped. "Hey, wait a second," I leaned over, propped an elbow on the bar and raised an accusing finger, "You should be paying for this dinner, pal, with your fancy expense account." "But then you'd feel obligated," he said.

"Obligated to do what?" I watched him rearrange his silverware precisely equidistant from his water glass. "To put out," he said, an evil smile on his face, "You know, a guy spends big money on a dinner like this he expects something back."

"I'll get right on that." I blushed.

"Oh, you will." he flipped to page 192 in the beverage encyclopedia, "Do you know what you want? Look, they have a porter that's eight percent alcohol."

"Sounds good to me," Mischievously, I nodded to the looming bartender to bring me a pint. "You better watch out though," I snatched my drink off the counter deliberately screwing up his silverware chi with my elbow. "I get handsy after a few drinks."

He smiled.

"I might accidentally say something mildly inappropriate and embarrass you," I watched him from the corner of my eye.

He shrugged nonchalantly.

"Medium inappropriate?"

He raised a finger.

"Massively inappropriate?"

Smirking, he put his forearm on the counter, leaned over and told the bartender, "Keep 'em coming."

TWENTY-NINE

Summer in Seattle is a strange exotic beast where everyone arrives at dinner dressed respectably but ends up leaving the bars at ten o'clock at night staggering down sunlit streets looking like cheap whores. "I look like a whore," I laughed quietly to myself before stumbling over the sidewalk, my bag fell off my shoulder onto the cement. I gripped his arm tightly, leaned over and picked up my wallet. He smiled, "You're a what? Did you just say you're a whore? Are you drunk?"

"No, I'm shitfaced," I said solemnly, "There's a difference."

"Ok, sweetheart. Whatever you say," he put his arm around my waist and pulled me aside to let people pass. "Maybe we should get you home now."

"It's your fault," I said plaintively, "You're the one that ordered me those drinks on an empty stomach!"

"I didn't expect you to have three of them before we'd even gotten our food," he laughed. "You're a lush! I'd never have guessed it. A lightweight and a lush at the same time." I weaved to the side slightly before reaching out an arm to steady myself. "I'm pretty sure this road was straight the last time I was down here," I said.

"Probably so," he answered straight-faced and signaled for a cab.

"Hey! Are you really going to send me home in a taxi by myself?" I whined. "Is that wise? I don't know if that's wise. I could end up in a landfill somewhere and then you'd feel really bad, you know that? You'd feel really bad."

"I'm not sending you home alone in a taxi, baby," he smiled down at me. "I'm taking you back to the Fairmont where you're going to sleep off your bender. I'll bring you home in the morning."

I clutched my jacket around my shoulders, straightened up as much as possible and said regally, "I hope you're not expecting special favors because three drinks and a steak salad will get you a hand job. But nothing more. Maybe if you'd bought me dessert…" I realized I was having trouble controlling the volume of my voice and blushed bright red as a woman nearby smiled and said, "You tell him, sweetie." He howled with laughter.

"And what a hand job it'd be," he shoveled me into a cab. "It'd be epic," I slurred and leaned over the front seat toward the driver, "My hand jobs are always memorable, I've been told." The cab driver flicked her eyes up to the rearview mirror and raised an eyebrow.

"The Fairmont on University Street, please," he reached around my shoulders and clapped a hand over my mouth. "To the Fairmont and beyond," I sang out into his palm before slowly sliding down the seat, my head on his shoulder as everything blurred into a delicious kaleido-scope of colors slowly fading into deep dark black.

THIRTY

I woke up a few hours later fully clothed draped across his bare chest in a giant bed. I cracked open one eye and slowly stretched out, sliding under the sheets backward towards the edge quietly peeling one arm out from where he'd trapped it. I really had to go to the bathroom. This was an emergency. I managed to get one full leg out before a large hand came swatting across the top of the comforter landing squarely on my head. "Where, exactly, do you think you're going," he said softly. "To the bathroom," I muttered, my face pushed down into the mattress, "and I can't breathe, you're suffocating me."

"Sorry," he said, not sounding sorry at all as he pushed down on the back of my head just a little harder before letting up. "Make sure you come straight back," he said, laughing silently. "Naturally. Totally. I'll be back in just a jiffy," I slipped out from under the covers, and ran a hand over my hair pushing my foot around the floor for my shoes. "You just close your eyes and rest. I'll only be a minute."

"Looking for these?" he said, rolling over on his side and raising himself up on one arm. I saw in the light of the alarm clock a single high heel in his hand wagging ever so slowly in my direction.

"Yes," I said grudgingly.

"Can't have 'em, sweetheart," he tossed it onto the floor and leaned back on the pillow pushing the sheet down to his waist, folding his hands behind his head. "Wouldn't want you to end up in a landfill, now would we."

Drawing myself up nice and tall, I smoothed down the front of my blouse and said, "This is not a conversation I'm prepared to have at this present moment, sir, because I am about to pee my pants," and ran around the corner into the bathroom slamming the door. I stayed in there for a good ten minutes listening to him softly whistling in that bed. I leaned my face against the mirror and shook my head. I did not want to go back out there. Good god, the humiliation. I wondered what I had said to him the night before.

What I had done. Well, to be honest, it was still night I told myself after glancing over at the wall clock. Three thirty-seven in the morning, to be exact.

"Are you planning on sleeping in the bathtub?" he asked from outside the door. "I'm thinking about it," I answered miserably. He knocked, peering through the crack. "Do you really feel that bad?"

"No, I feel fine. I'm just wondering happened last night," I cringed away and held a hand over my eyes, "I vaguely remember a cab and something about a hand job." I peeped through my fingers and saw him prop his hands on his hips as he shook his head in dismay, "Yep. You told the driver your hand jobs were legendary and, I must admit, it did not disappoint. It did not disappoint." He walked forward and put both hands on the counter trapping me in between.

"Oh God, I didn't," I groaned, "did I?"

He leaned in and put his mouth to my ear. "Sadly…no. But the night is young."

I realized we were standing in a hotel room and he was inches from my face wearing nothing but a pair of pajama pants and no shirt. I also realized he was in really good shape, my face getting redder and redder as he stared at me. "Feeling better, huh?" he said softly. "I'm happy to hear that."

"I do feel better," I said in a rush, crossing my arms over my chest. "Better, yes, I feel much better, thank you for asking. But not totally better. Just slightly better. Halfway, really, but not all the way better," I rambled on as he leaned closer.

"How much better?" he said.

"Not hand job better," I replied, immediately wanting to retract those words back into my mouth.

"Hmmm…" He narrowed his eyes. "That's too bad. I spent a lot of money on that steak salad, you know. I feel like I should receive at least some benefit, some consideration from this transaction."

I grinned with all my teeth showing and scrunched up my shoulders before dipping under his arm in a desperate dash for the door. "Nope," he said, grabbing my wrist as I scooted by, "there is no escape. No escape for you now, cow lady." He popped his shoulder under my arm as I went by, slinging me up across his front. He kicked the bathroom door open, marched out and unceremoniously dumped me face down on the bed. I grunted as he cannonballed right onto my back bouncing me a few inches off the mattress. "My god," I yelped from underneath his body and he laughed, "You weigh a million pounds! What are you eating up there in Anchorage?"

He reached up and swept my hair to the side, baring the back of my neck, "Meat. I eat lots of meat." I felt his fingertip sliding softly along my ear as he jammed an arm underneath my waist and rolled over bringing me flat on top of him, face up. And there we were. In a bed. A big one. Alone in the dark in a really nice hotel and he was wearing a pair of thin pajama pants with no shirt. Not good. This was not good.

"Lots and lots of meat," he said softly, bending a knee up and stretching it over my leg. Pinning it down with his calf he slowly ran his hand from my hip up my ribcage very lightly over the top of my breast. I arched backward as the other hand slipped under my waistband and slowly unsnapped my pants. He ran a single finger across the top of my hipbone and slipped his hand down in between my legs. Turning my head, I sighed as he licked lightly up my neck. I thought about his words in that kitchen and drew in a sharp breath. "That's right," he said into the darkness, "major leagues, baby. Major leagues right here."

Gently he slipped a finger inside me. I couldn't breathe. I gripped the hand resting on my breast as he hooked his fingers inside the front of my shirt next to all those buttons, all those buttons that needed to be unfastened immediately. He pulled hard and I heard something rip. His other hand came up and then my shirt was completely open, the buttons pinging off the headboard. "Surprising," he whispered, "If I'd realized you weren't wearing anything under this shirt six hours ago I might have done this sooner." I shrugged a shoulder. "It was laundry day," I said, grabbing his hand and pushing it back down toward my waist. He smiled against my shoulder, biting down where it joined my neck. "Every day should be laundry day," he said and rolled us over suddenly. "In fact, let me assist you with the rest of your laundry, madam."

He sat up, grabbed my waistband and pulled. Further and further down he pulled until he was halfway off the bed tugging my leather pants off my ankles. I felt his tongue run a thin hot line from my knee up the back of my thigh before he gripped my waist lifting me up. Yanking my underwear off with a single stroke, he laid down on his back between my legs. I felt him pushing me upwards and suddenly he was underneath, his tongue inside me as he pulled me down into his mouth. Leaning back, I shuddered and scraped my nails down his bare chest as he licked and sucked stroking me over and over.

He pulled me tightly down as I opened my eyes and came unexpectedly in a hot rush, leaning forward with my hand on his shoulder, squeezing, clenching tight as his fingers slipped deep inside, his thumb rubbing against me. I gasped and he smiled, tipping me over to one side. "Like licking a light socket," he purred as he slipped off his pants with both hands.

He swung his knees between my legs and leaned over putting a hand on either side of my shoulders, bending down. Reaching across my face, he hooked a finger inside my mouth. I licked it as he grabbed me by the back of my neck pulling, reclining as I glided up onto his lap. Clutching my hips, he yanked me down and then he was inside me hard and deep. I could feel him throbbing as I touched myself. He sighed softly and threw his head back, eyes closed. I wrapped an arm around his neck and pulled myself halfway up, sliding slowly as he took my nipple between his teeth and bit gently, his hands wide across my shoulder blades.

As I ground my hips down I could hear him panting, could feel him shivering and I smiled. As I moved I breathed into his ear, "Is this your worst day? Because I feel like I'm handling you pretty well right now." He turned toward my mouth, "Not even close to my best day," that delicious smirk crossing his face, "I'm going to fuck you so hard you won't be able to walk down to breakfast."

"Who says we're going to breakfast," I replied breathlessly. He ground against me moving slowly deep inside as he buried his face in my hair and smiled before tipping me over onto my back. Stroke after stroke he pushed himself into me. Lifting my hips up faster now I grabbed his ass with both hands pulling him in. God, he was so beautiful. He laid his forehead against mine, sweating, his arms shaking. "Jesus," he said and thrust inside me for a last time holding himself there with a gasp, shuddering. After a long minute, he laid the side of his face against my shoulder, panting.

I tipped his chin up with my fingers and kissed him gently as he took a deep breath and put his nose to mine. Eye-to-eye he told me in a very serious voice, "I feel like I need more data points before I consider this event a success."

I laughed. "More data points?"

"Yep," he said, rolling over into the darkness with me in his arms, "Lots and lots of data points."

THIRTY-ONE

The next morning outside my marina, he stepped around the back of the taxi, opened my door and held out a hand. I took it awkwardly and got out, shifting nervously from one foot to another using one hand to make sure my shirt was still securely closed.

"Well, I had a lovely time. Thank you for a very nice evening." I said uneasily.

"A lovely time? A very nice evening?"

Blushing, I glanced up past his face.

"Hey. I'm over here," he said, putting his hands on either side of my head as he leaned over in my line of sight, "I'll call you when I get home in a few days, ok?" He leaned forward, kissed me and softly stroked his fingertips down the side of my cheek. I nodded, feeling like I was sixteen, unbalanced and wobble kneed.

He climbed back into the cab, shut the door and rolled down the window. As he pulled away he leaned out and yelled, "Thanks for the screw, cow lady!" and blew me a kiss.

THIRTY-TWO

September came bringing with it three days of glorious fall leaves that graced Westlake Avenue before the trees said fuck it and dropped trou. "I'm going to go to Colorado," he said on the phone one night as we mutually screamed at the Seahawks losing once again to the goddamn St. Louis Rams.

The Rams.

"What the fuck," I said in disbelief gripping my hair with my hand, "how can we possibly lose to the Rams every single year? Every year! EVERY. FUCKING. YEAR." He sighed, "I know. I know. And it's soon to be the Los Angeles Rams which makes it even worse. It's beyond all comprehension. Armageddon is once again upon us. The end times are here. Stock up on Spam." I turned away from the television in disgust and said, "Why are you going to Colorado?" the words suddenly sticking in my throat. "Oh my god," I said, sickened.

"It's ok, it's ok," he said over that telephone line, calling on that phone from Anchorage. There was silence as I sat on the couch with my head between my knees, breathing deeply. "Do you want to go with me?" he asked, "no pressure."

Deep in thought I answered, "Might as well. I can't get onto the grounds without you anyway, right?"

His voice faded into the distance as I heard him say, "Ok well ok then," before he hung up. A day later an Expedia email popped into my Inbox congratulating me for choosing lovely Denver as my vacation destination. "I bought you a ticket," his text said, "Meet you there?"

"Ok," I said and slowly typed, "Thank you."

No problem, cow lady came the reply a half hour later. At one o'clock in the morning I rolled over to see a text notification shining up from the screen. Holding my thumb on the passcode button I read *I got two rooms at the Holiday Inn outside the gate but...*

I answered back with a smiley face and a snarky *we'll see* as I rolled over and went back to sleep.

The next morning a mere four words popped onto the screen as I showered in my tiny bathroom. I pulled the curtain aside and looked down.

Steak salad it is.

THIRTY-THREE

"Just ten minutes," I told him in a tired voice, "I just need ten minutes and then we can go to dinner. I'm so sorry my plane was late into Denver. Sorry. Sorry you had to wait around for so long." He pushed me toward the bed. "No problem," he told me, "Ten minutes won't kill us." He flipped off the light as he kicked shut my hotel room door. I sat down on the edge of the couch, took a shoe off and stood up, unzipping my jeans. "Whoa!" he looked up in surprise as he drew the comforter back. "What's with the de-pantsing?"

"I can't get comfortable with them on," I said, exhausted. He agreed sleeping with pants was not ideal, that comfort was paramount and promptly dropped his own jeans down to his ankles in solidarity. In boxers and a t-shirt he pushed me onto the bed swinging one knee and then the other over my body as we crawled underneath the sheets. Rolling onto his side, he slung an arm underneath mine and hauled me up against his front, my back pressing up against his body. "Only ten minutes," I whispered, closing my eyes, snuggling backward, pulling his arm tighter around my waist interlocking our fingers as I fell asleep, his breath hot against my neck.

The sun had already set behind the mountains when I cracked an eye open a few hours later. Stretching out my toes toward the bottom of the bed I rolled over and saw him sprawled on his back next to me snoring softly. He looked so peaceful. I inched over and gently pinched his nose shut. He came awake with a huge jerk, flailing out an arm in a panic as he took a gasping breath. "Jesus fucking Christ!" he shoved me away. "What the fuck! What the fuck was that?" I smashed my face into the pillows laughing hysterically as he swiped at his face with his hands, muttering threats of death and dismemberment in my general direction. "I couldn't help myself," I jabbed him with a finger, "I owe you from that night you tried to suffocate me in the woods, you know."

"Suffocate you? You think I was trying to suffocate you?" he grabbed a pillow and slammed it over my face pressing me down into the sheets. "How do you like me now? Huh, cow lady? How do you like me now!" He straddled my back and then laid flat on top of me, spreading out his arms and legs to keep me pinned as I wriggled underneath the pillow.

"I like you fine!" I choked out, "Shit, get off me! Get off right now!"

"No problem," he grabbed the back of my t-shirt and pulled it over the top of my head. Sitting up, he ripped his own t-shirt off and threw both articles of clothing toward the far corner of the room then whipped the covers to the side sending them sliding to the floor. He placed a large hand in the middle of my shoulder blades and pressed down as he reached around the front of my inner thigh rubbing his palm down my crotch. "You first," he pulled my lace panties to the side and stroked two fingers across me putting more weight on my back pinning me to the bed with his forearm. Spreading my legs wide with his knees he slid his fingers deeper and deeper as he ground against my ass.

My hands clutched the sheets as he moved his hand from my back grabbing the front of my hipbone as he jerked me off the mattress, his thumb flicking against me lightly as he pushed his fingers inside over and over. Face down, I turned my head and told him "Don't stop, please Jesus don't stop don't stop" and then I was shaking and falling forward as he wrapped an arm tight around my waist.

He pulled my panties down and stroked into me from behind in a smooth hard thrust. At some point he'd taken his boxers off and I'd totally missed it. I said, "I feel faintly deprived" as he slowly laid us down flat on the bed. "I think you'll survive" he pulled out halfway as his hand slipped forward to grasp my breast. His chest flat on my back he fucked me from behind, reaching down to drag my underwear off one leg, holding my legs open with his thighs while he licked across my upper shoulder, the weight of his arm keeping me motionless.

Grinding me into the bed I could feel him start to breathe faster and faster. He pulled out suddenly and sat back on his knees. "Turn around," he said, "I want you to watch." I rolled facing him. Arching backward, he put his hand on his cock and stroked himself. I sat up and grabbed him jerking his hips forward as I smacked his hands away and took him into my mouth. Both his hands came down on the back of my head pressing himself deep down my throat as he came in a giant rush. "Holy shit," he whispered, falling forward across my shoulders as I licked across the length of him, squeezing tightly with my fist.

"I win," he said, resting his forehead on my shoulder. "I win."

THIRTY-FOUR

The next morning I rolled over to find the bed empty. I stared at the ceiling and took a deep breath as a soft knock sounded on the door. I pulled on his t-shirt and padded to the peephole. He was standing there in uniform carrying a paper bag with a familiar yellow logo. "Miss me?," he smiled and brushed his hand over my bedhead, "You were racked out so I figured I'd just let you sleep." Holding up the bag he shook it and raised an eyebrow. "Hungry?"

I threw open the door and said, "Get in here and bring those McMuffins with you, I'm starving." He winked as he passed by, tipped my chin up and gave me a soft kiss. "You need a shower," he sniffed, "you stink."

"Food first," I answered back, digging my hand into the bag pulling out nothing but Chicken McNuggets.

I rolled my eyes and looked at him. He raised his hands, "Hey, they haven't gotten the breakfast all day memo up here yet. Don't kill the messenger." Grabbing a nugget in one hand I tackled him knocking him backward on the bed. I sat on his chest and held him down, cramming the nugget in his mouth. "Eat it!" I yelled, laughing as he tried to pinch his lips shut. "I can't! It's not even chicken! It's freak of nature meat!" he held up a desperate hand trying to ward off my attempts to force the nugget down his throat.

"Stop! You'll get grease on my uniform and this is the only flight suit I brought!" he blurted out as I jumped backward and started fast balling nuggets at his upraised arms. Putting his head down, he darted past clotheslining me across the chest hauling me into the bathroom. He shoved me in the shower then flipped on the water and held the glass door shut while I squealed under the icy spray. As the temperature rose I grabbed the bottom of the wet t-shirt and struggled to get it up over my head. I felt fingers trailing up my spine as I pulled it off and saw him standing there, his uniform crumpled outside on the bathroom floor next to his boots.

Pushing me up against the back of the shower, he sank down on his knees as the room filled with steam. He leaned forward and slowly licked up my inner leg as his fingers caressed down the back of my ass. I saw him glance up as he slipped a finger inside me as he gently sucked along the edge of my thigh. "Do you like that?" he said softly, pulling me toward him. I threw my head back and gasped as he pulled his finger forward inside me. I took a deep breath as he gently flicked me with his tongue biting gently. I started to clench inside but he smiled and backed away.

"That's so not fair." I complained and turned my face to the side as he stood and put his hand under my knee. Gripping tightly, he lifted my leg smoothly pushing into me as he leaned us against the wall. "I was just trying to help you with your laundry," he whispered as he moved inside me. I felt the water beating on my hands as I gripped his back, pulling him deeper. He pushed his hand firmly against the wall above us and thrust into me grasping my leg tightly while I pressed my face against his chest. "Don't you dare stop right now," I threatened him, "don't stop." I felt my whole body tighten around him as my knee buckled. "If I fall down and bust my face I will be really upset," I gasped. He lifted my leg higher. "I won't let you fall down," he whispered, smiling. "I'm nonskid." He winked pointing a single finger toward the floor and I saw he was still wearing his socks.

THIRTY-FIVE

"So…" I asked him as I got dressed, "you're really going to wear those barefoot?" "Yep," he answered blithely pulling on his boots over his naked feet. "I only brought one pair of socks."

"Who even does that," I snickered, "How could you not bring another pair of socks?" He shrugged, "Well, I have those slip-on shoes I usually wear and I only needed socks for the boots." He held out a foot and wagged it back and forth and stood up. He pulled his flight suit legs down adjusting all those delicious zippers. "See? Can't even tell!" he said proudly.

"Yeah, until your feet start to sweat and then it'll be bad, so bad," I laughed. "So, so bad."

"Come on, cow lady. Your chariot awaits," he swept an arm toward the door.

We drove up to the Academy gates and we paused as he leaned out and told the gate guard we were headed to the cemetery. As we drove through the grounds I could feel him glancing over at me. "You suddenly got real quiet," he said softly. "I'm ok," I replied distantly and looked out of the side window, "Just thinking."

"Dare I even ask about what?" he said apprehensively. "Just wondering how I could forget today is all," I pinched the bridge of my nose. "I feel like a horrible person, forgetting like that. It's not like I didn't love him. I did, you know I did."

He shifted uncomfortably and quietly told me, "I know."

"I guess I'm just still mad maybe," I wiped a hand across my forehead. He turned into the graveyard and parked along the access road. He pulled the key from the ignition and sat frozen for a long minute. "Do you feel guilty about us?" he asked. I thought back to the hotel room and his socks hung over the towel rod and replied, "No. Not really." He raised his eyebrows, "Not really? That's hardly a rousing recommendation."

"What do you want me to say? How about you, do you feel guilty?"

He paused, placing a wrist on the steering wheel, one hand on the door handle. As he pushed himself up out of the car I saw his mouth say maybe.

We walked silently across the grass together toward where your brass plaque shone in the sun. As we got closer he bent down, put his hand in his flight suit pocket and pulled out a bunch of nickels. I took two as he told me he'd be back in a bit and walked away. I sat next to your grave and imagined I could feel you under the grass. Basking in the sunshine, just sitting there resting under the earth where they'd packed you in, where you'd packed it in. I knew that coin was in there with you, the devil tarnishing around the edges. I was happy with you. *I was happy* I whispered knowing you could hear me. *But I'm happy with him, too.*

You just sat there under that grass and said nothing. You said nothing as the tears poured down my cheeks. I did feel guilty. I bent over, placing my hands on either side of your grave, clenching the perfectly manicured grass between my fingers. I should have loved you more. I should have tried harder. I should have given you my whole heart. I tried. I tried. I tried.

I wouldn't have left, I would have stayed, lover. I would have stayed. I would have stayed. I laid my forehead on your plaque and felt your name pressing across my face. I could feel those brass letters burning *Andrew* into my mind as even at that very moment I thought about him and despised myself for it. The sun beat down on the back of my head, glaring down, burning it down above those sharp peaks as they kept watch over you. Those cold mountains shining like a bad luck penny over where you laid in the dust.

I stood and leaned over your marker looking down at the nickel I'd laid carefully over the A in your name. I took a deep breath, turned away and walked down the next row reading the plaques as I looked for your classmate. Down one row and then another I stared at my feet *beloved beloved beloved* until I found your buddy's name. I bent over to put a nickel there, to place your nickel on top of your fallen friend and saw someone had already laid one down. I knelt and suddenly realized that all of you had been in the same class, in the same squadron here at the Academy. The three of you raging into the sky, two gone now from your flock and him remaining. Left behind, always him following behind. Following behind picking up the pieces.

Fixing all the broken things as I realized that there had been three nickels in his hand after he had given two to me. I sat there and pulled my knees to my chin and wondered if the third nickel was for him.

I swallowed hard, suddenly afraid that third nickel was for me.

THIRTY-SIX

"I'm pretty tired," he said from the doorway of my hotel room, "I think I'll make it an early night." I nodded and reached out to touch his arm but he stepped away. "I'll see you in the lobby tomorrow morning at nine," he whispered and walked down the hallway never once looking back finally disappearing around the corner leaving his socks behind.

THIRTY-SEVEN

What're you doing? I asked and Send in late October.

Going fishing.

Pictures! Let me live vicariously through you.

Four hours later a photo of him holding up a dying red with one hand appeared, that pistol tightly strapped over his heart.

I never bring anyone here, he'd told me as his smile taken through a long lens fell from the skies into my phone.

THIRTY-EIGHT

I'll be in Anchorage for business in January I texted just before Christmas. *Will you be around? Maybe for a drink? Just a drink. I'd just like to see you, just one drink.*

He replied he'd be gone for the holidays but had no plans after the New Year and asked *what business?*

IRS business I replied and added a series of kitchen knife stabbing emoticons. *Season Three of When Tax Lawyers Attack coming to a court near you. Get your tickets soon. It'll be a packed house.*

We'll see as he went dark.

THIRTY-NINE

"Hey," I told his voicemail as I stood at the baggage carousel in Anchorage three weeks later. "I'm here in town. Didn't know if you were around but figured I'd let you know I was here. So…you know how to reach me." I smacked the phone to my forehead after hanging up. You know how to reach me? Jesus Christ.

That phone message was a bigger disappointment than Russell Wilson opting to pass against the Patriots. As I walked out to my rental car I pondered how my social skills had degraded to the point that I could no longer speak to a boy with any sort of confidence. Maybe I should stop going to school.

Hell, maybe I should just stop working, period, I thought as I drove off toward the Captain Cook through a straight-up whiteout blizzard. Fuck this shit.

He texted the next day. *Whatcha doin' tonight? Why don't you come over for dinner around 6?*

Ok I answered back and slid down an icy sidewalk toward the hotel entrance in a pair of boots and that black crepe three-quarter sleeve dress with a heavy wool overcoat buttoned up tight to my chin.

I'll tell you all about my case. It was an epic event at the courthouse this morning. Epic, I say.

Zzzzzzzzzzz... came back his reply.

FORTY

"Good god, it's snowing hard," I shook off my shoes at his front door. "Letting the heat out, hot shot," he towed me into the house by my arm. "How about a drink?" I asked him, suddenly nervous. Thoughts of illicit adult activities forbidden in all fifty states and most of the territories flooded my mind when I brushed past him into the living room, "How about a really big drink."

He smiled, and told me he was preparing to ask about my day but didn't really want an answer because it was tax stuff which was boring but he felt the need to be polite anyway. I held out a hand for the beer he'd pulled from the fridge.

"How was your day?"

I tipped back the bottle and looked at him from the corner of my eye. "Fine." I smiled and held up my middle finger. He stared at me for a long minute before gently putting his glass on the counter and stepping across the kitchen. He reached out his hand and rubbed his thumb across my mouth as he leaned forward and whispered quietly, "I've missed you." I swallowed back the tears and nodded mutely as I put my arms around his waist and pressed my face into his shoulder. We stood there for a long minute, his face resting against the top of my head before he backed away and dropped the bomb.

"I'm seeing someone. And it's serious."

FORTY-ONE

I was stunned. Flabbergasted. Like someone had hit me with a semi, I stood there with that cold bottle in my hand and just looked at him. "I'm sorry to hear that," I said stiffly and stepped back toward the kitchen stool.

"She's a doctor in town," he told me and turned away toward the stove. "Is she the one who took that fishing picture?" I asked and inhaled that beer. He nodded before pulling on a hot mitt over his hand and tugging on the oven door. He checked the temperature, turned and opened the refrigerator.

"I thought we'd have this great piece of salmon I have left over from the fall season," he pulled out a large plate. I stared at the fish and wondered if he had caught it. If she had caught it. I thought back to the graveyard, to the third nickel and felt lightheaded. "That looks great," I said faintly. "Salad?" turning, he held up a bowl. I grunted and helped myself to another drink.

"I guess I just wasn't expecting it," I said an hour later as I picked at my dinner. "Why?" He arranged his silverware in precise angles. "I don't know," I answered, "Maybe I thought we, you know, that we had something. But I guess not, huh."

He looked at me and then down at the table. "I've been thinking about that a lot," he said. I suddenly felt like running, running away from this kitchen island, away from her fish on that plate laid out in front of me. "And…"

I put down my fork as he continued. "And I think maybe we were just…" his voice trailed off. I thought back to that kitchen when I had told him I cared for him, when I had opened my fat mouth and said those things in front of that iPhone.

"Available. We were just available."

"You are fucking kidding me with that shit," I shot to my feet. "How dare you sit there and tell me what we had was based on availability. How dare you use those words in this fucking kitchen, saying that to me while we're sitting right here, right here at this kitchen counter."

He shrugged, "It's true. I mean, I know you said some stuff and I said some stuff but…" I jumped right in there before he could continue. "I said some stuff? I said some stuff? I told you I was in love with you, that's hardly some stuff," I sputtered, slamming down my bottle on the counter. "I stood here in this very kitchen and told you I loved you and you kissed me. You kissed me! Shit, you did a whole lot more than just fucking kiss me, you asshole."

He stood and took his dishes to the sink. "Don't get upset," he said calmly, "it was a difficult night. You'd just found out about Andy and that girl and things just got all crazy for a while." He set his fork in the dishwasher and turned to face me, "I know you. I know you better than you think I do. You don't really love me, you just love the idea of me."

I looked at him standing in the corner and I wanted to hurt him like I was hurting because he should hurt, too. "Love the idea of you? What the fuck is that supposed to mean? I've loved you since the first day I saw you! And I meant what I said that night standing right here in this kitchen." Those words like bullets shot out of my mouth toward his face. "It's you that slept with me because I was available. Fucking your best friend's girl must have been quite a victory for you."

He sucked in a sharp breath.

I really ground it in. "You're one to talk, you know. Maybe you should check your own motivations before pointing a finger at me, asshole." I jumped to my feet and slid my plate away from me across the countertop with a quick shove. "At least I cared about you while you were just out for a piece of ass."

"You should be ashamed of yourself," I spat at him. "Fucking opportunist." I grabbed my coat and yelled *shithead* on my way toward the door.

"Don't you dare tell me what to feel," his voice snapped as he stood staring up from the sink. "I've always loved you…" he suddenly screamed at me, launching my dinner plate off the kitchen island into the wall, lunging forward. "So don't tell me what it's like to cry at night over someone. Don't tell me what it's like to want someone so badly you can't even breathe! Every time I watched you touch him, watched you kiss him I pretended to smile and I had to turn away because I wanted you!" Ceramic shattered in every direction, razor sharp shards rebounding off the floor as another plate shot off the counter.

I stepped back.

Something sharp slunk around the corner of the room loosed free into the night out into the darkness as he stalked toward me, his angry finger pointing, accusing. He looked hateful and violent like he was going to cry and I couldn't understand what was happening. "Every time you went home with him, every night you went with him when you got on those flights home with him when you left with him, I went home alone. Alone! I knew you were fucking him, that you loved him and I had nothing," he got right in my face. I saw his eyes begin to redden, his face getting hard so I closed up my shell for safety but he kept coming, advancing swiftly in sharp angles as I retreated.

"I lay in bed at night…" he ground out between clenched teeth now only inches from my face, his arms on either side of me pinning my arms over my head up against the wall, his body pressing the full length of mine his hands on my wrists so tight I couldn't breathe, "…and when I touch myself I try—I beg myself—not to think of you but I can't. I see your face when I'm fucking other girls and I hate myself for it. I hate myself…I hate myself…" falling away, turning away, he bent over grabbing his head in agony as if he could no longer stand to be inside his own skin.

A tear rolled down his face as he threw his head back, gasping for air. I stared as it wound down the outside of his cheekbone stopping at the edge of his mouth. I reached to catch it with my finger but he threw my hand aside and lurched toward me. He was shaking me by the shoulders suddenly, choking out that he wanted me that it was only ever me and he can't breathe now because you're dead while he's alive. He's still alive and he's touching me.

He's touching your possessions. He's exceeded the consent of the limited easement you granted him when you allowed him to tiptoe carefully along the unmarked border between my land and his for all these years. He'd broken the sacred brotherhood trust you left to him, only him, tucked inside that envelope. Leaning in close to my face, he named himself traitor.

I saw him fracture inside as he whispered harshly, "You're a cancer… I've cut you out a thousand times but I can't cut anymore. I can't bleed anymore because there's nothing left. I can't cut you out."

His thumbs dug into my collarbones. They were on my shoulders pushing gripping and it hurt but not as badly as me feeling a killer. I was killing him. I could see him dying. It was me with that gun to his chest pulling the trigger over and over. I could tell that something meant only to bend was being twisted too far. I had gone too far. That something I thought was only about me was him all along. There was an edge and he was on it teetering just outside my grasp. A line snapped leaving something large and destructive adrift unfettered and I was in its path, a small boat with no motor no wind no oars. He crushed the back of my neck with his hand as he bled out in deep crimson telling me he wanted rid of me, that it was wrong to love me.

He told me I was the devil, an unwanted intruder mincing around his corners refusing to fully vacate always leaving something behind. That he couldn't stand the sight of his own face in the mirror even as he always answered my texts. He always answered and he always returned those meaningless tokens that kept tight the fragile threads between us. The threads I had broken every night when I had gone home to you.

"For years I burned," he whispered with his mouth on my ear, "rejecting all the good things." Saying he deprived himself as penance, swallowed down poison in glasses, slaughtered things with guns and hooks, flew too fast and too high challenging the gods to strike him down for his sins. He told me he wanted me gone from his head. That he was drowning. Paralyzed, he couldn't breathe. That I was in his blood, in his veins.

He told me that I was part of him as his hand slid up between my legs, grabbing at my waistline ripping open my jeans. Reaching down past my zipper that hand slipped south on my skin and then I could feel him stroking hard up against me pushing his fingers up inside me, tugging down my neckline with the other hand, his shoulder pinning me against the wall, his breath hot against my neck.

His tongue touched mine as I breathed in and it smelled like home. He smelled like home to me as I fell halfway and then all the way in. I was all in when he stepped back. Chest heaving, he stepped back, brushed me aside and walked out the door slamming it behind him leaving me gasping for breath in a suffocating silence.

FORTY-TWO

I finally left after standing around in his kitchen for half an hour like a moron. Jesus Christ, why am I even still here? Maybe he was just waiting for me to leave. For me to slink back into my fucking hellhole, I thought spitefully as I dumped the broken plates into the garbage can I found under his sink.

What an asshole. I slammed his glass fronted cabinets and kicked a ceramic shard under the fridge. Fuck you, saying those things and touching me like that and then running off like a coward.

I flipped all his lights on and flung open the shades so he could see as I used his fancy bread knife to cram that stupid fish down his shitty garbage disposal. So he could watch as I buttoned my pants, slipped on my wizard shoes and fucking left his goddamn house slamming the door behind me.

I looked in the rear view mirror as I drove away and caught the faint edge of a shadow moving under a streetlight. Squinting, I saw it was him rounding the corner of the house in the driving snow heading toward the backyard. I watched him hop the fence and disappear into the darkness. Seconds later, all the lights in the house went out and as I slipped around the block again with my headlights off I saw the curtains were shut. He'd pulled the curtains completely closed and that garbage can was sitting out on the curb.

I bought the last ticket on the first flight out of Anchorage and was back in Seattle the next day by noon.

FORTY-THREE

On Valentine's Day I called a broker and told him I was ready to sell. I held that stiff card in my hand and stared at the dealer's name asking *Remember me? On the big classic boat in Lake Union, the one from last year's boat show?*

He came by the next afternoon with a stiff cardboard sign he tied to the front bow railing and stood beside me in the transom, his finger pointing at all the lines where my signature was needed. I gripped the pen tightly and gave him permission to bring strangers wandering through our private spaces, to look down into the engine room at that oil stain still visible on the floorboards.

"She's got great bones," he flipped open one hatch and then another looking for leaks and signs of fuzzy dry rot along the hull's interior. "We took good care of her," I said softly and slumped in the doorway after he shook my hand watching him walked down the dock, his words ringing in my head, "She should sell fast in this market. I wouldn't be surprised if it went within a few months."

I started with the dock box and began to whittle down our life to-gether separating out the drills, the circular saw, the wood chisels you'd bought me for my thirty-second birthday. You'd laughed as you held them out to me wrapped in a crumpled Home Depot bag telling me I was weird for wanting tools as a gift. I gripped those sharp chisels and wanted suddenly to drive them down into the dock, pin them down through my palms into the splintery wood and bleed out into the water below, flooding down a sea of red into the lake where we had been so happy, where I had been happy and you had passed through on your way to push it up. I knelt on the dock gripping those sharp points, rubbed a thumb softly across a razor edge and watched as a thin line of red emerged. I put my finger up to my mouth, leaned over and dropped the narrowest chisel off the edge with a soft splash and watched as it quickly disappeared into the dark green water. A faint shadow of a salmon passed in the distance keeping to the shadows of the boats above as it glided through the lake searching for food.

I put the other chisels back into their soft leather wrapper leaving an open empty space at the end of the row for the lone soldier now consigned to the muck of Lake Union, forever stuck in the slip where we'd laughed and cried and blown those circuits only twenty feet above and gently placed them in a blue Tupperware container sitting by the dock box. The jigsaw went next, followed by socket set and the strap wrenches I'd used to change the new filter canisters we'd put on the engine last year.

I left the paint for the new owners, whoever they would be, because I know how hard it is to match paint on a hull. Her curved expanse showing all the defects and dents, variations in the white so obvious in the sunlight of Andrews Bay as we slowly puttered around the exterior in our tiny tender. "I could have sworn we used Interlux," I'd shook my head, you rolling your eyes at our patchwork hobo hull job as clouds rolled in covering the sun. I moved some boxes to the side and pulled out the extra lines I'd snatched up at the West Marine closing sale and stuffed them into a sailcloth bag next to my random orbital sander and jumbo variety pack of sandpaper.

Weeks passed as I separated the wheat from the chaff, setting aside the things I would take with me and those I would pass on to the next

family coming to love her, to love the beautiful wood boat we'd purchased sight unseen. "She's fat," you'd joked every time we powered her
gently into the slip ever so carefully. "No, she's Rubenesque," I'd answer
over our headsets telling you to come to port three degrees, flipping
those huge black fenders over the side between her and the dock. I can
still hear your laughter as you expertly handled those duel props, so
similar to the jets you flew that the motions came without thinking,
moving that forty-two tons of mahogany in precise lines. "I like big
butts and I cannot lie," you'd sung over the airwaves and I shimmied for
you up at the front doing an unstable two step with boathook in hand.

Four people came through to judge her before I started my spring
maintenance schedule. I knocked down the outside rails with 220 grit
and brushed on gleaming refresher coats of varnish as canvas rolled
around inside the washer down in the galley. Then buffed the windlass
until the wood shone, a mirror finish gleaming off the stainless as I used
a grungy toothbrush to knock leftover Poulsbo mud off the anchor
chain.

I scrubbed the decks with teak cleaner, re-caulked a splitting seam
near where a damn unfixable drip kept emerging in the galley every
time I hosed her down. Where is this coming from, I wondered one
evening before pulling down the ceiling panels and shining a flashlight
up into the corners trying to trace the source of that pernicious water.
Victorious at last, I finally

discovered it was inside the front bench where we'd stored the deck
chairs and extra shore power cord. HA! I said to myself as I bent over
with sealant in hand, I've caught you now, you fucker.

I cleaned the carpets and rubbed oil into the mahogany paneling in
the salon. Stripping the stern down to bare wood, I scraped away long
lines of old varnish in great sweeping strokes watching as those strings
fell onto the plastic covered swim step, the vinyl name sticker splintering
off in pieces. With a two-part epoxy standing nearby I sanded some
mahogany into dust and blended it into the thick paste.

Not too much dust or it bends and won't stick, too little and it's brittle and snaps read my handwritten instructions scrawled on the side of the bottle.

"So noted," I muttered before patching all the tiny holes and dings. Two days of curing later I broke out that random orbital sander and plugged in the shop vac. Dressed like I was splicing Ebola, I stood on the swim step grinding the mahogany down through the grits, the shop vac a dull whine in the background muffled by my ear plugs and full face particulate respirator.

I ran a hand across the smooth wood my fingers tightly gripping a tack cloth while I looked at the sky silently calculating dew points and ambient air temperatures. Deciding I could get in a sealer coat, I broke open the Epifanes and brushing liquid and poured a stream of amber varnish through a paper filter into a plastic bucket. Brush in hand I walked down the steps and slowly drew the mixture across the bare wood watching the grain emerge in brilliant red and golden streaks. Across sixteen feet of bare wood I sealed that grain against the impending fall rains as she shimmered in summer's final rays of sunshine.

Every morning I checked my messages. "Can I bring someone by at three?" the broker asked. I replied that I would walk down to the Starbucks and have a cup of coffee while the he ushered yet another prospective buyer through those impossibly narrow transom doors. *I've been varnishing so make sure they don't rub up against the stern* I added as he texted back *they aren't those kind of people.*

Not those kind of people, I thought, saddened that she might be passed on to a careless hand who would let her decks darken, that glistening teak slowly clouding over time. Summer came and went in a single day it seemed. That summer so brilliant with a sun that just hung around for what seemed like days began to slowly slip away as the Seattle winter crept in. I moved to my inside projects, replacing a compressor in the refrigerator and filling our house batteries with distilled water on a set schedule. On Tuesday mornings I plugged in the trickle charger and ran it up to the tender outboard to top off the battery.

Every week I'd fire up the twin 671s resting under the salon floor with a great thundering roar and stand in the pilothouse watching the oil gages rise as the system pressure increased. That port side is always so much lower. I leaned forward and tapped the dial gently with my finger. I'd flip up the galley stairs, pull those ear protectors down firmly on my head and crawl into the engine room to check the fluids as those steel giants purred next to me in perfect unison, the engines hot against my palm as I shot them with a laser thermometer.

Looking good, baby I would tell her as I slowly backed away, looking good.

FORTY-FOUR

The trees gave fall colors their best shot that September but alas, it was not to be. One day as I shuffled through red-tinged leaves on my way down to the mailbox I pulled out my phone and dialed the Air Force Academy. "Yes," I said to some random person on the phone, "What's the procedure for getting onto the grounds to visit the cemetery?" She inquired as to my relationship with the deceased as I swallowed and once again tried to convince a stranger that we had been legit. That I wasn't just some random bar fly who'd shacked up with you. That we'd mattered.

There was a pause as her acrylic nails click clacked on a computer keyboard in the background for a minute.

"You're already cleared onto the grounds, ma'am," she said through her chewing gum. "What?" I asked stupidly. "You're on the preapproved visitor list," she explained and told me I'd been sponsored by a member of the military and could come onto the grounds to visit the graveyard whenever I wanted without an escort. "No advance notice needed, ma'am," she finished, sounding distracted.

"Thank you," I said softly when she told me who had sponsored me past the Academy gate, gently hung up and laid my phone on the deli counter next to the tuna sandwiches. Two days before the second anniversary of your death I flew out on a crappy Frontier flight to Denver and drove down to Colorado Springs in a Chevy so small I could touch the backseat and the windshield simultaneously. "Go hamsters go!" I shouted as we blazed onto the highway at a blistering forty-five miles per hour.

The Holiday Inn was full so I drove over to the Embassy Suites and checked into a room with two queen beds. I flipped off my shoes and called down to the front desk and asked for polyester pillows after tossing the down ones onto the couch then stood under the showerhead for a long time enjoying the unlimited hot water and fantastic pressure. All this extra space is very nice I said to myself, my back pressed against the glass door while I sat on the floor and shaved my legs. Very nice indeed.

Early the next morning I went over to that shitty diner and choked my way through a plate of undercooked eggs and limp bacon staring out the greasy window lost in thought. Regretting my sentimental choice almost instantly, I lumbered to my tiny vehicle and wedged myself into the front seat. "You make me feel tall, Chevy," I announced with great aplomb, "and for that I almost forgive you the unpardonable sin of selling a car in this horrible shade of lime."

The gate guard took my license at the Academy gate and held up a clipboard as he stared at my picture on that plastic and then back at my face. Then at the picture. And back at my face. Suddenly I wondered if the lady had been wrong, that I wasn't cleared and I felt dumb for not calling earlier that morning to check. The guard leaned into the car and handed me a pass and told me I was only allowed to visit the graveyard and to leave the laminated card on the dashboard when I left the vehicle. "Thank you," I paused as I considered asking the question stuck in the back of my throat and stared at that clipboard. "Is there anything else, ma'am?" the guard asked as he stepped back.

"No." I rolled up the window. "I have what I need," I whispered and drove away up the winding road toward where you were waiting.

FORTY-FIVE

"Hey lover," I said and flopped down on the grass next to your marker, face pointed upward at the gray skies as I slung an arm over my eyes. "Bad news…I put the boat up for sale." The wind rustled through the trees and I sensed you smiling. It was too much for one person, I explained, and I would really really like to have a bathtub. Rubbing a thumb across the face of a shiny new nickel, I told you that the galvanized steel cow watering tub I'd bought from Stoneway Hardware and put out on the dock next to my propane powered flash water heater just wasn't cutting it. The Duck Dodge sailors always stare at me when I sit out there in that thing with my knees cranked up under my chin, I confided.

You snickered. I held my stomach and howled with laughter as I told you all about the harbor patrol taking a long slow drift past the dock one night staring at me with binoculars as I sat in that tub reading a book. I knew you were laughing because I know you. I know you. You're so weird, you know that? came the words on a quickening breeze. "Yeah, yeah," I replied, "It's part of my charm."

"Uh huh," your distant reply.

We sat in silence for a long time until I started to shiver from resting on the cold ground. I guess it's good that you were always the one that ran hot. I stood up and brushed off the grass clippings. I'd hate to think of you stuck here freezing all winter, miserable. I thought about that blackened devil's coin and the three feet of dirt piled over your head and wondered if I should bring you a pair of those sweaty polyester pants you'd hated in the summer but were secretly grateful for as the snows rolled over the Academy quad but figured the wooden box was pretty insulating and you were always adaptable. Resilient.

"Don't sell yourself short," I remembered you telling me as I opened another law school rejection letter. "They're all fucking morons. You'll be awesome, just hang in there." I pressed a hand to my throat, closed my eyes and bent my head. I looked down at my shoes and I told you I was alone, too. That we could be alone together. "It's ok, baby," I heard your voice inside my head as I stared at your plaque next to my toes. "You'll be ok."

"We'll be ok."

"I'm ok," you told me softly. I knelt down and rubbed a hand over your name, your Andrew slipping softly across my fingertips as I raised my palm to my face and saw it was perfectly clean. Along the far side of the marker I spotted the edge of a shiny nickel tucked into the grass. "I do believe you've been co-opted," you smirked, "You've never been on time for anything in your entire fucking life."

My head shot up and I peered into the distance past the long rows of brass letters laid out in perfect lines stretching toward the trees. "There's no one there, lover," I turned back to you, swallowing down the lump in my throat as I laid my nickel over your A.

"I'll see you when I see you, baby," came your voice faintly as you drifted back to sleep.

FORTY-SIX

A pipe blew under the sink one November morning as I stood in the galley making coffee, a gentle hissing noise breaking through the silence. "Shit!" I slammed down my mug on the counter and ripped open the cabinet door to saw a jet of water shooting out against the side of the hull and dripping down the side into the bilge. No no no! Oh god, hang on baby, hang on I pleaded with her as I raced up through the salon to the circuit board, flipped off the fresh water pump breaker and grabbed a roll of silicone tape from the tool bag as I stumbled back toward the galley. I cranked closed the water shutoff valves as I wrapped that tape tight around a cracked nut and turned on the kitchen tap, trying to take pressure off the line.

I jammed my hands to my face and cried as everything went to shit, as everything kept breaking and as hard as I tried I just couldn't get it together, couldn't get it all put back together, couldn't keep it together. It's just too much maintenance for one person, I'd said to the broker when he asked why I was selling, turning my eyes away from where your coat had hung on the rack.

Sitting there in the galley with tears in my eyes by that busted nut I realized that it was too much, everything was too much.

Eventually I stood, walked down into the lower cabins, turned on the bathroom taps and left the system to drain as I went out to Stoneway Hardware and bought a lovely Delta sink faucet with a removable spray handle and a new set of hot and cold water shutoff valves. "Make sure you give me the right nuts," I told the counter guy and showed him photos of the carnage on my cell phone.

He assured me the nuts were the right size, that mine were old and needed replacing anyway, and to only hand tighten the sink connection to the shutoff valves because too much pressure would break the new fittings. "You can't tighten down too much because it'll crack," he told me as he placed some extras in a small clear bag and pinched shut the ziplock. "Too much pressure and the metal just splits right down the side," he said. I replied, "I understand," and thanked him for his help.

Back on the boat I pulled my phone from my pocket and set it on the floor beside me while I craned my head up under the counter looking for the sink fittings. "It's a good thing I have tiny arms," I told her, "because massive man hands would not be good. Not good." I heard a creaking noise as I finally ripped the sink fixture nut loose and heard it plink off the drain pipe bouncing off the hull into the bilge. "You're welcome," I told her and pushed the faucet up out of the hole. "Never say I never gave you anything," I said to the lines as I ran the new copper pipes from the sink down to the busted fittings. "I'll just replace all of this," I whispered, "in case the other one is broken and I just don't know it yet."

Grasping a crescent wrench, I gave that valve a horrendous pull and smiled as it crumbled under my grip. "Who's your daddy now," I held up the nut and peered at the crack running from top to bottom. I could hear her creaking as I heaved my way through the other fittings, scraping off the old plumbing tape and rewinding long lengths of white Teflon around the threads. "The guy at Stoneway said not to use this tape, you know," I said conspiratorially, "But I think we all agree that it's needed in this particular situation. Don't want to come home to four feet of water in your belly, now do we."

I could feel her approval as I wound the tape around, hand tightened the new shutoff valves before carefully connecting the hot and cold water lines from the sink completing the circuit. I took a deep breath, stood up and announced to the galley that the moment of truth was upon us. After opening the hot and cold water shutoff valves I walked back to the pilothouse and reluctantly flipped the fresh water pump breaker back on. I sprinted down the stairs and flew into the galley and pressed my face under the sink staring at those valves intently rubbing an anxious finger along the threads exposed beneath the nuts.

Watertight. No leaks. I put my hands in the air in mute victory and did a little hip shuffle before I closed all the bathroom taps. "Time to push it up, beotches," I crowed as I locked everything up and closed it all down. Back in the galley I sat on the floor with a Coke in hand and admired my handiwork while the water tank slowly drained out through the sink tap into Lake Union. I held a finger over the text icon on my phone for a long minute.

Whatcha doin? I typed and hit Send.

Fixing my goddamn garbage disposal he swiftly replied. *Some crazy bitch jammed my bread knife in it and it's still all jacked up.* I smiled and lifted the phone.

If it makes you feel better I tapped back, a drop of condensation from the soda can dropping onto the screen *I just fixed a busted sink pipe.*

Karma and a middle finger emoticon came back a second later. Laughing, I swiped my sleeve across the phone.

Doctor lady not so handy?

She was too busy trying to fix all the broken things he said ten minutes later. I sat back and thought about that statement as another text dinged through.

You let me know if you ever need help with your pipes, baby. You just let me know.

FORTY-SEVEN

Wow, I thought as I looked at my bank account that December and saw the seven digit balance. I sat back and I thought about the life insurance and the military SGLI you'd left me, given to me as your sole beneficiary in that will you'd had drawn up in Alaska.

"If I die you can have all my CDs," you'd said to me once and patted the side of my face with your hand. "All of them. Even the Beastie Boys ones."

I glanced around the transom out onto the lake and thought about my options. I could go home to Florida to see my parents once she was sold, once she had passed to someone else. I could go anywhere I wanted, suddenly realizing that money was freedom. That you had left me freedom in that open envelope.

I went to the bookstore at University Village later that afternoon and stood in front of the travel section running my fingertips over the brightly colored spines. Tibet? I thought for a moment about yaks and buses packed with sweaty people traversing narrow roads across mountain passes and moved on down the line. Santiago? I've heard Chile is nice. I pulled out the thin volume, split it open to the middle and leaned back against the book stacks. I heard a thump as a book fell onto the floor behind me and turned to see a fat volume lying on the floor with a single word singing out into the silent air.

Seward.

It said Seward and as I stared down at its cover I thought about campfires and middle-age rage. Night skies brilliant with stars, clear icy waters winding down from great heights. I slowly reached down, picked up that book and looked at the front. *Sailing the Inner Passage* it said in small letters under that glaring screaming *Seward*. Clutching it to my chest, I walked to the register and handed over $14.95 in cash as I told myself it was just research.

Only research.

FORTY-EIGHT

A week later that book was still sitting unread on the coffee table when the broker called. "I have some people I'd like you to meet," he said. I replied that I really wasn't feeling up to another showing, that I wanted to rest, was busy, was sick, was not available when he told me, "You need to make yourself available."

Two hours later I'd thrown my dirty laundry in the dryer and pulled the comforter tight over the wrinkled bed sheets in a semblance of faux order. When the knock sounded, I sighed and climbed slowly up the stairs into the transom. At the door was the broker trailed behind by a young couple. "Mark and Gary…" the broker started to say as a sandy-haired man stepped forward and grabbed my hand chattering, "Hello hello, we're so happy to finally meet you." I smiled as his husband stepped into the transom and nodded a quiet hi.

The broker started talking as I watched them holding hands in my transom, their golden rings shining on tightly intertwined fingers. Gary trailed his hand across the teak freezer cover, lost in thought as the broker prattled on about holding value and excellent investments. I saw Mark standing silently at the back gate looking down at the varnished stern. Turning, he said, "Did you refinish this yourself?" I replied that I did, that it was freshly done, that everything was good to go, it was

GTG. He unlocked the gate and stepped down running a palm flat across the nameless wood as he walked the length of the swim step. "She's beautiful," he said so softly I could barely hear his words. Looking up at Gary he gave a brilliant smile, "Let's look at the cabins."

Laughing, they rambled through the boat touching all the wood, turning on the taps, snickering as I told them about my busted sink pipe adventure, Mark giving me side eye when he opened the dryer. Blushing I shrugged, saying sheepishly it was laundry day. They trundled through the salon down toward the cabins. At the stern of the boat was the master with its separate bathroom and a giant king size bed. I stopped in the doorway letting them walk ahead, saw Gary lift an eyebrow as Mark leaned into his side. I backed into the darkened hallway when they put their heads together tightly whispering in each other's ears, laughing wickedly.

I put a hand over my mouth and turning away, skimming my fingers down the long hallway wall as I walked back toward the broker who was standing upstairs in the salon. "Sell her," I said choking back the tears, "Sell her to them, they'll love her like we did."

"And she'll love us back," said Gary as his arms came around my shoulders, Mark's hand resting gently on my arm, "She'll love us back."

"We'll take good care of her," they promised me when I handed over the door keys and parking pass two weeks later, carefully signing the papers placing her into the hands of a couple that would sleep in our bed, make coffee in our kitchen, who would undoubtedly blow our damn toaster breaker. Lovers side by side in our transom they stood resting their hands together on my varnished rail looking out at the Lake Union sunset as I walked down the dock for the last time.

Turning the far corner with my wood chisels tucked into that Tupperware box and a cashier's check clutched in my hand, I headed out into the parking lot where I bought three hours of time for space 69.

FORTY-NINE

What's up the text said around New Year's. *What's cookin', good lookin'.*

I quit my job and sold the boat I replied.

WHAT!? Why? WHY? You love that boat, why would you sell it, why did you sell it???

I thought for a minute. *It was too much for one person. I sold it to a nice gay couple who were overjoyed with all that wood.*

I paused.

Bad choice of words.

His text returned with a solid *HAHAHAHAHA.*

You're a child. I lifted my coffee cup to my lips and paused. *I'm buying a smaller boat.*

What kind?

A sailboat. I sat and stared at the phone.

A long minute passed before I threw five dollars on the table and stood up. I put the phone in my pocket and walked out the door, nodding hello to the familiar porter who was patiently explaining to a bunch of confused tourists that the Fairmont had two entrances. I felt a slight vibration and glanced down at his reply.

Rage on, cow lady. Rage on.

FIFTY

By the end of February I'd lucked out and bought a sturdy Hallberg-Rassy 35 Rasmus from a man who'd decided after making a solo Pacific crossing that sailing was the devil, the boat was possessed, and declared I was clinically insane to even touch that fucking thing as he threw the keys at me and sprinted out the title company's front door after final signing. Enclosing the cockpit windscreen, new black canvas hatch covers and Dacron sails set me back many a thousand but I figured I'd be wanting that thicker plastic and rubber welted seaming if things got dicey heading north.

Peering into the bilge I remarked to my carpenter on its shallowness and he agreed it was nothing even close to the seven feet my previous boat had but was much easier to keep dry. "Well, I hope it stays dry considering this baby's hull is fiberglass and not wood like my last gal," I grabbed ahold of a cockeyed cabinet off the forepeak v-berth cabin wall and gave it a hefty pull.

"Remind me why we're removing this," he said, wiping his hand across his forehead. "Because I'm putting in long lines of shelves on this side for all my shit," I looked up. "Because you're putting in long lines of shelves, bro." He smiled at me and rubbed his fingers together in the universal money sign.

"Yeah yeah yeah," I laughed and helped him move that cabinet up the dock toward Fisherman's Terminal. "When do you think I'll be ready to go?" I flipped up my hood against a misty rain. "By April, I would imagine," he said, loading up the dock cart with his tools and the piles of crap we'd dug out from the berth compartments. "Good," I said, "I'm ready to blow this joint ASAP-ly."

"Those are great bluewater boats," he looked over his shoulder as we trundled away down the dock, "I just don't like that separate aft cabin entry. Always thought that was bizarre that you had to go back outside up into the cockpit just to get to your bedroom." I told him that it was a drawback, yes, but as a solo sailor I wouldn't be using that back cabin much. Most of my extra sails were being boxed up and stowed in there with all the extra winter gear and pairs of socks stacked along the sides in canvas bags. That it was only me and the galley dinette lowered into a bed. "Sleeping in the kitchen," he grinned, "nice."

I replied with a smile, "Sleeping is a figure of speech and the proximity to the coffeepot is my primary concern."

"There are no meals when you single hand, just robust snacks," I told him as we turned the corner toward the parking lot, "catnaps are the only sleep you usually get on the long legs and even then you just usually crash in the cockpit." "Sounds atrocious," he said with a shudder, "how far are you planning to go?"

"Heading north," I answered. "I'm going north."

I stared up toward the gray skies and whispered, "I'm going as far away as I can get."

FIFTY-ONE

Do you even know what you're doing he asked in March.

I texted back that yes, I did know what I was doing, that I was a sailing instructor in Florida when I used to live there before I went to law school, that I was no shrinking violet and would be just fine, thank you.

Bitch he shot back with a smiley face and Spock hand emoticons.

FIFTY-TWO

April came and went followed swiftly by May. As June dawned on the horizon I was ready, so ready.

After flipping through a book of names one evening swinging on a hook in Andrews Bay, I finally tossed the pages down in frustration and asked the boat what it wanted to be called. "I know boats are supposed to be women," I told it as I stretched out my hands toward the mahogany floor in a long forward bend. "But this is Seattle and you can be whatever you want, who am I to judge." I stood back up and heard the halyards start to clang in the rising winds.

"Hold that thought," I said, climbing up the ladder to the cockpit. Craning my head backward I saw the anchor light brightly swaying side to side as whitecaps whipped up across the lake. "Dog the hatches!" I chirped, moving at a right sprightly pace tucking away a thick wool blanket I'd left folded next to the helm and snapped the canvas covers shut. "Incoming," I placed both hands on the rails I'd had the foresight to install on either side of the ladder and slid down into the galley as the boat rolled slowly to one side.

I braced my hands on the narrow cabin walls and reminded myself the Rasmus models were known for being roly-poly. "You're a lot skinnier than my last gal," I said and flipped shut all the cabinet drawer latches. "She was pretty hefty. It took a lot to get her moving, I tell ya." There was a slight snap when the anchor chain jerked against the bow sending a sharp jerking quiver back through the hull.

"Ok, so you're not a girl," I pressed a paper towel to the slanting counter with my palm and smacked two pieces of bread down propping the fridge door open with my knee, "Which means you're a guy, right?" I squeezed some mustard out and mashed the two pieces together using them to smear the paste around. "See? Easy peasy and no dirty dishes," I shoveled some lunch meat in between the slices and latched the fridge shut, keeping one foot firmly planted on the dinette cushions pushing my back against the sink counter as we swayed.

I flopped into the dinette bed and leaned back onto my pillow staring at the ceiling, sandwich in hand listening to the wind whistled through the lines before flipping the cotton duvet over my legs taking care to avoid the bread's mustard edge. Quietly I whispered into the darkness, "Do you think we're ready for this?" The water brushed past against the side of the hull while we swung on the end of that chain, bow into the wind. He was silent.

"I read a story once," I told him hours later, "about a hero who didn't know she was a hero until the chips were down. A book about a warrior witch with a dragon, a dragon with scarred wings who wouldn't fly for anyone but her."

"His name was Abraxis."

We rolled slowly to the side and I felt him take a deep quiet breath. "Abraxis it is," I rubbed a gentle hand across the glistening mahogany wall above my head and closed my eyes drifting off into a dreamless sleep.

FIFTY-THREE

We left six days later after loading up on paper towels, dried beans, canned pears, and motor oil at Costco. After firing up that big 75-horsepower Volvo-Penta diesel I pushed firmly away from the wharf waving goodbye to the small crowd of friends there to see me off. "Bye! Bye! I'll text you from Port Townsend," I shouted over the water as Abraxis and I moved slowly out into the channel. I looked toward the Ballard Locks and took a deep breath please god let us be in the small locks please god as I followed the meatball down that narrow concrete chute toward the Puget Sound. Firing the engine a short burst in reverse I slung a bow line over the forward bollard and raced down the port side jack line to the stern where a burly Lock Master took the line from my hand with a smile. "Locking down alone, huh," he said, ordering a small dinghy to snug up against the starboard packing us in like sardines.

"El lobo solo," I replied, laughing. "That's me."

Bells clanging, the gates shut water swiftly sucked under the lock walls through stone pipes gushing out into the Sound and I looked up at all the faces crowded around the edges of the small locks. I waved at a small child, seeing her tuck her face shyly into her mother's side as Abraxis hummed in anticipation. Dropping dropping we sank lower ten feet then twenty feet down before the bells signaled reopening. We were first out because we'd been first in and as I goosed the throttle I heard the Lock Master shout out good luck, my reply a silently victorious finger pointed upward to the clouds.

Motoring briskly out past Elliot Bay we stayed firmly to the right-hand side of the channel avoiding the big power boats shoving past, wakes smacking against us as Abraxis narrowed his eyes at their rudeness. I patted him on the helm I said, "Relax, devil child, we'll be out of this mess in no time." A small twang of the forestay was the only response.

Once we'd gotten far enough from the day sailors, University of Washington students taking Daddy's boat for a beer run and away from the ferry's path I turned up into the wind and stood in the cockpit for a long moment. "Last chance, buddy," I said to him looking up at the wind meter. Swiveling to stay nose into the wind I could feel him saying Get on with it, let's get on with it, Jesus Christ let's go let's go LET'S GO RIGHT NOW!

Safety first, I snapped onto a jack line with my safety vest tether and climbed onto the deck and made my way forward to the mast where I checked the stays for the last time before turning back toward the Seattle skyline. I saw the Space Needle sticking narrowly up above Lake Union, stray rays of light silhouetting its long slender legs and swallowed hard then grasped the mainsheet halyard in a gloved hand.

Arm over arm I pulled on the line as a brilliant white canvas unfurled toward the patchy blue sky. Shivering, Abraxis luffed his sheets in the quickening breeze as I grunted, heaving that line down, burning my palms as I brought that line briskly down. "Could use some help here, buddy," I told him as I cleated off the halyard, wiping a forearm across my sweaty brow thinking to myself I probably should have done a little more weightlifting before starting out on this enterprise.

Leaving the mainsheet snapping in the wind I walked on the jack line forward to the jib and checked the forestay before mincing carefully back to the stern and climbing down into the cockpit. Halyards spun through with a zing as I slowly unfurled the jib tying off the starboard line loosely through a cleat mounted on the cockpit helm.

I took a deep breath and turned slowly away from the wind as the breeze filled the mainsail, pushing the boom out over the water snapping hard against the end of the traveler while I tied off the sheet and checked the downhaul. "Chillax, bro," I cautioned Abraxis as he quickly heeled over clawing at the water, "Too far and we'll have some massive drift." There was a pause as the jib filled, snapping out of the cleat the full length of the line with a quick jerk.

I shook my head. "It's always the little things," I muttered and leaned forward to pull in the jib halyard, tying a quick figure-eight at the stop position. "Don't worry, baby," I told Abraxis as I compensated for our windward deviation, "It's not the size of your keel, it's how you use it."

As we pointed toward Port Townsend I swear I saw his lip raised in a sneer as we left Seattle behind in our wake.

FIFTY-FOUR

The weather held and one calm morning two days later we made a team decision to make the mad dash straight from Port Townsend across the Straits of Juan de Fuca to Victoria. I stood on the bow as we left Washington state in bright sunshine and could almost see British Columbia as a dark smudge spread across the horizon. Clinging tightly to the forestay with a clenched fist, bow rising up over the waves, the main close hauled with jib furled I leaned as far out as my jack line would allow and raised my face to the sun.

Water hummed past our sides as we flew on a brisk fifteen knot push out into the Straits. A brilliant shining beast, we skimmed across the waves as the Clipper blew our doors off blazing in the distance throwing up a giant rooster tail on its way to Friday Harbor with Abraxis trailing far behind. A thud suddenly rumbled through the hull and I looked down to see logs slipping past us just below the surface realizing that Canada in her infinite wisdom decided not to give a shit about letting their forestry industry chuck wood into their waters with apparently zero oversight.

Fuck I thought and quickstepped it down the deck, leaning precariously over the rails to evaluate the damage. Abraxis shifted slightly as he dipped down into a trough and I saw a shallow gouge running down the starboard side where a log had hit the fiberglass hull a glancing blow. "Goddamn it!" I threw my hands in the air and slapped them down on top of my head. "Fucking Canadians and their fucking logs and shit!" Abraxis snorted as he heeled back over and picked up the pace as if to say, "Get it together, you moron, I've got this," as he charged on, as we just moved right on through.

I found a boating supply store next to the visiting vessel slips in Victoria that sold me a quick cure fiberglass epoxy and two days after we'd cleared customs in Victoria Harbor I'd patched the gash in my baby's side and buffed him up nice and pretty. "Aren't you handsome," I complimented him wiping a microfiber across his gleaming teak toe rail. I could tell he was preening as passersby admired the Gothic crimson lettering across his stern spelling out Abraxis with the silhouette of a dragon's wings hovering behind.

"Don't get too used to all the attention," I told him that night as we shared a Coke on the bow, condensation beading down the can's sides in the heat. "We're leaving civilization shortly and it'll be just you and me. You and me for a long time, buddy."

He merely closed his eyes and crouched silently in the harbor as I dripped water on his head.

FIFTY-FIVE

A day later Abraxis and I raged out of Victoria with our diesel running at a whopping 7 knot pace and headed north the seventy miles toward Nanaimo, British Columbia. A golden Canadian sun shimmered in the early morning air bouncing small rays off the calm waters around us. I sat on the teak bench and crossed my heels on top of the wheel. I folded my hands behind my head, tilted my face back and breathed a deep sigh. "Don't worry, baby," I told him, "we'll be under power for a while but I'll give you a chance to fly when we leave Nanaimo." He shimmied a little when a passing pleasure boat wake tipped up our stern just a smidge. "Following seas," I whispered.

May we have fair winds and following seas.

Three hours in I flipped off my wool cap in the rising temps, pushed the hair out of my eyes and said, "Hey, Abraxis, you awake?" "Yes, you idiot, I've been carrying your fat ass around for almost half a day now," he sniped back. "Jesus," I huffed, "someone's grumpy today. You'd think you woke up at four o'clock in the morning or something."

He motored on without comment.

"Ok, well, I wanted to read you something," I said to him, flipping sideways on the bench before leaning my back against the port side against a dark crimson cushion. I held up a dog-eared paperback and pointed at the title. "Heir of Fire by Sarah Maas," I said to him, reading the words very slowly. He looked over his shoulder and told me he wasn't a five-year-old and to fucking get on with it because he was busy concentrating. "Don't get huffy, dragon boy, I'm going to read you the story of your name." I opened the earmarked page. "Although I did change the spelling a little," I confessed.

"Why?"

"Well," I flipped through the book, "She spelled it Abraxos but I thought it looked better with an *I*."

"Is it because 'I' am awesome?" he asked.

"Uh, yeah. Yes, yes that's exactly it. Totally yes, you got it in one, baby."

I didn't have the heart to tell him that his name with an O wouldn't fit across the stern. That I changed it because his butt was too skinny. "Totally because you're awesome," I fluffed him and began to read in a soft voice.

An hour later I heard a buzzing noise and looked up as a shining Seaair DeHavilland Turbine Beaver zipped across the sky above me on its way from Victoria to Nanaimo. I threw up an arm and waved to it shouting out a hello as the pontoons disappeared north out of sight. I thought back to Kenmore's bright yellow planes zooming across Lake Union weaving back and forth to avoid the kayakers at 8 am promptly on weekdays and a polite 9 am on weekends. Better than an alarm clock, I'd thought as I rolled over in bed and adjusted my eye shade more tightly drifting back to sleep in the darkness of that huge wood cabin.

In the cockpit I stood, pivoted and flipped open the hatch to the aft cabin to check on all the stuff strapped tightly onto those new shelves. It was way smaller than I had before, that's for sure. I climbed down the ladder, dug around and found a light jacket and started back up the ladder hand over hand, "No need for all that space when it's just me. It's just me now."

Abraxis skipped a beat and I paused halfway up cocking my head listening intently to the rhythm of the diesel engine. "What's that?" I stepped onto the cockpit bench and down past the wheel, "You trying to make a point here?" The engine evened out and I reminded myself to stock up on impellers when next in port.

"Fine," I slipped my arms into the jacket and zipped up the inner vest, "It's just us now. Us. Happy? Are you happy now?"

"I will be when you finish the book," he sniffed, "Now, please continue telling me about myself. I sound like quite the badass."

<h1 style="text-align:center">FIFTY-SIX</h1>

Nanaimo was delicious I told myself the next afternoon and sucked down a hot dog piled high with sauerkraut from the stand located across from the public library. Genius, genius to put hot dogs here. I raised my bun at the literature depository in salute before turning away. I let out the top button of my pants and decided it was time for a ramble down to the Thrifty for provisions. Along the way I drew in a deep breaths of salty clean air taking care to weave through every sun puddle on the sidewalk. At the store I bought a bag of apples, some Vaseline, potatoes, and a giant steak. I smiled to myself and picked up a small stuffed sheep from a bin next to the dish sponges. I knew someone who would adore this tiny animal so I stuffed it in my cart softly rubbing its furry head with my thumb.

I paid for my groceries after a very serious discussion with the cashier over exchange rates which culminated with me tossing a handful of American dollars on the counter saying, "I trust you not to take all my cash will you please just take whatever it costs and give me the correct change." The lady smiled and told me this happens all the time. I smiled back in embarrassment, swiped up a pile of loonies and shoved them into my jeans pocket. I spotted a Canadian nickel in the remaining pile of coins and picked it up. Gently I rubbed between my thumb and index finger before shoving it in my jacket pocket pulling the zipper all the way to the top, sealing it in.

An extra day in port sounded like just the ticket so I made a detour to buy a Nanaimo bar and shoved that chocolate cake right down my facehole with great dispatch. I licked my fingers and grunted happily, clutching two more bars in one hand and with the other I slung my Fred Meyer canvas grocery bags onto Abraxis with a giant heave. "Here we go," I climbed up over the side, "I got us some stuff with pits and eyes now that we're past those customs jerks." Abraxis sourly reminded me that fruit and potatoes were lame. I whipped out the giant steak, "and I got THIS!"

He took a deep breath. OMG STEAK STEAK STEAK he shouted gleefully as the wind gusted shrilly through the halyards.

"And I also got you something else," I flung the stuffed sheep over my head victoriously.

He was silent.

"What's the dealio, dude?" My feelings were slightly hurt. "I buy you a gift and you just dog me like that." I felt him pause.

"But I can't eat that," he replied grudgingly. "Then be friends with it," I huffed. "What's its name," he asked and refused to look at me staring instead straight out into the harbor, "Better not be a cooler name than mine."

"I'll let you name it," I said magnanimously and wrapped a thin line around the sheep's neck in a hangman's noose before attaching it to the windscreen ceiling. A long minute passed before he whispered a word into the rising winds. "Didn't hear you," I replied, my voice muffled from where I was digging under benches for the wool blanket. "Come again?"

"Meat."

"I'm sorry, did you say you want to name your friend Meat?"

"Yes."

"Ok. Meat it is."

FIFTY-SEVEN

I topped off our tanks with fresh water that evening before whipping out the shiny new Magma grill I'd bought at Fisheries in Seattle and screwed on a tiny green propane bottle. "Thought I'd cook this big steak out here so you can enjoy the smell," I told him, slicing the tape wrapped around the butcher's paper. "I like my steak raw," he answered.

"Well, I don't," I flipped it onto a plate and covered it with a dishtowel, "so you can live vicariously through me and pretend medium rare is actually really rare." "I like it when dinner runs and I have to chase it," he smiled. "Well, that's because you're weird and scary," I replied, cutting potatoes into paper thin slices laying them carefully into a cast iron pan. "We'll get you running soon enough when we head out to Campbell River in the morning."

I carried the pan down to the galley tapping Meat gently on the butt as I passed and fired up one of the burners to cook the potatoes. "Don't forget to check Whiskey Gulf," he said to me as the potatoes started to sizzle in the oil. "Yep," I flipped the slices with a fork, "Don't want to get blown out of the water by the squids, now do we."

Once the pan was safely heating on the stove I hopped up the ladder and grabbed the steak with one hand and opened the grill lid with the other. I heard the ribeye sizzle when it hit the hot grate and a delicious smell wafted up from the railing where the grill was clipped. "That smells heavenly," Abraxis groaned and rolled his fenders against the dock. "You're welcome," I turned away and climbed down the ladder headed for the sink holding up my steak juice-covered hand. I heard him ask, "Can I at least lick your fingers?"

"No! That's disgusting!"

His only reply the reverberating screech of a fender grinding against the fiberglass.

That evening I sat staring down at the Canadian Current Tables adding up the numbers in my head. "Must add one hour, must add one hour," I muttered to myself and wrote ADD ONE HOUR FOR CANADA on a Post It note and pinned it above the navigation station light. "Why," Abraxis asked and winked at the Chantiers Amel Super Maramu sailboat the next slip over.

"Stop flirting bro, she's out of your league." Distracted by the Daylight Savings Time conversion, I continued a minute later, "They don't believe in time changes here." After adding in the extra hour to our projected departure time tide prediction, I leaned over reaching for the Ports and Passes volume wedged onto a tiny bookshelf intending to double check my calculations and promptly fell off my stool.

"Jesus Christ, Abraxis," I yelled out as I hit the floor. He just snickered and sent a small sneaky ripple toward the lovely lady next door.

FIFTY-EIGHT

Early the next morning we checked the winds and discovered it was forecasted for 18 knots. "Not gonna do it," I told him when he tried to convince me that the sail would reef down enough, that the navy gunners wouldn't be out, and he needed to fly!

TO FLY he roared at me as the winds sped shrilly down the gulf outside.

"Pipe down," I whispered and crawled back under the duvet slapping my eye shade back on. "Sleepy time. It's sleepy time, crabby pants." Around ten o'clock in the morning I felt the boat shift slightly and rolled over in bed as a shadow passed by the cabin porthole. "Visitor," Abraxis whispered when a knock came on the outside deck.

"Hello!" came a voice through the open porthole screen, "Anyone home?"

I sat up abruptly. "Just a second, be up in a second," I looked around for my pants, slightly confused. Note to self, sleep wearing pants. I pulled on a set of stiff yellow canvas foul weather pants over my underwear, jammed that gray sweater over my head and slapped a baseball cap over my quickly braided hair before I climbed up the ladder shoeless and pushed open the hatch.

There on the dock next to Abraxis stood a stunningly gorgeous man in a royal blue cashmere cowl-necked sweater holding a silver tray loaded down with steaming hot croissants.

FIFTY-NINE

"Don't know where you came from but you are always welcome here, anything you need, anything you need, you just come to me," I said a half hour later as I ate my fourth delicious homemade pastry. "You, Alain, are a culinary genius," I told him through a mouth of crumbs. He laughed and handed me an actual linen napkin. "Merci," he replied in a soft French accent, "Since we are neighbors I thought you might want to share in my breakfast."

I snaked an arm across the table, lifted the silver coffee pot and poured myself another generous dose into a delicate china cup. "How do you keep this stuff from breaking," I shook my head, "I can't even keep a pencil from snapping and yet here you are with real dishes." Waving his hand with a flourish as only a Frenchman can do he said, "It's an Amel. It's French. Naturally, it's fabulous." I nodded in agreement and mashed another croissant down my throat.

A few hours later I shouted a brisk "Alain!" over toward his slip. "I'm going to wander the town aimlessly. Care to accompany?" He *oui oui'd* and emerged wearing a spiffy pair of linen pants, a cream straw fedora and Italian leather loafers with no socks. He tucked a lemon yellow pocket square into a navy sport coat he'd thrown casually over an untucked button down shirt and held out his elbow. I curtsied as I put my hand on his arm and we pranced away. "You need better clothes," he said looking down at my sweatshirt, flip flops and worn blue jeans, "A woman like you should be dressed in the finest silks."

"Yeah, silk holds up really well on sailing trips, but I do have a pretty awesome pair of wizard shoes."

"About the silk, yes. Yes, this is true, this is true," he patted my hand gently, "I don't know anything about wizard shoes but just promise me you won't forget you are a gorgeous butterfly while you are out there flying across the water on that beast." I told him I wouldn't, that I would endeavor to brush my teeth and shower at least once a week. He grinned down at me, gave a loonie to a vendor and pulled back his hand with a flourish presenting me with a single perfect sunflower.

SIXTY

"So, what's a fancy cat like you doing out here alone in Nanaimo," I asked later that night as we sat on his bow, Abraxis eavesdropping from across the dock. "Escape," Alain looked away.

"I was in love," he continued after a long moment, "but, alas, it was not meant to be. I wanted more than he could give." He smiled sadly. "So I told him I was leaving him for a woman, bought Nanette the next week and came here to hide."

"She's beautiful, you know." I looked around at the shining stainless and perfectly seamed navy upholstery. I cupped a hand up around one side of my mouth and leaned over in his direction watching his eyes light up in a devilish smile. I whispered, "Don't tell, but…Abraxis has a crush on Nanette."

"But he's American!" There was a click as Abraxis flipped his water pump on, "Actually, I'm German."

"Oh la vache! Might as well be a Republican."

I reached back and picked up the wine bottle. "Best top up now, pal," I raised an eyebrow in his direction and began to tell him about a dark and crazy night in an Anchorage kitchen.

SIXTY-ONE

No one was in any shape the next morning to do anything even though the weather dawned sunny with both Whiskey Gulf and the wind perfectly silent. "How in the world do you look so good," I moaned from where I was sprawled across Nanette's stern bench with an ice pack on my head.

"I'm French."

Enough said. I swallowed down the aspirin he handed me with sparkling water he poured from a cut crystal carafe. "I'll probably leave tomorrow morning," I told him squinting at his face in the sunlight. "Where is your final destination?" he whipped a suede brush across the top of a pair of loafers.

"Seward."

"Ahhhhh…so close, yet so far away."

"I can neither confirm nor deny Seward is my destination of choice for any particular reason. Besides, I can't sail right up to Anchorage."

"Yes, of course, desperation is never attractive. Let him chase you, let him come to you," he set a shoe to the side and nodded sagely.

"Actually, the Cook Inlet is too shallow," I said sheepishly and he tilted his face to the sky, laughing.

"Perhaps Nanette and I will accompany you on your trip as far as Prince Rupert," Alain suggested. "Only if you bring that fancy croissant pan," I held out my hand and after a moment's consideration we shook on it.

SIXTY-TWO

Nanette and Abraxis took off out of Nanaimo into Whiskey Gulf early the next morning as the sun began to inch up over the horizon. "I really would prefer to follow," Abraxis said when Nanette fell in behind. "That's because you want to stare at her ass, you perv," I watched Meat swing gently to starboard.

"She has a lovely stern, yes."

"Don't act dignified. I know you," I released the jib halyard and let out the main.

"I would help her with her inboard anytime," he glanced over his shoulder at that gorgeous French coquette tacking windward playing hard to get.

"You reefed ok back there?" I released the transmission button on the VHF radio clipped to my safety vest and waited for Alain to answer. A moment of silence passed before his voice came back, "Yes. And now I am enjoying a lovely espresso."

"I'm so jealous. My electric won't support that kind of fancy machinery, you know." Abraxis shushed me, "Don't reveal my faults, a guy needs a little mystery with a gal like that." Alain laughed, "Tell Abraxis

Nanette says bonjour." I clicked the VHF twice and patted Abraxis on the helm.

Four hours and a lovely Croque Monsieur later we were officially in the shit.

"Jesus Christ, weathers 1 through 5 all said light winds, every one of them said light fucking winds," I yelled over the gale to Alain via VHF as we screamed across Whiskey Gulf at an inhumanly fast rate. "Liars! All Canadians are liars," the staccato reply. Nanette shot across our stern. "Just hang on for another few hours and we'll be out of the worst of it, I think," I gasped, wind driven spray flying across the side hitting me square in the face. "Dog down all your shit and for god's sake save the croissant pan," I choked out. He double clicked in acknowledgment.

The wind kept rising until we topped out at twenty-seven knots. "Hang on baby," I looked up at the main desperately straining to hold in the high winds. I'd reefed it pretty far down when we'd left Nanaimo intending to just power through with the diesel if we needed speed but that main canvas suddenly looked really big. The angles were all wrong. I cringed when the mast quivered and flexed in the strong gusts.

This was not good. Not good. I wiped spray off my face and turned my head when another wave came over the edge of the bow and rolled down the decking smashing up against the windscreen pouring over the edge filling up the cockpit before draining slowly out through the scuppers. We pitched up over a swell and crashed down the back side with a giant heave before rolling hard to starboard. "This is awesome," Abraxis screamed out with glee out as he flew up the face of another swell.

"No, this is bullshit," I coughed, spitting water out on the deck. "Let's surf," he turned up slightly into the wind to reduce pressure on the main and I pulled in the sheets preparing to tack. Turning off the wind to port I felt the boom blast over my head like a cannon as we clipped the top of a passing swell. I slowly inched the main back out but even reefed we immediately picked up what seemed an impossible speed. I looked down and saw the number fourteen flip up on the speed display and realized we were really moving.

"Pretty sure we've exceeded the manufacturing specs. As in, defying-the-laws-of-physics exceeded. Can't do anything about it now," I told him nervously, hoping desperately that the wind held in a single direction and we didn't jibe. "If we broach we're going to lay it down so be prepared," I warned him when he turned a smidge too far to starboard. I compulsively tugged on the extra jack line snapped to my safety harness. I backed off slightly trying to catch the leading edge of a swell and gingerly let out the main. Holding an almost constant tension on the sheets we carefully surfed at a firm 45-degree angle sliding swiftly through the white-capped troughs toward Campbell River with Nanette following closely behind.

SIXTY-THREE

I'm sure we looked like a cloud of avenging furies as Abraxis and Nanette blasted into Campbell River that evening as a blood red sun lurked in the background. I spied the giant rock breakwater in the distance and tapped the VHF, "Alain, you alive?" His tired voice came back a moment later, "We will survive."

"You break anything over there?" I let out a huge sigh of relief into the radio and held a shaking hand up to my sweaty forehead, "Personally, I'm afraid to look down below at whatever was crashing around in my galley. I'm pretty sure it was the coffee pot."

"What a tragedy," he replied wryly, "that the world will be deprived of that swill you call coffee." I laughed and suggested we find a spot to drop our mainsails before we broadsided a nearby cruise ship. He agreed and within an hour we'd flipped a bitch and were motoring sedately toward Discovery Harbour where I tagged up with the harbormaster over the radio and passed on Alain's slip assignment. "Looks like we're both on a side tie," I said, consulting my handy marina map shivering in my wet foulies. "You have fancy bow thrusters on that sexy lady, right?"

"Of course," came back his smug reply, "Perhaps you should dock first so that poor Nanette doesn't get crushed by your dragon." I felt

Abraxis tighten into a tiny ball whispering, "I'd crush that. I'd crush that so hard." I cleared my throat and replied, "Let me go first and then you can just slide right in." There was a slight snicker from Abraxis.

I told him to grow up.

"On a platter," he shot back while we rode up to the harbor entrance, "laying them right out there on a platter." "Well at least you'll have something nice to look at while we're in port," I smacked a palm down on his helm, reached over and wrung a bucket of water out of poor bedraggled Meat.

"Looks like we're on H dock," I said to Alain, slowing our speed below the harbor 3 knot maximum. "I'll just pull all the way forward, I guess." Abraxis huffed as we snubbed up bow first to the Silverton powerboat moored further down the dock. "Sorry buddy," I threw a dock line out to one of the harbormasters standing by to help, "you're gonna have to check out her booty some other day." I lurched down the port side in my sloshing boots before signaling the harbormaster to let out the bow line a few feet so I could reverse our stern into the dock. I popped the engine into neutral a few feet out and let Abraxis drift in as I stepped to the edge of his deck with line in hand, ready to hop out and tie off.

"Thanks for the assist," I said breathlessly to the harbormaster who just shook his head. "Couldn't believe my eyes when I saw you both shoot that gap," he shuddered, "both of you are crazy. Crazy to be out in that wind."

"Wasn't what we'd planned, that's for damn sure," I leapt off Abraxis tying him quickly to the dock cleats as Nanette began her gliding approach. A few feet from the dock Alain fired his cheater thrusters and Nanette gently slid sideways into the dock in a single move. "Fancy," I said, catching the thrown bow line as Nanette hovered at a perfect distance. "As well she should be," said Alain, "for she cost me a pretty penny." "All the good ones are pricey," Abraxis said over his shoulder. Nanette huffed her bow thruster in indignation.

That evening Alain and I sat bow to stern on our respective vessels in exhausted silence with our foul weather gear hung dripping off every available line. "This is incredibly trashy," he sniffed, a Henri Lloyd jacket swinging from the jib halyard smacking damply into the side of his face. "Well, I'm actually from West Virginia, or my mom is at least," I told him over my shoulder as I toweled off my orange survival suit and clipped it securely to the side of my cockpit, "So I feel right at home having laundry strewn about in public."

"I never would have guessed," he gestured emphatically at my ancient Crocs. "Such style, such grace," he continued when I accidentally tossed a microfiber over the edge of the deck into the harbor. "I'll have you know I'm incredibly athletic," I grunted, sweeping a boat hook under the sinking towel flipping it up onto the deck where it landed with a sopping wet splash. "I stand corrected," he replied and poured himself another martini from a stainless shaker. "If it'll make you feel better, I'll go put on my wizard shoes," I smirked at him, "you won't even be able to compete, fancy pants. My wizard shoes bring the heat."

Alain shivered once in the cold night air and told me to trot those puppies out, that sequins were perfectly acceptable with fleece and any heat I could provide would be graciously appreciated. "It's the epitome of high-low fashion," I said with élan as I posed on the cockpit bench a few minutes later, hauling up the ankle of my gray sweatpants and wiggling my silvery wizard shoe suggestively. "It's the epitome of something," he agreed as he drained his glass in one giant gulp.

One hot shower and a generous slug of straight Pimms from my secret liquor locker later, I met Alain on the dock and we meandered down toward Moxie's. "I'm not quite sure why we are being forced to traverse a giant parking lot in order to reach this dining establishment," he wondered, clutching a green cashmere scarf against his chest. "I'm not quite sure why you're wearing a scarf in the summertime," I replied. "I am a fragile flower," he sniffed, "also I had an incident with some water during our trip here and was forced to stand in wet boots for four hours."

"Valid. All valid points," I nodded a thank you as he swung open the door.

Two hours later we slowly waddled back across the parking lot toward the marina. I shifted my gigantic chicken enchilada leftovers box from one hand to the other and reached back grabbing Alain's arm, tugging him along. "That salmon salad with the bacon was delicious," he slurred, "I thought perhaps it would be terrible with the egg because restaurants always overcook the egg like sawdust but it was not bad. Not bad."

"You drank way too much gin, pal," I tightened my grip as he started to weave. "Yes, well, their bartender was also quite delicious," he smiled and held out his hand. "Whatcha got there, Casanova," I peered over in the dim light to see a series of digits written along Alain's wrist in ballpoint pen.

"Oooooooooo! Somebody got a phone number when I was in the bathroom," I punched him lightly on the arm and called him a whore. Alain shrugged sheepishly. "I have a fondness for blondes," he said, flipping my ponytail sideways over my face. "Be that as it may, let's not be driving anywhere this evening, ok," I helped him weave down the dock. He assured me that Delicious Bartender might perhaps pay a visit to Nanette after his shift was completed which would give Alain plenty of time to sober up.

"Hopefully he's still delicious when you're not toasted," I giggled. Alain straightened up, wished me a genteel good evening and fell down the ladder into his galley. "I'm ok," his voice drifted up through the hatch, "Nothing to see here. Nothing to see."

SIXTY-FOUR

"Don't forget to pump out," I reminded Alain the next morning as Delicious Bartender lounged on Nanette's cockpit bench, croissant in hand. Alain gave me a thumbs up so I hopped onto the dock and headed off to West Marine. When I looked back over my shoulder I saw him holding a linen napkin over his mouth leaning over laughing at some undoubtedly raunchy joke while Delicious Bartender waved his hands expressively in the air. I smiled and walked away shaking my head, wizard shoes smacking against the gangway on my way out of the marina.

"Yo! Alain!" I yelled from the dock a few hours later and knocked my knuckles on the deck. "Up and at 'em, tiger." His head popped up from the hatch and he climbed into the cockpit. "I see your trip was successful," he raised an eyebrow at my giant stack of West Marine bags. "Yep, bought out almost their whole supply of impellers," I told him and jammed a hand down into one of the bags. "Bought you some extras, too. Definitely don't want to lose an engine out there since we'll be under power almost the whole time from here on out to Prince Rupert." He ooh'd and awe'd over my new strap wrenches while I told him about busting a transmission gasket in our old boat heading into the Ballard locks one summer afternoon.

"There we were, forty-two tons of mahogany moving at six knots toward a giant concrete wall when Andy says, 'Well, we've just lost the port engine' calm as a cucumber."

Alain gasped, holding out his mimosa glass for me to top off. "And then what happened, what happened to your beautiful boat," he leaned forward. "Andy just did whatever it was he did with the wheel, cranking it around and pushing up the starboard engine and whatever else he was doing up there while I was running around trying to put out all the fenders screeching like a crazy person in front of all the tourists. Put it right through the chute and lightly up against the lock wall like nothing even happened. Didn't break a sweat. Sixty-two feet of boat on one working engine and he didn't even blink. It was amazing." Alain nodded, "It's because he was a pilot in a twin engine plane," he said sounding quite knowledgeable, "I'm sure he was used to compensating for the lack of thrust."

I set my mimosa glass on Nanette's fancy folding table. "And how do you know all these technical terms, Alain Fourchette?" I tilted my chin up and folded my arms. "I, too, have done some flying in my day," he said modestly. "My family had a small plane for a while and we would meander about the countryside on the weekends."

"Really?" I leaned back against a navy cushion and propped my feet up on his table. "What, exactly, do you do for a living that affords you the cash to putter around in your own plane?" He smiled, reached down a hand and slipped off one of my blue flowered slip-on Crocs. "I work in the fashion business," he said, tapping the rubber shoe gently on my knee, "and I must say, you have terrible terrible taste in shoes."

I put my hands to my face and groaned. "I knew you were too good to be true," I wailed, "Judging, judging. You French are always judging." He laughed and said the magic words every woman dreams of hearing from a Frenchman's lips, "Perhaps you and I will go shopping together one day." He reached over and tugged the tip of my ponytail. "And maybe I can convince you to do something about this mop."

"Well," I vogued with my hands on either side of my face, "I've always wanted to shave my head."

He pushed my face sideways with his fingers and looked closely at me from several angles. "Why not," he flipped his hand up in a devil-may-care gesture and told me I had the cheekbones for it. "Yeah, I'll think about it," I slid my foot back into my shoe before lifting my glass into the air. "Now make me another mimosa as penance for mocking my choice of footwear."

SIXTY-FIVE

"So, I'm thinking we should probably put our heads together and check the charts at some point tonight or early tomorrow morning," I said in early evening as we enjoyed a lovely salad nicoise in Nanette's perfectly proportioned teak galley. "Don't talk with your mouth full," Alain said, pointing an actual silver fork at me. "I'm regretting the moment I asked you to civilize me," I griped back and tried not to slouch. "You're too American," he announced like I had leprosy. "You need to bring back your mystery, the innate suspense of being that creature known as *woman*. You would never have said those things in that kitchen if you'd have been French, you know."

"Yeah, I would have had his pants on the floor a hell of a lot faster if I'd been French," I said and he laughed and laughed.

We sat in companionable silence until he cleared his throat. "There's a small place just down the street from here," he began, "with free wifi." "Well, none of the American cell phones work here in Canada without costing a zillion dollars and I didn't bother to get a Canadian cell phone or I'd just poach wifi off that," I attempted to use a fork and knife simultaneously. He looked at me.

I looked at him.

He stared back.

"What is your dealio, dude?" I shifted my eyes away knowing exactly where he was going with this. "First, the words 'dealio' and 'dude' should be stricken from your vocabulary," he said, enumerating my faults on upraised fingers. "Second, you need to go write an email to a certain gentleman who currently resides in Anchorage lest he find himself ensnared by another mysterious doctor before you can entrance him with your newly found je ne sais quoi."

I thought for a moment and then turned to him opening my mouth as he said, "They close at nine." I yanked on my thick green wool sweater as protection against the Canadian night, slipped on my wizard shoes and kissed Alain on the cheek before climbing up the ladder and down onto the dock, iPad in hand. "If I'm not back in an hour, send out the Mounties," I said. He replied, "Only the ugly ones. I will keep the handsome ones for myself."

"You and these Canadians, Alain," I teased him as I walked backward down the dock. "It's the accent!" he shouted back. I turned and tramped up the gangway toward the small cafe. I felt bad about freeloading wifi so I bought a latte, flipped open my iPad and logged in reluctantly to my email. I sat in front of the keyboard for a long time before I clicked Compose in the Gmail window.

Hi.

That was lame. I hit the Backspace button. I could start with the traditional fighter pilot "What's up muthafucka?" but that wasn't subtle in the slightest. I reminded myself that I needed mystery. Don't look desperate.

I took a deep breath, set my fingers on the keyboard and started typing.

Hey! Surprise…I'm alive (although barely). Ran into some bitching weather over Whiskey Gulf but the upside is we made it from Nanaimo to Campbell River in one minute versus 10 hours.

Met a divine Frenchman named Alain who is going to tag along while Abraxis and I rage north. His boat is Nanette and Abraxis has a serious crush on her. It's adorable. Sooner or later Alain and I are going to come back from breakfast and find four or five tiny tenders floating in the water between the two of them. I hope those crazy kids are being responsible.

The goal is to hit Port McNeill in a week or so (maybe). I'll try to poach some wifi there and update you. That way if you see my face on a milk carton you can tell people not only am I alive…I'm in Canada.

Boom.

Ok, I'll be checking email tomorrow before we leave. Hope you are well.

I read the message twice before hitting Send. I sighed deeply, gathered my things and trudged back to where Abraxis hovered in silence waiting for my return. As I climbed back onto the deck I heard the sound of a hatch slipping open and saw the top of Alain's head pop over the edge of Nanette's cockpit. "And…," he whispered quietly.

"I sent an email that said *hi* and nothing else. Trying to keep my mystery, Alain, just like you taught me," I smiled down at him, watching his middle finger slowly lower until the hatch snapped shut.

SIXTY-SIX

Early the next morning I performed my standard groaning forward bends and downward dogs in the dark galley in preparation for the day's activities. "Old, I'm so old," I complained to a boat that was my age. Abraxis rolled his eyes. Meat glistened with the morning dew.

"Heading up to town," I said innocently to Alain as I climbed onto the dock, "Need anything?" He unfurled a newspaper and peered over the edge of his table. "Not from that terrible café, I don't. But thank you for asking nonetheless." He went back to the Arts section. I blushed and turned away. He sniffed at my total lack of subtlety.

I had one email. I needed more friends if all the email I have in three weeks is a single solitary message OMG IT WAS FROM HIM.

Dumbfounded, I looked at the Received time and noticed it came through at two o'clock in the morning. What was he even doing checking email at that ungodly hour? I thought for a minute about late night activities and shook my head. Demons be gone, don't think about that, don't think about that. I gripped my jacket collar and pulled it away from my neck. Lordy, I might need a cold shower in a second. My upper lip began to sweat.

Jesus. I took a deep breath, clicked on the email and saw five simple words.

Who the fuck is Alain?

"Ahh….the green devil rears his ugly head at last," Alain-Of-The-Email leaned over my shoulder staring at the iPad screen mere minutes after I had dashed back to the docks and dragged him by his well-manicured hand up to the café. "What should I say back?" I propped my chin on my hand, "I can just tell him you're gay and that will solve the problem, right?"

"Problem? This is not a problem. C'est magnifique!" Alain announced victoriously taking great care not to touch any of the chairs while he gesticulated. "We must cultivate this carefully," he mused. "He's not a tomato, Alain," I laughed, "what the hell does that even mean, this 'cultivating' you speak of?"

"We want to make him realize that you are not going to fall into his lap," he paused when I silently mouthed *but I so totally will, right down in that lap face first, oh yeah.* Alain rolled his eyes, "…but not so distant that he believes you to be gone from him forever."

"I'll be gone from him for the next six weeks probably." I said straight-faced and he slowly reached up a hand and squeezed my neck, shaking me gently. "Ok ok ok what should I say, Mysterious Alain-of-the-Email," I laughed and he grinned. Bumping me aside, he sat gingerly down on the chair and raised his fingers to the keyboard. Pausing, he typed five words in reply.

None of your business, lover.

And hit Send.

SIXTY-SEVEN

That afternoon I sat in the café for a good hour staring at the Gmail icon hitting the Refresh button every six seconds. Around two o'clock Alain finally came in and dragged me out by the arm. I desperately watched the screen until we walked out of range. "We'll check for a message later this evening and maybe not even until morning," he said firmly. "What if he's mad?" I asked nervously, "your message was kind of rude, Alain."

He looked down at me, "It's none of his business who I am. He made it very clear when he spoke of 'availability' in his kitchen where his place in your life actually is. You are no longer so available, are you?" I shrugged a shoulder. "But I don't want to be so unavailably rude that he just runs off with a delicious bartender." Alain gave me an evil grin. "Trust me, that message was like waving a flag in front of a bull. He'll pull out all the stops now. Just watch."

Sure enough, there was an email sitting in the Gmail box that evening. Unfortunately, it was from my mother.

SIXTY-EIGHT

"I really feel like I should send another email before we leave," I protested and dug in my heels late that night when Alain tried to pull me down the uneven dock after a quick trip to the grocery store. "No," he said firmly, "Mystery. Mystery, you must have mystery."

"Mystery is bullshit," I loaded on the last gallons of distilled water while he checked the tender strapped tight onto Nanette's deck. "I agree," said Abraxis, "so give it up, baby. Give it up for daddy." "Jesus Christ, Abraxis," I grouched, "pipe down." Nanette passed him a secret message under the waterline. "You guys are the only ones getting any," I whispered to him while Alain nattered on about Delicious Bartender possibly meeting us up the road for a visit.

"A visit," I rolled the extra screening and stuffed it into a canvas bag in the aft cabin, "is that what the kids are calling it nowadays." Alain huffed, "Maybe you should go pick up a delicious bartender of your own."

I shook my head, "No thanks, I do believe I'll hold out until Seward." He looked over the bow at where I was cleaning off my stern solar panels, stretching on my tiptoes way up over the aft cabin with a microfiber. "You do realize that he may never be yours," he said solemnly, "that perhaps it was not to be. Not to be. That what has already been, is what will be and nothing more."

I paused, "I know." I adjusted my baseball cap down over my eyes. "I still see his face when I go to sleep at night. It's sublimely horrid." Miserable, I sat down on the edge of the stern and kicked my heels against the dragon's wings. Alain looked down the dock, "I do, too. But every morning you must open your eyes and face the day. You never know what you might see."

"Stand tall," I whispered into the darkness as Alain sat alone on the bow and gently polished Nanette with a chamois cloth he'd pulled from a black satin bag.

SIXTY-NINE

The next morning we were all packed up and stuffed full with a fancy Gruyere omelet by eight o'clock. I loosened my top pants button and peered over my shoulder making sure Abraxis didn't smash his ass into Nanette's face. "Don't even say it, reprobate," I told him when he opened his mouth. As his bow pushed away from the dock and we slowly motored backward down H dock I could feel him sulking.

"Seymour Narrows," I leaned down and yelled into the cabin at him, "Tidal streams potentially at 16 knots! Suck it up, you whiny little bitch!" He paused then shook off his funk moving at a right sprightly pace scooting up to hover off Nanette's port side as we headed out of Campbell River pointing north.

"Let's take great pains to not miss the slack tide today," I held the VHF with one hand and bent forward to check the charts spread across the console. "Yep," Alain replied. I smiled and gave him shit for sounding more like an American every day. "We should be there right on target," I folded the chart back inside its plastic cover, "One hour before slack tide and then if the water's smooth we'll barge around hull-eating Ripple Rock and bust out toward Chatham Point."

I could hear him ruminating. "It's an underwater mountain practically smack in the middle of Seymour Narrows," I explained, looking over my shoulder making sure I cleared the breakwater before goosing Abraxis forward. "They tried to blow it up a few times but I don't think it ever completely took."

"A nuclear explosion, I've heard," Alain answered over the airwaves sauntering forward toward Nanette's bow after making sure he was securely snapped into his jack line. I paused. "Don't think the Canadians have ever admitted it…but yes. Allegedly there was an 'incident'." I held up my hands in dramatic quotations. Alain wagged his finger at me and yelled across the water between us, "I will be very upset if poor Nanette is irradiated."

We entered Seymour Narrows at nine that morning and quickly motored through calm waters on a wicked ebb tide crossing our fingers that The Whiskey Gulf Nightmare would not be repeated. With a giant a sigh of relief we finally exited the Narrows and passed Chatham Point where we heaved to for a quick confab. "I'm not a big fan of Current Passage," I pounded down a turkey sandwich sans crust, flipping the charts around till they were right side up. "And this is why?" Alain answered over the VHF, peering over from where he was spritzing oil on a squeaky fitting. "Haven't heard anything good about it," I shrugged, "Every salty seadog has told me to take Race Passage instead and, quite frankly, I'm inclined to take their advice."

"These are the same bastards who recommended we cross Whiskey Gulf on a calm day, yes?" he asked suspiciously. I admitted that perhaps the advice should be taken with a grain of salt. Eventually we agreed to take our chances on Race Passage and decided to make it a long day pushing on north to Kelsey Bay where we would raft up for the night with whoever happened to be anchored. "We'll just barge in and tie up next to the nicest boat we find," I said, dropping sails securing them tightly to the booms and rechecked the winds. Alain raised an index finger in my direction as we entered against the current and pointed down at Nanette in the universally snooty sign of *I am the nicest boat you'll find and I will break your face if you touch me, you slovenly Americans.*

SEVENTY

"My ass hurts," I said late that evening after we'd rafted up with a respectable Pearson resting gently against Abraxis to starboard, an anonymous Catalina carefully tied on Nanette's port side. Alain agreed, shifting gingerly on a large striped cushion, his stockinged feet propped on his cockpit bench. "I didn't think it would be so bumpy," he complained and drowned his pains with gin. "Well, we were going against both the current and the wind simultaneously," I explained and tried touch my toes, groaning. Alain sighed and I heard the bottle clinking against his glass, "Perhaps I should take over the navigation duties." I shot back, "Suit yourself, fancy pants," and fired up a giant slab of dill rubbed salmon on my grill.

The next day we checked the winds and finding them to be straight 20 knot northerlies decided we'd suck it up and make French toast from day-old brioche. "If this is your equivalent of lemons, lemonade," I leaned over and grabbed for the syrup, "I like it." Alain stabbed at my arm with his fork and I jerked my hand backward.

"Don't reach over plates like an orangutan. It's just bad manners."

I sat back, primly dabbed a napkin to the corners of my mouth and politely asked him to pass the fucking bottle, s'il vous plait.

Midmorning we bid adieu to the Pearson who decided to ride those northerlies of goodwill south through the Straits toward Seymour Narrows. We wished them good luck yelling out to avoid Ripple Rock. The Catalina soon followed leaving Nanette and Abraxis tucked closely into each other's sides dancing gently in the current holding tightly to their respective hooks.

That evening after we'd awoken from the uninterrupted dead-to-the-world naps so enjoyed by solo sailors at anchor the world over we took the tender off Abraxis's stern and motored sedately around the bay wrapped up in thick sweaters checking out everyone's stuff. "Judgey judgey, you French are so judgey," I needled Alain as he sniffed at a particularly atrocious orange canvas cockpit cover. "It looks like he was assaulted by the Tropicana Orange Juice man," he said and swung the tender around the starboard side of the offending vessel. I poked him gently in the arm. He expressively shrugged a shoulder and headed back toward where Nanette was silhouetted against the setting sun.

"What do you think he'll say?" I asked Alain that evening out on Nanette's deck bundled up in wool blankets. "You seem convinced that he'll write back although the jury is still out, Alain-of-the-Email because of your rudeness." I angled my eyes toward him and pulled my fur thrown over my head until only my nose poked out.

Smiling, he held a coffee cup in his hands and blew softly across the steaming surface. "He will write back because he cannot help himself," he shifted the pillow behind him. "You said you were leaving and he failed to reply before your departure and now he must wait. He must wait for your return to civilization." I sighed as he continued, "Besides, he is probably struggling with what to say. I would wager he has written and rewritten a reply many times over at this point."

A moment of silence stretched out into the darkness. Ripples blown by soft winds tipped up against the sides of Abraxis with tiny plinking sounds. "When you said you wanted more," I pushed the words out into the breeze, "What did you want?"

Alain leaned his head back and closed his eyes. "Freedom," he whispered sadly, "I wanted freedom."

SEVENTY-ONE

I hopped over to Nanette early the next morning and slammed my palm on Alain's hatch a few times until I heard faint sounds of movement from the cabin below. "There had better be a Delicious Bartender up here to compensate for all this racket," he grumbled, clutching his thick green cashmere robe to his neck padding up the ladder in his suede slippers. "Actually, it's southern winds," excited, I reached out and grabbed his upper arm and shook him slightly, "If we beat feet we can maybe make it all the way up to Port McNeill today!" "Transparent, transparent," he shook his head as he backed down the ladder. "Don't think I don't know about Port McNeill's free wifi," he said with gravity watching me leap across the gap onto Abraxis.

Thirty minutes later Alain bumped Nanette forward slowly over her anchor and hit the windlass control. The clanking of the chain pulling off the bottom and feeding into the locker rattled into the quiet morning as he slowly motored along the line. "The weather says gale warnings but I think we'll be ok. I think it almost always says that," I told Alain over VHF from where Abraxis turned in slow circles just outside of Nanette's anchorage. "To fly, to fly," Abraxis agreed, enjoying his slow pirouette. "This way Nanette can see me in all of my 360-degree glory," he wobbled slightly on the third revolution. Stopping the spin I smiled, "Getting a little dizzy, busy bee?"

He made a small urping noise.

"Are these also salty seadog words of wisdom," Alain replied over the VHF as we lined up and motored out of Kelsey Bay pushing firmly against the strong currents, a wispy morning sea fog beginning to dissipate. "Well, actually I learned it from Google," straight-faced I swirled a finger with great panache above my head. Adjusting the squelch, I steered slightly to starboard with my knee, saying in a deadpan tone, "I've been told it's the Source of All Truth and Knowledge." I laughed as the bright sunshine burned against my eyes and clicked the VHF once, cutting off a very rude French reply in mid-speech.

"Send me some tunes," I said, looking at Nanette hovered a safe distance off our stern, "these southerlies will prove useful in my continuing search for refinement." Alain replied he'd be happy to oblige and moments later the dulcet tones of The Grateful Dead rolled forward. Wing on wing we flew north to Port McNeill as the southerlies filled our sails with a marvelous consistent wind. "At least the puffs are few and far between," I said, adjusting the jib and letting out the main a tad to compensate for a random gap in the breeze. "This is very nice," Alain agreed and switched up the music selection.

Eclectic, I mused, as raucous French rap completely disturbed the peace as we sailed up the Johnstone Strait. "Who is this?" Alain replied mischievously, "A duo of fine gentlemen who abbreviate themselves as NTM." I asked what that stood for and adjusted to port to avoid some sea lions poking out their curious heads along the coastline. There was a pause as the VHF clicked on in what sounded like a mid-cough. Sounding a bit strangled Alain replied, *"Nique ta mère."*

"Which means what, fancy pants, in English. In English for my dumb American ears," I turned around to face him and stepped up onto the cockpit stern bench peering over Nanette's bow until I could see him from his shoulders up. "Fuck your mother," he bellowed out to the emerald forest lifting both arms over his head, fists clenched in victory.

"Let's fuel up in Port McNeill and then check the forecast," I suggested hours later when we neared the harbor. Alain concurred and we both kept a sharp eye out for logging operations and their inevitable waterborne missiles. "Let's not repeat the Victoria Smashup," Abraxis suggested, gingerly picking his way toward a protected anchorage at the mouth of the bay. A full load of ice later we were both more than ready for a small slice of heaven. "A man and his martini must not be parted," Alain explained patiently as he loaded the tender down with the cold bags while I bounced from foot to foot with excitement.

"Ok, ok, you're an alcoholic, I get it. Let's go! Let's go!"

Ten minutes later, I heaved the ice bags up onto his deck and ran across the gap to Abraxis, grabbed my towel and a blue loofah on a stick. Martini ice safely stowed, Alain and I hopped back in the tender and headed for shore. I blasted past Alain on the right at a full sprint moving those wizard shoes at top speed up the dock toward the marina showers smacking him on the butt with my loofah as I passed by yelling *dibs*.

After twenty minutes of excellent water pressure with room to stretch out my full wingspan I was completely pruned and blissfully happy. Finally exfoliated within an inch of my life I reluctantly shut off the shower and put on the clean t-shirt and cotton pants I'd brought with me. When I left the bathrooms I saw Alain deep in conversation with a red-headed woman off to the side. Motioning to myself with a finger I made the universal typing-hands-on-a-keyboard sign. He nodded and pointed up the hill tapping the Rolex on his wrist as if to say *no email, no waiting. Mystery. Mystery.*

I turned my head away and pretended not to notice as I skipped down the dock toward the tender swinging the loofah over my shoulder hobo-style. After pinning my towel to the steering wheel with a potato chip clip I quickly braided my hair into a low bun. I really need to do something with all this craziness. A strand slipped free and blew into my eyes. Maybe once we head out into the wilds from Sitka I'll pull the trigger and do the deed. Abraxis shouted out across the bay, "Aren't we picking up a shotgun on the US side?" I told him I regretted my choice of words and turned away marching up the dock without waiting for a reply.

I stood in the doorway of Mugz Coffee and Tea House a few minutes later and raised an eyebrow at both the eclectic chalkboard menu and the strangely psychedelic purple wall it hung on before ordering a latte and inquiring as to the wifi connection. I snagged a zebra print chair with my free hand and pulled it over to a small table then took out my iPad and opened up Gmail. Still nothing and it's been days, I realized with dismay. What the fuck! He must be really mad.

A half hour passed and I managed to physically restrain myself from sending a pathetic email to him questioning his mental status. I closed out the Gmail window and opened Facebook. Four cat videos and one divine yet tortuous time lapse of a mixed berry crumble later a small window opened up at the lower right corner. *What's up muthafuckaaaa* it said with his user name across the top of the chat.

Nothing much. We are here in Port McNeill. I smiled and I pecked at the screen with two index fingers.

So… Rude. Your email was rude, baby.

Sorry…but not sorry. Baby. I paused and wrote *gal's gotta have some mystery, you know.*

He replied *Alain better watch himself or I'll come down there and bust up his grain crib.*

Laughing, I typed back *Grain crib? Are you drunk?*

Getting there. Thinking of you raging around with some random divine French cat drives me to drink, woman. I blame you. I blame you for this descent into addiction.

I leaned over and started to type then stopped. *Feed the green monster* I heard Alain say inside my head. Hitting Backspace I cleared out the window and said *maybe you should come down and take a jaunt with me yourself then, Nanook of the North. Take a walk on the wild side. Unless you think it would be pistols at dawn...Alain's pretty good with his gun, you know.*

I snickered to myself and hit Enter.

There was a moment of silence before he replied *I'll seriously consider it.* I sent back a quick *you let me know, baby. You just let me know* and closed out the chat window before I dug myself into another deep dark hole.

SEVENTY-TWO

"Do you want to continue up to Sointula or stay here overnight? It's about an hour away on Malcolm Island, maybe less with these zippy winds," I asked Alain while he pushed the cart through the Thrifty and expressed his displeasure at their lack of foie gras. "None of these grocery stores is going to have foie gras, sweetie," I lifted a block of Tillamook extra sharp, "but this is delicious on Triskets." Horrified, he took the cheese from my hand pinching it carefully between a thumb and forefinger and dropped it into the cart. "I may lower my standards for this questionable block of cheddar but I will not stoop to Triskets. Triskets are the devil," he continued, digging through the deli section on a hunt for prosciutto. "How about some bacon instead," I held up a plastic shrink wrapped package.

"We are no longer friends," he sniffed, threw something into the cart and walked off with a haughty stride, "Americans, pfffft". We schlepped the groceries back to the boats and agreed to apportion them according to our respective storage space. "Wow," I said, amazed at the size of his lockers. "I didn't realize Nanette was so spacious."

"She did not mean that as an insult, my dear," he looked askance at me and stroked a hand down her cabin wall. "You are voluptuous," he told her, puffed out his cheeks and held his arms away from his stomach.

I clapped my hand over my mouth to stifle my laughter and cracked open a side door, "Holy shit! This entire cabin is a closet!" I realized the beds had been removed and long shelves and hanging bars were installed along the three walls. "Necessities, just the necessities," Alain said, placing cans of beans next to a box of neatly folded pocket squares.

"You realize you're a walking cliché, right?" I helped myself to a gorgeous thick maroon cashmere fisherman's cowl neck sweater and slipped it over my head. "Tsk, tsk, tsk," he said, "So many assumptions." He held out his hand toward me and snapped his fingers a few times. "I showered today," I shied away from his arm, "and exfoliated. I even shaved my legs so back up off the sweater, buddy. Let me live a little. Consider it part of my education."

"Fine, fine," he handed me bags of pasta I gently shoved down into his shoe cubbies, "But you cannot leave this boat wearing that. It's Armani." "Who you know personally, I'm sure," I tossed the words over my shoulder and was not in the least surprised when he replied that he did, that Georgio was quite lovely and his fabrics were adequately constructed in his humble opinion. "Good," I slipped out the door when his back was turned, "then you can get another one of these sweaters at a smashingly good price." I cackled gleefully to myself as I bounded up the ladder carrying the prosciutto, leapt across the gap onto Abraxis and slammed shut the hatch.

"Let's eat out tonight," I said over the VHF when we departed Port McNeill an hour later pointed across the Strait to Sointula, "As penance I will purchase dinner. Your choice of establishments." He answered a few minutes later sounding distracted, "I see here in this dubious poorly illustrated guidebook I picked up at the liquor store.." I interrupted and said picking up a guidebook at a liquor store was his first mistake. He just talked right over me, "…and I see here we have two possible choices for fine dining."

I smiled, knowing what was coming. "This Burger Barn—while intriguing in a purely bourgeois fashion—I fear I will have to decline," he announced. "So you will choose the other excellent gastronomic locale, I assume," I clipped the VHF to my shoulder, stepped forward and checked the halyards before quickly hauling up the main. Pulling in the mainsheet we heeled sharply as I trimmed out the jib taking advantage of the brisk southerlies still shooting up the Straits. "Indeed I shall," came his reply, Nanette luffing loudly in the breeze before she caught the wind cutting slightly south of Abraxis. As she sped by on her sleek lines stealing our wind and stalling us out slightly, Alain caught my eye and made jerking off motion yelling over the VHF, "Rub Pub it is!"

SEVENTY-THREE

One delicious Shepherd's Pie for me and salmon appetizer plate for Alain later we left Ravintola and headed to the Whale's Rub Pub for some tunes. "How was the Greek salad?" I asked politely and he shook his head. "Olives, feta and salmon together is…eclectic," he replied and flipped the end of his turquoise silk scarf over one shoulder. "But yet you hoovered it down, my friend," I answered, "with nary a peep," and held the door for him as we walked into the bar.

"There is a giant saw blade hanging over my head," he whispered to me while he sipped a martini. "The sword of Damocles," I tried to ascertain how, exactly, the ten-foot blade was attached to the beam. "Hanging by a thread, indeed," he looked down at my slightly worse for the wear wizard shoes. "Perhaps you should retire your wizard shoes lest they fall apart and also be gone from you forever," he suggested, signaling for another drink. I admitted he was probably right and dug some change out of my pocket heading toward the jukebox.

"I thought there was live music here," he questioned when country music shot out of the speakers. "I think we missed live music night," I leaned over and chucked him under the chin. He gingerly wiped up a spot on the table where my elbow had hit his glass a glancing blow. "Yes,

I can sense that," he plucked an olive out of his glass with his fingers and threw it up in the air catching it neatly in his mouth.

"What in the world have you done with Alain Fourchette, you imposter," I said, aghast. "Delicious Bartender taught me some tricks," he flipped an olive in my direction hitting me squarely in the forehead. "That wasn't as bad as getting smacked in the face with a pistol," I flicked at a drip of vodka slipping down the side of my nose. "Do tell," he replied with great interest and leaned forward, "this sounds like a distinctly American event that I have no desire to personally experience but I will nonetheless gain great pleasure from your misfortune."

"Well, unfortunate as it may have been, you'll be glad for it when we hit Fitz Hugh Sound and I break out the fishing rods. Apparently there's great salmon north of here, or so the seadogs tell me."

He replied that he did not know how to fly fish and he would defer to my expertise. "I think you'd be good at it," I assured him, "It's like dancing."

"Then I question your expertise," he held his hand to his forehead dramatically, "for I have seen you at your graceful best and I fear all may lost if we depend solely on your prowess to provide our sustenance." He winked and tossed another olive in his mouth, got up and put another quarter into the jukebox.

SEVENTY-FOUR

"I guess we should fill up with water here and not wait for Port Hardy," I said the next morning and wrinkled my nose at the suspiciously yellow water pouring from the hose. "This water tastes like a donkey's ass," Alain replied, bending over Nanette's water intake with the dock hose. "It's the only water we'll have for a while so I guess we'll just have to deal," I screwed on my water tank fitting and patted Abraxis on his decking, "Although you have a fancy watermaker so why even bother filling up." Alain sensibly reminded me that all good things must end and should the watermaker break while we were out that I would have to share my shower with him. I pictured him sitting on the toilet in my shower/toilet/sink combination with a detachable hose held over his head and grinned.

"I'd love to have you shower over here. The blackmail photos alone would fund my retirement." Flipping the hose in my direction, he sent a small spray of water over my wizard shoes. I yelped and jumped backward. "I know what you consider a shower," he said, walking back to the spigot, "and while I would suffer the indignities of that experience to gain cleanliness you are greatly mistaken if you believe I would let you have a camera within one hundred miles of me while I was lowering myself to such depths."

I just shook my head as we walked up the dock to the Burger Barn for our pre-departure lunch and muttered under my breath about the security cameras I may or may not have installed in Abraxis. He glanced at me suspiciously, "You realize that boats go down all the time out here, right?"

"I do," I replied, tucking my hand under his arm and leaning my head on his shoulder. "Don't worry, I'll be sure to save your pocket squares."

Away we went mid-morning northward toward Port Hardy on a stiff five-hour beat. "This is going to be an athletic day," I heard over the radio when Alain took the lead. "I know. Hopefully it helps work off the giant hunk of beef and chips I just put down my facehole," Abraxis and I tacked opposite Nanette as I talked, "We can top off your water in Port Hardy if you'd like." He agreed that when we reached Port Hardy perhaps he would run a load of laundry or six and get rid of the funky tasting water. "Excellent," I cheered and sliced to port. "I need to wash that sweater I stole from you. Got some mustard on it yesterday and even though I've scrubbed and scrubbed with my kitchen sponge I just can't seem to get it out."

There was a screeching howl from Nanette's stern and Alain threw his arms up in dismay barely managing to pull them back down before his boom swung across. "Merde," he yelled over the radio. I did a happy evil dance. The winds steadily picked up and before long we were beating into a pretty stiff northerly. "Good think you're a steady upwind boat," I said to Abraxis as we prepared to tack for the millionth time. "Well, I'm good at a lot of things," he replied sourly, "although I am quickly tiring of smashing my face through the wind over and over and over…" His voice trailed off when some chop hit us broadside as we swung through. "I know," I grabbed Meat and poked my finger in a rip that had mysteriously appeared along a leg seam, "Just hang in there. Cape Caution could prove to be adventurous and maybe you'll have a chance to sail in a relatively straight line."

"Sorry about Meat," he said sheepishly, "I didn't realize he was so fragile." "Did you do this?" accusingly I pointing at a chunk of stuffing squeezed out above Meat's front leg. There was no answer as Meat kept the bro code and steadfastly refused to discuss the unfortunate situation that might very well result in the loss of one of his appendages.

We rolled into Port Hardy that evening cold and tired. "Sorry, Alain!" I shouted, not sorry at all as he cut over to the splintery slightly decrepit public docks while I sucked up the last government space next to a rather large steel fishing vessel. "That's what you get for buying a really big fancy expensive boat," I intoned over the loudspeaker blasting out his financial status to the rest of the harbor.

"It is not a problem," came his zippy reply over Nanette's loud hailer as he cheater thrusted himself into a slightly off-kilter slip, "I have often heard I am too large to fit in small spaces and yet I persevere. I persevere."

"Well, I'm going to persevere over to the showers, kind sir," I clicked off the VHF, grabbed a towel off the bathroom rack and carefully considered my loofah. "Maybe less loofah and more lotion," Abraxis gently suggested. I scratched the back of one wrist. "Yeah yeah. You try standing in water wearing neoprene for six hours and see whether you feel itchy."

He rolled slightly and reminded me that he sat in the water all the time, yelling at me that I should suck it up and not be such a pussy when I hopped down on the dock and shambled away toward unlimited hot water.

"Let's eat in tonight," Alain suggested that evening as we luxuriated in Nanette's spacious galley on the bad side of town relishing the feeling of being warm, dry and clean. "I feel like I have consumed so much sodium and fat that I am now a solid." I reached over and pinched his perfectly flat muscled stomach. "Yep, looking pretty chubbers there, pal. Best lose that gut before Delicious Bartender comes for a conjugal."

Alain looked down his nose at me as he sprinkled spices onto some chicken, "I'll have you know that I weigh exactly the same amount today as I did when I purchased Nanette and set off north with you and your ill-tempered beast." "Uh huh," I smiled, "Pop that chicken you've been molesting in your fancy oven and pour me a drink." Turns out a watched coq au vin takes just as long to cook as an unwatched one and an hour later we were carefully slurping our way through giant bowls of chicken chased by liberal amounts of red wine. "This is delicious," I complemented the chef with consummate grace balancing my bowl on one knee reaching out to refill my glass. "It's the mushrooms in browned butter," Alain explained eying my circus act carefully, no doubt prepared to rescue Nanette's fragile decking from my heavy bowl should I lean too far in my search for an adult beverage. "I still can't believe you cooked this in your oven," I gestured a spoon in his direction before I got up and dished out generous second helpings. He reminded me, as always, that all things French were naturally superior.

"Tomorrow's going to be a long day," I explained later while we washed up in Nanette's galley. "If the weather looks good we'll head up toward Fury Cove and throw down a hook for the night. I don't want to be stuck out in the Queen Charlotte when the afternoon winds pick up so we'll check the forecast at four o'clock tomorrow morning. If it's good, let's leave early and hopefully we'll make it to the mouth of Fitz Hugh Sound by nightfall. We just need to make sure we hit Fury Cove with enough light to miss all the rocks at the mouth." I set a dry fork carefully down on a fluffy dish mat and picked up a plate. Alain turned away from the sink and raised a yellow-gloved finger, "This is up by Rivers Inlet, yes?"

"Yep. Someone's been reading the charts, I see."

He smiled and told me that he'd been anxiously awaiting the fishing adventure I'd been promising him and that the Dubious Guidebook agreed with me that Fish Egg Inlet might be a good choice. "An interesting name," he mused. "Perhaps Caviar Inlet would be more to your liking?" I poked him in the arm with a spoon. He replied that a man must have standards, water dripping down the side of his leg from where he'd propped one hand on his waist.

"I'll do the best I can on the fishing," I told him after dinner during our meander down the dock back toward Abraxis. "Still not completely sure exactly what we can and can't fish for or where we can do it but at least we have a whole passel of permits." Alain agreed that our buying permits for everything whether it was in season or not was indeed wise, albeit expensive. "Plus, Fish Egg Inlet is a rockfish conservation area I think," I tapped a finger on my chin, "which means technically I don't believe you can fish in there at all. But we can certainly troll along Fitz Hugh Sound so maybe we'll run some lines out and see what we catch."

"Of course, our departure depends on the weather tomorrow morning," I thanked him politely for walking me home. Presenting me with a debonair bow he replied that he hoped the weather was gray and drizzly, that he'd stop by to discuss after his morning shower and wrinkled his nose when I told him I'd have coffee ready and waiting.

SEVENTY-FIVE

Gloriously rainy skies greeted us early the next morning. I pulled my jacket hood over my watch cap and leaned over my railing in a quick confab with my delicious Frenchman. "So, the weather looks good to me," I traced a line up the map from Port Hardy through Queen Charlotte toward Fitz Hugh Sound. "I think we should cut here by Pine Island and around Egg. What do you think?"

Alain peered at the pages as the water beaded on his wool jacket. "I think that looks good to me," he said, sipping espresso from a tiny cup. "I recall something about easterlies around Egg Island so we need to make sure to leave plenty of room when we cut around to Rivers Inlet, right?"

I nodded and placed my hands on my lower back, leaning into the stretch, "And we should make a decision now as to who's going into Fury Cove first." "And why is that," he said, distracted by some random noise coming from across the dock. "Because there are serious rocks at the mouth of Fury Cove and it's a super tight channel so we need to go in single file," I explained, shaking water off my map book before carefully rolling it up into a tight cylinder.

Alain raised an eyebrow.

"Rocks. Keel busters. Hull holers. The Sinkerator." I raised my hands to the sky and bellowed, "SAVE US FROM OURSELVES!" Alain rolled his eyes. "Drama drama," he said, "Always the drama with you."

"So, you lead? I lead? Want to test out your navigation skills in the crucible of Fury Cove?" Dancing back and forth from one foot to the other I air punched in his direction. He said primly that I could take one for the team. I paused for a minute before saying, "Then I'll just move on through and you can follow. I'll just move right on through like I always have." He smiled softly and kissed my hand before turning away. "See you on the other side," he threw over his shoulder as he sauntered off back toward Nanette.

Good Queen Charlotte behaved as any well-bred lady would which is to say she blew perfectly fine at a respectable twelve knots until two thirds of the way toward Fitz Hugh Sound when she abruptly threw a tantrum for about forty-five minutes for absolutely no reason, sending random wind gusts backward and forward before launching a very nice scarf right off the side of Abraxis into the water where it floated gaily away before slowly submerging. "Don't tell Alain," I whispered, giving Nanette long-range side eye, "I think that belonged to him." Abraxis smiled showing all his pointy teeth as the fussy monarch blasted us up the ass with a twenty knot gust. There were modest rolling six foot seas but I set my feet shoulder width apart and kept to the flats as best I could, the swells slipping under the hull.

"Roly poly today," Alain's voice came over the airwaves sounding rather sickly. "Not your cup of tea?" I shot back, howling out a *yee haw* as we slid up over another slow glassy roller. His voice cut out mid-reply. "You need the patch, my friend," I slowly angled through a trough, "Seasickness will kill you out here." Respectfully I waited another ten seconds for him to stop puking before launching another salvo. "Guess that's why you Frenchies never really managed to get a firm grip on the Channel, huh." The sound of his soft laughter was the only reply.

After cutting wide around Egg Island we skootched past Pine Island toward Rivers Inlet as the sun slowly dipped toward the mountains and began its long horizontal run across the June horizon. Clinking halyards and the rustle of the jib singing in the wind broke the silence as I sat on top of the aft cabin roof, a foot propped on either side of the wheel. I looked toward the sky, the sun beating down against my eyes. I swallowed and saw sparks rising into the sky, pianos snapping in the heat, Putin's face slowly blackening around the edges and curling up into white ash.

I opened my eyes spotting wings carrying aloft snowy heads far above over the long treed slopes on left and right. I wondered what they thought of our sails drifting by so far below. I'd like to be up there if it weren't for heights which I greatly despise, telling myself it wouldn't likely be an issue were I an eagle.

But still.

I laid back on the aft cabin roof, those shadows back-lit through the sails when the sun struck just so. Striking distance soon too from Seward, whispering to Abraxis sincere apologies for his lack of air time. I stared at the sails against the sky but saw nothing…just salt winds snapping at the canvas.

I pictured you in that box thousands of miles away resting under patriotically upright grass in the sunshine of a warm Colorado Springs summer day. I spread my limbs across the aft cabin roof, arms wide. You would have really enjoyed this trip. A small breeze tipped the ends of my hair and blew it across my face. Would you have been happy with just me for weeks and weeks? I ruminated on this for a great while. Maybe I did need a little more mystery. The splash of a Dall's porpoise slicing through the water whispered softly in the distance. Is that why you went to her, with her perfect hair and impeccable cat eye liner flicked just so? Was it because I curse too much and hate high heels?

You didn't answer.

Could you even hear me all the way out here in the ocean so far away from your box? Maybe you're even closer here. Where you left me, where you broke me. The sun passed behind a cloud and shadows covered my face as I curled into a miserable ball and cried.

SEVENTY-SIX

I pulled it together in time to prep for Fury Cove. I splashed my face with cold water from the bathroom tap and peered at myself in the mirror. I looked tired. And old. I pulled the corner of my eye back toward my temple and watched my little crows feet wrinkles magically disappear.

I wondered how old she was and pictured her smooth glowing olive skin and the way her stomach was completely flat all the way down to where your hand dipped under that sheet. I realized I was almost forty and rubbed a finger along the thin scar slicing across the bottom of my jawline where I'd fallen off a skateboard as a child and ripped it open on the concrete sidewalk. I pressed my forehead against the glass and closed my eyes resting quietly for just a moment before pulling my watch cap down low and slipping out of the bathroom.

"Check six, check six," I said over the VHF as we closed in on Fury Island. "I don't know what that means," came Alain's puzzled answer. I smiled and remembered you yelling *check six* as you raced through the boat chasing me down into the back cabin before throwing me onto the bed. "It means look out behind you," I said, coming up around his starboard side passing him slowly to take the lead. I waved an arm through the air even though I knew he couldn't see my face from so far away, from a half-mile away.

Two clicks came over the VHF as I pulled out the chart I'd been pouring over for almost an hour. *I'd never admit it to Alain but I'll admit it to you, lover* I thought as sweat built up along my hairline *I'm afraid I'm going to fuck this up and hit something.* I laid out the Fury Island charts and looked at the GPS. Checked the tide chart for the eighth time. I plotted our path on the screen and double checked it the old-fashioned way swinging the calipers across the paper charts in great swooping half circles along our line. My grease pencil at the ready, I leaned over the plastic and carefully marked the route. Double check everything and have a contingency. I reminded myself of this wisdom considering what would happen if I lost the electronic navigation at a crucial moment. Shuddering in dismay, I raised my hands to the sky and fell slowly forward reaching my fingers toward my toes letting out a slow exhalation as I tried to relax.

I felt sick to my stomach when thought about hitting those rocks. Of failing. I told myself to fucking pull it together. Abraxis gently reminded me that his butt was literally on the line. "I got this, buddy," I patted him gently on the side of the windscreen and tugged on Meat's busted leg telling both of them to buckle up, buttercup.

I flipped on the depth sounder reluctantly and said, "Let's bring 'em down," over the VHF. I dumped the jib first, slowing turning into the wind slipping sideways through the swells as I rolled the sail up foot by foot until it wrapped tightly around the forestay. *Focus. Focus.* Holding the halyard tightly as it slid through my gloved palm I let loose the main and flaked it in big swooping folds over the boom. Like taffy flowing down it collapsed softly in a great whistling rush from where it had been pinned up against the sky. Abraxis bobbed slowly in the current while I flipped the cargo netting I'd attached under the boom over the top of the sail and peeked under to make sure the leaded sinker line I'd sewn over the far edge carried the netting all the way over to the other side. Reaching under, I grabbed the sail ties I'd looped on the forward edge of the netting and pulled it under snapping it to the rings I'd had soldered to the bottom of the boom, securing that sail safely down until I could properly wrap the canvas tight. "My own design," I told Abraxis as I strutted back to the cockpit and picked up the VHF.

"One," I said with a smile. "I don't know what that means," came Alain's exasperated voice, "Are we now performing acts of public math? Why are you doing this to me!" "You're supposed to say 'two-p'," I released the button and waited. "What the fuck is toop," came back a very puzzled voice.

"It's what the boys say when they get all lined up on the runway. Like counting off who's ready to go but with a P at the end. One, Two-p, Three-p, Four-p. Nice and short. You try it."

There was only silence before a very French *toop* came over the airwaves. "NO! You're supposed to say ONE!" I shook my head and let out an exasperated sigh right into the microphone.

"Fuck you," Alain said but followed it very quietly with *one* and I replied, yelling out *TOOP, BEOTCHES!* into the quiet air.

"Ok, seriously, we know what we're doing, right?" I kept one hand on the radio I'd snapped onto the shoulder of my safety vest and clenched the harness tightly with the other. I waited a moment before raising a hand to the radio preparing to send over another message as Alain's voice came drifting over. "Relax," he said in a calm voice, "I trust you."

"Your funeral. Let's do this." I placed both hands on the wheel and slowly peeled off to the south on a slow approach toward Rouse Reef. One last glance down at the chart plotter before I took a deep slow breath and pushed the throttle forward. "Now passing Rouse Point," came Alain's voice in a preachy tone, "On our way to death and destruction." I laughed. "Ok, fine, I'm freaking out a little much, yes, ok." I could hear him smiling as I shot back, "Best batten down those pocket squares cause we're going in."

Rounding south of Cleave Island we hooked to the left and slowly motored past the back of Fury Island entering a narrow pass. I hawked the depth finder watching the numbers dropping and dropping and dropping as suddenly I feared I'd calculated the tide incorrectly. "Is this number right," came Alain's voice as the depth finder hit twenty feet. I said calmly that it was correct and tried not to pee my pants. "Ok," he said slowly as we hit seventeen feet. Pucker factor…engaged. I closed my eyes and pushed right on through. As we came out the other side the numbers slowly rose until we were in a respectable twenty-five feet of water before slowly coming to a stop in the middle of the cove's open space.

"I think we should just stay here forever and never leave, we should never leave," Alain said breathlessly over the radio and I started to laugh. In a state of mild hysteria I bent over and slung my arms over the wheel as Abraxis sat silently in still waters, my face pressed against my forearm, shoulders shaking.

"Jesus Christ, I need to change my pants," I finally said before we laid out our chain and set the anchors. I threw a fender over the side hanging it next to the hull while he snubbed Nanette over bumping gently against my starboard side. I tossed him a line under the railing and squatted down looking across the decks as he cleated it off securing us together in that deserted anchorage.

He smiled across the gap and said, "When I said I trusted you…I lied."

SEVENTY-SEVEN

"Fishing time!" I sang out into the morning light and pulled a canvas bag from the aft cabin lockers lifting the strap towards Alain's waiting hands. "Got it?" I schlepped my way up the ladder and into the cockpit. "I do. But I don't know what to do with any of these things," he tried to look innocent. "They're rods," I rolled my eyes when he snickered, "which you most definitely how to use so don't play coy, mister."

"Ok, fine," he said and we laid out the gear on the bow, "You have a valid point, I must admit." I pulled out the fly rods and announced a lesson was in order before the real fishing could begin. He pointed at the white shell beach that had appeared like magic overnight from beneath the ebbing tide. Rays of sunlight sliced through the tall trees lining the edges of the cove turning the shallow waters over the leading edge of the shell beach a deep green and brilliant turquoise blue. "Wow," speechless, I stood and stared at that unexpected beach, "Is it just me or do you feel like we've suddenly been transported to the South Pacific." Alain looked at me and smacked his palm down on my wool cap shaking it gently back and forth. "Trust me," he said, "There's no way I would ever mistake these cold temperatures for the South Pacific."

We decided letting down Abraxis's tender from its stern mount made more sense than unfastening Nanette's from where it was secured to her front decking and twenty minutes later went zooming off over the glassy water performing a high speed taxi around the edges of the cove at a decidedly unsafe rate before approaching shore at a more sedate speed.

"It's clam shells!" Delighted, I bent down to run my hands along the surface of the water as we slowly motored the tender parallel to the white beach. I turned toward the bow and leaned over the side. Alain goosed the engine nearly sending me over the side. I flailed out a hand and barely caught the edge of the dingy line. I pointed a threatening finger in his direction while tightly grasping the line in my other hand, "Watch it. I know where you live."

He raised a palm rattling off something in French that suspiciously sounded like, "Sorry. I don't understand. I don't speak English."

We ran the tender up onto a small sandbar and hopped out, gear in hand. "Ok, let's practice," I said, tied a piece of red yarn on the end of a line and handed him one of the rods. "What is this," he said, jiggling the yarn on the end of the line. "You don't think I would actually give you something with a hook on it, right?" I gave him stink eye. "It would end up buried in the side of my face. Or your face." He grimaced and agreed that maybe starting out with yarn would be best because while my face was pretty, his was prettier.

I stood to one side with my rod. "This is called the two stroke cast," I said and pointed a finger at him stopping him mid-sentence. "Get your mind out of the gutter," I grouched, "you're worse than Abraxis!"

I showed him how to pull out the line until it was about three times as long as the rod. "You seem pretty athletic for a fashion dude," I muttered when I encroached into his personal space to check the line for tangles. He smiled. "Just because I like clothes doesn't mean I can't enjoy sports, too. Just because you like sports doesn't mean you can't enjoy clothes. Lots of things go both ways, you know."

I turned my face away, "I was never the pretty one growing up so I guess I just never paid that much attention to clothes and stuff." I told him about being short and blonde while my sisters were lean statuesque brunette gazelles leaping across the plains of high school escaping with homecoming crowns and sashes while I dated the football quarterback for three weeks. "We struck a deal. He needed someone to write his English paper and I needed a popularity boost in order to win the vote for student government president," I explained as I tied yarn to the end of my own line while Alain experimentally whipped the tip of the rod through the air with a swishing sound.

"He was a moron," he said conversationally and swung that rod a little too close to my face for comfort. Holding up an arm to ward off the assault I continued, "Yeah, well, it was my one brief moment of popularity. Turns out, I actually preferred eating alone in the cafeteria. Found it too hard to be with other people, to talk about girls and boys and clothes and all that stuff, you know. I just never..." my voice trailed off.

"Never what," he said, facing me.

"I knew I was the smart one. That was my place, my bailiwick," I looked down at my boots and saw the clamshells glistening in the sun's last rays as the clouds passed over. "Beauty fades but smarts last forever." I forced a laugh and looked up. "So I just got smarter and left the eyeliner to all the cheerleaders, you know?"

We stood in a companionable silence before I asked him if he was popular in high school. "You seem like a cool cat," I bumped him with one of my hips and told him he was probably the school stud and had all the girls and boys drooling. He shrugged. "Not really," he said, scrunching his face up on one side as he ran his fingers up the rod to work out a kink in the line. "I was quiet. Lurked in corners. Awkward. I never really grew into my height until I was out of college and away from home. On my own."

"Huh," I shook my head, "never figured you for the awkward type. You seem so debonair, so suave, so..." I waved my fingers through the air, trying to think of the right phrase when he said, "Not everything is what it seems at first glance. You of all people should know this."

Putting an arm around my shoulder, Alain leaned in and whispered in my ear, "Not everything is what it seems but that doesn't mean it isn't good. It doesn't mean it isn't right." I looked away with a deep swallow and nodded. He gave me a squeeze and told me to get on with the fishing lesson because he felt the call of an impending nap.

"Jesus Christ!" Ten minutes later, I ducked when the yarn flew past my face. Alain chuckled. "You did that on purpose!" I screeched. "I did, I did," he admitted and flipped the rod back swiftly stopping abruptly when the tip just passed his shoulder. Peering up we watched the yarn floating over his shoulder, that red so bright against the green of the forest. "Snap it!" leaning forward I swung my arm out toward the water and he brought the rod forward just before the line straightened out entirely.

He smiled up at the yarn as he cast over and over until he'd dropped the string in the water too many times and it refused to float weightless through the air. "I think it's given up the ghost," I pinched the soggy thread between my fingers like a dirty worm and shook my head sadly. "Rest in peace, string from Alain's Armani Sweater. Rest in peace."

After letting out a deep sigh, I abruptly dropped the yarn and dashed toward the tender as Alain swung the rod around in a sharp motion and smacked me right across the ass.

SEVENTY-EIGHT

"Ok," I said that evening as we lazed around on the decks rolled up in blankets like mummies. "Let's head out early tomorrow morning and take the dinghy up to Pierce Bay. Try our hand at some blue back Coho."

"Some what," Alain said, his hand reaching out from under his pile of blankets grabbing some prosciutto wrapped melon off a nearby plate. "Blue back Coho. It's a type of salmon," I rolled over and took a bite of my Questionable Cheddar and Triskets. "This is delicious, sure you don't want one?" His lump of blankets shivered slightly as a muffled "Absolutely not, merci," came across the gap.

I smiled. "We're a little early for Coho since they don't really start running hard until July but we're in shoulder season…" Alain grunted questioningly. "It's the build-up to the regular season," I explained. "We can probably pull in some five- to eight-pounders. Nothing as crazy as the Tyee Chinooks in August that can reach almost eighty pounds."

"That's obscene," Alain said, sitting straight up from his nest, "How is that even catchable?" I told him we usually troll for fish like that on downriggers behind a boat. "They say it's a minute of fight for every pound of fish," I propped myself up on a deck cushion and wiggled my toes inside my thick wool socks. "That's an hour and a half of madness," he said and flopped back down, "madness I say."

"But damn good eating, I'll have you know. Damn good eating." I sighed in delight and told him about all those trips to Alaska where I'd stuffed my face with silvers. "What's a silver," he replied peevishly, "these terms mean nothing." "Coho has a nickname," I breathed in a deep lungful of crisp dusk air. "They call them silvers. So if you say you went fishing for silvers people up here will know you're talking about Coho."

"Are they good?"

I sat up and threw a grape at his head. "Blasphemy! Of course they're delicious. Super mild and not limp and squishy in the slightest." "Limp and squishy is an excellent recommendation for dinner, in my opinion," Abraxis whispered through the open windscreen. I ignored him. "The filets are nice and firm. They stand up well on the grill or you can stick them in your fancy oven and bake them." Alain launched the grape back over the rails while my head was turned and it smacked me wetly on the ear.

"Or we can eat something else entirely because we may catch nothing," he added.

"True. All true ," I replied, "although I think our chances are better here than anywhere else in the area at this present point in time."

He let out a pensive sigh. "I'll take a good chance over an assured failure any day."

SEVENTY-NINE

"Oh my god! Pull! Pull harder!" I screeched when Alain began to lean way too far back, his line singing out through the reel. "I am! I fucking am pulling harder," he yelled back and reeled furiously. Zipping out another ten feet the Coho desperately took off out to sea. "Put your back into it!" I slogged through the water behind him and pushed my shoulder into him bracing my boots on slippery bottom. "Come on, man," sweating, I pivoted until we were back to back and held him up as he struggled haul that Coho in. "It's dinner. This is dinner. Bring dinner home for mama."

"It's not my fault I lost the last three in a row," he turned his head losing sight of the salmon as the reel sang out another few feet. "You were distracting me! Distracted! I was distracted!"

"I fell down in the mud, that's hardly mesmerizing." I ducked under his arms and gripped the rod, my hands just above his. "You reel and I'll help pull," I said and we heaved that fucking fish straight out of the water onto the shoreline.

Cheering loudly, Alain and I made complete asses of ourselves sloshing out of the water toward the shoreline. "Oh my god," he said, exhausted, "I will enjoy eating this fish. I will enjoy it immensely." I paused and looked down at the flopping salmon with its mouth gaping open, its gills trying desperately to pull in oxygen. Alain loomed over my shoulder as I started to laugh.

"This fish is not even two pounds!"

He sniffed. I turned and put my hands on either side of his face shaking my head in amusement, "You fought this fish for ten minutes, sweetie." "I am a beast of a man," he nodded his head haughtily, "please, no pictures."

I rolled my eyes, leaned down and picked the salmon up by the tail before slamming its head against a nearby log. "Holy shit, you're a psychopath," he said, shocked at the sudden violence. "Just you wait, sugar," I pulled a knife from a sheath on my fishing vest and slit the stunned salmon under the gills on both sides, holding it up tail first as blood ran down the side of my hand and dripped into the water. "This is nothing," I looked over at him, "when I fished for rainbow trout in Montana I'd have to twist the head back and snap its neck to kill it but salmon are weak. They just pass right out when you bonk them on the noggin. Personally, I prefer to whack them before I slice them open because I don't like it when they wiggle." I shook the Coho slightly as the red stream started to slow. "If it's halibut over 80 pounds we cap it in the head with a pistol before we haul it into the boat. Otherwise it'll fuck up all your shit when it starts flailing around."

"I feel ill," Alain said, weaving slightly before sitting down smack in the mud. I leaned my free hand over and pushed on the back of his head forcing his face down toward his knees.

"Take a deep breath," I told him, "Just relax and let it happen."

EIGHTY

"Ok, I admit, this is fantastically delicious," Alain conceded that evening as we enjoyed oven roasted Coho with asparagus and new potatoes dripping in butter. I squeezed lemon over a filet, leaned over and courteously offered him a second helping after inquiring as to the preparation of his meal.

"I see your comportment lessons are beginning to take hold," he said approvingly and watched me wipe my fingers genteelly on a cloth napkin, "Therefore, I will forgive you your extreme acts of violence committed on the beach this afternoon." "Even the gutting," I asked. He held a hand up across my mouth muffling my voice. "We will not speak of that. Abhorrent. Simply atrocious."

"But necessary," I wedged my fork under his palm and pushed his hand away.

"Most abhorrent things usually are," he said and looked out of the porthole into the darkness before pouring me another glass of wine.

We both made it an early night exhausted from the long trip over to the bay and salmon death match. Around three o'clock in the morning I startled awake when the anchor chain clunked loudly off the bow roller. I rolled over and climbed out from under the duvet slipping on my foul weather overalls before shoving my feet into the waiting boots. Slinging my jacket over my shoulders, I climbed up through the hatch.

Weather had started rolling in and while Fury Cove was a protected anchorage I knew I wouldn't get any sleep until I fixed the periodic slamming of that anchor chain. I flipped on the nav station and checked our position to make sure we weren't drifting. After assuring myself we hadn't come off the hook in the middle of the night I snapped on my safety harness and clicked onto the jackline. As I walked forward I looked up at the stars as clouds rolled in partially obscuring the sliver of moon peeking over the distant mountains.

At the bow I dug around in a locker until I found the length of line and firehose I used as a snubber. Cleating off one end, I attached a longer safety line to my vest and leaned out spreading my legs open to either side against the rails until I hung upside down off the front of the boat over the anchor chain. Pinching a shackle with my fingers I snapped the v of the line onto the chain as far down as I could reach. I wiggled my butt toward the deck and hauled myself back up on my knees before walking the other line down to another cleat on the opposite side where I tied it off. After making sure I had a few feet of slack I bumped out the anchor chain about two feet until the snubber shackle was a foot or so above the water. I tightened the side lines pulling the chain back toward the bow so it hung straight down into the water before checking the firehose making sure no lines were left chaffing against the shrouds before turning away and stepping down into the cockpit.

"That was quite a show," Alain said and I let out a shriek. "Good god, man, you scared the bejesus out of me!" I pressed a hand over my pounding heart and he laughed. "Did I wake you up when I let out the chain? I'm sorry. It kept coming off the roller and making a terrible racket."

"I was already awake," he replied, his face hidden from the moonlight in the shadow of Nanette's boom. "Couldn't sleep?" I leaned over the side rail and rubbed my eyes with the palms of my hands. "Just thinking,"

Alain stood up and walked to the edge of the cockpit and propped his forearms on the edge of the deck.

"Dare I ask about what?" I peered over at his face. "Loneliness," he replied, staring down at his feet.

I climbed through the rail onto Nanette, sat down on the edge between his hands and put my arms around his neck. He laid his forehead gently on my shoulder. "You don't have to be lonely when I'm around," I whispered in his ear, "if you want, I can fall on my face again and make you laugh."

He looked up, smirking, "I saw you starting to go down and I couldn't stop it. It was like slow motion, your foot just shot off to the side and you went right down on your face in the mud—I couldn't believe it."

"Well, laughing and pointing at me wasn't exactly the help I needed at that particular moment, sir." I smacked his arm lightly with my hand. "I'll have you know it took me a good forty-five minutes to get all that mud off my waders. I had to sacrifice a toothbrush."

He leaned back and ran his fingers lightly down the side of my face. "I have an extra and you are welcome to it," he whispered. There was a moment of confusion as I wondered what exactly was happening here. I thought back to the Delicious Bartender and snooty shoe comments. A flash of a basement room with boxes stacked against the wall and wizard shoes ran through my mind. I pictured the brightly patterned pocket squares and the job in fashion design. He wears pocket squares and suede slippers. And drinks martinis.

Leaning back on my hands casually, I asked him, "When you said you wanted freedom, that you needed freedom…what did you mean?"

He stepped back into the shadows, "I think it's possible to love many people at once. To be content with just a single person forever is not realistic, perhaps. No one can be all things simultaneously. I don't believe you can put someone in a box on a shelf in isolation and assume they will be happy. He did not agree. We had an argument and I left."

I glanced up at where the moon used to be and whispered, "When you told him you were leaving him for a woman was he surprised?" A soft laugh slipped through the night air. "Not really," he said.

"Not really," he whispered, turned away and disappeared down into the cabin.

EIGHTY-ONE

What. The fuck. I pondered this development for a few moments and listened to his footsteps move back through Nanette. I heard a door shut softly, saw the hatch was still open and wondered what that meant. "This is incredibly confusing," I told Abraxis. I hopped quietly to my feet and tiptoed across the gap down into my own galley. "What's confusing," Abraxis yawned. I slowly took off my boots, slipped off my overalls and threw my jacket up onto the hook by the companionway ladder. "Oh, please," I whispered, opened the refrigerator and pulled out an apple, "you can't seriously think he was flirting with me. He's gay!"

Right? He's gay. He's gay. I took a big bite out of the side of the apple and slowly sat on the edge of my makeshift bed. He wears pocket squares. And he slept with a man.

Abraxis snorted.

"What's so funny about that?" I felt insulted. My logic was sound, my facts unimpeachable. The numbers matched. Pocket squares plus sex with a man equals gay. "Don't forget the suede slippers, excellent cooking skills, Nanette's impeccably decorated interior, the flourish-y gestures…" "That's not a word," absentmindedly I interrupted Abraxis's list and recalculated with this new data. "The distribution is still wonky. All the points are on the gay side."

Abraxis answered, "Wonky's not a word either."

"Shut up, I'm thinking."

"Just sayin'."

I took another bite of the apple and cocked my head to the side. "This is going to be really awkward tomorrow morning," I said, "isn't it."

"Unclear," he replied.

I complimented him on his Spock-ness as the rising winds plunked Meat against the windscreen. "You need to get laid," Abraxis commented. I answered, "And what, tell him 'Hey, Alain, pretty sure you were gay but now it seems you're only partly gay and I'm suddenly noticing you're incredibly hot in a maybe-I'm-interested kind of way but I know you slept with a guy so I'm totally confused'."

"Unclear," Abraxis said unhelpfully.

Am I actually interested? What about the wizard shoes and that night I told another guy I loved him in his Anchorage kitchen? Shouldn't that mean something? Abraxis pondered this line of questioning for a long minute.

"Maybe Alain is right, you know. Just because you love someone else doesn't mean you can't like Alain, too."

"But shouldn't love outweigh whatever this is?"

"It's called lust," Abraxis said. "So I'm a whore," I put an elbow on my knee and bent over, rubbing a hand over the top of my head. "That makes me a whore, right?"

"And don't even say *unclear*, you asshole," I pointed my finger up at the ceiling and felt him sliding backward until the anchor chain stopped us with a soft clunk. "Maybe you should ask Andy," Abraxis sniped, "This conversation bores me. I'm going to go say goodnight to Nanette."

He turned his back on me and drifted away.

Frustrated, I tossed the apple core toward the sink and listened as it hit the side of a cabinet and roll along the countertop. Goddamnit. I stood and slid my hands along the stainless ledge in the pitch black until I hit the handle of my frying pan and knocked it to the floor.

"This is ridiculous," I announced loudly and flipped on the galley light. "I'm a grown ass woman and I don't need to be skulking around in the dark like I've done something wrong. Enough of this bullshit already." I snatched up the pan and yanked opened a cabinet door and an entire stack of nesting bowls tumbled out onto the teak and bounced away in every direction.

"Shit!" I leaned over and started pitching the bowls over my shoulder up onto the dinette cushions and muttered, "Fucking bowls making all this noise while I'm trying hide down here and think." I shook a bowl in the air and told it sternly, "Don't screw with me tonight. I'm dealing with a crisis."

"And what crisis would that be, butterfly," an amused French voice drifted down through my open hatch.

I spun around with that bowl in my hand, looked up and saw Alain bending down into the cabin, his arms propped up on either side of the open hatch. I whispered faintly, "Cooking crisis," and he grinned.

"Cooking crisis? That sounds like a job for a Frenchman," he gripped the rails and slid down into the cabin.

"This is nice," he said quietly and walked past me stepping carefully over the frying pan. I realized he'd never been inside Abraxis. Suddenly self-conscious, I looked around nervously for any embarrassing items I may have left out. He peeked into a cabin where I'd thrown my unfolded laundry in a big canvas bag up on one of the beds. He leaned over and picked up one of my sweaters holding it up with one finger. "Pink," he said, "Surprising."

"I like pink," I blushed bright red, "I just never wear it in public because it makes me look like a twelve-year old."

He dropped the sweater onto the bed and sauntered past me back toward the galley leaning in to whisper, "No one in their right mind would ever mistake you for a twelve-year old."

"Are you gay or not," I blurted out when he walked by, "Oh god, I'm sorry. I'm sorry I asked you that. That's a personal question and none of my business. It just came out."

His eyes narrowed. He leaned over me and I wondered if he was angry. Humiliated, I looked away when he said, "Do you think I'm gay?" I realized he was amused as he turned and sat on the edge of the dinette cushions.

"This isn't funny," I pointed a finger in his direction, "I thought you were gay. And safe. But now you're only half-gay or partly straight but sleep with dudes and I'm having a crisis."

"A cooking crisis?" He laughed.

"Yes! A fucking cooking crisis," I realized I was freaking out and threw my hands up in the air. "And I'm in a goddamn kitchen!" Shrugging his shoulders, he said helpfully, "You're more than welcome to lose your shit in my galley, butterfly."

"No, I'll do it in my own galley for once, thank you." I put my hands on my hips. "Also, what are you even doing here? In my house at…four o'clock in the morning?"

"I heard a terrible racket and thought perhaps you were having a…crisis."

Abraxis smothered a laugh. Nanette bumped him and told him to be quiet. I took a deep breath, "So are you gay or not."

"I'm not anything. Just myself," he said, leaning back on his hands looking quite delicious in his tight black t-shirt. "But you have to be one or the other!" I went and sat next to him on the cushion and stared straight ahead at the sink.

"Why?" Alain shrugged his shoulders, "Not everyone needs a label. You don't have a label, why should I?"

"Of course I have a label," I snorted at the ridiculousness of that statement, "I'm a straight woman." "Who is attracted to a man who sleeps with other men," he said matter-of-factly. I paused. "And women, right?" I finished his sentence with a question.

"Sometimes…yes." Alain bumped his shoulder into mine. "Relax, butterfly, I'm not going to attack you without warning." I raised an eyebrow. "Don't think I didn't catch the 'without warning' part of that statement." He looked me up and down.

"And what makes you think I'm attracted to you in the first place, Mr. Assumptions."

"Well," he stood and stepped across to the sink and opened a cabinet. After rummaging around he found my coffee pot and put it under the sink faucet. "I happened to overhear the part of your conversation with yourself where you admitted I was incredibly handsome." He looked over his shoulder and thanked me for the compliment before turning off the water and peering around him. "Then you said you were maybe kind of interested so I thought I would come help you make up your mind."

"And, of course, you were in crisis and I am a gentleman so…" He stopped and turned to face me. "I don't know what to do with this," he raised the coffee pot with a puzzled look, "Where do I put this?"

Jesus Christ. I got up from the cushion and took the pot from his hands. "Sit down, Jacques Pepin, I'll take care of the coffee," I scooped grounds into a filter. "This is positively medieval," he said with amazement as he looked over my shoulder at my Mr. Coffee. I plopped the filter in the machine and shoved the pot under and flipped the switch with my finger. "And you are incredibly spoiled," I patted his face with my palm and he grinned down at me.

"You are also shockingly good looking. Are you seriously flirting with me?"

He raised his finger and tapped the tip of my nose, "I'm trying to do a lot more than that, butterfly."

"Why do you keep calling me that?"

He shrugged, "I could call you by the French word for butterfly but you would probably be insulted." I raised an eyebrow.

"The French word for butterfly is 'papillion' which Americans associate with a very small annoyingly yappy dog."

"Which, alarmingly, also seems to describe you," he finished. I reached around him and pulled two coffee mugs from the shelf. Handing him the least chipped, I poured him a cup of distinctly sludgy American coffee and innocently asked him if he needed cream. "I do not, thank you," he pointed at the mug, "but I would like to know who this crotchety old woman is."

"That 'crotchety old woman' is Justice Ruth Bader Ginsburg," I shook my head at his ignorance, "Only the most badass Supreme Court justice to ever walk the planet Earth." "Ahhhhh…" he nodded, "this explains the saying here," he tapped his finger on the slogan written under the drawing of Justice Ginsburg wearing a jaunty crown, "The Notorious RBG. Clever. Clever."

"Wait, you can identify the Notorious BIG but you don't know who Justice Ginsburg is? Do they even educate you in France?" I pulled a can of condensed milk from the cabinet, popped the tabbed lid off the top and tossed it in the trashcan. Opening a drawer I grabbed a spoon and held it up to the light before scooping out a dollop plopping it into my coffee cup.

He looked appalled. "What the fuck just happened in this kitchen?" he put a thumb and forefinger to his temples and closed his eyes. "Did you just check your spoon for cleanliness and put condensed milk in your coffee?" "I did and it's delicious. Besides, I always check my spoons for roaches. They're everywhere and I can't seem to get rid of them." Innocently I raised the mug to my lips and took a sip as he spit a mouthful of coffee into the sink. "Please tell me you are joking," he carefully set Justice Ginsburg on the counter and stepped away from the sink looking at the floor around his feet.

"You should see your face!" I couldn't even stand it. "Of course I don't have roaches. I might be cluttered but I'm not dirty." "Aren't you?," Alain said, "I think you might have untapped depths, butterfly." He moved in for the kill.

"What's happening here," I backpedaled as he trailed his fingers down the countertop and drifted closer. "I'm coming over to say thank you for the coffee," he said softly. I tossed my mug on the counter and stepped away from him heading for the dinette. "Why do you feel the need to say that from so close," I leaned backward.

"Because I am French and we believe in personal communication," he slid toward me, smiling.

"Well you certainly don't believe in personal space," I shot back as the dinette cushion hit me in the back of my knees and I started to fall. Alain's hand shot out and grabbed my upper arm, yanking me back on my feet as his other arm wrapped my waist. "The last time I saw you fall down you lost a toothbrush," he whispered, "and I only brought two, so out of concern for our collective dental health I would prefer you stay on your feet. For now."

I narrowed my eyes at him. "Why are you interested in me? I'm not fashionable or particularly beautiful. I curse too much and I have an ongoing love affair with a set of wood chisels. Can't tell a soufflé from a sandwich and god help us if you break an arm because we'll be eating peanut butter out of a jar until we can get into port. And," I held up a finger, "I'm probably in love with someone else! What on earth has possessed you, Alain?"

He stroked his hand down the back of my hair trailing the end of my ponytail through his fingers as he stared down at my face. "Probably in love doesn't sound like totally in love to me but if you tell me to go away, butterfly, I will certainly do so."

There was a moment of silence as I contemplated his perfectly aquiline nose and glossy hair from my extremely close vantage point. I opened my mouth and paused. He raised an eyebrow. "Have you nothing to say?" he pulled me closer.

I shut my facehole.

"Then I will tell you what has possessed me," he bent over until his mouth was barely touching mine, "I don't need you. I can fix my own engines, furl my own sails, cook my own meals. Unbutton my own shirts. I don't need you. But I want you. There is a distinct difference."

He grinned as I shifted nervously and gave him some serious side-eye. "And what is it, exactly, that you want from me?" Stepping forward he tipped us both backward onto the dinette cushions and braced himself on his forearms above me.

"You. I want you the way a man wants a beautiful woman." Shushing me, he looked down at my face and continued, "You are beautiful, you know. I wish you could see yourself as I see you. Like a sparkler, you light up a room when you enter and when you leave everything seems dull and gray. You fascinate me. I want to know what you think about when you are by yourself out here flying over the seas on your dragon. Are you as fearless as you seem?" He ran his thumb over my forehead.

"No," I closed my eyes, " I'm afraid of almost everything. Failure. Dying alone out here if something goes wrong because no one is here to catch me when I fall. I'm the only one left now. I'm the only one left. I'm the only one that fixes all the broken things. I'm afraid of love. Because it hurts."

He smiled, "Well, I'm not in love with you so you don't have to be afraid of me. But that doesn't mean I don't hunger for you in the dark of night as I lay in my bed alone. Alone when you are here only feet away."

"But what about the Delicious Bartender," I wrinkled my forehead and slid my hand along his side from his hip toward his shoulder before scrubbing my wrist across my eyes. "There will always be bartenders," he rolled us over until I was staring down at him nose to nose. "But there is only one you, I think."

He was so unbelievably gorgeous I couldn't even believe he was right there on that dinette in my tiny sailboat. A mere foot from my face was a unicorn and a French one at that. Right there between my arms. I didn't know what to say so I said nothing.

I just stared at him.

"What are you thinking about in here?" he tapped his finger on the side of my head. "You're a unicorn," I said in a dazed voice. "Excuse me?" he laughed, "I'm a unicorn? What does that mean?"

"You're a unicorn. And you're just wandering around out here from port to port like it's nothing. How is this even possible?" I shook my head, "No one seems to think this a big deal!" I sat up, my legs straddling his midsection and flailed my arms through the air. He folded his hands behind his head and grinned.

"Remember when we were in the grocery store buying prosciutto?"

"Yes, of course, you bought those terrible Triskets," he shuddered.

I continued, "It's as if everyone just said 'oh look, a unicorn' and carried right on like it was totally normal." I looked down at him lying underneath me that black t-shirt pulled over his impossibly perfect body.

"I actually thought to myself, if no one wants this unicorn I'll take it. I'll go get my net right now and catch that unicorn, goddamn it. Snatch me that unicorn right up and put it in my closet where it belongs. Throw it some Skittles every once in a while." I spread my arms wide and shouted dramatically, "Taste The Rainbow, Unicorn Boy!"

Alain put his hands over his eyes and shook his head, "And what happens when you take the unicorn out of the closet?" Looking down at him I smirked, "I'd ride it. I'd ride it whenever I wanted. Every night I'd ride it so hard because it'd be my goddamn unicorn and I could do what I wanted with it. It's so weird though..." I paused and put my finger to my chin as if in deep contemplation.

"What is so weird..." Alain wrapped his hands around both sides of my waist.

I leaned forward, "Oddly enough, it turns out that unicorn wasn't ever in the closet in the first place."

He rolled his eyes and laughed, "You are correct, butterfly. This particular unicorn was never in the closet but I'm more than happy to stand in yours if it means you'll ride me. That sounds exciting."

I ran a finger down the side of his neck trailing it across his chest down toward his waist and he took a deep breath. Sliding my hand under the bottom of his shirt I rubbed my hand across his muscled stomach slipping my fingers under the waistband of his jeans giving him a tiny smile before I told him a girl must have mystery and it was time he leave and get some sleep. I slipped slowly down his body, got up and held out a hand.

Languidly he sat up. Leaning forward he grabbed my wrist and pulled himself out of my bed. "Maybe you should walk me home," he headed toward the ladder. "I think I might do more than that at some point," I trailed behind him and surreptitiously stared at his ass. He smiled and held out an arm, "Ladies first."

"Oh I will be. I will be," I pushed him up toward the cockpit, wished him good night, closed the hatch behind him and flipped off the cabin lights. Letting out a deep breath I sat silently with my back against those doors and listened to him softly laughing. "I can hold out longer than you, butterfly," he said wickedly, "Two can play at this game." I felt the boat sway slightly as he stepped quietly off Abraxis and faded into the blackness.

EIGHTY-TWO

"That was nicely done last night," whispered Abraxis into the morning light. I pressed my fingers over my puffy eyes. "Thank you, being mysterious is new to me but I gave it my best shot," I replied, sliding further under the covers avoiding the cold air.

"I don't feel so good," he whined. "I'll run the generator today and boost up your batteries, sweetie. You'll feel better once I give you some juice," I told him while I contemplated breakfast. Eventually I sat up and swung my feet over the edge of the dinette and hopped down as a shrill whine suddenly knifed through the air. I froze for a moment trying to place where the sound was coming from.

It was the high water alarm. In a panic I jumped across the cabin and snatched my foul weather overalls off the wall shoving them on over my long underwear before jamming my bare feet into boots. I started ripping up the galley hatches. Shit shit shit. I saw the ocean leaking into the bottom of the boat seeping quickly around the edges of a hose clamp at the end of the raw water engine intake hose. I bent over and stuck my head down into the bilge and saw it hadn't yet touched the bottom of the engine. Can't let the water get to the engine. Gotta save the engine. Thoughts of being stuck out here in Fury Cove with a flooded engine ran through my mind.

I could put the tender outboard on the back and maybe limp up to Shearwater but goddamn if there's bad weather I'll be in the shit for sure.

I sat back on my heels for a minute. Panic helps no one. Panic helps no one. I started sucking in massive quantities of air. Why didn't my bilge pump go off? I scrabbled around on the floor flinging the hatches aside, launching them clattering onto the galley counter. Peering over the flooring's edge down at the bilge pump I saw the mallet I'd attached to the underside of the hatch had come loose and landed on top of the float switch. I snatched it out of the water and watched the switch spring up and the bilge pump start to suck up water and eject it out of the boat.

"You fucking piece of goddamn shit," I yelled at the mallet. "Oh the irony," Abraxis said, coughing weakly. I ripped the wooden plug that was still attached to the underside of the hatch right out of its fasteners and slogged back to the leaking intake.

I had to close the valve. Bending down over the bilge I grabbed the handle of the seacock and pushed down as hard as I could. "It won't move! Goddamn it Abraxis why won't this move," I sat there on my knees. "I could stomp on it," I said. Abraxis swiftly vetoed my suggestion. I said I'd give it one more try and he suggested I eat more spinach.

I gripped the handle and cranked it down as hard as I could putting my whole weight onto the metal. Slowly began to rotate before suddenly snapping completely off sending me face first down into the water smashing my shoulder against the side of the boat.

"I'll have to do it from the outside." I shot up, whipping my wet hair out of my face and frantically told Abraxis, "I can't fix the line until the water stops coming in from the outside. I can't take the line off to replace the clamp because the pressure coming in will flood the boat and we'll go down. We'll go straight down. I have to stop the water coming in before we flood the engine or we'll be stuck here. We'll be stuck here," I said shrilly, my voice getting louder and louder.

"I know all of these things," Abraxis replied, "so get on with it please."

I pressed my hands to my eyes and wondered why I hadn't bought that marvelous role of silicone tape at the West Marine when I snatched up all the impellers. "I'm being punished for my fucking sins," laughing hysterically I bent over that hole and stared down at the rising water.

"Less guilt, more move," Abraxis shouted as he slightly tilted to port.

"Right. Ok. I can do this. I have a plan. I have a contingency. I have a plan. Follow the plan." I yanked my orange waterproof crisis bag off the wall next to the ladder and threw it up into the cockpit. Tossing the mallet and wooden plug up after it I ran outside stripping off my boots, overalls and jacket tossing them down behind me onto the dinette.

"Jesus," Alain said from where he was standing on Nanette's stern with espresso cup in hand as I went flying past jumping into the aft cabin wearing a pair of bright red long underwear. "What is that horrible noise? What the hell is going on over there? Why is your hair wet?"

"No time! Get over here right now and bring your safety harness!"

I grabbed a large mesh bag out of the aft cabin and heaved it up into the cockpit feeling my shoulder twinge sharply. Climbing back up I swiftly glanced down into the galley and listened intently making sure the bilge pump was still kicking water out.

"What the…oh my god there's water in your galley," Alain said in a shocked tone peering through my hatch dropping his espresso cup onto the decking where it shattered into three pieces. I upended the contents of the mesh bag onto the cockpit floor at his feet. Yanking my long underwear down off my shoulders and kicking it off my feet I said, "Yeah, I know, I really stepped in it this morning." I jammed a leg into my wetsuit and grimaced, "…literally."

"What happened?" he asked as I turned around, his hands reaching down and pulling the tab upward zipping the suit closed. "The mallet I keep fastened to the bottom of the hatch came loose and landed on the bilge pump float switch," I said over my shoulder and dug around in the side pocket of the crisis bag for a small knife. "And the engine water intake hose clamp is busted around the seacock. I tried to shut the valve but I broke the handle off."

He raised an eyebrow and pinched my bicep, "Impressively done, butterfly." I continued, "I have to plug it from the outside before I can fix the line. I have to fix it before it floods the engine." I shoved the knife up my sleeve and looked up. I saw he had his safety vest on, reached over and snapped him into the port jackline.

I slipped my own harness on and handed him the length of line I'd cleated to the boat before running it under the railing. I hopped over the bowsprit and tied the rope's bitter end swiftly to a snapshackle. Handing him the line I turned back toward him as he attached the shackle to the harness rings. Holding the mallet and wooden plug in one hand I shouted *One*. A split second later he answered *Two* and I leapt over the side into the water.

"Holy mother of god," Alain yelled as I went under, hands clenched tight over my mouth trying to keep the water out of my lungs as I involuntarily breathed in from the cold. Surfacing, I gasped and looked up at him standing on the deck with his mouth hanging open. "What the fuck are you doing!" he leaned over the side and stared down at me.

"I have to plug it," I held up the wooden plug in one hand and shivered. "I have maybe ten minutes before you'll have to pull me out because I won't be able to do it myself. You might have to swing the boom over and haul me in using the block and tackle in the orange bag. Twenty minutes and it'll be bad. Really bad. For me and Abraxis."

Staring up at him I saw him say *I should be doing this* but I answered, "I can't pull you out. I'm not strong enough to get you out if things go to shit. Man the line, I'll be under for a minute or two." I purposefully hyperventilated and dove under the surface.

I couldn't see fuckall. I ran my hand along the side kicking deeper into the freezing darkness and felt for the engine intake through-hull.

Motherfucker please please be here somewhere I pleaded with Abraxis *help me help me* as he silently listed taking on water. I burst back to the surface and swam back from the boat a few feet yelling to Alain let out the line. I frantically looked up and down the waterline for the tick mark I'd made on the hull marking the location of the intake when I'd hauled out and had the bottom painted in Seattle.

Spotting the vertical slash a few feet over from where I'd originally searched I splashed back over and went under again. Sliding along the slick bottom I pressed my hand over the through-hull before jamming in as many fingers as I could fit. I felt sick to my stomach when I realized the wooden plug I'd grabbed was too small in diameter to safely plug the gap. Shit. I turned back toward the surface, shooting up into the air next to the boat frantically scraping my hair away from my face as my arms tangled in the line.

I yelled out for the time and he shouted back "Five minutes." Rolling onto my back I dipped my face under the surface sending my hair flowing back behind me in a great shining wave. I threw the old plug at Alain's face telling him to open the orange bag and get me the biggest one there was and throw it down. Hands shaking, fingers going numb, I shoved my foot into the bowline loop I'd tied in the line and rested against the hull for a second listening to him digging swiftly, tossing objects to and fro.

Gotta be done. Gotta be done. Goddamn it had to be done. I grabbed the rigging knife from under my sleeve and snapped it open in one hand while I gathered my hair together with the other. I took a deep breath, slid the knife back and sawed off my ponytail in three quick slices. I tossed two feet of blonde hair over my shoulder as something splashed down next to me.

"Maybe I am in love with you after all," Alain said in a slightly stunned voice as I snapped shut the knife and shoved it back under my sleeve. "Hold that thought, unicorn," I slapped my hand over the floating plug and went under for the third and last time.

EIGHTY-THREE

Pull me in, pull me in I tried to get the words out of my mouth but they got stuck somewhere inside. The line slipped through my frozen hands. Looking up I saw Alain had loosed the mainsheet swinging the boom out over the water and strung up the line through the extra block and tackle I'd kept in the crisis bag. "Hold on, butterfly," he hauled on the line heaving me foot by foot out of the water. "Don't really have much choice," I whispered to Abraxis as I hung there like a sardine, shaking. The clicking of the line cleating off rang through the air as Alain dragged the boom over the decking swinging me along with it.

He grabbed me around the waist, unsnapped the shackle from the safety harness and threw me up over his shoulder before jumping into the cockpit. He hooked his fingers into the front neckline of the wetsuit and said, "Twelve minutes." I gave him the thumbs up, or some semblance of a thumbs up. "Did you plug it?" he asked and flipped me around.

"Yes, yes it's good," I stuttered. He pushed me face down on the cockpit bench and unzipped the wetsuit. I tried to sit up when he grabbed one arm and ripped the suit off and then down to my waist. "Help me out here," he laughed when I rolled onto the floor like an overcooked noodle. I tried to smile but my face wouldn't work and my hands couldn't squeeze shut to pull the rest of the suit off. "This is going to be very undignified," he sat down on the cockpit floor. Jamming his feet under my arms he grabbed the suit at the waist using his feet to hold me away from him as he pulled it inside out and down off my ankles.

"Ok, here we go," Alain grabbed me by an arm and slung me over his shoulders in a fireman's carry. Stepping through the open railings onto Nanette's stern he angled us down into the galley and shoved me into the main cabin shower. I shook uncontrollably and he hurried to turn on the water. Leaning down he said, "It's on full cold. Can't warm you up too fast, yes?" I nodded and told him my teeth hurt. I sat huddled under spray that felt as if it was 100 degrees and tried to think warm thoughts. "Be right back," he said and shut the door. I heard his feet go racing through the cabin and Nanette rocked slightly to the side.

This is not at all mysterious I realized I was only wearing a pair of underwear and no bra. Guess that's what happens to seduction when your house starts to sink. I started snickering, picturing his face when I'd run out screaming like a banshee whipping off my clothing in public like a demented drunken stripper. The bathroom door opened and he stepped back in. "Should I be concerned that you are laughing," he sounded worried. "No, no I'm ok," I said as he gradually turned up the heat. I stared up at him when he told me the bilge pump had kicked out most of water, the engine was dry and the plug was holding just fine.

"Thank you," I choked out resting my head on my knees as I cried in the bottom of that steaming shower while he stroked my hacked up hair and whispered god knows what to me in French.

EIGHTY-FOUR

"This is the only time in my life I will ever admit I need a man so don't get used to it, unicorn," I told Alain, watching while he cranked the broken ball valve shut at the end of the engine intake line holding the sheared off end firmly with a pair of vice grips. He looked up and grinned at me standing there in his bathrobe wearing a stocking cap, gloves, cashmere muffler and boots. "You look ridiculous," he tugged at the bathrobe belt. I smacked his hand. He stood, brushed off his pants and looked down in the bilge, hands on his hips. "What next, MacGyver?"

"Well, I'll just leave the valve shut for now," I replied. "I can't take the chance of opening it again since there's no handle." I retracted my chin under the edge of the bathrobe like a turtle. He reached over and pulled me in front of him, "Cold?"

"Goddamn right I'm cold," I laughed. "Squeeze tighter. I need as much warmth as I can get." "Shall I get your wizard shoes?" his voice whispered in my ear, "I hear they bring the heat." I elbowed him gently and bent forward to look at the valve.

"I think I'll just switch over the intake line to here," I pointed at the extra ball valve I'd drilled a few feet over from the leaking line. I told him I'd had the yard put it in specifically for this reason. "I think I can epoxy around the busted one to make sure it won't crack open and then when we get to Shearwater I'll have to haul out and have the yard either fix it or seal it up permanently. I need some other work done anyway before I make the open ocean crossing up to Seward." I leaned back on my heels and contemplated the potential magnitude of the repairs and thought about the miles of potentially rough seas between our anchorage and the boatyard.

"Will this valve stay closed under way?" Alain sounded worried as he ran his fingers through my uneven hair. "Should, yeah," I sighed, "I'll just assume they'll plug the fitting permanently and keep the intake on this other through-hull. That's the safest bet. Maybe I'll even have them grind it down and glass it over on the outside."

"Will the plug hold?"

"I think so," I absently ran my fingers along the edge of the intake line and I thought about the tools I would need while Alain wandered off and came back bringing with him a delicious toasted turkey and cheese sandwich.

An hour later I'd moved the intake line and pumped out the rest of the water when Alain leaned over my shoulder and complemented me on my excellent handiwork. I reached around his leg, grabbed a flathead screwdriver from my toolkit and tightened down both new hose clamps at the end of the intake line. I held up the busted one, "Three guesses what this piece of crap is made of." He rolled his eyes, "Judging from the rust, not one hundred percent stainless, clearly."

"I'm going to have a serious talk with my Seattle boatyard. Who only uses a single clamp on an intake hose?" I said snootily, "Goddamn Home Depot hose clamps be sinking my house while I'm busy trying to snag me a unicorn." I leaned my neck to the side and cracked my spine loudly. Alain laughed and dug his thumb into the giant knot at the base of my shoulder where I'd whacked it against the edge of the galley floor.

I closed my eyes and leaned backward against his knees. "Let's give this a day before we turn on the engine," he answered, "I'd like to have a break from the arctic seas in case this line blows and we have to repeat the process." "Agreed," I said as Alain helped me slowly stand up.

"I have the perfect activity to pass the time," he whispered in my ear as he took me by the hand and hauled me up the ladder through the cockpit across the gap toward Nanette.

EIGHTY-FIVE

"What is going on here," I asked when I stepped down into his galley to find a sheet laid out on the floor, "Are you a serial killer?" Alain laughed. "No, I'm not a serial killer." He pulled a stool over and sat me down. "Oops, stand back up," he raised a finger and zoomed off into his cabin.

A midnight blue silk dress shirt suddenly appeared over my shoulder and his voice said, "Put this on please."

"Why?"

"Less talking, more undressing, butterfly," came his crisp reply as he promised he wasn't looking. I slipped my sweatshirt off before pushing my arms into his shirt and buttoning it up halfway. "Decent?" he asked and I saw him peeking through his fingers.

"Well, you've already seen half the goods so I'm not quite sure it matters," I said saucily. He bent down and pulled off my boots and socks. "What the hell," I said in surprise when he yanked the stocking cap off my head. "This is most bizarre seduction I've ever experienced."

"And I as well," Alain ran his hand gently over the top of my shoulder and down one arm. Leaning forward, he pressed a soft kiss to the top of my head, told me to close my eyes and promptly shaved off a one inch strip of hair down the middle of my head with the clippers he'd hidden behind his back.

"Jesus Christ!" I jumped up and felt the top of my head as I swung around to face him. Looking perfectly innocent he shrugged and reminded me that I'd always wanted to shave my head, that my impromptu hack job couldn't be salvaged and he was more than willing to operate the power tools in my pursuit of sartorial splendor.

"Well, I guess you'll have to finish the job now," I rubbed my fingers down that prickly line. "Just don't go all the way down to the scalp. Think crew cut. Not like the Marines." "I like Marines," Alain smiled.

"I'm sure you do, unicorn. I'm sure you do."

He reached a hand back, grabbed his t-shirt with one hand and pulled it over his head. My eyes widened at the sight of all those rippling muscles. "Don't want to mess up my clothes," he explained as he tossed it onto the counter and stalked my way. Like a lithe jungle cat he silently drifted around my edges before bending down toward my face, his eyes staring into mine.

"Ready?"

I nodded. His hand came around and grasped my jawbone. Tilting, pulling the side of my face with his fingers I heard the hum of the clippers before they touched my skin, running swiftly up the line of my neck stopping just behind my ear. Alain brushed the hair back away from my face and told me to take a deep breath. I felt the vibrations skim across my right temple arching over the ear trailing down toward the base of my neck.

I sighed and he laughed softly. "What does it feel like," he leaned forward, tilting my face upward before running his palm carefully over the newly sheared side of my head. "Unique," I whispered as section after section of my hair fell to the sheet below.

My eyes closed, his hands moving over my neck in long smooth lines as the soft vibrations chased the tips of his fingers across my skin. I felt him lean closer, pulling the side of my face toward his chest pressing my forehead against his bare skin as he skimmed over my head in the opposite direction, his hand pulling the shirt collar slowly off one shoulder as he exposed my neck in a long straight line. I could hear him breathing when he bent over and gently ran a finger down the outside edge of my ear making sure everything was smooth and even.

He walked around behind me, his hand drifting across to the other side pressing my head in the opposite direction as he brushed the fabric off the edge of my other shoulder sending it floating toward my elbow, those hands firmly stroking up my skin as I shivered. "Look up," he said and stepped in front of me pushing my legs open and sliding in between. "Open your eyes," he stared down at my face pushing, pulling those fingertips lightly along the base of my neck as I arched backward.

He placed his palm against my shoulder blades holding me tightly against him as he stroked across the top of my head, his feather light movement echoed by the feeling of the clippers pushing firmly against my scalp. He swept a hand down my neck slowly unbuttoning my top button and whispered quietly, "You look beautiful." He gently ran the backs of his fingers across my forehead down the side of my face.

I smiled, "I feel beautiful." I leaned into his palm and he took a last look making sure everything was smooth. He turned the clippers off and gently set them on the counter, put his hands on the edge of the sink and smiled. "I love it," he said. I looked upward toward the sky pressing my palms firmly down the sides of my head sliding them all the way down to my collarbone where I slowly traced the edge of the shirt with my fingertips.

"Do you," I asked, leaning forward putting a hand on the stool in between my legs curling toward him as the shirt slid further down my arm. "Very much so," he turned away and opened a cabinet door. "But I haven't finished yet," he ran a linen dishtowel under the sink faucet and gently wrung it out. I leaned back as he stepped toward me and grabbed me by the chin and forced my head to the side. Gasping, my hands came up toward his arm as he told me, "Hold very still, there's something on your face." Very carefully he brushed the linen over my skin sending thousands of tiny blonde hairs drifting downward.

A cold dampness skimmed my neck, his skin pressing hot against my bare back as his arm slid forward around my shoulders pulling me in tightly. "Don't move, butterfly," the words came past my ear as he drew the towel across my forehead down my temple to my cheekbone before heading south along my neck dipping past the hollow of my collarbone lingering just above the swell of my breast. He drew in a deep breath and pulled the cloth back up along my jawline over the crown of my head then used both hands to draw the linen slowly down my spine.

"Make sure you get it all," I sighed when I felt a thumb push upwards slowly massaging the knots out of my back. "You are lucky that I have an unlimited supply of water," he helpfully reminded me, "in case you want to visit my shower again." I looked back at him, "Last time I was in that shower I was in crisis."

He raised a linen covered finger and slowly drew it down the inside curve of my ear. "What kind of crisis," he placed a hand on my upper arm and began to push that sleeve down toward the floor.

"An unlimited water kind of crisis." I stood, the shirt sliding down around my ankles and I stepped over it trailing a hand across the side of his face on my way toward the shower. I paused at the end of the galley, placed my thumbs in my waistband and bent over with my back toward him slowly slipping my pants down toward the floor. Silently thanking the gods that I had dared to put on a really slutty pair of lace underwear on the off chance I'd be riding a handsome unicorn I turned slightly, crooked a finger at him and stepped into the bathroom.

EIGHTY-SIX

"Holy shit!" Looking back at me in the mirror was a stranger with striking cheekbones and wide gray eyes framed by dark lashes. I leaned, turned my face and touched my skin. "I should have done this years ago," I was stunned. For the first time in my life I actually felt beautiful.

"I can't even believe it. I don't even look like myself," I peered closer. "You look very much like yourself," Alain said from the doorway where he leaned against the companionway wall. "It's always looked like this, you know."

"What? What's looked like this?" I glanced up in the mirror and he smiled, reaching an arm around into the shower turning on the water. "Your face, butterfly. Your face has always looked like this, you just never saw it."

I turned back toward the mirror and watched his reflection step closer. "Do you like it?" I hesitated, "It's not very feminine." He ran a hand past the small of my back up under my arm reaching across and gently grazed his fingers over my breast. He bent down, pressed his cheek against mine and stared at me in the mirror. "You have the distinct privilege of giving me one of the most erotic experiences of my adult life," he nipped at my ear, his eyes never leaving mine. "I consider this particular style on you to be a complete and total victory."

I grinned. "Is this the only style you like on me?" I leaned back against his chest and looked up at his face. "Well, I particularly enjoyed the red long underwear," he admitted and slowly shoved me toward the shower. "They're authentic," I touched my tongue to my lips, "with the flap in the back and everything."

He snickered and shut the shower door behind me, "Precisely so."

I tilted my face back and sighed, letting the warm water stream over my head trickling down my back and lifted a hand stroking it over my scalp. Very lightly I ran my fingers down the side of my neck. Water poured across my cheekbones sliding over my shoulders dripping slowly from my arms toward the floor and I realized suddenly that I felt free. I felt free and weightless standing there in that small shower on a French boat in a cold Canadian sea. "What are you smiling about," he whispered, slipping in behind me, wrapping his arm around my waist kissing one shoulder softly.

"Being frigid," I answered. He laughed into my neck. "If there's one thing you're not, it's frigid," he said as I started to turn. "No, stay where you are," he pushed me slightly forward under the water. The smell of lemons filled the air and I felt his hands slowly massaging my head, soap bubbles streaming down over my body. "Even your shampoo is perfect," I sighed.

Alain snorted. "I got it at Walmart." He pushed a hand up against the shower wall pressing his face into my back and bent over laughing.

"Are you kidding me," I twisted to the side and felt him shaking his head. "I absolutely got it at Walmart," his shoulders quivered, "in the sale bin." Stunned, I imagined him gliding up the packaged chips aisle debonairly snatching boxed rice from one shelf and canned tomatoes from another as he sashayed out the door to his Grand Caravan loaded down with Cheese Whiz and two-for-one tuna fish.

He straightened up and pushed my head under, rinsing my face and head free of soap before he expertly flipped spots with me and tilted his face up into the water pushing his wet hair back from his face with his fingers, eyes closed.

Jesus Christ on a cracker. I started at his forehead and surveyed him all the way down to his toes. I felt like I should memorialize this somehow so I can prove that I actually was here. In this shower. With this naked unicorn. He cleared his throat and I glanced up at him quickly, "Yes, sorry. Did I miss something?" Dammit, I was blushing. "I don't think you missed anything," he reached out a finger and tapped me on the nose, "but I'm happy to stand here longer in case you need to double check."

Water beaded on the ends of his eyelashes, his hair perfectly slicked back against his head, the angles of his face under that tan skin sharp in the dim light of the porthole. I swallowed. "Why so silent, butterfly," his mouth gently touched mine his fingers sliding down my wet arm as he moved my hand up his thigh around to his lower back pulling me into him.

"Do you shower in here all the time," I asked softly and he smiled.

"I do indeed. I stand here in this very shower every day mere feet away from you, in fact." His hands spanned my waist and gripped me tightly, his mouth opened hungrily against my lips. "And lately I find myself wishing you were closer," he swept his tongue past my mine and I sighed.

He pressed his hands to either side of my face and whispered against my cheek, "I want you much closer, to slide my fingers along your skin and discover your body. To draw your shape with my hands and be inside you. Please, butterfly, put me out of my misery."

EIGHTY-SEVEN

I suddenly realized I could say no. That sex with Alain was not a foregone conclusion. Here I was naked in a shower with the most gorgeous human being I'd ever seen and he was giving me the opportunity to reject him.

Did I want to reject him? His hands slid down my spine, fingers strong against my tight muscles and pulled me closer. I really did want to fuck him super bad but…he sleeps with guys. For some reason, I felt like this should be more of an issue.

Because I'd been raised Baptist.

I shouldn't even be here. In this shower with a naked man. A man I'm not married to.

A man who has sex with other men.

Was this truly an issue? Really…was it? Alain's hands drifted up the inside of my thigh while I ran the numbers in my head. He sleeps with guys but he's clearly interested in me. And I'm obviously not a dude. I have no commitments to anyone else. I'm single. I can do what I want.

Slowly, he tilted my face to the side and kissed underneath my ear as he stroked me with those long fingers. Would he stop if I said no? "Yes," he slipped one finger around the edge of that slutty black lace underwear and up inside me taking my earlobe between his teeth sucking gently. I realized I had actually said that out loud. "Would you be angry?" I whispered and started to quiver deep inside.

"I would be disappointed but not angry, butterfly. I would keep trying, of course, but we are equals. And if you want me to stop at any point I will always listen." He leaned me backward toward the teak bench and gently licked my collarbone as he slipped another finger inside me pushing gently.

It dawned on me with a brilliant flash that even if I should care about him fucking other men that I didn't. I didn't care. I didn't care that my head was shaved, that I lived on a boat by myself, or unabashedly enjoyed Triskets with Questionable Cheddar. I was perfectly capable of fixing my own broken things, thank you very much. The rest of society say what it will, I realized I didn't give two shits what everyone thought.

This was my life and goddamn it I was going to ride that unicorn.

EIGHTY-EIGHT

"Let's do this," I looked him straight in the eyes and he laughed. "This sounds like the beginning of a sports match," he flipped off the shower and snatched a thick towel from a rack on the opposite wall. "It's going to be an athletic day," I opened the shower door, stepped out, turned and grabbed his arm yanking him from the bathroom completely naked and soaking wet.

"Good god, butterfly. What has possessed you," he put his hands in the middle of my back and pushed me down the hallway toward his cabin. "When I make up my mind to accomplish something," I threw my fist in the air and my towel on the floor stripping off my underwear along the way, "by god I accomplish it."

He sighed, bent down and picked up the wet towel hanging it with the slutty underwear on a hook inside the closet door. "This is teak," he wagged a finger in my direction before grabbing me and throwing me up onto the bed.

I landed sprawled out on my back and quickly rolled over feeling suddenly self-conscious in the bright light. "I don't think so," he grabbed an ankle and flipped me back over, "Let me see you." He ran a finger over the arch of my foot, my toes curling involuntarily. "I'm really nervous," I slung an arm over my eyes. "Well, you're certainly not shy about saying how you feel," he slowly pushed his thumbs under my toes and rubbed firmly.

"I have a pathological truth problem," I groaned softly at the marvelousness of that foot rub. "Truth problem?," He leaned forward and gently sucked on my middle toe. "Oh wow," I said, "that feels…wow. In a good way. A very good way." Alain smiled. "Don't evade the question, butterfly. What is your truth problem?" He ran his fingers up my ankle gently pushing my legs apart and slid up onto the duvet.

"I can't lie," I admitted miserably. "Every time I do I blush and stammer and people can tell. It's super problematic in my personal life. And I can't stop myself from telling the truth either. It just comes out. I can't control it."

"This is not a problem for me," he said. "At least when I ask you if you like something," he ran his tongue up the side of my knee, "I'll know if you do. Besides, your body will tell me the truth even if your lips say otherwise." Slowly his mouth slipped up the inside of my thigh, hands floating upward over my hip bones.

"Stop. Awkward truth moment," I stammered, putting my hand on his forehead. "Do you…Are you going to…" Humiliated beyond belief I closed my eyes and blurted it out. "You're going to wear a condom, right?"

He sat straight up. "I think it's time we had a frank adult discussion," he leaned back on his knees. I felt sick. I'd ruined my chance with the unicorn by opening my fat mouth. Cringing and drawing my knees up to my chin I scrunched over into a small miserable ball.

"Don't move," he pointed a finger at my face, jumped down off the bed and stalked down the hallway. I leaned over as he turned and caught me staring at his perfect ass. "Saw you looking, butterfly," he teased before stepping into his cabin closet. Maybe he wasn't angry. I raised an eyebrow recalling the smile on his face and suddenly caught a full eyeful of his front as he strode confidently back down toward the bedroom with an envelope in his hands.

He put both hands on the edge of the bunk and vaulted back up onto the duvet crawling on his hands and knees toward me. "Come here," he wedged himself behind me until I was sitting between his legs. "Let me be perfectly clear, butterfly," he said firmly, "You should ask that question of all your lovers, no matter who they are. And you should never be embarrassed when you ask it. Not with me. Not with anyone else. It is disrespectful to be frivolous with your own health or anyone else's. Do you understand?"

"Yes." I replied awkwardly, "You sound like an afterschool PSA."

He ignored me.

"And if someone refuses to answer you or agree to your wishes, you politely decline and then kick them out." He slung an arm around my front and wagged the envelope. "Open it," he said. I reached out and took the envelope, pinching it between two fingers and pulled it toward me.

"What is this?" I looked at his face and he said, "Open it and see."

I open up the envelope and pulled out a bunch of papers unfolding them slowly. *Test Results* it said at the top of the page. Oh my god these were STD test results. I skimmed quickly down the text. I spun around, "Seriously? You're seriously just going to hand these to me like it's no big deal."

"It's not a big deal, butterfly," he pointed at a section of the paper. "Negative. Negative. Negative." He clapped his hands together as if he was brushing off an offending substance ending with a sprightly *Voila!*

"You're not even slightly uncomfortable talking about this? Because I'm feeling really uncomfortable," I stuttered, looking at his placid face. "That is very American of you," he said matter-of-factly, "You are prudes. I understand that. It's only a big deal if you make it one and to me…no big deal."

I took a deep breath. "Hold that thought, unicorn." I slid down to the edge of the bed and snatched the towel from the back of the closet door.

" I feel deprived," Alain yelled down the hallway as I moved at a right sprightly pace toward the galley. "You should be naked! This is inequitable!" I flipped him the finger over my shoulder, climbed up the galley ladder and jumped over onto Abraxis.

I cannot even believe I am doing this. I rummaged through a canvas box in the aft cabin. Romance killer. Seduction murderer. What a fucking disaster this is turning out to be. Mood officially dead and buried.

I clutched the towel to my chest as I climbed back up the ladder. It's not like we can start over and shave my head again. I felt slightly ill as I descended slowly back down into Nanette's galley. I felt like running but there was nowhere to go but still pictured myself jumping into the dinghy and taking off into the woods clad only in white cotton. High thread count cotton, I admitted, rubbing the thick terrycloth as I gave him mental props for purchasing quality towels.

Alain smiled from the end of the companionway watching me slowly trudge down toward the bedroom. "Get in here, butterfly," he hopped down and snatched me by the arm. Tugging me upwards onto the sheets, he stripped off the towel and rolled me over until I was underneath him and dug his fingers up under my ribs. "Oh my god stop! Stop!" I howled with laughter and desperately tried to block him. "Feel better?" He looked down at me and grinned. I narrowed my eyes and whacked him on the forehead with my own envelope.

"Ahhhh…quid pro quo," he purred and rolled over, pinched open the envelope and slid the contents out onto the bed. With a flourish, he whipped open the stack of papers and peered over the edge at my face. "This is very detailed, butterfly," he said. "Well, I had everything done at my last appointment before I left Seattle. The one I have every year. You know, the female stuff." I tried to snatch the papers from his hand to edit the information but he swiftly pulled them away. "No no no," he stiff armed me, "let me see your test results, they're right here." He tapped the third page and peered closer.

While he read and made small *mmhmmm* and *aha* noises I reached over and grabbed his results and reread them. "Quid pro quo," I flipped through the papers and he smiled to himself. "You have an excellent thyroid," I complemented him and he replied that my white blood cell count was quite healthy. "I see this is recent," he looked up and winked, "Good to know. Good to know."

I looked at the top of his pages and saw the date coincided with our stop in Port McNeill. "What the hell…" I pointed at the testing date. He laughed, "You're too smart for your own good, butterfly. Yes, I went to the local health clinic in Port McNeill after a very nice lady pointed me in the right direction." I paused, recalling the redhead outside the showers.

"Why? Were you feeling…" I looked at him uncomfortably but he shook his head. "No. I get tested every twelve months or so and I figured now was as good a time as any. I saw Port McNeill had a walk-in facility and so I went over there. Took fifteen minutes. And then I came back and had a lovely nap."

I paused.

"But we haven't been in port since we left there," I poked a finger into his chest and leaned in nose to nose. "How did you get these results if we haven't been in port since you got tested, Mr. Healthy?"

He looked away and turned slightly red, "This is also something we should discuss."

"What is something we should discuss," I smacked his shoulder with the envelope. "I have kept something from you and I feel terrible about it, actually," he shrugged his shoulders guiltily. Thoughts of wives in other countries, forged test results, restraining orders and angry mothers towing illegitimate children behind them as they screeched for the courts to enforce unpaid child support ran through my mind.

I swallowed and asked faintly, "What have you kept from me?"

EIGHTY-NINE

"I have Internet access on Nanette," he said in a great cringing rush. "What the hell!" I shoved him over onto his side and sat on him. "You have Internet and you didn't tell me? Have you had this the whole time? What the hell, Alain!" I started laughing, relieved, and he sheepishly reached into a side cabinet and pulled out a cell phone.

"Didn't you ever wonder why I got Delicious Bartender's phone number?" He looked up at me. I thought back and remembered those digits in black ink scrawled across his wrist. "No, I did not, you sneaky sneakerton."

I wrapped my fingers around his throat and gently shook him. "Why do you have a Canadian cell phone? Are you James Bond or something?" He rolled his eyes, "You and your assumptions, butterfly."

"What!?" I sat back, "What assumptions?" He stretched out a long arm and lightly smacked my cheek. "First you assume I'm gay which I can understand, of course," he put his finger up to my lips and shushed me, "no, let me finish. Then you assume I don't like sports because you assumed gay men don't like sports, but I do like sports and also I am not gay. And you assume I am from France solely because I speak French." He pursed his lips and raised an eyebrow.

"You're not from France?" I was confused. "Not really," Alain pounced and knocked me backward and I squealed. "My parents are French but I grew up in Montreal."

"So you're Canadian."

Tweaking my nose, he replied, "Yep. And my cell phone works perfectly well in British Columbia although I'm sure my roaming charges will be utterly obscene."

"So the test results…" my voice trailed off and he finished my sentence, "were emailed to me on my phone and I printed them out in my office."

"Nanette has an office?"

"I have a printer in my closet," he admitted sheepishly. "So you're saying you have a printer in your pants," I slid my hand south along his side. He nodded and silently snickered.

"Got any ink left in the cartridge?"

"Oh I am more than prepared to fulfill all your printing needs," Alain whispered in my ear. I ran my fingers teasingly down his lower back. "But I require a full service facility, sir." I gripped his ass with my hands, his tongue slipping across the inside rim of my ear. "Full service is my specialty, madam," he answered lightly.

"I'm afraid I have a job that requires attention of a very personal nature." I pulled on his arms ignoring the pain in my shoulder Reaching down, he pulled me upwards biting my breast between his teeth and stared into my eyes, "Let's do this."

I laughed and pushed down his body trailing my fingers across his rippled stomach. When I reached his hips I gently bent over and took him slowly into my mouth running my tongue gently along the shaft of his cock up along the edge of the head. I took a deep breath and sucked him in as far as I could while gently cupping his balls in one hand and digging my nails into his thigh with the other. Placing a hand at the base I raised my head and spit as I squeezed upward. "Do you like that," he asked softly. "I cannot tell a lie," I answered and deep throated him again running my hands rhythmically up and down keeping pace with my tongue as I sucked.

"If you continue much longer this might be a short match," he said breathlessly, his hand pushed down on the back of my head. I looked up and saw his head thrown back, eyes squeezed shut as he breathed heavily. "How about some quid pro quo, unicorn." He lifted his head and saw me staring at him so he sat up. "I'd grab you by your hair and drag you up here but you don't have any left," he put his hand under my chin. "I'm sure you'll figure something out," I gasped as he shoved me onto my back.

"I have to say, butterfly, so far I am very impressed," he whispered from between my thighs as he licked firmly against me. I could hardly stand it and arched my back when he softly bit down pushing his fingers inside me. He slid his hands under my ass and gripped me from below pulling me upward. I slung my ankles across his shoulders as he dug his thumbs into the sides of my hips. Pulling his mouth back he blew softly across me before lightly, so lightly flicking me with the tip of his tongue before I shattered into a million pieces.

"Let's go for two," he smiled, and slipped a finger inside me curling it slightly upward. He lowered me slowly back down onto the bed and e leaned over, his palm rubbing against me as he pushed firmly with that finger while I gripped the sheets between my fists. "What are you doing," I stammered as I started to sweat. "Should I stop?" He bit his lip between his teeth and pressed harder before bending over licking a trail across one hipbone toward my navel. "Fuck no don't stop," I took a deep breath, threw my head backward and cried out squeezing tightly around his finger over and over.

Everything grayed out for a second and I blinked rapidly. I heard him laughing softly and his face drifted up across mine.

"Good?"

I nodded, dazed. Pulling him toward me I licked up the side of his face across his lips and he sucked my tongue inside his mouth. "Can you taste yourself on me," he whispered, running his palm across the back of my newly shaved head.

"I'm delicious."

He smiled and purred softly in the back of his throat while he tongued the roof of my mouth. "I must say, you've never been properly French kissed until you've had it done by a Frenchman," he covered my body with his own. "But you're Canadian," I corrected him but Alain assured me it was just semantics. "Semantics, just semantics butterfly," he said and whispered something in French into my ear that was probably a grocery list but sounded unbelievable erotic.

"I don't know what you're saying," I ground my hips upward against him, "but keep saying it and for god's sake fuck me already. Please." Alain smiled and said he had other plans but was happy to put me out of my misery as long as I promised him a second round. "Unicorn, you're never leaving this bedroom," I announced imperially as he reached over and snatched a box from a cabinet.

Upending it over my head he shook a rainfall of condoms onto my face and I laughed. "Pick one," he said and stroked himself with one hand. I flung the first package I touched at his chest and old him he had thirty seconds to put that on before I rocked his world.

He ripped it open and rolled it down over himself as I came flying across the bed and knocked him flat on his back. "Time to ride the unicorn," he said before I pushed him deep inside with a loud groan. "And I'll do a thorough job of it, I assure you," I braced a hand on the shelving running parallel to the bed as I slid upward. "I hope so," he said and I saw a bead of sweat run down his temple toward his jawline. I leaned down and licked it up with my tongue as I fucked him, squeezing him tightly inside me while he panted. "Jesus Christ," Alain said, grasping my hips tight enough to leave bruises. "Harder," I told him, "I like it rough." He reached upward and placed his fingers around the base of my neck and held me tightly as he slammed himself into me. I looked down at his face, ripping his hand away from my throat and bent down telling him to *Come for me, bitch* as he closed his eyes and took a breath driving swiftly into me letting out a deep gasp as he finished.

NINETY

"I'm not quite sure what just happened," he flung his arms out wide and I collapsed across his chest. "I fucked the shit out of you, that's what happened," I answered. I saw him smiling. "Is that what that was?" He looked over, trailing a hand up my back.

"You're welcome." I rolled to the side and flipped the duvet over both our bodies before snuggling into his side. "Aren't you hot? I'm sweating," Alain shoved the blanket off him doubling it up on top of me. "I'm always cold," my voice sounded muffled under all the layers.

"But certainly not frigid," he swung his legs over the side of the bed and hopped down. I sat up, "Where are you going?" "Don't worry, butterfly, I'll be right back," Alain stepped into the bathroom and shut the door. I flopped back on the bed, pulled the duvet up to my chin and thought about what just happened.

I closed my eyes and recalled the look on his face as he came, that bead of sweat running down his face and how it felt when his fingers did that magical thing deep inside me. I shivered and rolled onto my side, "Best day ever."

"Best day ever compared to what?" Alain bent over and pulled the covers away from my face. "Compared to every other day," I looked up.

"Get in here, you beast," I grabbed his wrist and pulled him under the sheets.

We laid there in silence for a few minutes. I listened to his heart beat next to my ear. "Did you enjoy yourself," he asked softly and turned to face me. "What do you think?" I wedged a leg between his and smiled. He looked at me and waited. "It was passable," I choked back a laugh as his eyes narrowed.

"Passable?"

I nodded. "I think you can do better. That we can do better. There's room for improvement." He shook his head and laughed, flinging an arm over my side before kissing me gently on the forehead, "Life with you is never dull, that is for certain."

"Seriously, I think we should refine some of our techniques," I told him solemnly.

"I think I heard you say you like it rough. Did you really tell me that?"

I blushed. "A little, yeah. I'm such a control freak I kinda like it when someone manhandles me a little. Just a little though," I pointed a finger at him. "Just a little. I'm not quite sure how much yet but maybe just a little."

"A control freak, eh? Never would have guessed it. What a surprise to find you have control issues." He rolled his eyes and tugged me closer until our heads rested on the same pillow.

"Think you can help me get over those 'issues'?" I asked him, holding a hand up in air quotes.

He smiled. "I think so. But we will have to build some trust first, I think."

"Which takes practice, I'm assuming."

A very wicked grin crossed his lips and he whispered, "Anything worth doing well is worth doing at least once a day. Maybe twice. Think you can handle that, butterfly?"

"We'll see," my hand brushed the hair back from his gorgeous face running those silky dark strands through my fingers, "But first I'm going to need a sandwich."

NINETY-ONE

"What the hell is this," I pointed at my plate as we stood wrapped up in heavy bathrobes in Nanette's spacious galley. "Not a sandwich, at least not the American version of one that's for damn sure." "Gift horse, butterfly," he slid over a plate of freshly cut tomatoes laid neatly on top of thinly sliced mozzarella lightly dusted with pepper and balsamic vinegar sprinkled with a few basil leaves he'd snipped from the plant hanging in front of the porthole over the sink. I felt ungrateful and embarrassed. "I apologize. That was rude." I looked down sheepishly and pulled the beautiful plate closer. "Thank you. Thank you for making me this. It looks lovely." He chucked his hand under my chin and smirked, "Not what you were expecting?"

"Not really," I said. He handed me a heavy fork and sliced himself off a piece of tomato. "I'm not much of a vegetable fan," I explained and dug a slice of mozzarella from under the basil leaves and raised it toward my mouth.

"Not so fast. We have a problem I think we need to discuss." His fingers pinched the bottom of my fork and slowly brought it down toward the plate. I followed it with my tongue making grumpy whining noises.

Alain paused. "This is a bit delicate for me," He put his chin on his hand and stared at my face. I shifted uncomfortably. I started to get weirded out so I leaned away when his arm came around from behind his back and landed on the counter. I jumped back and raised my hands defensively.

"Holy shit," he froze, surprised. "Sorry, last time you whipped something out from behind your back I lost all my hair," I laughed and put a hand over my pounding heart. He looked at the floor, "I do apologize for that. It was probably not the most respectful thing to do and I am truly sorry if I forced you into something you were not truly ready for."

I reached across the table and grabbed his hand. "Hey," I shook his wrist, "I love it. I absolutely love it. So stop feeling bad because I'm not upset at all. It's my favorite haircut ever and I'll have you know that I expect you to tidy up the edges of this fabulousness on a regular basis."

"I am happy do that as long as there is a shower afterward," he kissed the inside of my wrist with a lecherous wink.

"So what's this delicateness you're dying to discuss," I reached across the counter, picked up a tomato slice and took a bite. "This is surprisingly good," I tilted my head and examined it closely. "It's the vinegar," he pushed it toward my face, "eat it. Broaden your horizons beyond cheeseburgers and condensed milk. You'll like it."

And I did. I also promptly proceeded to devour the entire plate including the basil leaves as he shook his head. "I have more," he got up from the table and carried the heavy plate to the counter. "I'll take seconds…amazingly," I told him and peered over his shoulder. Reaching into a wicker basket he drew out a very ugly tomato striped in shades of green.

"I'm sorry, is that lumpy thing a tomato?"

"It is," he reached into a drawer and pulled out a knife. "It's from the farmer's market. An heirloom tomato called a Green Zebra." He swiftly cut thick slices off the sides. "They're much better than the mealy ones you usually get in the grocery stores, in my opinion."

"But it's green." I poked it with a finger.

"It's delicious." He swiped a thin slice across the balsamic left on the plate and sprinkled on a bit of sea salt before handing it to me. I took a big bite, holding a hand under my chin as juice dripped off the edge. It was sublime. I did need to broaden my culinary horizons, I conceded.

"I've been doing most of the cooking, yes?" He said blandly and arranged the slices on the plate. "I do feel bad about that," I snatched a piece and he smacked my hand.

"I can pay you for the incredible amount of food I'm consuming. And I'm happy to contribute if you can stomach my meals. I'm warning you though, I can't cook worth shit. Never learned how. Never had the patience." I told him I could make a mean pound cake but that it took an obscene amount of butter and eggs and my oven probably couldn't handle it anyway. "But I have a cast iron pan and cornbread in a properly seasoned cast iron pan is to die for." My voice trailed off as I pondered where I could find some bacon grease.

"Ok, butterfly," he smacked the knife blade down on the counter, "This has to stop." I looked down and saw he'd been using a bread knife to slice the tomato. What is it with my lovers and bread knives? Clearly I'd missed the memo.

"What has to stop," I looked up, suddenly realizing he was slightly agitated. "Alain, what are you talking about?" He stared at the ceiling and told me that having a crisis in a kitchen was apparently communicable because he was suddenly at a loss for words.

"Good god," I pulled up a stool, "you look like you're having a stroke." He bent down and placed both hands on the counter and looked at his feet. "Sit down and don't move," he pointed a finger in my face and walked away down the hall returning a minute later with a stack of papers in his hand.

I sat silently and watched him move closer.

He pulled up a stool next to mine and put a hand on the counter. "I want you to listen to everything I have to say without talking," he pinched my lips shut before I could open my mouth. "I'm serious. When I am done, I will listen to everything you have to say without talking. Can you do that?" I nodded and felt his fingers brush against my mouth. My forehead creased as fear started to creep in. Maybe the sex wasn't as good as I thought it was. Was he dumping me already? Stomach churning, I stared at his face as it dawned on me I liked him a whole lot more than I'd originally anticipated.

"You actually do have a truth problem, don't you," he smoothed a thumb across my wrinkles. "I can literally see every thought cross your face. It's amazing. I've heard the saying before but I always thought it was metaphorical yet here you are, an open book." I smiled weakly.

"Relax, butterfly," Alain leaned forward and whispered in my ear, "I'm not going to say any of the things you fear are coming. I promise."

I let out a deep breath.

"I like you," he told me. "A lot. More than a lot, actually. I'm not in love with you because I don't fall in love easily but…someday. Someday maybe I could be. Today was unique," he paused, "Good. Amazing, really. And not what I expected."

I stared at him.

"I am not a serious person. It is a fault perhaps," he shrugged a shoulder casually, "I am who I am. But you are different. You make me want to be different which scares me. I want to run but I won't. I won't this time. At least, I'll do my best not to run away from you."

He got up and walked to the sink. He stared out the window, "When we reach Prince Rupert I need to go home. I have some things that need to be…handled." He turned and leaned against the counter. "And I have some work to do at my job. I've put off a project for too long already. Sadly, I cannot stay here with you indefinitely, however delightful that might be."

I gave him a big frowny face.

"Nanette will stay, of course. But I don't know when I'll be back. You'll be in the boatyard for a while," I rolled my eyes and let out a groan as he continued. "Perhaps I will go home then while you are fixing what is broken. I do know one thing for sure." He walked over, knelt down and took my hand.

"I want to see you again. Here. Somewhere else. Anywhere you like. Maybe you can come to Montreal. You would enjoy it, I think. When we get to Shearwater I'll let you make that decision and I'll accept it either way, of course. But I won't lie and tell you I won't be very disappointed should you decide I am not for you. Butterfly, I want you in my life. In whatever capacity you choose."

I looked down at that smashingly gorgeous face and could not even believe my ears. Alain rested his forehead on my knee and started laughing. "Lover, your face is too much," he stood up and patted my cheek. "Don't ever change," he said, "I love your face and its truth problem. Don't change, not for anyone but yourself."

"Ok," I whispered before I realized I wasn't supposed to be talking and clapped a hand across my mouth.

He chuckled. "I'm not finished."

My eyes widened.

"To be with me, however, I have one nonnegotiable requirement." Shit, here it comes. He turned away and my shoulders sagged.

"You have to be alive." He held out the papers he'd brought back from the bedroom.

I was perplexed. I was pretty sure he wasn't a vampire because I'd seen him in the sunlight. Also was pretty sure he didn't fuck dead bodies which would absolutely be a deal breaker for me. This statement was so obvious that I was missing something. Of course I'd have to be alive. I slanted my eyes to the side, thinking swiftly. This statement is illogical. I must be missing some data.

What am I missing here.

He shook the stack in my face. "Numbers are falling out of your ears. Look at the papers. This is the information you're searching for."

I reached out a hand and took the bundle before looking down realizing it was my test results. The ones I'd handed him earlier that day.

Looked up questioningly.

Glanced back at the papers.

Alain leaned over and pointed at a section on page three. "Normally I would never even think to pry into a lover's concerns beyond that which immediately affects me, of course. And I am very uncomfortable pointing this out because it is personal to you. But this is not good, butterfly. Not good."

It was a number. 241. I shrugged. "So what."

He looked at me.

I stared back at him.

"That's your cholesterol level."

"I can see that. It's right next to the number. That's the label next to the 241. So what?"

He looked shocked. "Didn't your doctor talk to you about this?"

"No. I left Seattle right after I got these," I waved the papers in the air, totally confused.

"Holy shit," he put his hands on his head. "You're on the edge of dead, butterfly. It is you that is practically a solid. This is a terrible score. Angiogram terrible. Heart attack terrible. Immediate medication terrible. Lover, you cannot ignore this."

"Really?" I lifted the papers to my face and stared at the number. "What's a good number? What's your number?" He reached into his pocket and handed me a paper.

It said 143.

Wow. That was a big difference from 241. I looked back at my score with apprehension.

"What do I do about this? Alain, what am I supposed to do?" I set the paper carefully down on the counter. "I'm in a foreign country. I can't go waltzing into a doctor's office and ask for meds for whatever fixes this…thing," I looked up at him.

"Well, I can tell you one thing you can do. You can stop eating corn-bread cooked in bacon grease." He looked at me disapprovingly. "The foods you eat are terrible. Your diet is horrendous. But you are in excellent shape so that's a positive," he winked at me. "Maybe if you eat better the score will come down."

"From now on," he decreed, "we eat better. Less cheese. More vege-tables." I put my forehead on the counter. Shoot me, just shoot me. I'm better off dead. Swear to god if I ate more than one vegetable a day without cheese on it I might as well roll over and die.

"I will eat better, too. We'll do it together. At least for the next few days until Shearwater. Yes? Will you try?" I looked up and told him that since he did all the cooking I didn't really have a choice.

"Seriously, butterfly. Will you let me help you? Just for a few days? I can't bear the thought of you keeling over out in the ocean all alone from a stroke or something."

He actually looked concerned and I felt bad. "Of course. I didn't realize this was a problem," I looked down at the 241 and felt my heart twinge, "or I would have fixed it. Or something. I would have done something."

I heard a deep relieved sigh and realized this conversation had totally stressed him out. Clearly he felt horrible about invading my privacy but had cared enough to ask the question. Liked me enough to actually attempt to prolong my life.

"I'm presuming your motives are purely platonic," I said innocently and tried to make the situation less awkward. Alain snorted and replied, "Not in the least. It would pain me greatly if I were fucking you up against a wall somewhere and you keeled over dead."

I peered up at his face and asked him if he was feeling better. "Much better, thank you. I do feel better. Not all the way better but partly better." He tipped his hand back and forth, "Certainly I will be completely better after I take advantage of you at some point this evening. Gently. I'll do it gently. So you don't have an infarct and croak."

"Oh, our romance is truly alive and well," I leaned over and snatched the last Green Zebra from his plate and stuffed it down my throat as he laughed.

NINETY-TWO

"For dinner I think we can have this chicken," he handed me a paper wrapped package tied with actual string from his crouched position over his refrigerator. "And these." He tossed a few zucchini on the galley counter and stepped toward the sink. "And…" my voice trailed off .

"And what?" He looked confused.

"That's it? That's all we're eating? But I'll starve!" I put one hand on my hip, cocked an eyebrow and told him we can't go cold chicken all at once. He sauntered over and took the paper-wrapped bird from my outstretched hand before dropping it on the counter.

"You have to ease me into this eating better process or you'll shock my system, you know."

"Ease you in, huh," Alain backed me toward a corner, put his hands across my back and pulled me toward him. I winced and let out a tiny involuntary squeak. "What's wrong? I'm sorry!" He backed away lifting his hands in the air, "I assumed you would be ok with me touching you like that."

"I am, I am." I turned stiffly and pulled my robe slightly to the side, "But that hurt." Alain peeked over my arm.

"Holy shit!" He looked down at my face as he turned me around, "What happened here? You're completely black and blue across your entire back! Did I do this?" Alain looked sick. "Oh butterfly, your wing is all busted up. I am so sorry…"

"I did it when I fell into the bilge. When the handle of the ball valve broke I fell down and hit my shoulder on the edge of the floor."

I pushed him gently to the side and headed for the bathroom mirror.

"Oh my god. This looks horrible." Shocked, I pulled the robe down to my waist and fully turned my back to the sink. I reached a hand over my shoulder and pushed a finger into the massive bruise running down the right side of my body. Giant blossoms of dark purple and black streaked across the top of my shoulder and ran down my side trailing off at my hip bone.

"Look," I leaned closer, "you can actually see the edge of the floor where it's beveled to meet the hatch." We both peered into the mirror as I started laughing, "That's hilarious!" This was too much. A busted boat, a head shave, a unicorn ride and now I looked like I'd been beaten with a rolling pin. It could only go up from here. I started to pull the corner of the robe up and Alain grabbed the lapels and fluffed up the thick cotton under my chin tsk tsk-ing with concern. He tied the robe closed with a jaunty overhand knot and sadly informed me that there would be no up-against-anything fucking this evening. "I would be surprised if you can even sleep on your back at all it looks so bad."

"I'll just sleep face down on top of you." I kissed him longingly but he pushed me away with two fingers. "Alas, I'm almost afraid to touch you," he smiled. "Besides, I like to sleep alone."

I felt sad. Bereft. "You probably snore anyway," I told him that maybe he wasn't totally perfect after all.

"I thrash around a little I've been told. Plus I would probably smack you and hurt you." Alain kissed me softly on the forehead and whispered that I should rest as much as I could tonight because I'd be very busy tomorrow doing many other things.

"Adult things." He ran a finger along the skin peeking from behind the robe's collar.

"But no up-against-a-wall things, sadly," I turned my lips down in a giant frown. "We'll see," he turned back toward the galley, "We'll see."

NINETY-THREE

"Are you still hungry?" Alain held out another piece of oven roasted chicken. "I'm stuffed. I'm so stuffed you'll have to roll me over to Abraxis," I leaned backward and let the belt of the robe out another inch, "That was really good. Super good."

"Ok, maybe a half a slice more," I held out my plate.

He laughed, picked up the bread knife and cut a paper thin piece of chicken off the side of the thigh. I paused, "And please explain to me what's with the bread knives because Nanook has one too and apparently it's quite the thing."

"Nanook?" He sighed. "Is this Mr. Anchorage? These nicknames...you are so strange."

I shrugged, told him that Nanook of the North had a bread knife and asked him to please explain why this cutlery was suddenly so ubiquitous. "I've never had one and no one I know has one until voila! Nanook and the Unicorn, bread knife brothers for life."

I twisted my fingers together and tossed out a random gang sign. Alain shook his head. "It's serrated which means it's good for cutting things you don't want squashed," he held it up and ran a finger along the edge of the knife. "Tomatoes, chicken, bread…" he paused.

"You leave the crusts on your bread though."

"Of course I do. That's the best part," he turned away and wrapped up the leftovers. "Nanook cuts his off," I blurted and immediately felt uncomfortable.

"I don't know what to do here," I reached across and speared the last grilled zucchini slice. "Am I supposed to talk about him to you? Or is that not allowed. This is new to me. Help a sister out."

He smiled. "Ground rules, eh?"

"Ok," he raised his fingers. "One, we don't talk about other lovers unless we are fully clothed and even then…not so much. Two, we don't talk about other lovers in bed. At all. Ever. Not to discuss techniques, not for any reason. Or talk about what they do in bed even if we are out of bed. No comparing me to anyone else." He pointed a finger at me. "And this means also with your face, butterfly. You need to concentrate when you're fucking me or I will be very upset. And I will know it. I will know. I know you."

"Scouts honor and trust me, that won't be an issue," I promised solemnly.

"Three, I don't give or take relationship advice unless it is about us. That is what your mother or your girlfriends or your boat is for. Four…"

"My god, I feel like I need to be writing this down so I don't forget anything!" I put my chin in my hand and motioned him to continue. He stuck his tongue out at me for interrupting.

"Four, we don't lie to each other. I will never lie to you. If you call and ask me who I'm with I will give you an honest answer. That's the only way this works. And five, we talk to each other about how we feel. I might be jealous when what I actually feel is ignored. Or lonely because I miss you. We can't let those things just linger because it will kill us. What we have now. What we might have in the future."

He looked at me.

"But this doesn't mean you're going to tell me whenever you go out with someone else, right? Because I'm not sure I want to know about all that," I considered what might be an extreme and potentially unwanted amount of openness. Alain turned away and stuck the chicken in the fridge. "Of course not. But when I am with you, I am only with you." He stood up and pinched my chin between his fingers, bent down and pecked me on the forehead. "And when I am not with you, I am not with you and you have the same freedoms, of course."

"This is quite Continental," I said with a little swagger. "But I'm picking up what you're putting down. Besides," I shrugged, "I've recently decided that I won't ask a question if I don't truly want to know the answer."

"I would have to agree with that statement,," he wiped off the counter with a towel and turned away. "Oh, one more thing."

"Jesus Christ," I threw my hands in the air. "My church had fewer rules than this relationship. What, what's the 'one more thing'?"

"We don't share. Unless we are all in bed together by choice. Then, I might consider it if we talk about it beforehand."

The thought of Nanook and the Unicorn in the same bed as me at the same time doing adult things to each other was genuinely shocking. Legit shocking. "Trust me, that will never happen," I assured him confidently, "Nanook is about as hetero as you can get."

"You'd be surprised, lover," he turned away and smiled secretly. "You'd be surprised."

He shrugged casually and the horizon broadening statements just kept coming. "Besides, who says it has to be another man?"

Ok. Now we were in totally new territory. Massively and unexpectedly previously heretofore unexplored Yukon wilderness kind of territory. "Let's just get a whole bunch of people between the sheets so I can rack up all my sins simultaneously and get eternal damnation out of the way in one fell swoop," I stammered, slightly stunned.

"Eh, I don't want to share you right now," he threw the towel over a rack adjusting it just so before sauntering over and plopping down onto a stool. "But someday, maybe. If you can manage to not be such a prude."

I snorted and told him he was a sinner quickly on his way to hell. I could tell my mother was crying in her soup somewhere on the East Coast because she could no doubt feel the evil vibrations of our thoughts. I finished with the statement that I may not actually be opposed to future discussions about this particular topic, prude or not.

"You continue to amaze, butterfly," he announced and told me it was time for bed.

NINETY-FOUR

"Hop on in, unicorn," I patted the edge of the bed. Alain stood in the doorway his toothbrush sticking out the side of his mouth.

"I sleep alone, remember?" He turned away and I heard the water running followed by the clattering of his toothbrush in the cabinet.

"I know, but I can still tuck you in, right?"

"Am I six years old?" Alain stripped off his pants and jumped into bed under the covers.

"That's not fair," I wagged a finger, "you can't just take off all your clothes and expect me not to at least try to molest you."

"Not tonight, broken butterfly."

I shrugged, "Your loss," and climbed up onto the covers. He laid back on his pillow after fluffing it a few times and pulled the blankets up to his chin. My eyes adjusted slowly to the darkness as he snuffled around fidgeting until he finally situated himself satisfactorily. "Jesus, you do thrash." I saw him grinning in the dim light.

I looked down and saw the outline of his face, his hair curving down on one side grazing the top of his cheekbone. "What's it like to be so beautiful?" I asked in all seriousness. "No, really, what's it like? You have to know you don't look like everyone else, right? You must know that."

He was silent for a long moment before answering. "Awkward. It's awkward," he swallowed hard. "I don't like being stared at. It bothers me. I'm shy, you know."

I was surprised. "I don't think you're shy at all. I've never felt you were shy."

He shifted a little and I adjusted slightly to the side. "I don't go out alone very much. When I was younger I used my face like a weapon to get whatever I wanted but I found I didn't like myself after a while. So I just…"

"You just what?"

"I just pick the people I spend time with more carefully now. Or I choose them for one night and move on."

I brushed his hair away from his face rather surprised that someone that physically perfect would actually find their looks to be disconcerting. I wondered how my sisters really felt in high school when all those boys' heads turned lusting for them as they strode through the hallways. I remembered how uncomfortable I was during those three weeks as the quarterback's de facto girlfriend.

"But you must get a lot of attention because of your job, right? Fashion shows, blah blah blah." I paused, "Or is that another faulty assumption." He laughed.

"I work in the fashion industry but I'm not a designer," he rolled toward me, "I'm a chemist."

"You're a what?" The thought that he was beautiful as well as smart was almost too much to comprehend. "I'm a textile chemist. You know, I help develop new fabrics. All those ombre leathers and exotic finishes that make silk look like water or whatever… I create things like that," he pulled an arm out from under the covers and rubbed his hand along my leg.

"Are there universities that teach textile chemistry?" Genuinely curious, I flopped down next to him and pulled the edge of a blanket over my feet. Alain grinned. "I have a degree in chemical engineering with an emphasis in polymers."

I sighed and said softly, "I'm a tax attorney."

"No shit? I don't believe it. Really?" He sounded shocked. I stared at his face, "I never told you what I did for a living? Huh. Well, congrats. You're fucking a totally nerdy tax lawyer."

I patted his arm and told him that I didn't know anything about his particular money situation but if he ever needed help with a complex structured finance transaction I was his gal. "I don't understand what that means," he said, smiling.

"It means I find loopholes in tax codes and help people shift their money around between different countries in order to avoid shelling any out to the government."

"So you're a criminal," he patted me back.

"This is why my truth issue is so problematic. It's hard to tell an entire country to go fuck itself when your face actually says you're bluffing," I explained and crawled under the covers next to his body siphoning away the warmth. "They usually keep me in the back room with all the dusty books."

"Do not even think of putting those cold feet on me," his voice warned me from across the pillow. "I mean it. I will kick you out of this bed so fast." I inched a toe up his calf and he pulled his leg away. "Butterfly I will smash you flat if you touch me with those," he yelped when I shoved my leg in between his and slung an arm across his back preventing him from moving. "Heat transfer! It's chemistry!" I said in his ear as he grunted grumpily into the pillow.

"That's actually physics but I'll give you a pass since you're just a dumb tax lawyer," he said condescendingly.

His fingers ran lightly over the side of my head and asked what my bosses would think of my haircut. "Don't know," I shrugged. "I took an indefinite leave of absence from the firm before I headed up here. Besides, Seattle's weird. They probably wouldn't even notice. Nobody said anything when I showed up with a ring in my nose. I think this buzz cut makes me look rather badass, quite frankly." I puffed myself up and he shook his head, amused, and asked me if I'd always wanted to be a tax lawyer.

"No, actually, I didn't." Rolling away I looked at the ceiling. "I wanted to be a writer but I couldn't ever get out of my own way. That's what a professor told me at least. He also told me my writing was shit because it wasn't authentic. That I was the worst kind of fake because I didn't know I was a fake. He told me I had to truly know myself before I could write anything worthwhile so I just…stopped—what does that even mean? Know yourself. What a crock of crap. Plus a lawyer once said I was a numbers person not a words person so…"

"That's ridiculous, of course you're a words person," he sounded personally offended before reluctantly admitting, "And also a numbers person. Quite frankly, I've never seen anyone run through data the way you do. It's alarming, actually, the way you calculate every tiny thing. Terrifying. I hope I don't end up on the wrong end of a distribution."

I told him he was an outlier for sure and he'd originally been pegged on the gay side. "With a statistically significant standard deviation, I'll have you know," I educated him about his past categorizations. "But I moved you. I balance. That's my job. Weigh things back and forth until they're equal. I've always been that way. And indecisive."

I sighed and told him that's why I never wrote anything. That every writer felt they had one great story in them but were afraid to squander it. "No one wants to waste it, you know? If you haven't found your writing style or it's just bad timing or whatever. Then you've lost The Story and it's gone. You can't ever get it back." I smiled wryly. "Sometimes I feel frozen, like I'm petrified in amber with my fingers hovering over the keyboard but I can't ever shake it out. It gets stuck somewhere in here." I waved my hands around.

"So you have a story, then," he asked. "I thought I did," shifting, I groaned a little as my shoulder cramped. "Now I'm not so sure. Plus the whole knowing yourself and all that business kinda screwed my brain up, I think."

We laid there in silence for a few minutes. I heard his breathing deepen and realized he was falling asleep. Slowly I crawled out from under his arm trying not to wake him as I inched out from under the covers. He whispered, "Was I snoring? I'm sorry." I leaned down and kissed his forehead and told him not to be silly.

"Alain," quietly I spoke his name into the silence. "I want you to know I like you for what's in here," I tapped the side of his head. "Your outside is gorgeous, don't get me wrong, I could stare at you for hours." He closed his eyes and turned his face away. "Hey, let me see you," I leaned over into his frame of view tipping his face toward me with my fingers.

"But if there wasn't anything up here," I pushed a finger into his forehead and felt him smiling, "you wouldn't be getting in here." I pointed at my lap. I pressed my cheek against his, softly smooched his face and carefully climbed down off the bed making sure I didn't put any weight on my right side.

"Do you need some light," he whispered as I shambled slowly down the hallway trailing a hand down one wall for guidance. I glanced backward and told him it was sixteen and a half steps from the bed to the galley ladder and if he didn't shut his trap he'd screw up my tally and I'd have to come back and start over.

The sheets rustled as he rolled over laughing. I counted loudly all the way down the hallway up into the cockpit before jumping the gap silently onto Abraxis where I stood for a minute next to my sink before climbing under the covers. I reached up my left hand and patted the mahogany wall above my head. "Don't be jealous, baby," I whispered to Abraxis. "I'm not jealous," he yawned before telling me to stop thinking so much.

"You're exhausting," he whispered. I turned my face toward the wall and closed my eyes, my busted wing aching with every breath.

NINETY-FIVE

"Butterfly? Are you alive?" Alain knocked on the hatch softly late the next morning. A moment passed before I heard the top flip open and his voice say, "Are you sick? What's going on in here?"

I could barely think I hurt so badly so I just laid there in a miserable huddle, a single foot hanging over the edge of the cushions. I took shallow breaths and tried not to move. "I think I've really done something terrible to myself," I whispered and heard his footsteps click down the ladder.

"Why are you still in bed?" The cushions dipped slightly and his concerned face came into view peering over toward where I was leaning my forehead against the back cushions clutching my right arm to my chest. "I think I'm going to be sick. I'm in serious pain here and I feel like I'm going to be sick." I turned my head slightly away from him and gagged.

"Let's get you up and take a look," he gently put his arm under my left shoulder and the other under my hips and pulled me toward the edge of the bed. "I know it hurts. I'm sorry but we have to see what's going on here," he apologized when I gasped.

I sat up slowly breathing deeply as Alain propped me upright and peered at my face. "Ok, what's hurting?" I pointed to my right shoulder and he carefully pulled down the collar of my t-shirt before letting out a deep sigh.

"You are right," he confirmed, "You've done something terrible, that's for certain."

"I can't even lift my arm." I bent over and tried to stand up. "Hold on, hold on. Just hold on a minute." Alain told me to stay put and briskly climbed up the ladder heading for Nanette. A few agonizing minutes later he came back with a cashmere scarf slung over one shoulder holding a leather belt in his hands.

"I'm not up for bondage today, unicorn," I laughed weakly. "It's for your arm," he knelt down next to me. Lightly he slipped the scarf over my head in a big loop and slid it under my arm as I made tiny *ouch ouch ouch* noises. He carefully reached around my body, slid the belt around my chest and gently threaded it over the scarf pinning my limb tightly to my torso.

"This is very impressive. Please tell me you're not also a doctor because I'm feeling very insecure right now." Joking, but not really, I put my other hand on his shoulder and leaned forward before inching to a standing position. He assured me he wasn't a doctor but he had a wonderful first aid manual before proceeding to utter the most spectacular phrase known to mankind.

"And I have Percocet."

An hour later I felt marginally human. And hungry. With Alain's help I managed to climb up the stairs and over to Nanette where I sat at the counter holding a bag of ice on top of my shoulder watching as he made me a sandwich cutting it carefully into small squares before sliding it toward me on a plate.

"Thank you," I picked up a square with my left hand and took a big bite. "Ahhhh," I sighed in delight, "Cheese. I should blow out a shoulder every day if I can convince you to serve me cheese."

"It's mercy cheese," he smiled, "so don't get used to it." I told him that I must have torn something when I took my impromptu dive into the bilge, "It can't be that bad because I would have felt it yesterday and it was only achy when I went to bed."

"It's really swollen so that's not helping," Alain wiped up the counter, "But clearly you have damaged it somehow and it's probably not going to fix itself without some sort of medical attention."

"Great. Busted wing and a terrible cholesterol score. What a catch I'm turning out to be." I wiped face with my opposite hand as the room slowly blurred. "I'm enjoying the Percocet though, I can tell you that much."

Alain sat down at the counter next to me and tapped his fingers, deep in thought. "Do you have a place in Seattle still?" he asked.

"Nope. But I could probably crash at a friend's house."

He *hmmm'd* for a minute.

"You'll have to go to Anchorage. You need to go to Nanook," he announced matter-of-factly, "if he will have you."

"If he will have me," I sat back, irritated. "What's that supposed to mean?" Alain looked over, "You need help. If he will help you, let him help you. At least ask him if he will help you. Certainly there has to be a hospital in Anchorage. You can't very well get care in Canada or I would take you to Montreal. So, you might as well go to Anchorage where you have support." He paused. "What if you have to have surgery?"

I thought back to when you blew out your rotator cuff and were completely incapacitated for practically an entire year and swallowed hard. "Hopefully it's not that bad," I envisioned me hobbling along all by myself in Seattle living out of a hotel trying to wipe my butt with my non-dominant hand and failing miserably. "Maybe you're right though. I'll call him when we get to Shearwater, I guess."

He asked me if I still had health insurance. Weakly, I lifted my left hand in the air and gave three shouts for Obamacare. "Ok, good to know," he then felt compelled to remind me that healthcare in Canada was free for citizens. We sat there for a few minutes before he abruptly stood and announced I couldn't captain Abraxis to Shearwater.

"Excuse me?" I raised my eyebrows in astonishment.

"You cannot take Abraxis to Shearwater," he explained patiently, "I will not allow it."

"You are not the boss of me," I felt a little peeved. "I am the boss of me and I will drive my own damn boat, thank you very much."

"No, you will not." Alain shrugged. "You cannot do it. There will be no more discussion. You will take Nanette and I will take Abraxis. We will leave in the morning if the weather looks good."

"Who the fuck do you think you are," I started to yell. He wheeled around and pointed a finger in my face. "No, you do not speak to me like that," he snapped quietly, "I will not be disrespected. I do not speak to you like that and you will not treat me that way." I sat back in surprise and started to say something when he tilted his head to the side, "Think very carefully about what comes out of that mouth, butterfly. We do not yell and we do not say hurtful things just because we are angry. I will not stand here and let you cut me down with your tongue. I won't have it."

He looked really serious so I shut up. I thought mean things but didn't say them as he stood in the corner of the galley and stared at my face. I started to reply but paused when he shot a warning look my way.

"Maybe you could rephrase so it doesn't sound so authoritarian," I said carefully. "I don't respond well to that sort of thing. I would also like it noted for the record that my statement applies to all future conversations."

Alain narrowed his eyes.

"You cannot physically captain a boat that has no automatic capabilities," he said after a long minute, "even if you are only under power."

"How so," my voice came out nice and even.

"Because the throttle is on the right side. You are dominant right-handed. And your boat is damaged. What will you do if something goes wrong? If the weather gets bad? How will you pull up the anchor or dock when we get to Shearwater?"

I pondered this. He continued, "Nanette has automatic everything. Auto helm. Auto furlers. Auto mainsheet. Auto windlass. You just have to sit there and make sure you don't hit something." He paused. "I am happy to take Abraxis."

"So you're saying you'll take one for the team." I smiled. His shoulders relaxed and he stepped across the galley toward me. "I will take one for our team," he chucked me under the chin and leaned down pressing his forehead gently against mine and closed his eyes. "And I am sorry about what happened just now. I'll try to word my statements more carefully in the future. But I meant what I said."

I looked down. "You were right. I was going to say something nasty without thinking."

He kissed me on the cheek and said, "No big deal. I'm over it." Reaching around me, he grabbed a sandwich square and stuffed it in my mouth. "So eat this cheese before I feel less generous, butterfly. And know that if you say something in the future on purpose just to be mean I will spank you. And I won't be gentle about it." He turned away toward the nav station and pulled out a big roll of charts, "Now, let's figure out how we're going to get out of here without sinking."

NINETY-SIX

I slept in Alain's bed that night after he built a huge pillow wall behind my back to keep me pinned upright before removing himself to Nanette's galley couch. "If you need something just yell," he told me I should have no problem projecting my voice into the galley. "If you're saying I have a big mouth…that is valid," I slurred as he poured me under the sheets.

"Tomorrow…maybe not so much Percocet, yes?"

"No. Tomorrow lots of Percocet," I replied, "Auto everything can auto me to Shearwater while I enjoy all these pretty colors." His laughter trailed off into nothing as I passed out.

Early the next morning we stood in the galley peering at the charts while I iced my cashmere wrapped shoulder. "I actually feel a little better," I admitted, fumbling left-handed through an egg white, tomato and zucchini omelet. Alain told me that it was Advil only from here on out. I gave up and just used my fingers.

"Not dignified, no, but I'm hungry and this fork is just not working," I explained. He shook his head. "You need auto everything…" he sang under his breath. I rolled my eyes and reluctantly admitted he had been right.

"Ok," he announced. "Let's get you suited up." Gently he slipped a thick sweater over my head helping me thread my busted wing through the sleeve before holding out my overalls. "Hold still," I jammed one foot in and then the other, "Remember, last time I tried this I pistol whipped myself." Alain chuckled. "When I meet Nanook I'll have to shake his hand for that," he said.

"What do you mean, 'when you meet Nanook'," I stuck my feet into the boots bracing myself on his shoulder. "We're not allowed to share, remember? I can't have you poaching my boyfriend, Alain. Because you will. You will. He's super hot and you totally will try to poach him." I wagged a finger in his general direction, picked up my safety harness and contemplated how I was going to squeeze my arm and thick coat sleeve through the narrow hole.

"Well, I'm not putting you on a plane to Anchorage alone," Alain snatched the harness from my hand and turned it right side out, "So he will have to come here to get you. Or I will take you there and hand you off to him personally. Like a suitcase." He leaned over and carefully slipped the yellow webbing under my arm before reaching behind me to redo my makeshift sling.

"I am a saucy piece of baggage, aren't I."

He leaned forward and kissed me and agreed I was completely out of control.

"So…Shearwater and not Bella Bella," we conferred with each other a last time and agreed the aforementioned marina had the facilities to fix Abraxis and sufficient moorage to handle Nanette for a week or two while we figured out what our next steps were. Alain baldly told me he'd be happy to throw cash at whoever required it until we found someone willing to give us what we wanted.

"I'll pull my end of the deal especially if I have to get cut," I assured him. I thought about how long Abraxis might actually be stuck in Shearwater and wondered how in the world I was going to sail him anywhere much less open ocean up to Seward. I smacked my lips together considering all the possibilities. "Shearwater first, conquer the world later," Alain rolled up the charts and tapped them on my head, "Let's go."

We unrafted from Abraxis after Alain dropped my tender and attached it on a long line behind Nanette. "Here's how the windlass works," he pushed a button on his high tech space ship console and bumped forward over his anchor chain reeling it in foot by foot.

"Wow, fancy schmancy." I broke the cardinal rule of boating and asked him how much he blew on Nanette. "Don't ask," he turned to me, "It's obscene. Absolutely obscene. High six figures obscene."

"And you're giving me the keys to this castle with full confidence."

He nodded. "I am. And I will take it out of your ass if you ding her."

"I spent about fifty grand on Abraxis not including all the upgrades. Fancy canvas. Roller furler. A superfly storm jib and drogue. Spinnaker with a giant dragon face on it. You know, a gal's basic necessities."

He stopped and looked at me. "Really?" He turned back toward the windlass and chunked in the last few feet of chain and muttered that he'd been royally gypped. I reminded him that nothing on Abraxis was automatic and I'd be happy to walk him through docking if he needed it. "Don't be shy, unicorn. Cause it's your ass that'll be hurting if you smash my house up," I said while we slowly motored through the tiny channel out to sea leaving Abraxis staring after us forlornly from the end of his hook.

"Ok," Alain pushed a bunch of buttons after checking random gauges and flipping levers here and there. "When I come back, hit this button and then that button and you are good to go. I've put in the waypoints for Shearwater already so you don't need to worry about any of that underway. You monitor the speed and Nanette will drive herself."

I held out my hand for the ship's manual.

"You seriously want this?" Alain laughed. "I need to know what's happening at all times," I snatched it out of his hands. "Control. I must have control. I need to develop my contingency plans."

"Fine, fine," he backed away and began pulling in my tender as Nanette's systems kept me firmly pinned to a specific GPS point hovering a safe distance off Fury Island.

"You remember how to attach the tender and pull in the anchor and all that, right?" I was suddenly concerned that maybe he couldn't handle the tasks ahead because he'd been totally spoiled by all this electronica. Perhaps he wasn't truly a good sailor and just limped along because Nanette was so ridiculously technologically advanced. I reached out my good arm and clutched desperately at his hand.

"Tell your face I know what I'm doing," Alain slipped past me down the ladder, "Abraxis and I will be back in just a minute."

NINETY-SEVEN

Half an hour later I saw Abraxis sedately motor past the head of the channel before turning slightly toward where I reclined on the back of Nanette under an Hermes blanket sipping a glass of iced tea. I heard the VHF squawk and leaned over to answer as Alain's voice came over the airwaves.

"This is exhausting," he said, bitching and moaning about having to manually do everything. "I am tired already and we haven't even started." I laughed and clinked the sound of ice against crystal through the radio. "I, on the other hand, am extremely relaxed," I said when he informed me a critical error had been made.

"What error? Did something happen?" I sat up from my nest of cushions in a panic. He sadly announced he had failed to consider the sad state of my pantry before we parted. "I am in no way adequately provisioned for this voyage," Alain announced in a wounded tone of voice. "I will suffer. I will suffer for you, butterfly."

"Well you're clearly not doing your suffering in silence," I told him. He sent back a deep dramatic sigh. I put his fancy binoculars to my eyes, looked across the water and saw him resting his forehead on my wheel slowly shaking it side to side as he contemplated the interminable hours he'd have to endure without Green Zebras and linen napkins.

Sixty minutes later he informed me that he and Abraxis had come to an accommodation. "What's that," I languidly tipped my eye shade up and yawned.

"We have agreed that if he doesn't sink I will not smash his face against the Shearwater docks."

"That sounds like an excellent accommodation," I said and asked him how he was doing. "Not bad. Not bad," he answered as a suspicious rustling sounded in the background.

I reached over and grabbed the binoculars and innocently queried him about various systems and whether the bilge was still dry and on and on as I tightened in the focus angling my eyes toward the back of Abraxis. He kept yammering about all the new and unwanted things he was learning.

Oh my fucking God. I leaned forward in shock before sitting straight up from the bench. Thinking swiftly I pulled the binoculars away from my face and looked at the model number. Of course the binoculars were also uber expensive. I crossed my fingers and climbed carefully down into the galley headed for the nav station. I dug through the cabinet above the charts and quickly found what I was looking for. "BINGO!" I shouted out. Nanette started to giggle. "We have him now, sister. Oh boy do we have him now."

Please don't stop, please don't let Alain stop. I begged the universe for a favor and sped through the manual until I hit the photography section. Boom. Hoist on your own petard, fancy pants. I lifted the binoculars to my eyes searching for Abraxis and snapped a series of digital photos of Alain sprawled out on the aft cabin roof his feet propped on the wheel happily munching from a box of Triskets with that big chunk of Questionable Cheddar sitting beside him on a paper towel.

I snatched the VHF from the cradle and placed it carefully in my bad hand before lifting the lenses back to my eyes. "Desperate times, desperate measures," I watched him unclip my portable radio from his safety harness. "I see you have found my binoculars, butterfly," he answered and flipped me the bird.

"I have photos. I have much photos for the makings of millions from you." In a horrible accent I informed him that blackmail was imminent watching as he shoved another handful of Triskets in his mouth and laughed.

He leaned over and grabbed the Questionable Cheddar off the deck and bit off a big chunk before telling me to make sure I got his good side as we sailed onward through the afternoon sunshine.

We reversed the departing process at Shearwater. I sat comfortably on the back of Nanette enjoying the sun while Alain stressed out over the radio heading in to dock Abraxis. "I cannot deal with this," he told me and I heard the throttle power down slightly, "There are no bow thrusters. And I cannot see the front over this windscreen. I just cannot with this lack of technology! How have you been surviving all this time?"

"Because I'm awesome and you're spoiled," I stretched out fully on the back bench and contemplated the physical exertion, or lack thereof, Alain had been expending during our voyages. "Now you know how I feel out there in bad weather while you're over here enjoying a mani-pedi."

"Silence," he ordered. "I'm trying not to smash up your house."

I silenced.

A surprisingly short amount of time later I saw him zooming out in the tender toward Nanette. "Bonjour," he hopped out and shoved the tender away trailing it on the line behind us. "Salutations," I replied from my padded perch watching as he leaned over and spread out his arms across his fancy console. "I have missed you, my one true love," he crooned to Nanette.

I laughed. "It's not that bad. And you get in really good shape hauling the sheets around by hand." I inquired about the pantry situation with a grin.

"I am happy to announce that I have rid you of your Questionable Cheddar problem," Alain proclaimed and spun Nanette on a tight axis toward the shore.

"Because you ate it all."

He smiled. "And I must say…not so questionable. It was not bad, not bad. I would not buy it myself," he raised his nose up in disdain, "but I would have a slice or two in the future should you purchase it."

"On a Trisket?"

"Eh," he wagged a hand. "I like Wheat Thins better."

"You and these snooty food issues. What's with that?"

He reminded me that he was a chemist and fully understood the process of making all these items. "I eat things that come out of the ground, not tubes," he explained. I informed him that ground-grown things are fertilized with shit.

"Be that as it may, butterfly," he dictated, "your mercy cheese days are over."

"Nanook will let me eat whatever I want." I laid back on the bench. "Not after I talk to him he won't," Alain said confidently.

"Well, I can assure you that if you announce that to him in the Royal We he'll probably punch you in your pretty mouth. I'm serious. He'll lay you out, Alain, so be polite."

Alain grinned. "I'll flatten him right back. Pistols at dawn, remember? And I'm a damn good shot."

The vision of Nanook and the Unicorn engaging in serious physical violence over my cholesterol level was both hilarious and terrifying. "You cannot beat on each other," I warned him, "because he won't hold back. He's got a bit of a temper. Plate thrower and all that." I continued, "Also, I like both your faces intact and if you bust each other up I'll have to look elsewhere for companionship."

Alain reluctantly agreed that perhaps he and Nanook might also come to an accommodation.

"He doesn't allow cheese and I don't snap his neck. Works for me," he tossed me a thumbs up, hopped off Nanette onto the dock and secured the lines before helping me carefully step down off the side.

I carefully stretched my back and inquired as to when we would begin Percocet happy hour. "After food and after your phone call," he said, disappearing down the hatch emerging with cell phone in hand.

I sighed loudly, reached out grabbing the device and whipped out a quick text before handing it back. "Seriously?" Alain raised an eyebrow, "A text? You're asking for help over a text?"

"I don't know if he would answer if I actually called," I admitted. "He's kind of a loner. Sometimes it takes weeks before he responds. Occasionally I wonder whether he even likes me that much."

Alain paused. "I don't care if he likes you. If he loves you he'll help. Like and love are not the same thing, you know. I've been in love with people who were horrible, just horrible. Sometimes you just can't choose who you love even though you would like to."

I considered the inherent truth of that statement. Did Nanook actually like me as a person? He called me a cancer and the devil and I told him he couldn't get it up. That fucking his best friend's girl was a victory. "Maybe he doesn't like me," sickened, I looked at Alain, "I never even considered that he might not actually like me as a person."

Alain paused.

"You've got quite a mouth on you," he said evenly as he rearranged all the lines. "And from what you've said, you haven't been that nice to him." He looked up. "Butterfly, you've got a mean streak and it's a bad one."

"But you like me, don't you?" Suddenly I was very concerned that I was surrounded by people who loved me but secretly couldn't stand me.

"Yes, of course," he turned toward me, "but I have to tell you, I will walk away if you get nasty. I will leave and I might not come back."

I sat there and thought about that. Maybe I didn't have a truth problem. Maybe it was me. I was the problem.

"Am I a bully?"

He threw a fender over the edge of Nanette's railing. "You can be."

"Then why are you still even here?" That tinge of hysteria was right there behind the tears I knew were coming. I sucked in a deep breath and thought of happy things. Cheese, think about cheese and French fries. Don't cry. Don't start crying.

Alain put his hands on my cheeks. "Because I saw what was on your face in that galley when we were arguing. I saw it. I saw what you were thinking, those hurtful words you wanted to say to me. Inside my heart I was begging you silently not to say them because it would not have turned out well for us."

I stared into his eyes and realized he was totally serious. That I'd come really close to possibly losing him. Or at least driving him away. Of making him not like me as a person.

"And thank god you didn't say those things," he kissed me longingly. "I don't think you're really like that inside. This vicious person comes out sometimes for some reason but I honestly don't believe that is really you. That's not you, butterfly." He stepped away and held out the phone.

"Make the call."

NINETY-EIGHT

Alain puttered around in Nanette's cabin while I walked down the dock deep in thought clutching his cell phone in my hand. Sick to my stomach I thought about those comments I'd made to your mother on the phone after you died. That terrible night in Anchorage when I'd broken your best friend and secretly enjoyed it.

Doctor lady not so handy. I remembered those spiteful words and realized I'd typed them knowing they'd be hurtful. That I'd wanted them to hurt.

Wanted them to sting.

I stared at the phone and didn't want to call. He won't wouldn't a strange number anyway. I reread the text I'd sent that I now noticed wasn't the friendliest greeting.

Slowly I typed in his phone number and hit the button as I raised the phone to my ear, halfway hoping he wouldn't answer.

And he didn't.

NINETY-NINE

"I think maybe tonight I'll sleep on Abraxis," I told Alain after dinner. "Can you help me build a pillow wall again so I don't squash my shoulder?"

"Of course, butterfly," he said with a small smile. I looked up, "I'm not running away. I just need to be by myself for a while." I choked back a few tears and fidgeted with my fork.

Alain told me he knew that. "I know you're not running," he gathered up a giant bundle of pillows and blankets. "I'll give you as much space and time as you want. No judgment."

"I feel really lucky that I met you," he told me later and tucked in a corner of the soft blanket he'd rolled up and wedged behind my back. "Really lucky. I want you to know that." Tears pooled up in my eyes and I looked away.

"I feel lucky, too. And I'll try to be better. Be a better person. Be nicer and not so nasty."

As he walked up the stairs after kissing me goodnight I heard him tell me that Nanook would call.

"He'll call, butterfly," he disappeared up the stairs and I remembered the first half of his statement earlier. *If he loves you he'll help you.*

If he loves you.

ONE HUNDRED

Two days later Nanook still hadn't called. "Maybe he's on a work trip or something," I justified the silence desperately, "I can always go home to Florida. My mom will help me."

Alain looked over. "Your mother cannot take care of you right now. That's not fair to her. You know that." He dried the breakfast plates and I tried to be helpful with my good arm. He reached a hand across the counter, put it on top of mine and said me that if Nanook didn't call soon that he'd take me to the United States himself and then back to Montreal if he had to.

"You can stay with me. I have a large closet you can stand in."

I smiled.

"Of course, this may all be moot if I don't have anything wrong with me," I shrugged. "Maybe I just tweaked something and all I need is rest. I do feel a lot better, you know." He stared at me.

"I will participate in your wishful thinking if you want but you and I both know that something was seriously damaged."

I bumped the silverware drawer shut with my butt and wiped off the counter with the towel he tossed me. "Yeah," I sighed with delight, "I'm going to need a lot of cheese."

"What you need is a nap, butterfly." He put his hand behind my good shoulder, pushed me up the stairs and helped me over to Abraxis. "I just got up!", I hopped gently onto the bunk before he arranged the pillows and strapped me in. I reached out a hand and grabbed his arm. "Thanks for helping me fix up my cabin," I whispered, "Having a smaller bunk and this netting helps a lot. And it's darker. I really do sleep better." Alain kissed my cheek and sat on the edge of the bed and stroked my hair whispering a bedtime story in French while I nodded off to sleep.

I was out for almost an entire day waking only to go to the bathroom and eat some soup in Alain's galley before taking another slug of meds. "Sorry I'm so boring," I nodded off into my bowl, "I don't feel very good."

"It's finals syndrome," Alain explained. "Stress level drops, immune system crashes. Standard procedure for every college student after exams." "So that's why I practically died of the flu after I took the bar," I pushed myself up from the counter and asked him politely if he would help me back to Abraxis. I weaved slightly and my eyes started to close. "How about you just head back here for a while," he suggested, lifting me up into his nest of fabulous high thread count sheets and mohair afghans.

"You textile chemists do have fantastic taste in bed linens," I whispered, watching as he flipped all the porthole covers down and quietly shut the door on his way out.

ONE HUNDRED ONE

"You're a goddamn asshole shithead is what you are," someone said rather loudly from the galley. I cracked a puffy eye and swallowed gently. My throat ached. I sat up and scratched my head and I tried to figure out where I was. I confirmed I was on Nanette by slipping the soft cotton sheet through my fingers. So what is that godawful shouting?

"Fuck you," a French voice replied, "You cheated. I saw you. Don't deny it."

"Lies. Motherfucking lies…You want another beer?"

"Merci," Alain said and something metal clinked onto a counter.

"Deal 'em up, loser."

The sound of cards shuffling sounded through the door and I pressed my ear against the teak. Something was happening. Something was clearly happening but my Percocet fog was interfering with my data collection. I schlepped over to the en suite bathroom and took care of business then crawled into the bed and pitched onto my good side as the room started spinning.

ONE HUNDRED TWO

"Is she dead?"

Alain answered from the doorway, "Judging from the snoring…I would say no." I listened to the strange conversation as if from a great distance, the light from the hallway shrinking into a tiny pinpoint before finally fading away. Darkness descended and I heard Alain say, "Maybe we shouldn't be drugging her soup so much," then someone else laughing softly from behind the slowly closing door.

ONE HUNDRED THREE

I feel much better…I think. I pushed up on my good arm, scratched my neck and suddenly smelled myself. Oh god I needed a shower. Had I been rolling around in shit? What is going on here? I pinched my nose shut and slid carefully out of the bed.

I must have been really sick. I slowly walked toward the bathroom, tired from even the smallest movement. I didn't even know what day it was. What day was this? I peered through the bathroom porthole and suddenly realized Nanette wasn't in Shearwater. I leaned forward squinting my eyes and looked up the strange dock toward a large building perched on a hill just across from where we were tied up.

This must be the twilight zone. I pulled open the shower door and started the water while I dug around in the cabinet and pulled out Alain's toothbrush. I should use this. I convinced myself he wouldn't mind. He has another one, right? He did have another one I remembered. He offered it to me right before he confirmed he liked sports. No, that was later. I was confused. He offered me a toothbrush as a way to get in my pants.

I reminded myself that I needed pants and dropped my sweaty shirt on the floor.

That's not my shirt. I kicked it to the side.

I shook my head and decided ask for forgiveness and not permission and squeezed some toothpaste on the bristles before stepping into the shower.

I ran the hot water out and felt halfway human by the time I finished soaping up with those Walmart lemons trying to hit all the important spots with my left hand before drying myself off unevenly.

Did I need pants? Were they truly essential?

Unclear.

I dug through the cabinets along the side of the bed and examined my clothing options before deciding that a t-shirt and soft cotton slacks were just the ticket. I awkwardly rolled up the pant cuffs and told Nanette these pants now belong to me. Only me. These are so comfortable they should be mine. All mine. Just mine.

"I am appropriating these," I announced to the empty room and opened the cabin door inching slowly down the hallway holding my bad arm close to my side, exhausted.

Halfway to the galley I realized this was not the twilight zone. It was hell.

I am in hell, I realized, as I spotted Nanook and the Unicorn lounging on opposite sides of Nanette's stern, their feet propped up with drinks in hand insulting each other loudly, fully engrossed in a fractious game of Texas Hold'Em.

ONE HUNDRED FOUR

"What's up, cow lady?" Nanook spotted me in the galley before he called Alain a fucktard and threw a twenty into the pot. I glanced at Alain and he winked at me, "I see your twenty and raise you another twenty."

"Don't be giving me that Canadian shit."

Alain shot back, "It's not my fault your dollar is overvalued."

This was beyond bizarre. I didn't know what to do with my hands. Or my face. I just stood there silently in Alain's clothes with my mouth hanging open as I stared at the two of them happy as clams up there in Nanette's cockpit.

"Do you feel better, butterfly?" Alain's voice was soft and smooth. He swept the pot up victoriously. I watched Nanook toss his cards down in frustration before he informed me that my boyfriend was a goddamn cheater and asked could I please get him two more beers.

Slowly I reached over and opened the cheap red cooler sitting on the counter and pulled out two cans of some sort of adult beverage before lifting them up one at a time with my good arm. "You look much better, baby," Nanook said handing both drinks to Alain before jumping down into the galley and giving me a big kiss right on the lips before smacking me on the ass.

"What the hell is going on," I said, completely taken aback.

"She wants to know what's happening," he told Alain.

"We've come to an accommodation," my delicious Frenchman answered.

I paused and examined their faces for signs of a beat-down. "What is this accommodation…" slowly I looked from one gorgeous face to the other before narrowing my eyes at Alain.

"Alain Fourchette, did you fuck my boyfriend?" I pointed a finger at him as Alain said *no* and Nanook said *yes* simultaneously.

They looked at each other then back at me as Alain said *maybe* while Nanook answered *he tried* before they both started howling with laughter shouting at each other to *look at her face, look at her face.*

"Oh God," Nanook said, hands on his knees as he doubled over, "I didn't sleep with your boyfriend, cow lady. Jesus Christ." He straightened up as Alain let loose the details of their accommodation.

"We've decided to share."

"Share?" I said blankly.

Nanook nodded and palmed my head. He shook it back and forth and announced that it was like a vacation condo. "I get you two weeks a month and every other holiday," he explained. I raised an eyebrow. Alain leaned over and interrupted, "But he cannot come to the door. He has to wait at the curb for you to leave the house." Nanook nodded and said from the side of his mouth, "I can't even touch the driveway."

My brain exploded.

I couldn't think of anything to say so I just turned around and walked down the hallway to Alain's cabin and shut the door. Behind me I heard Nanook say, "Told you she'd run," as Alain pulled an American twenty from his wallet and grudgingly handed it over.

ONE HUNDRED FIVE

They can't be serious. Were they really going to share me? I was perplexed. Never in my wildest calculations did I envision them being
friendly much less ganging up against me.

Or maybe they actually truly were serious. I pictured myself shuttling
from the Unicorn to Nanook and back again traversing the Canadian
skies every two weeks. I'll have a shitload of miles for sure. I tallied up
all those flights . "This is ridiculous," I announced to myself the idiocy
of this whole idea while contemplating whether it would work. I shook
my head. They must be joking.

It went on like this for a good thirty minutes while I pressed my ear
to the door listening intently to them bickering in the galley like an old
married couple about sandwiches with or without crusts. "I don't eat the
crusts so cut that shit off," Nanook complained. Alain informed him
that he was a guest on Nanette and the fucking crusts were staying right
where they were. There was the sound of a small scuffle before détente
was reached apparently by agreeing that Alain would not prevent
Nanook from removing the crusts as long as he didn't throw them out.
"Don't be wasteful," said the unicorn, the bread knife swishing against
the wood chopping block, "Trust me, when you're hungry you're
thankful for every single thing, even bread crusts."

"My bad," came Nanook's apologetic voice..

I wondered about the crust comment. I pictured Alain cold and small wondering where his next meal was coming from and felt a little bad about not cleaning all the food off my plate. I reconsidered the potential reasons he always seemed to use every tiny piece of leftovers in something else.

I took a deep breath, arranged my clothes as neatly as I could making sure the cashmere scarf was tied securely around my neck and arm and opened the door before proceeding confidently down the hallway toward the galley on a mission to figure out what the hell was going on up in this joint.

"I'll eat the crusts," I stepped up to the counter staring them both in the face. "Take one for the team and all that."

The unicorn smiled at me. Nanook shoved a toasted ham and cheese sandwich sans crust down his facehole.

Alain slid a sandwich across the counter. I pulled the plate toward me as Nanook's hand whipped across and flipped off the top piece of bread snatching the cheese right off the meat.

"Good call," said Alain.

"No cheese for you, cow lady," Nanook stacked the extra slice on top of his own sandwich and took another bite.

"I feel superfluous," I looked from one guy to the other in disbelief. "Do you two need a moment alone? Are you registered at Macy's or Pottery Barn?"

Nanook snorted and walked over to the sink to wash his hands. "Like he," Nanook flung a finger over his shoulder at Alain, "would ever be caught dead in a Macy's. Get real."

"I love Macy's," Alain replied, sounding wounded, "They're one of our biggest customers." "And that's where my favorite wizard shoes came from," I interjected in an attempt to stay relevant. Nanook smiled down at me and patted my face. Alain informed him I needed a new pair because my old ones were disintegrating.

"She wears them everywhere, you know," Alain leaned over and snatched up a towel from the counter. Nanook launched a beer at his head. Neatly snatching the projectile from the air, Alain precisely folded the linen and laid it gently next to the sink before flopping down on a stool and snapping open the can, "You should buy her another pair. Absolutely loves them. Loves them, don't you, butterfly?" I realized they were both staring at me so I agreed that yes, I did love them and would certainly accept a replacement.

"In red this time if that's possible, please," I asked politely.

"When we were in Campbell River she told me those wizard shoes brought the heat," Alain raised his eyebrows. Nanook laughed. "Oh yeah? How's that?"

I reminded them both that she was sitting right here listening.

Alain explained the circumstances of our wild trip in colorful terms including some unique descriptions of my sailing abilities as Nanook chuckled and laid back on the salon couch his drink propped up on his chest. "I thought for sure she was going over. No doubt about it. Going over into the water for certain," Alain described my extreme surfing maneuvers on the way through Whiskey Gulf.

"Nah, cow lady ran the numbers before pulling a stunt like that. She was never in any danger."

Alain reluctantly admitted I was an exceptional sailor.

"Well that's good cause she's shit at fishing, aren't you cow lady?" Nanook grinned at me over the edge of that can and I huffed at his remarks.

"Actually, she taught me to fly fish I'll have you know. And I caught something."

"Thank you, Alain, for standing up for me," I said. The unicorn informed Nanook that I probably destroyed one of his sweaters to do it.

"After she scrubbed it with a kitchen sponge," Alain whispered dramatically, "Cashmere. Armani!"

Nanook whistled. "More of a Bass Pro Shop guy myself but even I know not to scrub Armani anything with a kitchen sponge." He called me a heathen under his voice then asked when we'd be having dinner.

Alain replied, "Don't know. I'll call up to the house in a bit and see."

I turned away from Nanook and asked who owned that beautiful house on the hill. Alain looked me straight in the eyes and said, "Friend of a friend of an old lover."

"Ex-lover," he quickly qualified, "He and I were together for a while a few years ago." I looked at Nanook from the corner of my eye. "His loss," Nanook said blithely, got up and walked down the hall announcing he needed to use the bathroom.

I waited until the door shut before spinning around and asking Alain, "What the fuck is going on here" in a loud whisper. "Relax, butterfly," he leaned forward and thoroughly kissed me assuring me that Stephen was just a friend of a friend. Just a friend.

"I'm not talking about Stephen…Wait, is that his name?" I pointed toward the house and Alain confirmed that yes, the friend of a friend was Stephen. I waved my hands around frantically, "Not important. I mean, what the fuck with Nanook? How did he get here? And why are you so chummy?"

He told me that they'd had a delightful conversation while I was apparently on death's door and Nanook had hopped on a flight the very next day. "I guess it took a series of successively smaller planes followed by a water taxi of some sort to get to here," Alain shuddered. "You are lucky he loves you, butterfly, because the story of that trip sounds hellish. Just horrible."

"It was pretty shitty, I must admit," Nanook confirmed and flopped back down on the couch. "Trust me, they don't put the best pilots on these regional airlines." He lifted a hand above his head. "Me," he lowered his hand below his waist, "Them." Alain laughed as Nanook finished by saying clearly those guys had graduated below him in pilot training and he was lucky to have made it in one piece.

I held out my hands. "Ok, full stop. Full stop guys." Alain looked across at the couch and warned Nanook a truth moment was coming. "I'm fucking serious," I yelled and immediately apologized for raising my voice.

I breathed in deeply.

"And we're in a kitchen," Nanook butted in as I tried to speak.

"Goddamn it, shut up!" I apologized again.

Nanook stared at me and then across the room at Alain. "Did you do this? Did you do this to the cow lady?"

"Do what? What are you talking about?" I was confused.

He rolled his eyes. "You just apologized more in thirty seconds than I've heard you do the entire time I've known you." Turning to Alain, Nanook asked him if maybe a clot had broken loose and pulverized part of my brain. "Rude," I answered before Alain could reply, "So rude."

Nanook said, "My bad," but didn't sound sincere in the slightest. "I feel like we should be in a drum circle or something," Alain snickered from the corner of the galley and carefully pruned his basil plant with tiny silver scissors.

"Seriously. Seriously. For real, no seriously. I'm serious." That goddamn uncontrollable inappropriate laughter was headed my way, I could feel it. Trying to head it off at the pass I put my face down on the counter and thought calm things when suddenly Nanook told me, "Pull it together, you moron."

I couldn't help myself and just completely lost it.

ONE HUNDRED SIX

It took me a good ten minutes to stop the hysterics and I finally had to remove myself apologizing profusely back to the stern cabin to recover my composure. What the hell is going on here? I put my hand over my mouth to muffle the sound of my snorting. Deep breaths. Deep breaths. Take nice deep breaths. I flopped backward onto the bed letting out a yelp as my shoulder tweaked.

Six nanoseconds later the cabin door busted open as both boys shot into the room demanding I tell them immediately what was wrong.

"Get in bed," I said with all seriousness and stared at the ceiling, "Both of you get in this bed right now."

I have to give Nanook credit. He barely hesitated before hopping up on the comforter and racking out next to me in a big sprawl. Alain vaulted over my legs and landed on the other side. Nanook informed us that he wasn't going to be fucking either of us at that present moment so we should just all move on from that shit.

"Silence," I ordered and then shushed Alain before he could open his trap. We all just laid there in a nice row next to each other staring at the ceiling for a long minute before Nanook raised his hand.

"I recognize the gentleman from Alaska," I said.

"What are we doing here, cow lady," he asked. I informed him that was also my question to him.

"I'm here because you need help. Because Alain said you needed my help." He sighed deeply and rubbed his face. Turning slightly he reminded me that he hadn't seen me for almost a year and a half. "Nice hair, by the way," he rubbed his palm across my head gently. "You could have come to Seattle," I snipped him. He shot back, "Flights go both ways, sweetheart."

I was quiet for a few thoughts before I softly told him, "Thank you for coming down to help me. I do appreciate you taking time off work and spending the money to get here." He replied I was very welcome, picked up my hand and kissed the back of it gently.

"You realize I'm screwing Alain, right?" I just came out and said it. Right out there on the table I laid all those cards down.

"Yep".

"I also don't plan on stopping. This doesn't bother you?"

"Nope."

Alain whispered, "A man of few words is very attractive." Nanook swiftly reminded him to keep his mitts to himself.

In great detail I told them there was significant confusion on my part. Nanook eventually sat up, leaned over me and held out a palm. "Stop. Chillax. Seriously, give it a rest. What's happening here is I'm taking you back to Anchorage where you and your busted wing are going to get checked out." He flipped a thumb toward Alain. "Rico Suave is going home to Montreal to fix some corduroy crisis or something." A small sniff sounded beside me and Alain said under his voice, "Valentino is hardly a small crisis."

"Simmer down over there," Nanook gave him a pointed look before continuing. "I don't know anything more than that. This situation, this madness is a whole new world for me so just…stop. Stop with the questions and the analyzing of every little thing and just relax for once."

Very slowly Alain started to clap. Nanook gave a small bow and thanked the Academy for their support.

"He's right, you know," Alain agreed. "About the thinking and crunching and worrying. Also, I like him, surprisingly. And he likes me. I think so, at least."

"I do like you," Nanook admitted sheepishly. I started to feel like a third wheel.

Alain sat up and stuck his hand out over my face, Nanook reached over and shook it. "I can't promise that at some point I won't smash every bone in your face," Alain said conversationally, and tried to crush Nanook's fingers. He replied, "Bring it on princess."

I groaned.

Alain smiled, "But I can say that what the butterfly decides is best for her is what I will respect. Can you do the same?"

Nanook paused. "Only if you get me some of those sweaters. In green."

"You do look good in green," Alain winked and Nanook ripped his hand away before laying back down in a loud huff then thanking Alain for the complement.

It was all so nice and polite. So lovely, this complementing each other and being so civil. So nice. So nice. Just such a wonderfully delightful time we were having as I informed them that my new goal in life was to fuck them both simultaneously.

I smiled when Alain elbowed me. "Here here," he said from one side. Nanook held up a firm index finger from the other, "Not a chance, cow lady."

"Fine. Fine," I told them. "If you won't take your clothes off I guess I'll have to be satisfied with a burger."

A brief moment of silence rang through the cabin before Alain said, "Let me call up to the house." Nanook hopped swiftly up out of bed and ran off looking for his shoes rubbing his hands together in anticipation whispering *burgers burgers burgers*.

"Come on, butterfly," Alain pulled me to my feet and steadied me as the blood rushed back to my head. He leaned in and told me I had excellent taste in men and gave me many kudos for at least trying to get Nanook out of his pants. Carefully he shoved me down the hallway and up the ladder down onto the dock holding my hand tightly the whole way up the hill toward that beautiful brick house.

ONE HUNDRED SEVEN

The next morning a bright blue floatplane slid to a stop off the docks in front of the house while the three of us stood watching it taxi in. Nanook caught a line and tied it off while Alain tossed a canvas bag full of my things to the pilot who carefully stowed it in the back luggage bin. "You're sure Abraxis is up and out and secure," I fretted to Alain while Nanook discussed certifications and flying hours with our ride.

"Yes, Abraxis is on the hard and fully secured," Alain wrapped his arms around me from behind whispering in my ear that he was lonely already. "What about Meat? I left Meat out!" I looked back at his face in a panic as Alain assured me he'd thrown Meat into the cabin onto the dinette cushions.

"I don't even want to know what the two of you are discussing over here," Nanook shook his head and plugged his ears with his fingers before announcing we were GTG. "And Stephen is ok with Nanette being here for a while, right," I said as both Nanook and Alain said *give it a rest* in unison.

I felt a little picked on but turned and hugged Alain as closely as I could with my busted wing, "Will you call me sometime?" He smiled, "I'll call you all the time. Especially if you have to have surgery because who knows what delightful things you might say under the influence of all those drugs."

Nanook gave Alain a thumbs up and informed us he'd already wired the house for sound.

"Seriously," I whispered in Alain's ear, "Can I call you? Is that allowed?"

My lovely unicorn grabbed the back of my head and pulled me in for a long thorough kiss. Nanook made puking noises off the side of the dock and Alain informed me that not only could I call him but to expect a visit should I actually go under the knife. "You can stay in the room with all the boxes," Nanook offered, "Cow lady can stay upstairs with me."

"You're jeopardizing your sweaters," Alain smirked and the two of them shook hands and slapped each other's backs. With Nanook pulling on one arm and Alain pushing gently from behind I managed to get into the plane without falling into the water. "Thank Stephen for the sling," I said over my shoulder to Alain. He assured me he would.

"This is just still so incredibly strange…" I opened my mouth to continue when Nanook said *Jesus Christ* and slapped a headset over my ears. Alain rolled his eyes and slammed the door shut.

The propeller spun up with a loud whir and as we pulled away I smashed myself against the window and blew kisses at my gorgeous Frenchman until he faded away into the distance.

I managed to make it all the way down to Denny Island before I asked the crucial question, "How exactly are we landing this on a runway that's not water?" Nanook grinned and said that we were just going to crash it and hope for the best. I shot a look at the back of the pilot's head before telling Nanook he needed to check himself. "I'm serious," I leaned toward the glass and tried to look down at the pontoons. "How are we landing this thing? I need information about this process."

"There's landing gear under the floats, cow lady," Nanook said into the headset. I heard the pilot softly laugh at my nickname. Seeing the continuing consternation, Nanook helpfully simulated the physics of landing with his hands telling me all the various steps and where things could go wrong, possible mitigations and how to exit the plane if we actually did crash. "I feel better," I proclaimed with a big smile. Nanook replied, "That's fabulous because I'm fucking exhausted."

We came in for a rather hard landing and I gripped his knee with my good hand while he assured me everything was proceeding normally.

"Thank god that's over," I politely thanked the uniformed pilot for not squashing me against the tarmac at high speed. He replied that I was very welcome and tipped his hat before handing Nanook my bag and hopping back into the cockpit.

"Canadians pilots are so much nicer," I ribbed Nanook as he dragged my bag across the tarmac by one strap. "The rich ones can afford to be," he replied.

"Stephen must have a lot of money to set this up so fast."

He looked over at my face and turned away without comment as he opened the terminal doors. "You're a quick one, cow lady," he said and tossed my bag to the side before pulling over some chairs.

I cracked open a Coke and commented that I didn't know commercial airlines flew out to small places like Denny Island. He slowly put his face in his hands and groaned loudly, "Are you fucking serious?" He flicked me in the nose and told me Alain was worth millions and we were flying home to Anchorage on *that*. I looked down his outstretched arm following his finger out the window as a sleek Gulfstream rolled to a stop outside the terminal.

I blinked. There on the side of that goddamn plane were the letters ANF in solid black type and I had a very bad feeling that someone had purposefully given me an incomplete data set. I gently reached my good hand into my pocket and pulled out my cell phone. I stared at it for a moment mentally calculating international roaming fees while Nanook silently laughed and poked my leg over and over and over.

"This isn't funny."

Nanook assured me it was hilarious and Alain owed him a twenty because it'd taken so long for me to realize the unicorn was ridiculously wealthy. "He said you'd crunch the numbers by the time the floatplane got to the house but I knew you'd need that fucking Gulfstream in your face to put it together." He lightly tapped the back of my head and helped me stand up as a uniformed attendant came and silently collected my bag whisking it out to the tarmac. I stood mutely watching that brilliant white bird magically materialize a set of stairs from behind the cockpit and thought deeply about this new data.

As we walked out to the jet I informed Nanook that he was the one that should feel moronic for betting a zillionaire a measly twenty bucks on what he apparently felt was a sure thing. "Never bet more than you're willing to lose, cow lady," he answered. "First rule of poker…gotta know when to fold."

I stepped up the stairs into the cream and blue interior and slowly trailed my fingers down the leather seats across the mirror finish of the wood trim finally sinking into a chair. Nanook plopped into a seat facing me. He stretched out his legs, set an elbow on the table and inquired of the attractive attendant what she could offer him in the way of adult beverages.

"Scares me when you're quiet, cow lady," he handed our passports to the pilot who politely asked me if I needed anything. "No, thank you," I answered faintly when he pointed out the large bedroom at the back of the jet and told me I was welcome to it.

The stairs retracted and the engines spun up. I looked down at that phone gripped tightly in my palm. Using a single index finger I pecked out *structured finance transaction* and hit Send.

No clue came the reply thirty seconds later followed swiftly with *I never listen when the lawyers talk.*

I stole a look at Nanook's closed eyes as he reclined sighing with delight and answered *Triskets and Questionable Cheddar.*

The jet turned slightly at the end of the runway and I heard the engines revving for takeoff. The unicorn sent back six dollar signs followed by a question mark.

Deep in thought I considered my options as the sunlight gleamed off the water receding quickly beneath us.

A watermaker and autohelm.

My phone buzzed.

Done…as long as I get the originals.

As we passed out of cell range a last text popped up on the screen. I set the phone gently on the table and bent over to read the message.

Tell Nanook he can suck it.

"You going to use that bed, cow lady?" Nanook rubbed his face with his hands and glanced at me over the table, "I feel like I need a serious nap and this chair ain't cutting it." Twenty thousand feet in the air over Ketchikan I sat in that fancy jet and stared at him in his standard sweater and average blue jeans. I looked around the edge of the table at his sockless feet pushed into those inexpensive slip on shoes. Watched him tap his long fingers on the table as the light bounced off the Breitling watch he'd always worn for as long as I'd known him. The same watch you'd worn except the call sign on the back of his said *Jester*.

He was so beautiful. How did I ever get this lucky? I leaned forward and took his hand in mine. I rubbed my fingers gently across his palm and whispered, "You never called, did you."

He looked away.

He looked away and said, "No".

"Alain called me," Nanook finally said after we'd stared at each other for a few minutes. "He actually called me eleven times. In a row. Over and over until I finally answered the phone intending to tell whoever it was to fuck off but…"

"Because you thought it was me calling."

He braced his forearms on the table and laced his fingers together and nodded his head as he stared down at that watch. "What have you been doing for the past year and a half?" I asked him, knowing the answer that was coming and dreading it still the same.

"Getting over you, cow lady."

Nanook got up from the table and slowly walked past me, his hand lightly gripping my shoulder. As he moved back toward the bedroom I stood and followed. I put my foot in the door when he tried to close it and pushed my way past him when he stuck a hand out to prevent me from entering.

I stood there with my back to that door and saw him sit slowly on the edge of the bed watching me with careful eyes. "I'm not running away from this," I slid against the door downward toward the floor and sucked my knees up under my chin, "And neither are you."

Silence. We sat in silence because there were too many things to say. Where do you even start in a situation like this? At the beginning? Where I broke him? "Why are you here," I tapped him on his toes with my shoe until he looked over at my face. "I don't know," he admitted, heaved out a big sigh and flopped back onto the bed his hands over his face.

"Help me up. Help a sister out." I grunted and tried to get back to my feet. He reached out a hand to steady my arm. "Jesus, cow lady," he laughed as I pitched to the side. I stood and sat on the edge of the bed. "Sit down, take a load off," I patted the comforter, "Put your feet up."

Nanook looked at me warily but kicked off his shoes and sat back down at a safe and respectable distance. "Relax, sweetheart," I rolled my eyes, "Your virtue is safe with me."

"That's too bad," he said with a smirk.

"See? You say you're over me and then you act all flirty," I was confused. "What's the deal?"

"I never said I was over you, just that I'm trying to get over you," he explained. "Trying. Operative word. Trying to get over you."

I raised an eyebrow, fell backward and looked up at the ceiling. A few minutes passed before I felt him pulling those wizard shoes off my feet muttering something about angry unicorns and mud never completely coming out of silk before he rolled over next to me and stared down at my face.

He opened his mouth as I started to say something. "Sorry, you go," he said, zipping his lips. I swallowed hard and sucked down every bit of my considerable pride and closed my eyes.

"I'm sorry I said those horrible things to you. In the kitchen. Both times. All the times, really."

Nanook laid down on his back next to me and we both stared at the ceiling. "Alain told me I have a mean streak," I continued, "that I'm a bully. A horrible vicious person comes out sometimes he says and he's right, you know." I felt the tears getting backed up in my throat but I pushed right on through. "I am a bully. I am. And what's worse is I like it."

He was very still and silent when I told him I'd meant those things in the kitchen. I'd meant them and I'd said them trying to shoot him down. Pulling that trigger over and over with the pistol to his heart I'd done it on purpose. I'd killed him in that kitchen and I liked it, I whispered to him as I cried, "I liked it even though I hated myself for doing it."

He slowly rubbed his thumb across the back of my hand.

"I don't know why I'm like this because I don't want to be like this. " I tossed my good arm over my eyes and sobbed. "I don't like myself and you don't like me either. How can anyone like me when I kill people for fun. When I killed you when I broke you. When I broke you on purpose. That's not love."

"No, that's not love, cow lady," he whispered. I told him I knew why you went to her, "Why Andy walked out and went to her. Because she wasn't me. She didn't slice him up and cut him down because she could. I did that. That was my job."

"You can't blame yourself for what Andy did," Nanook rolled over and looked down at my red face. "What he did wasn't right. It wasn't right. No matter what you did, it wasn't right to behave that way."

I gave him a sad smile. "It's not even the sex," I explained and rolled the side of my cheek into his hand, "It's the words. The lies. It's the lying that's so awful, that hurts the most."

"I always thought people were dumb when they said it wasn't the sex," he curled his fingers around the back of my neck and tucked me tightly into his side, "but I can see how the lies and the secrets would be worse. How the lies could cut more deeply. Those lies drew a lot of blood, didn't they. Didn't they."

He slipped a pillow under my head and skootched closer until we were nose to nose.

"I'm sorry too," he swallowed roughly, "When I said we happened because we were just available it wasn't true. I knew it would hurt, that it would drive you away and I wanted that. I wanted you to leave because I couldn't bring myself to make you go. I didn't want you to go. But we're not good for each other. We're just not good together."

I tapped a finger on his cheek and reminded him about those socks slung over the towel rod at the Holiday Inn, "We're damn good together."

"You know what I mean," Nanook grinned and moved an inch closer. I stared into his face as he leaned forward and kissed me gently. "Do you still feel guilty about us?" I asked, remembering that mouth saying *maybe* in the graveyard.

His lips said *not really* as his hand slipped up the side of my leg and loosely gripped my waist. "But why are you trying to get over me if you don't really feel guilty about us," I closed my eyes and held my breath when he pulled my thigh under his holding me firmly against him.

"Because you're Andy's girl," he said, "Because you'll always be Andy's girl to me."

"Do you think you could ever look down at my face and see me as more than just Andy's Girl?" I asked desperately. He ran his mouth up the side of my jawbone toward the corner of my lips. "I don't know," he answered, breathing heavily.

He suddenly rolled away in frustration, "You're like crack! It's fucking ridiculous. Here I am trying to break up with you and all I can think about is ripping your clothes off!"

There were a few seconds of silence before he admitted, "Also, we're currently in a bed on a super expensive jet that belongs to your really rich boyfriend who is strangely ok with me ripping your clothes off…which is a little uncomfortable for me." I told him Alain would be delighted that he'd gotten Nanook into one of his beds albeit extremely disappointed that it was only with me and the unicorn had not been invited.

"You don't think it's a little creepy," he wrinkled up his face a little. "Baby, he fucks other guys. That's…weird. And gross." He paused. "But I must admit he's uber charming and, in my staunchly heterosexual opinion, incredibly good looking." I laughed. "You sure you don't want to ride my unicorn," I teased him and he shook his head saying firmly *no no no.*

"Seriously," he rolled over and propped his head on his hand. "Seriously. That's not weird for you?"

"No. Surprisingly, no. Not weird at all." I flipped a blanket over one side of my body and he tucked it under me so I resembled a giant burrito. "I thought it would be strange. That it would be a much bigger deal. Deal breaker, actually. But it's not."

"And why is that, please enlighten me," he tapped a finger on his chin.

I considered his question. "Does it gross you out to think about me with another woman?"

"Fuck no, that's hot," he immediately shot back and asked me to put a percentage possibility on this particular activity occurring.

"Then why shouldn't the opposite be true? I think it's actually kinda sexy thinking about him with someone else. Even if that someone else is a guy." I turned and looked wide-eyed at Nanook who raised an eyebrow and told me I had serious issues. "You need help," he said and I proceeded to tell him I liked it rough so he should bring his whips and chains.

"Oh my god," he grabbed his hair in his hands and kicked his legs around on the bed flailing to and fro. "The girl I'm in love with is also dating a rich guy who screws dudes plus she wants me to rough her up in the sack while she fucks another chick." He threw his arms in the air clenching his fists as he gleefully shouted *JACKPOT!*

I snickered and wiggled inside the burrito nest before asking him, "In all seriousness, what's the plan here?" "How about we don't have a plan for once," Nanook grabbed me by the ankles and slid me through the comforter tube toward the end of the bed. "I need a plan. I need contingencies," I laughed. He slammed a pillow over my face.

"Be careful, I'm broken! Watch out for my busted wing!"

He tipped the edge of the pillow up. "Let's take it one day at a time, cow lady."

He reluctantly admitted that maybe he could deal as long as we drew some boundary lines and he didn't have to screw Alain. That he wasn't totally over me even though he'd given it a damn good try. If the three of us didn't vacation together but he was still invited to all the company's private box sporting events. Possibly he could think of me as more than Andy's Girl if he put a bag over my head in bed. I could also try to be nicer and not so nasty.

"How about we just start over and see what happens," he said.

"Just think of it as if we're seriously dating but neither one of us is in an exclusive relationship. You can just pretend he doesn't exist if that helps," I explained as he shoved my wizard shoes back on my feet and helped me out of bed. "Except I've met Alain and I actually really like him," Nanook admitted sheepishly, "which is not good. I'm kinda jealous you get him all to yourself."

He flung his arms around and gestured at the room, "I want to fly around on the fancy jet! Sail the big boat! Piles of cash and dancing ladies! It's not fair that you reap the rewards of this bargain and I get nothing!"

I informed him the pleasure of my company was hardly nothing and that there was a stack of super nice sweaters headed his way. He reluctantly admitted he was receiving some minor consideration. "Miniscule. Infinitesimal," he pinched his fingers together and shoved them into my face, "I'm going to need a lot more than sweaters if this time share is going to work out."

"He's got a really nice bread knife," I reminded him. Reluctantly he conceded an obscenely expensive cutlery set would sweeten the pot slightly. "And maybe a new garbage disposal," he sniffed and reminded me I was responsible for the damage to his current one.

"Well, make Alain a list," I poked him in the arm before he shoved me down the aisle toward a table covered with snacks.

"I just might," Nanook answered. He slid the cheese tray away from my hands and replaced it with a plate of fresh fruit. I wondered what he might put on that list and considered the myriad possibilities while I fiddled with my silverware.

He smiled. "I know what you're thinking."

"And what would that be," I speared a watermelon slice and carefully put it on a small china plate. Nanook rose and rummaged around in his bag for a minute before pulling out a small red notepad and pencil.

"Rack and stack, cow lady," he flipped it open to a new page, "let's do this."

ONE HUNDRED NINE

'No! No," I howled, "You should get a Maserati for the first time and a Honda Accord every third time thereafter." Nanook rolled onto his side and held his stomach. "If you think I'm going to settle for a Honda Accord you're fucking delusional. I'm going to need at least a Jaguar F-Type. And not every third time…every time." "Except the first time which is the Maserati, right," I scribbled a line across the notepad with the pencil scratching out our previous calculations. Nanook confirmed the Maserati was the first occurrence.

"Payment before or after? We might have an issue with buyer's remorse. Also, we should discuss what constitutes material breach and the potential calculation of damages," I looked up with pencil poised at the pilot walking down the aisle toward us. "Hey Robert," Nanook said from his spot on the couch, "what's up." The pilot informed us we were going to be landing in Anchorage shortly and would be collecting the plates soon. "No problem," I piped up, "we'll pick up all our stuff in a minute." He assured us the cabin staff would take care of everything. Nanook held up a finger.

"Yo, Robert, one sec." The pilot turned and Nanook asked him, "How much do you think a hand job from me is worth?"

Robert paused. "Certainly more than an Accord but unfortunately less than a Maserati, sir. No offense."

I jumped on that. "No, the Maserati is if he lets the unicorn fuck him in the ass."

The pilot grinned. "In that particular case, I do believe it is the classic seller's market and I would hike my prices as high as I could."

"Oh he'll be hiking something up high, that's for certain," I snickered. Nanook threw a grape at my face and missed, rebounding it off the cabin window into the seats.

Robert laughed.

"You are a fisherman, are you not," he glanced surreptitiously over his shoulder toward the cockpit where the co-pilot was tending the controls. "I am indeed," Nanook leaned forward in anticipation.

"The Fourchette's have a lovely home in Banff on the Upper Bow River," Robert whispered, "Perhaps you could request transportation to and use of the residence during brown trout season in exchange for certain…occurrences." Nanook's eyes brightened, "Brown trout, huh." He thought swiftly before informing me he would need two consecutive weeks during the March to November brown trout season for every hand job.

Robert cleared his throat.

"Too high? Two weeks is too high? Probably too high," Nanook analzyed silently.

"One week?"

Robert wiggled a hand.

"Three-day weekend?"

This got the thumbs-up from Robert and he headed back toward the cockpit. Exchanging high-fives with Nanook, I memorialized the change swiftly while the cabin crew locked everything down on final.

ONE HUNDRED TEN

"This is quite the list," Alain said through the phone in an amused tone that evening while I reclined on Nanook's couch propping a giant bag of ice on my shoulder. "We thought you would appreciate having an itemization emailed over so that you could estimate your potential future financial expenditures," I shifted slightly and heard Alain laugh. Nanook sailed into the room on his way from the kitchen to the grill shouting out, "I'll need that Maserati in red, Rico Suave," on his way by.

A soft rustling of paper came through the line while Alain flipped through the document. "I can see here I will need to purchase additional stock in Honda…and possibly Jaguar. The fee for the hand jobs is a little high but I think there is room for negotiation." I yelled to Nanook through the open screen door that Alain thought his hand jobs were overvalued. He sent me back a double bird from behind the grill. "Mine are epic," I confirmed on the down-low to Alain, "that's what I've been told in the past."

"Are you charging for yours, butterfly?"

I snorted. "You can't afford me."

Alain assured me he most definitely could.

"Seriously, is ANF your company? What does ANF stand for?" I slowly stood up from the couch and motioned to Nanook that I was going to the bathroom. He threw me an OK and the ten-minutes-till-dinner sign.

"No Google, Source of All Truth and Knowledge?" the unicorn teased as I walked slowly down the hallway after setting the ice on a towel Nanook had prepositioned next to the coffee table. "I considered Googling you, actually," I admitted. "But it felt like an invasion of privacy and all. If I want to know something I'll just ask. It just felt…creepy." There was a brief moment of silence before he softly said, "Unexpected. But much appreciated."

"Yeah, well, I can't promise I won't in the future because goddamn it was hard not to get on the Internet and stalk your ass."

The unicorn laughed and helpfully explained that the company was actually a family business still run by his father. "So you're the playboy dilettante of the Fourchette clan, huh," I needled him and he confirmed that he did very little work but still took home a gigantic paycheck.

"Although the work I do perform is quite good, I must say. When I put my mind to it I am actually a half-way decent employee."

"So the ANF is…" I bent over the sink and splashed water on my face.

"It's the first initials of my parents, Armand and Nanette."

I put a hand on the counter and sternly asked him if he'd named his boat after his mother, "Have I been screwing you inside your mother?" I tapped my finger against the mouthpiece and informed him there might be some serious interference on our line. He started laughing. "My mother died when I was a child," he replied, "but I'm sure she would have found this very entertaining if she were still alive. She would have liked you. I think she would have liked you very much."

"I'm sorry. I didn't realize your mother was gone," I said uncomfortably and felt rather bad that I'd made a sexual joke about a dead person.

"That's ok, butterfly," I could hear him shrugging over the phone, "You didn't know."

Nanook pounded on the door with his palm and announced dinner would be served shortly in the main dining room to be followed by a brief chamber orchestra performance on the back lawn. "I have to go," I told Alain, "James Beard's been slaving over tubs of macaroni salad for hours out there."

I threw the door open and walked down the hallway assuring Alain there wasn't any mayonnaise or cheese or butter or anything else bad for my health on the dinner menu before heading for the open bag of potato chips laying on the kitchen counter. "I will ignore the crunching noises for this one time only," Alain warned me, "Don't forget I have Nanook's number as well. I am not above threatening him, you know."

"Well you certainly won't get in his pants with that attitude even if you do promise him a Maserati," I quietly reached in the bag for another round. The only reply I heard was a dial tone. Stunned, I pulled the phone away from my ear and stared down at it as Nanook's ringtone trilled out from the deck.

"Hello? Yeah. Uh huh. Uh huh." Nanook looked up at me and narrowed his eyes. "She did? Sadly, I can believe that." Nanook shoved the screen door open, walked past me and snatched the bag of potato chips off the counter and dumped the whole thing into the garbage disposal staring me in the eyes the entire time.

"I'd prefer black," he said.

He flipped the tap on and ran the water through the disposal until all the chips were destroyed before handing me a plate and hauling me back out to the grill, "No, it needs to be leather. Yes, real leather. Don't be cheap."

He slid a large piece of fish off the cedar planking onto my plate, pointed the tongs at the table and raised an eyebrow, "And none of that basic shit. It needs to be fully loaded. All the upgrades."

Nanook circled the tongs in the air with a sense of urgency. I realized he was waiting for me to put my plate down and bring him the empty one off the table. I hustled over and returned with a dish. I held it while he served himself up some food with one hand, the other holding the phone against his ear.

"Well, you get what you pay for, princess. If you want a low budget screw I'll be more than happy to accept less than the full sports package." He winked at me. "Just send me a catalog and I'll circle what I want. I'll even earmark the pages for you if you need me to."

"And I'll need it personally delivered. No, to the front door." He rolled his eyes and gave me the money sign. "Of course it has to be brand new. You're getting pristine product, my friend, quid pro quo. Quid pro quo."

And he hung up.

"Great news, good news, bad news, ridiculous news or fucking ridiculous news," I sighed, giving Alain his choice of doom as we talked on the phone the next day. "Let's go down the list," he said and I heard the rustling of sheets in the background. "Probably going to regret asking this but…are you in bed?" I immediately qualified, "Not asking if you're alone but isn't a little late to be snoozing?"

Alain informed me that my lung fung had made him slightly ill, "Also, sailing is hard work. I forgot how tiring it can be so I've been going in to the factory late and sleeping in." I apologized for turning Nanette into a hot zone and he inquired as to my orthopedic status.

"Well, great news is I didn't do any major damage. Bad news is I did tear something. But only a little, which is the good news."

"And the fucking ridiculous news," his voice sounded slightly jumbled and I realized he was brushing his teeth. "Aren't we getting all domesticated now," I said. He snorted and sucked some toothpaste into the wrong tube. He coughed a few times and instructed me to continue my health analysis. "Pay no attention to me dying of asphyxiation over here, no really I'm fine and thank you for your concern," he added and I heard the faucet turn on.

"The ridiculous news is I am getting cut," I admitted, "and the fucking ridiculous part is the doctor gave me a choice and I actually picked the surgery option." Alain sounded puzzled, "Why on earth would you choose surgery if you didn't need it?"

I explained that surgery was best for traumatic injuries and Alain interjected that the circumstances surrounding the injury were indeed traumatic for him and he would shortly be receiving intensive therapy. "Butterfly, the sight of you coming half naked out from Abraxis in that long underwear with no warning haunts my mind." He sadly told me he would likely be permanently damaged.

I reminded him that the incident resulted in a very nice afternoon for him, thank you very much, "As well as an occurrence that was completely free, I might add." He quickly explained that his forking over of the watermaker and autohelm was hardly gratis.

"You did that to yourself with the Questionable Cheddar." I told him he should never have left those fancy binoculars on Nanette, "Clearly you should have realized I'd look at the manual and photograph you Trisket-ing."

"How was I to know the depths of your evil soul," he replied, "Now explain why you are voluntarily going under the knife, please."

I told him the doctor recommended surgery since sailing was repetitive overhead motions and physical therapy wouldn't help as much considering my shoulder was used so often. "If you took Nanette you wouldn't have to worry about that," Alain said, "She could auto you to wherever you like while you eat bon bons and watch soap operas over my satellite tv."

"Yes, because that's totally why I sail." I sighed dramatically, "It's the thrill of conquering nature! The excitement! The danger!" "The wet boots, manual labor, lack of adequate personal hygiene facilities," he continued, "Blows my mind everyone doesn't participate in this extraordinary activity to the exclusion of all other things like lounging on tropical beaches drinking mai tais."

Grudgingly I admitted Abraxis was rustic at best and thanked him for his Nanette offer. "I might take you up on that in the future as long as that delicious cabin boy comes with."

"That can certainly be arranged," he replied, the sound of a zipper coming through the phone as a voice in the background said *have a good day sir* followed by the rumble of a very powerful sports car charging down the line.

"Did someone just bring you a Formula One and wish you good day?"

"Yes," he said, wheels squealing as he gunned the car down the driveway. "That's Henri. We imported him from Paris. He's quite accomplished in the world of butlering. Buttleing? He's a butler," Alain concluded and I started laughing.

"You have a butler? No wonder the Mr. Coffee was beyond your comprehension, fancy pants."

"Pick up the pace, butterfly, I'm almost to the factory," the unicorn sniffed and I could tell his nose was pointed toward the sky. I finished explaining the surgical calendar. "I'll need a day or three to make sure Abraxis is all set in Shearwater for the winter because there will be no open ocean anything for at least four months. Even I'm not foolhardy enough to make the Sitka crossing in December. Plus, I'll have to make some sort of housing arrangement or something because I think the thought of twenty-four seven me is sending Nanook into severe depression. He's a solitary cat, you know. Pretty sure he's close to feeling impinged upon."

Alain paused. "Can you do physical therapy from anywhere after your doctor clears you from the actual procedure?"

"Probably."

"You will come here," he announced in a firm voice.

"Phrasing, unicorn. Phrasing," I reminded him. He cleared his throat.

"I would be happy to tolerate your presence for part of your recovery period as a gesture of good will," he said carefully. "Purely for your personal safety, of course, since Nanook is likely to smother you in your sleep at some point. Your interminable yakking brings out thoughts of homicide in even the most manly of men."

"I'll be sure to communicate your appreciation of his physique," I assured him and heard a window rolling down and his voice speaking to a random gate guard. "I have to go," the unicorn said and requested I send him a printed timeline of the upcoming events so he could plan a jaunt to the backwoods of Anchorage. "Broken down into six-minute increments, please," Alain politely requested, "I need to keep my billing costs down or my father will cut off my Amex even though technically it has no limit."

"I miss you," I said softly. Alain made kissy noises into the phone, told me he'd seen me soon and hung up.

ONE HUNDRED TWELVE

A few days later Nanook drove me over to PAMC at an obscenely early hour while I complained about being hungry. "Even just an egg, they couldn't even just let me have a single solitary egg," I tried to cross my arms and was quickly reminded of why I could not. "Do you want to spend the entire time recovering from anesthesia throwing up into a bedpan?" He looked over at me. I sat in silence.

"Didn't think so," he said.

"And they've noted on my admissions paperwork a low cholesterol diet!" I tossed the consent for surgery papers down in frustration after signing them in the surgical prep room and tugged on the tie of my backless hospital gown. "Why does that matter? Hospital food is horrible," Nanook shuddered and pulled a huge black marker from his bag before walking over to the gurney. "Are you kidding? I love hospital food! Mmmmmm…unlimited graham crackers and apple juice and jello and that high sodium beef meatloaf stuff with the tiny canned mushrooms," I smacked my lips. He pulled my gown down around my waist.

He stopped with the marker poised above my shoulder, "Are you sure your doctor is ok with me doing this? I feel like I'm busting procedure or something." I assured him as long as he stayed within the lines they'd drawn he could put whatever he wanted. "Go," he said and I instructed him to put large arrows going up toward my shoulder ending with a giant X next to where the surgical staff had already made their own notations in black ink.

He looked down at my face. "You realize that they're just going to scrub this off as soon as you're under, right? That's why this marker is water soluble." Nanook wagged it in my face. I told him to write *ONLY CUT HERE* next to the giant X. "I know. But I feel better if we're all on the same page when I can't actually observe what they're doing myself," I admitted sheepishly, "Now get the red one."

Nanook groaned and motioned like he was cutting his own throat before pulling another marker from his back pocket. "I think you'll be ok, cow lady," he said and wrote *NO NO NO* in crimson on my good shoulder. "Now put the words *OR I'LL FUCKING SUE* right underneath the *NO NO NO*," I demanded. He stepped back and firmly told me this madness had concluded. "I'm not threatening the surgeon with legal action," he said just as the nurse came into the room, her eyebrows raised.

"Take a picture with your cell phone. I need it for evidence," I ordered. He ignored me, pulled my gown back up and begged the nurse to put him out of his misery. I stared up desperately at his face telling him I was really scared and begged him not to leave me in this horrible place by myself. My hand gripped his tightly and I tried not to panic as he walked next to the gurney towards the OR. "You'll be fine, baby," he leaned down and gave me a kiss when we reached a set of double doors, "I'll be here the whole time."

The nurse hit the button and shoved me into a beige hallway as his face disappeared. I heard that awful buzzing noise of security doors slamming shut and suddenly felt like an unwanted sock disintegrating away into the darkness.

ONE HUNDRED THIRTEEN

"It's supposed to be an outpatient procedure," I heard someone say faintly, "but it looks like they're keeping her for observation at least overnight." Sucks to be her. I pitied that poor loser and contemplated the marvelous texture of my inner eyelids.

"Not quite sure but they've got her wired up like a Christmas tree."

The voice sounded familiar.

"Well, I can't leave her alone or I'd come pick you up. I promised I'd be here the whole time." I realized it was Nanook talking. My chest rose and I sucked in air but I couldn't stop it.

I couldn't stop it because I wasn't doing it.

Screaming silently in my head *help someone help me help me don't leave don't leave* I begged him not to abandon me as his voice disappeared into the distance.

ONE HUNDRED FOURTEEN

A soft beeping noise split the silence and woke me up. I felt more in control. The tube was gone and my throat was better. This was better. I felt better now so let's get this show on the road. Let's blow this joint.

I moved a single finger.

They were moving, right? I felt like my fingers are moving. I wiggled them again. Flipping you the bird, PAMC.

Your ass is grass when I get out of here. Lawsuit time, bitches.

"You must be the unicorn," an amused voice said and a French accent replied back that he was indeed the very same. "She made certain while we were prepping her to have you included on her family visitor list," the stranger said. I assumed it was the doctor. Alain responded with some smart comment. The doctor laughed and papers rustled next to my ear.

"Apparently the three names she insisted on including were Nanook of the North, the Unicorn, which is you, apparently, and Santa Clause." The doctor hesitated. "That's 'clause' with an *e*. Something about her adhering to the spirit if not the letter of the laws of Christmas and partially performing the good behavior requirement and there's a notation about some random words regarding the renegotiation of a gift of some sort."

I heard a snort from the corner.

"May I see that please," Alain said and I heard the sound of an iPhone snapping a photo, "because I am putting this in my blackmail file immediately." "Gotta balance out that Questionable Cheddar, huh," Nanook's voice commented before the doctor continued.

"You'll see here," the soft tapping noise of a finger hitting a folder came from the other side of my head, "that she specifically instructed us, and I quote, 'to look in the closet for the unicorn because he stands in there sometimes but not all the times'. She also requested the aliases 'cow lady' and 'butterfly' be added to her official record for identification purposes." Nanook burst out laughing. Alain muttered something in French under his breath. The blanket slipped off my torso as the doctor confided to the boys that he didn't know what the hell was going on with me but that I was the most entertaining patient he'd had in a long time.

He then inquired as to our connections, Nanook answering, "Boy-friend," while Alain said, "Lover." There was a moment of silence before the doctor responded cheerfully, "Ok. Well, clearly it takes a village with this one. I'll be back in a bit to check on her status."

ONE HUNDRED FIFTEEN

I heard the door shut and a chair squeaked across the floor followed shortly after by a gigantic sigh. "Eight years of this and yet you have survived with mental faculties intact," Alain said in a stunned tone. Nanook told him it was actually ten years or so because you'd been gone for a while now.

A moment of silence passed before Alain softly said you must have loved me very much.

"He did love her. Mad love. Hollywood love. But Andy dinged her up pretty bad at the end so…please be careful," Nanook whispered. They sounded sad and I wondered if I were dying or something. Then I felt sad so I wiggled my mental fingers a few times, told my face to look more alive and tried my best to be better.

Nanook told Alain he hadn't wanted to love me but it just happened. "Like some cheesy romance novel or something," he said. "Just…boom. I couldn't stop it. It was horrible, wanting her like that and Andy being my best friend and all."

"That does sound horrible," Alain responded.

There was a rustling readjustment noise of some sort before Nanook's words drifted past, "He wouldn't have shared her, you know.

With me. We weren't like that, me and Andy. We weren't those kinds of friends." He laughed, "And she wouldn't have done it anyway back then. A serial monogamist, Andy used to call her. Clearly she's changed in that regard."

"Is this going to be a problem, you and me," Alain said evenly. "Because you don't seem like the type to share either, quite frankly."

I worried that a beat-down was coming and started planning an exit strategy before I realized there was no exit. Well, there was an exit I just didn't know where it was located. I reminded myself to review the hospital emergency procedures again when I regained my powers of movement.

Nanook sighed deeply. "I don't know anything anymore. It's all so upside down. I tried to cut her loose on the plane but I just couldn't get there. Couldn't do it." I heard him shift in his chair. "It's weird for me…her with you and me wanting to be with her…and I'm super uncomfortable talking to you about this but…" He took a deep breath. "I love her and I want to be in her life so I'll adjust to you and her and me and this bizarreness, I guess. I'll try to anyway."

"You don't have a moral problem with this situation?" The unicorn reminded him that Americans were prudes and had some sort of strange obsession with monogamy.

"Well, yeah, I have a huge fucking problem with it but if I forced her to choose I don't know if I'd come out on top," Nanook sounded rather offended.

"I think she'd walk away from both of us if we asked her to make a choice," said Alain matter-of-factly.

Would I walk away from both of them and sail off into the sunset alone? Hmmmm… I felt sick to my stomach when I thought about the possibility of losing Nanook forever. That would be horrible not to have him in my life at all. But simultaneously I cringed at the prospect of never kissing the unicorn again. What a clusterfuck this was turning out

to be. My nose started itching. And what the hell was a serial monogamist?

"Have you ever been friends with anyone without screwing them?"
said Nanook.

Oh boy, this could be a bigger problem than two boyfriends. I adjusted my earlier stratification of comments precipitating a beat-down.

"Because as much as I like you, dude," he continued, "and totally
want that Maserati, you have to realize you're never going to get a piece
of this." I envisioned him gesturing at himself and silently snickered.

Alain responded that he was well aware Nanook would never put out
and he was ok with that. "And yes, I've been friends with people I didn't
sleep with," he finished in an even tone of voice.

I breathed a sigh of relief but felt strangely upset that there might
not be any more naughty banter between the two of them. Kings of
Repartee, they were. I congratulated myself on snatching up two
excellent conversationalists.

A pause ensued and I tried to master the art of finger movement
beneath the blankets.

"I think we could be friends," said Alain after a long minute, "although this would be new territory for me. You, who I will sadly not be
sleeping with. The butterfly or cow lady or whatever alias she chooses.
And me."

Nanook laughed.

"Uncharted territory for sure," he agreed and I heard him get up from his
chair. "All I ask is we don't undermine each other. She needs to choose, if she
decides she wants to choose, on her own. Equal chances." I heard another
chair squeak and felt rather disappointed my eyes wouldn't obey me and open
so that I could witness the bromance for myself.

"I was looking for a handshake but I'll accept a hug," came Nanook's
muffled voice as Alain promised to keep his mitts above the waist.

The door opened and I heard the doctor say that his day just kept getting better and better, his shoes tapping across the floor. I could feel Nanook blushing which was confirmed by some awkward throat clearing noises.

"I'm French," Alain explained smoothly, "We believe in physical touching during times of great distress." The doctor commented that he himself was often in distress and thus probably should have married a Frenchwoman, a statement to which Alain and Nanook both whole-heartedly agreed. "I love French women," Nanook mused and proceeded to tell an absolutely foul story about a deployment in Paris, a pint glass and a set of brunette twins that left the three of them in absolute paroxysms of laughter.

That's disgusting. I moved on to toe twitches. But also kinda hot. And you're Canadian, you liar.

"Respiration looks good, pulse looks good," the doctor declared as he reviewed everything. "Everything looks good. We'll decrease the meds and depending on how she feels you two can take her home this evening." The boys heaved sighs of relief.

I assumed it was relief...I decided I'd go with relief. The door clicked shut.

I heard Alain ask Nanook if he wanted to go grab something from the cafeteria. "Love to but someone needs to be here if she wakes up. Cow lady's not so hot on hospitals."

"Why not?" the unicorn sounded puzzled.

What would happen if I threw up right now? I desperately sent *silence silence you know only silence* through the atmosphere in Nanook's direction.

"That's something personal to the cow lady," he finally said, "she doesn't talk about it much so..." His voice trailed off and I shot him massive curling waves of love and gratitude for keeping his trap shut.

"I see," Alain replied slowly. "Well, if she wants to share I'll certainly listen but I, above all people, understand the priceless value of privacy."

Who was this guy? I'm Googling your ass the second I get out of this shithole.

The sound of a jacket zipping and chairs being moved around and then Alain said he'd be happy to run down and get something from the cafeteria so someone would be here. "You'll suffer the slings and arrows of institutionalized grilled cheese, huh," Nanook ribbed him. Alain sniffed and replied that it was taco day.

"Even better. Make mine with extra cheese."

Cheese cheese cheese. I considered the horribleness of having to smell them eating delicious hospital tacos and not be able to open my own mouthhole to partake. Less toes and more face, I ordered myself.

Alain vamoosed on a quest for ground beef and I felt Nanook's hand rest softly on my head. "You're probably in there listening to us talk about you," he said conversationally. "So I want you to know that I'm readjusting the medication back up so we can enjoy a few more hours of silence."

He pecked me on the cheek, walked back to a chair and slid it over toward the bed. A second later I felt his feet land on the edge jostling me slightly as he let out a deep sigh and promptly fell asleep.

ONE HUNDRED SIXTEEN

Alain returned shortly thereafter with a tray of delicious items I could only smell but not see because my face was still uncooperative. Tacos…beef? And something with enchilada sauce, likely with rice. And refried beans. I suddenly remembered Nanook only ate black beans.

Uh oh. Crust moment.

"I got one of everything," the unicorn announced and I felt Nanook's feet slide off the edge of the bed.

"Let's divvy up and see how badly I need to pummel you before you give me my top choices," he said. Alain told him to fuck off. Turns out the only thing in dispute was a plate of nachos which they reluctantly agreed to share. "But only if you don't double dip," commanded Alain. Nanook informed him that if their hands touched whilst grabbing chips the unicorn would go home to Montreal with a crooked nose.

"Why does she call you Nanook of the North," Alain asked while they crunched their way through lunch.

"I'm a Husky. Went to University of Washington down in Seattle for graduate school so I guess it's that and the whole Alaska thing. You?"

Alain replied in kind. "She was trying to figure out whether I was gay or not and told me it was strange that a mythical creature such as myself was wandering around alone. That she would get a net and keep me in her closet if no one else wanted me. I guess it was my handsome face." I heard a snort of derision. "I've been called worse things," Alain finished blandly.

Nobody better be insulting my unicorn or I'll bust their chops. I moved my big toe a tiny smidgen.

"College?" Nanook sounded curious.

"Chemical engineering."

"Nice. I got an English degree but compensated by breaking things and killing people."

There was a small noise of approval.

"Cow lady's a lawyer. Taxation." Nanook shuddered. Alain told him he thought I was brilliant.

And that's why you're my favorite. My heart beat with joy.

The unicorn continued, "Doesn't have the social skills god gave a donut but no one's perfect."

Nanook back on top as I demoted the Canadian.

"She's mechanically inclined too which is awesome," Nanook declared, "I keep trying to get her to fix my garbage disposal but she says she's afraid of all the tiny whirling knives." I heard crumpling wrappers followed by a hollow thunk.

Alain snorted. "Easy shot."

"Fine," Nanook fired back, "Off the door past the window into the can." A few seconds later he grudgingly admitted Alain wasn't half bad. The next ten minutes were spent in a classic display of machismo as they recycled the wrappers a dozen times eventually culminating in an epic attempted basket that went out of control and hit me in the side of my face.

"Oh shit," Alain smothered a laugh under his hand, "is she ok?" Nanook confirmed I was fine, that if I'd been awake I wouldn't have been able to restrain myself and offered the unicorn a mulligan which he graciously accepted.

I ordered my tongue to get the slice of lettuce stuck to my cheek. They would both pay for this. Big time. Steak dinner with multiple desserts big time, I vowed, as they collapsed back into their chairs lapsing into silence.

"Football?"

Alain said soccer but not NFL. "Not even CFL?" Nanook asked. The unicorn said he'd never been a fan. "Cow lady watches football religiously," Nanook confided, "Plays in a fantasy football league with a bunch of random dudes, screams at the players, curses like a sailor. Rabid. Absolutely rabid."

I mentally tabulated the days until the league auction and made a mental reminder to confirm the salary cap had been upped to fifty million. I drifted off distracted by thoughts of possibly snagging both Mark Ingram and Alshon Jeffrey. If I added in Le'Veon Bell, Ezekiel Elliott and AJ Green I'd be practically unbeatable. And broke. I moneyballed the upcoming year and plotted possible collusions.

Nanook informed Alain he'd be the football boyfriend. "I'll take ice hockey," the unicorn decreed with surprisingly little push back. They bickered for a minute before splitting me down the middle like Solomon's baby with Nanook getting custody of soccer and snow machining while Alain snagged baseball.

"I get fishing, too," Alain said and the room got really quiet.

Face…engage. Face…ENGAGE. Come on face go go go. A cloud of violence started to form by the window.

Nanook replied ominously that he'd be goddamned if he'd give up fishing with his best girl without a tussle but if Alain was willing to lose sailing he'd consider it. Frantically I willed every muscle in my body to move even if it was only to fart in an attempt to distract my boys from peeling the skin off each other's respective bodies in the fight to end all fights.

"Butterfly has informed me that occasionally my wording is less than ideal," Alain said with appropriate gravity considering how near he was to a painful and protracted death.

"So you'd like to move to strike and rephrase," Nanook sent measured tones back toward Alain. I puffed up with pride even though technically it's withdraw the question and then rephrase but I'm no litigator. I tried to remember my advocacy classes. Probably need a refresher on that.

Alain answered that he would indeed like to rephrase.

"Perhaps neither one of us should claim activities that the three of us equally enjoy," he said carefully. The unicorn explained that he'd enjoyed our fishing adventure although not the violence associated with the eating. "She bashed the salmon in the head. Against a log," he said in a harsh whisper.

Nanook told him in a rather blasé tone he personally never knocked fish out. "Stresses 'em when you whack them like that. I think it makes the meat taste funny so I just hold 'em real tight and cut the gills. Besides, they bleed out faster when they're moving."

Oh Jesus, I hoped Alain was sitting down. I envisioned the two of us in matching hospital beds with Nanook standing in between with a bowl of ice chips.

"You look a little pale, bro," Nanook started laughing. Alain informed him he was just resting his eyes. Nanook commented that most people didn't do that with their heads between their knees. "I guess I'll take custody of elk and pheasant seasons," he suggested. The unicorn assured him that he would not dispute ownership of any sport requiring a bullet.

Nanook sighed. "Tell you what, fishing and sailing can be equally shared. And maybe done in a group if we promise no screwing when the three of us are all in the same place." Alain agreed that would be acceptable and that he'd even teach Nanook to sail if he would return the favor with some fly fishing lessons. "I won't be ruining one of those fancy sweaters to do it," Nanook warned before thanking him for the giant box of cashmere that had apparently accompanied the unicorn on his impromptu dash from Montreal to my sickbed.

This was supposed to be all about me. Something was wrong.

"Butterfly tells me you're a Republican."

Yep. Something was terribly wrong here.

Nanook confirmed his political party affiliation and they moved on to a discussion of non-sport activities with Nanook taking live theater and Alain the opera and symphony with joint custody over comedy, popular musicians and social events.

I guess being a Republican was low on the shocking revelations list in this particular love triangle. My how far we'd come.

"I don't know how comfortable she'll be at big events," Alain admitted. "She doesn't seem like a fancy crowds person."

Don't say it. Don't say it. I tronned Nanook's cranium and he started laughing. Damn it.

"Wow, you guys are a matched pair aren't you."

The unicorn responded with, "How so."

I could tell Nanook was poking Alain in the leg and felt like cracking a chair over his head. "Cow lady's got money, too. Well, her parents do at least. But she's not much interested in material things I don't think. Although she's super hot about a set of wood chisels Andy gave her a few years ago." The unicorn sounded surprised about the money but confirmed I'd freely admitted to an ongoing relationship with those particular implements.

"It's those terrible shoes," Alain said. "No one in their right mind with money would wear those. Have you seen them?" He demanded

Nanook concur as to their horribleness before my most favorite boy-friend told the unicorn he was arrogant and vain. "She keeps them because they're rubber and they float cause she's always dropping things overboard."

Goddamn traitor.

He continued, "And she's clumsy so they actually prevent a lot of busted toes."

Unicorn boy and I are kicking you to the curb if you don't stop yakking.

Alain snorted but Nanook just kept right on going, "You could buy her some different shoes if you wanted but she won't like you any more than she does already. If there's one thing cow lady isn't, it's shallow."

And now we're back to a solid threesome. I never doubted you. Not even once, lover.

"Could be worse, Rico. You haven't seen her walk in high heels yet. Although she did great at Andy's service, I must admit. Must've practiced quite a bit because she's a total menace. Goddamn, it's funny."

Alain laughed. "She told me she can't run from mass murderers in high heels. That they're inherently unsafe at social gatherings because they impede egress and that's why she doesn't wear them."

They concluded their insulting bitch session with the agreement that flats were likely ok in the majority of situations as long as they weren't Crocs. This was ridiculous. Where was that fucking doctor and why was I drooling.

A set of feet weighed down one end of the bed. The unicorn said, "Great idea," and took up pole position on the opposite side. This would be pleasant if I weren't starting to feel like I've been smashed by a battering ram. My shoulder started to throb just a tad.

"What's up with her name," Alain fidgeted, sending twinges up the right side of my body. "It's her grandmother's name," Nanook explained. "She hates it."

I don't hate my name all that much but I'll murder both of you if you don't stop moving, goddamn it. Shit was getting real. I need to be re-vegetablized ASAP.

"It's French, you know," the unicorn said.

I did not know that and I don't fucking care. I will cut a bitch if I don't get some morphine.

Nanook sounded surprised. "Huh. Well, her grandmother's from West Virginia. Fell through a bridge or something. It's a wacky story, you should ask her sometime."

"I love her name," the unicorn announced.

Alain you are my destiny. Now come over here and smother me. Put me out of this misery. I'm dying. Oh Jesus just kill me.

Nanook offered some advice, "Well, don't call her by the full thing unless you want to get pummeled. She almost flattened Andy the first time he introduced her to me."

Alain reiterated that he thought it was sexy and said he would try it out on me in bed where I would be most likely to tolerate it.

"Party foul, bro. Party foul."

The unicorn quickly apologized.

Kumbaya it out boys and then find the nurse. I started to sweat and wondered if the doctor had flipped the switch the wrong way cutting off all the juice instead of just reducing it.

I could hear myself breathing inside my head and thought it odd that neither of them noticed me moaning. Hurts. Hurts much bad. Very much bad up here. What's the use of two boyfriends if they're engrossed in each other, I grumbled. This is about me. I started to feel a little sick.

"These are the things I'll never know about her," Alain said quietly. I contemplated jumbo bottles of Pepto Bismol. "There's a million things, actually. You have something with her I can never match. Never replace. Can't even come close to competing with."

They were quiet for a minute while I ran various happy things quickly through my brain trying to distract myself from the nausea.

"And what's that," Nanook whispered, "cause it's not money. I don't have very much of that. You're definitely the winner there. And it's not looks because we both know you're a lot prettier than I am." I wanted to tell Nanook not to worry, not to feel threatened but couldn't because my stomach was trying to crawl up my throat.

"It's not travel and fancy cars. I drive an average SUV and live in a normal house across town. Got a pretty sweet float plane but you could probably buy and sell me a million times over. So what could I possibly have that you can't give her, huh? You have everything. Including the cow lady."

"History," the unicorn whispered the word like it was precious. "You have history with her that can't be replicated with money or things or time, even. A part of her heart will always be with you even when she's with me. That's something I will just have to accept."

They were both quiet for a long time and desperately I cranked open an eye to see if they'd departed.

"Oh Jesus, I think she's awake," the unicorn jumped to his feet and I let out a small gasp, "and we're definitely going to need a nurse."

Ten agonizing minutes later a very dapper doctor whisked through the door and shined a bright light in my eyes while a nurse shot me up with anti-nausea medicine. "How do you feel?" he asked. I announced I should have eaten the egg and promptly threw up on his loafers.

"My bad," I tried to wipe my mouth off with the sheet. He smiled down at me. My two lovely boys took up positions on either side of the bed. "Happens all the time," he assured me before politely inquiring as to which alias I preferred. "Don't care what you call me just make it stop, doc," I moaned and someone handed me a bucket.

"What's happening here," Nanook said in a concerned tone. The doctor told him the reaction was bad but still within normal standards, "Put a lot of drugs into a tiny body and this is what happens, unfortunately." He explained that coming out of surgery my respiration had dropped really low so they'd put me on a ventilator as a precaution until things had evened out. The unicorn bent down and congratulated me on adding general anesthesia to my list of allergies. "Roll that up with milk, sunshine, cold air, vegetables, aerobic exercise…" his voice trailed off and Nanook picked up the slack, "Bees."

Alain looked surprised. "Bees?"

"Yep, she has one of those things," Nanook made a stabbing motion and Alain shouted "EpiPen!"

Nanook snapped his fingers and pointed at him victoriously, "Got it in one! Damn we'd be good at charades." He reached across the bed and high-fived the unicorn while the doctor stood mutely by my side.

"I feel like maybe I'm being secretly filmed for reality TV." The doctor sounded slightly stunned so Alain informed him in a perfectly even tone that he'd been standing in the closet periodically throughout the day and there were no hidden cameras.

"Uh huh," the doctor narrowed his eyes at me, "Well, it's been fun kids but I think we're ready to get this young lady checked out and on her way home." He looked up. "Who's responsible for transportation?"

Nanook and the unicorn conferred briefly. "I have the SUV," Nanook looked over at the doctor and received the thumbs up.

"I have nothing. I took a cab," the unicorn added.

And thus it was thumbs down for Alain as the doctor decided my best chance of survival would be the boys sedately raging together across town with me and my trusty bucket shoved into the SUV's lay-flat backseat like luggage.

ONE HUNDRED EIGHTEEN

"French Unicorn, Nanook of the North, Madame Butter Cow," the doctor gifted me with a wide smile as he bid me adieu a short time later, "a distinct pleasure." I assured him one or both of the boys would bring me to his office for post-surgical evaluation within the next few days and tried to take rapid shallow breaths while Nanook pushed my wheelchair toward the exit. Alain triggered an automatic door as we rolled down the hallway and slowly picked up speed. "Sorry, sorry I couldn't help myself," Nanook apologized when we took a corner practically on one wheel.

"Let me do this," Alain shoved Nanook to the side, "You get to drive on the way home." They sniped over my mode of propulsion for a minute or two while I puked into the bucket. "If you two don't shut your traps and get me home this fucking second you'll both be single," I whispered. They quickly apologized and we resumed forward progress.

By the time the hellish drive was close to completion I was dehydrated from throwing up and incredibly dizzy. We pulled slowly into the driveway while the two boys discussed the logistics of hefting my apparently ponderous physique from the SUV into the house. "I can hold the door if you'll slide her out," Alain suggested. Nanook discussed use of a wheelbarrow.

"Cow lady's dead weight so I can't just prop her up against the side of the car," Nanook pondered all his options as the unicorn unlocked the residence in preparation for my arrival. Between the two of them they managed to get me out of the vehicle into the house onto the couch with relatively few missteps although I did throw up on the front lawn as we trudged down the sidewalk. I apologized desperately and Alain patted my face gently and told me not to worry about it.

Twenty minutes after touchdown I lowered my personal standards and asked Nanook for help going to the bathroom. "I need to keep some mystery," I explained in a hoarse whisper to Alain after I politely declined his offer of assistance. "This is so humiliating," my face burned bright red when Nanook pulled my sweatpants down and off my ankles. I braced my good hand against the bathroom counter, "but it hurts to sit down and I can't get back up on my own."

"No problem cow lady," he laughed silently into my good shoulder holding me upright while I peed down my leg into the drain of his giant walk-in shower. After hosing me off, he gently dried my butt with a hand towel assuring me The Event would remain our little secret. A knock sounded at the doorway.

"I thought one of these might be little more comfortable," the unicorn explained in a loud whisper. I stood wobbling in front of the bathroom mirror half-heartedly rubbing toothpaste on my tongue with a shaky finger while he and Nanook considered the merits of various clothing ensembles in the hallway. "This is really nice," Nanook said, "but I'm warning you she'll probably wreck it." The unicorn assured him it was no problem even after Nanook explained *wreck it* was code for *pee on it in the shower*.

"You goddamn traitor," I gasped as the two of them gently disengaged the sling contraption and used scissors to cut my t-shirt down the side before peeling it slowly off my torso, "you said it was our little secret." Alain leaned in and kissed me on the cheek and whispered, "Butterfly, you left the door open." Nanook buttoned up the lovely emerald green satin knee-length nightgown the unicorn had thoughtfully provided before strapping my shoulder back into the brace.

It took both of them to shuffle me down the hallway to the guest bedroom. "Not quite sure what's going on here," Alain stuttered in a slightly shocked voice from the doorway, "but I feel it might be inappropriate for me to ask for further explanation." Nanook laughed. The two boys shoveled me into the bed, carefully arranged a pressure cuff around my shoulder and built a pillow wall around me to prevent all movement. "Let's get some ice water and I'll explain the Contraption," Nanook said.

I heard them talking in the kitchen down the hall during my final review of the device. Support beams…check. Bicycle chain…check. Can't see if the webbing is properly secured but I'll check on that…check. Faintly I heard the rattle of the ice maker as the cubes were shoveled into the cooler. I thought about the volume of the ice and was absolutely reasonably certain Nanook had followed the measurements. Footsteps returned slowly and the unicorn peeked an amused face around the door jamb.

"I hear there was quite an expensive visit to Home Depot," he said and asked whether I had found a use for low budget hose clamps. Nanook started hanging the cooler on the Contraption hook before pausing and glancing down at my face with a saucy grin. "Do you need to check the levels or can we just assume I didn't overfill past the line?" He turned to the unicorn and confided that I'd weighed the cooler on a bathroom scale to make sure the counterweight would work properly. "These are reasonable concerns that needed to be considered," I informed them with my eyes halfway closed, "otherwise the Contraption wouldn't have at least ninety percent efficacy which is my personal minimum for overhead structures projects."

"Wow," the unicorn sounded impressed as he watched the cooler start above my head sending ice cold water gravitationally down a tube into the pressure cuff around my shoulder. Slowly the cooler began to automatically drop toward the floor and I sighed in relief as the cuff tightened around my body.

"Blessed numbness overlords I welcome you. Please make sure you're timing this," I glanced at Nanook who held up his wrist and helpfully tapped the watch face. "On it, cow lady," he rolled his eyes at Alain.

"I saw that," I waited a few seconds before confirming that Level Three tension was appropriate for this stage of recovery. The cooler eventually transitioned below my shoulder draining the water from my cuff at a reasonably snail-like pace reducing the pressure in tiny increments before slowly, hopefully, beginning its reverse counterweight rise to the top of the Contraption continuing the cycle ad infinitum.

"I have to say, butterfly," Alain gave me an enthusiastic round of applause, "engineering may have been your calling." Nanook ordered him to not encourage my architectural leanings. I educated the both of them that the bucket of ice water had an approximate half-life of two hours give or take thirty minutes and thus the five hours of uninterrupted nightly sleep they would receive because of the Contraption and its extensive beta testing was not to be scoffed at. "My gift to you, my beautiful boys," I yawned.

"Get some rest," Nanook leaned over and gave me gentle kiss. "I'm going to need to copyright these building plans for use in potential future business development," the unicorn whispered and smooched me rather enthusiastically before they both tramped out shutting the door behind them.

I cleared my throat.

"Jesus fucking Christ," I heard Nanook laughing before the door reopened and he walked back in carrying a small two-way radio which he placed on the bedside table within reach of my good arm and a Camelback full of water he hung on another hook next to my head making sure the drinking tube was fully extended. He bent over and told me, "Secretly I'd like to bash you in the head but I won't because I'm completely in love with you, infuriating wench that you are." He stroked his fingers down the side of my face and told me he'd already set his watch to ring at our prearranged medication intervals before quietly re-exiting the room.

"I love you, too," I whispered into the emptiness and drifted off to sleep.

ONE HUNDRED NINETEEN

Four days after surgery Alain politely took his leave back to Montreal and left me to the tender ministrations of someone I adored but who eventually revealed himself to be a homicidal maniac.

"Three more," Nanook demanded. I told him to screw himself but pulled on the exercise band anyway. "Swear to god if I'd known recovery was going to be this painful I'd have never chosen surgery no matter how minimally invasive," I panted. He congratulated me on reaching my one month anniversary of misery. "Has it been that long?" I counted the days off on my fingers, "August already. Wow."

I bent over gingerly and practiced slow toe touches eyeballing the clock to see if Percocet hour was nigh. "And we're also cutting back the drugs today," Nanook announced victoriously and declared he was tired of me sleeping my days away stoned all the time before informing me he was headed out to get some fishing done before bad weather rolled in.

"This low cholesterol diet requires major salmon infusions, you know. Just trying to keep the budget down, cow lady."

"You've been fishing four times in the past two weeks and I'll promise not to pout about you going again if you take me this time. Please please please," I told him my arm was better and I was dying to get out of the house. "Plus, you've been gone flying all over the world for work, lucky dog. You've been to Singapore! And almost six whole days to Seoul!"

He continued the list of exotic destinations, "Oakland. Ft. Lauderdale. Los Angeles—"

"Ok, valid. But I've been waiting patiently! Patiently with minimal bitching!"

He rolled his eyes and sucked me into his death zone. He grabbed me and kissed me on the side of the face over and over reluctantly admitting I had adhered to the physical fitness schedule with religious devotion. He also reminded me that it was FaceTime monitoring with the unicorn and himself as well as the long suffering staff of PAMC that prompted this good behavior.

"And McDonald's cheat day helps too," I bounced up and down on my toes inside his arms eagerly anticipating the arrival of Wednesday when we would lounge around in our pajamas, eat hamburgers for dinner and watch cheesy horror movies. "And McDonald's cheat day," he smiled down at my face.

I grinned back. "Come on, cow lady wants to go fishing," I teased him a little. "I'll even let you bash my face with your pistol again if I get too mouthy."

He clapped his hands together and declared fishing sounded marvelous and we could go that very minute if I could find my wizard shoes. I dashed down to my room, dug those red sequined suckers out from under a pile of clean laundry and ran back toward the door whooping gleefully the entire way.

Nanook, being a man of his word, dug out the waders and off we went to the lake where I confidently allowed him to push me up into that tissue paper floatplane only hyperventilating a tiny bit when we hit some bumps on takeoff.

"You ok?" came his voice over the headset and I flipped him a thumbs up with my bad arm. "Looking good on mobility, cow lady," he caught my movement in the reflection of the windshield and grinned congratulations. "I slay," I modestly admitted as he prepared for landing.

Sadly, I wasn't allowed to actually fish but he did graciously let me schlep all his smaller bits of gear around and sit on a folding chair with my boots in the water watching enviously while he enjoyed the solitude. "Ahh…" he said as he waded back from the deeper parts of the river where he knew I couldn't follow, "…silence. Blessed silence."

I said nothing.

"You good?" He flopped down next to me on the riverbank.

I remained quiet.

He looked at me.

I stared back.

Nanook grinned and I started giggling. "You can't even keep your mouth shut for five minutes, can you," he elbowed my knee. I shook my head glumly.

"I tried. I tried my best I swear it."

He rose to his feet and held out a hand, "Grab the fish. It's time to head home." I groaned in disappointment but allowed him to haul me up from the chair and did my part to repack all the stuff into the bags he eventually jammed behind my seat before shoving me back up into the cabin.

I swallowed lightly and asked him for a little help with my harness as he started to flip the front seat back. "Sure thing, baby," he leaned over me putting his hand awkwardly on my thigh for balance. I told him I had a question to ask him and felt him pause for a split second before he started to reach across my chest. "And what's that," his hands pulled the straps tight then stilled, his fingers next to my shoulders.

"Didn't know if you were aware of this but I almost fell down in the shower this morning."

Nanook expressed an appropriate level of concern and agreed with me that slippery surfaces posed a threat when someone such as myself suffered from mobility issues.

"And I wondered if you'd given any more thought to maybe helping me a little more if I needed it now with that kind of stuff. Hands on attention, you know. Because I'm so tired from all this physical therapy and all…" My voice trailed off uncomfortably.

A brief moment of silence passed while he stared at my face before turning away giving me the same answer he'd given me every time before this time.

"I'll seriously consider it," he whispered as my heart sobbed quietly inside my aching chest.

ONE HUNDRED TWENTY

That night it was my face that cried just like it had every night since I'd been conscious enough to button my own shirts and use the restroom without assistance. I jammed my head under the pillows huddled in a miserable ball and clutched the comforter to my mouth trying my best to be better, fat tears rolling across my cheeks down through my fingers.

I thought about him telling me over dinner he was leaving in the morning for Tokyo *no choice, cow lady* even though I knew he was volunteering for all the long haul routes. I knew because I'd heard him talking on the phone with the flight scheduler one day when I was supposed to be exercising in the basement but had taken a break to get a drink of water. "I've got some time so if you need anyone to pull an extra just let me know," he'd said. I'd backed silently down the stairs and pretended nothing was wrong when we'd stuffed hamburgers down our throats a few hours later.

"Love you, baby," he'd whispered every night before walking away from my open door.

I got up around midnight and crept down into the basement where I folded and refolded the towels I'd dried earlier that afternoon. "For practice," I said into the silence, my shoulder throbbing from the repetitive movements.

An hour later bored with laundry I moved to the bedroom boxes and refined my rummaging skills as I sorted the sports equipment and random widgets Nanook had assured me were nothing private but needed organizing. "Give you something to do while I'm gone," he'd said as his uniformed back had strode out the door to Memphis. Moving my third container of the night I spotted something in the corner and realized it was the box with your things in it he'd given me long ago when I'd started this whole disaster with my big fat mouth.

Slowly I reached out my arm and pulled the box out of the stack carefully ensuring Nanook's snowboard didn't bust me in the face before flipping open the box lid. I softly touched that green t-shirt and remembered how nice it had looked against your skin. You were always such a hottie. I was a lucky gal. Not so lucky before I met you though.

Bad times…bad times in Santa Ana.

"I'm all better now," I convinced your box and pulled out the smashed black iPhone from where it had fallen inside one of the shoes suddenly seeing your face on that easel, *beloved beloved beloved* in brass letters surrounded by carefully tended grass.

I realized someone else wouldn't be there with you either as I told my fingers *make the call* while those wizard shoes crept silently up the stairs toward the charger I'd plugged into an extra outlet.

ONE HUNDRED TWENTY-ONE

Five days later, I was sitting very still at the kitchen island when Nanook of the North returned from the Far East.

"Hey, cow lady." He slowly slipped off his uniform jacket and hung it over the back of a chair. "You ok?"

"I talked to her," my mouth said, my eyes seeing photos flipping past on a shattered screen, "Her name is Rianne Johnson and I need you to put her on the list."

He inched closer.

"The list for what," his voice whispered.

"The cemetery," I answered as my feet got up and left.

ONE HUNDRED TWENTY-TWO

At breakfast that next Wednesday he asked me politely if I needed a cheat day and I replied *damn straight I do* so he brought home the standard dinner suitcase of heart attack mystery meat stacking the packages on the big TV tray in the living room while I flipped through the Cheesy Horror Movie section of his film library.

"Got you something extra," he said sheepishly and held out a giant milkshake. "Oh my god," my hands shot out snatching the heavenly dessert right out of his grasp. I noticed the burgers were from Arctic Roadrunner and not McDonalds.

He cleared his throat, "Figured you could use an upgrade."

I whispered *thank you* and started sucking chocolate down my facehole while he put old school Dracula up on the big screen. We crumpled wrappers and ran through half a bottle of ketchup in silence for an hour before he told me he'd done what I requested.

"Do you want to talk about it?" He wiped his fingers with a napkin and started gathering up all the trash.

I considered my options and decided a truth moment was the best choice. Nothing to lose so I might as well man up.

"There was a ring in Andy's stuff," I said like I was announcing the sky was blue, "in the bottom of one of the bags he had here at the squadron. A diamond ring. Nice one, too. Big."

He slowly sat down next to me on the couch and looked at the television.

"I never heard anything about a ring," Nanook whispered so faintly I could barely hear his voice.

I got up and swept together the rest of the wrappers and tossed them casually in the paper bag resting on the coffee table.

He was very quiet for a long moment as I disappeared into the kitchen and discarded the trash in the can under the sink. I walked back into the living room, sat in the easy chair across from the couch and stared at his face until he glanced up.

"She's a bartender downtown. Rianne is, I mean. Nice girl. A little young but I can see why he loved her." I told him I'd borrowed his SUV and gone down to Humpy's while he'd been in Tokyo but drove very carefully and obeyed all the speed limits so I didn't fender bender myself back into the hospital. Explained that'd the ring had probably been meant for her and not me but that I didn't know for certain. "Didn't tell her about it because she looked pretty devastated the entire time we were talking. Figured that would be mean and I'm trying to not be so nasty."

He put his elbows on his knees, laced his fingers across the back of his head and closed his eyes tightly.

"I took it to the jeweler he bought it from while you were out grocery shopping one time. Called a cab and went down to the store after they agreed to buy it back."

I took a deep breath and told him I'd carried the ring in the side pocket of my suitcase on that flight up from Seattle and sold it after he'd given me the box.

After the kitchen. After the kiss.

He shot to his feet, walked over to the patio doors and stood there with his hands on his hips staring out into the bright August sunlight.

"I gave her the money when I met her. In cash. Ten thousand dollars in a Mafia style envelope. Said you'd put her on the list for the cemetery so she could say goodbye and the funds would help pay for travel expenses. I lied and said the money was from Andy's will, that she'd been in Andy's will but I didn't know how to find her until recently. I knew she wouldn't take the money if she thought it was me giving it to her."

I laughed and rubbed my eyes with my hands before confessing I'd then proceeded to commit a federal crime. "I told her to stick it all in a safety deposit box since the bank would notify the IRS of such a large deposit into her account and she could probably avoid paying taxes on it if she was smart about spending it. Walked her down to Alaska Federal and helped her set it up, actually. Gave her my business card in case she ran into trouble."

He looked at me blankly.

I held my finger to my lips and whispered *shhhh*. I saw a tiny smile cross his face.

I was exhausted. This was exhausting. I stood up tall and told him I was never Andy's Girl then or now and nobody was putting a bag over my head in bed or otherwise.

"I'll answer the question you're afraid of," I moved toward the hall-way. "If he'd asked I would have said no."

I watched Nanook slide down that glass door sobbing as tears poured down his beautiful face. Holding that pistol up to my own heart pulling the trigger over and over I told Ian MacMillan I loved him for himself and he could love me for myself or not at all.

"Because I'm just Maxine now. Just Max," I clutched a trembling hand to my throat and walked out.

ONE HUNDRED TWENTY-THREE

I performed my standard silent crying ritual under the covers shortly thereafter deciding that an early bedtime alone in my room with the door firmly closed was just the ticket. About an hour into my pity party a tiny knock tapped on the door. I rolled over just in time to see a piece of paper slip over the hardwood through the gap under the door.

Huh. We'd regressed to grade school. I could roll with that.

I got out the pen I'd been trained to carry at all times in preparation for last minute legal document emergencies and silently slid over on stockinged feet.

It said *Do you still love me? Check Yes or No.* I smothered a small laugh and choked back a sob simultaneously as I considered the minuscule size of the paper. "This is completely inadequate for my response," I whispered to myself. A blank piece of printer paper winged past. *Addendum* it said across the top in big letters. I realized he was sitting outside in the hallway with his back against the wall and let out an snort. I scrawled *Stand by for Cow Lady* on the original index card and shoved it under the crack.

It slowly disappeared and I heard a pencil scratching before the card came back through halfway. Written on it was *Standing by.*

I pulled it through, checked *Yes* on the index card with a shaky hand and set it to the side.

I thought about things then looked at the Addendum and started writing. *Please answer the following question: Do you still love me? Choose one of the options below:* I began a new line, *1. Yes* or *2. No.*

If circling yes, proceed to 1.a. If circling no, proceed to 1.b.

I paused, indented a proper two spaces and wrote *1.a. Are you ever going to touch me again? Because I'm dying in here.*

I swallowed gently and wrote *1.b. Do you want me to leave?*

I started to send it under but couldn't help myself and quickly re-tracted it. I drew a signature line at the bottom for *Maxine F. aka Cow Lady* and *Nanook of the North aka Ian M.*, put the current date and the statement that this document was for settlement only and not admissible as evidence in a court of law.

Sailed it back through.

Heard a muffled laugh and *Jesus Christ this is fucking ridiculous* followed by that pencil moving across the paper and a slight rustling noise.

It returned folded in two with a stick figure hanging from a gallows with a noose around its neck drawn on the front. I laughed outright, "Rude."

"Read the damn paper, you wackjob," came his voice through the crack.

I unfolded it and saw the words *I have things to say to you. Please open the door.* There were no boxes checked but the words *Subject to arbitra-tion* was scrawled above the signature lines.

I felt rather sick. Usually negotiations of this duration didn't end well. I remembered telling him that the only good contract was one where both parties leave slightly unhappy. I raised my pen and crossed out *arbitration*, replaced it with *nonbinding arbitration* and memorialized the document with my standard hideous lawyer scrawl that looked like I'd had an epileptic fit during signing. Paused, scratched out *nonbinding arbitration* and wrote *mediation* above it and slid it under the door.

A split second later it shot back through with Nanook's neatly printed initials and hit my foot as my fingers slowly turned the doorknob cracking open the door.

And there he was, one arm propped up against the doorjamb silently looking at my face. I gave him the original index card and watched him slowly look down at the box I'd checked before he stepped backward into the hallway.

I felt like crying but I sucked it back inside because I was not going to jeopardize my professional integrity by showing inappropriate emotion at a crucial stage of negotiations. He bent down, reached his hand out to the side and pulled it back holding a pencil. Still bending over he picked up the Addendum and circled an option. And then another option.

Handed it to me.

Yes. And *1.a.*

He stepped into the room. When he passed me I noticed there was another item captured within the second circle.

It was *1.b.*

ONE HUNDRED TWENTY-FOUR

Ian turned slightly and flipped off the lights after quietly shutting the door. He walked over to the bed, stripped off his jeans along with his t-shirt and flung the covers to the side. "Hop on in, cow lady," that silky tone drifted my way, "what I have to tell you is best said in the dark."

I decided I'd take this as a sign of progress toward 1.a. and walked toward the bed. I pulled off my robe and hopped under the duvet. He fluffed the fur throw over the bed and jumped on top of me squashing me flat.

"You weigh less," I choked out and he assured me the high fish diet had removed excess chub around his middle for which he was secretly grateful. "Haven't been going to the gym much whilst traveling around the world being a man of mystery," he confided before he rolled over and got under the covers.

He pushed a pillow under my head and sucked me close in with his arm. I felt him tuck my back up against his bare chest. "Hold that thought," I sat up and took off my own nightshirt and laid back down. "I like it when our skin touches," I whispered softly as he intertwined our fingers pulling the joined hands tight up against my heart.

We laid there in silence for a while as I readjusted my legs. I finally reached over, grabbed a pillow and shoved it under my top knee before hauling his leg across tucking up right behind mine. "Jesus, it's like you forgot how to properly spoon or something," I grumbled. He snickered and squeezed me a little too hard to be acceptable in polite society.

"If I call you *cow lady* are you going to get nasty, Just Max?"

I laughed and then paused. I told him I'd overheard the history comment Alain had made while I was trying to re-master my face. He told me he knew I was awake because he'd seen my toes moving under the blanket toward the end but chosen to keep his trap shut. "Figured you'd appreciate a complete data set," he said. I softly thanked him for keeping my hospital issue under wraps.

Nanook softly kissed my head and told me it was probably time for a trim then confirmed he adored my no-hair haircut. "Heard the unicorn took his life in his hands and assaulted you with clippers while you were in a vulnerable state," he chuckled, "which I appreciate because you'd have pummeled me for sure if I'd pulled that stunt." I thought about the subsequent occurrence and he kissed the back of my neck, "Relax, cow lady, I know it's because you were dying to get in that big fancy shower. Don't deny it."

Clearly the two boys had been flagrantly breaking Rules One through Three and possibly Four although I was absolutely certain Five had remained intact. Or was it Six. I should have written them down. But, I realized we were probably in uncharted lawless territory and decided to just chillax and give it a rest.

"Your shampoos are better," I assured him.

He confirmed they were both from Bed Bath and Beyond because he enjoyed the smell of peppermint in the morning as a wake-up but needed sandalwood in the evenings to wind down. Sheepishly I told him he'd probably need a new bedtime bottle pretty soon because I'd been poaching the Relaxation Elixir and using it as bubble bath in his giant tub while he was off 007-ing.

I did have one pressing question, "Where'd you get that awesome charcoal soap?"

Awkwardly he admitted he'd stood a safe distance from Alain closely observing the location of the unicorn's hands before asking him whether he had a Dorian Gray or some secret rich dude potion that gave him completely perfect skin and the unicorn had sent him a giant collection of shit in an unmarked brown paper box after returning to Montreal. "He put stickers on the outside that made it look like fishing gear," he sounded rather embarrassed but simultaneously proud of their joint deception.

I complemented him on getting in touch with his bisexual side and confirmed he was looking rather youthful around the forehead and eye areas. "Apparently the secret is emulsified carrots and obscene amounts of red wine," he confided. I mentally allotted an hour on my daily schedule to rummage through his bathroom cabinets and appropriate those creams. "I know what you're thinking," Nanook whispered and told me Alain had sent an extra set for me in his most recent care package, "because he knows an equitable distribution of assets is important to you."

He buried his face in the back of my neck and took a deep breath.

"Gonna tell you some weird shit in a minute or two but you're crazy as a loon so I figure you'll be cool with it," he said. I elbowed him gently but confirmed my tolerance for wackiness was abnormally high.

"Can I ask you a question first?" I cleared my throat.

"I know what you're asking and no, it was awkward when it happened but I agree with Alain that being responsible isn't anything to be embarrassed about. So I'm over it, cow lady. Not a big deal."

I smiled and kissed the back of his hand remembering our conversation in the living room weeks ago when he raised an eyebrow at the contents of my most recent envelope.

He added, "Felt left out that the two of you had taken the plunge so I went and got tested myself. Flight doc actually congratulated me on getting laid so that's a plus. Increased my street cred as a ladies man in the squadron. All good in my hood, cow lady. All good."

I told him he was a reprobate when he announced his envelope was longer than Alain's. "By a good two inches," he whispered proudly, "and thicker, too."

I couldn't help myself and started laughing. "I love you madly," I patted his thigh and he smooched me on the back of the neck in rapid pecks.

It took us a good five minutes to quit goofing around before he cleared his throat and said he was ready to disseminate the insanity.

"Gonna tell you the story of when I first met you," he started, "so engage your mute button until I finish." I nodded my head in agreement.

Nanook of the North told me he'd been bored that day in the squadron and planning an early exit from the party when the door had opened into the bar. "I heard Andy's voice so I turned around to say *what's up* and there you were. It was like getting struck by lightening," he pulled me a little closer. "I felt really weird inside as I walked over. Didn't quite know what was going on because nothing like that has ever happened to me. Before or since."

"It's like you weren't there, all the light just got sucked in as if you were a black hole," his voice sounded strange. "It was just a blank space where you were supposed to be standing, just light all around the edges and nothing in the middle. Thought I was going bananas and maybe somebody had spiked my drink with something." I also agreed this is a little out there…but not nearly as wacko as Santa Ana. Decided I'd sit down on this train and ride it to the end of the line.

"Got closer and shit started getting super weird." He paused. "I'm not a religious guy. Never raised that way. No church or anything. Don't believe in heaven or hell or God or any of that bullshit. Dead is dead and nothing more. But when you reached out your hand and I grabbed it…I saw things. Heard things."

"Like time slowed down where our hands met and kept going for everyone else," he whispered sickly. "Sounded like people were talking underwater as I looked up at your face. I saw your face and smelled cotton hanging on a long line drying in the sunshine. Horses racing down a hill. Church bells from stone towers."

He paused and took a deep breath.

"Children laughing and baking bread sliding out of an oven. Heard rifles firing. Felt your hands like velvet, your lips on mine in the darkness. Couldn't ever see your face or my face but I knew it was you."

I remembered he was an English major and thought about all those books on his shelves, the extras stacked up in towers along the living room walls. "Hifalutin jibber jabber," he'd joked, telling all the guys they were there to impress the ladies, the spines cracked with dog eared pages. The way they would all mysteriously be arranged in a different order every time I'd come to visit. A slim volume of poetry hidden under the Playboy in his nightstand drawer.

"Crying. Sobbing. A voice screaming from behind a wooden door as boots pounded down a long hallway. Anger. I felt angry, so angry. Rage for no reason but not at you. Like I wanted to cry. That locked door and my feet kicking it over and over realizing I was too late. I wanted it to stop, to let go but my fingers wouldn't listen. Smelled fresh dirt as it slipped through my hands dropping down and hitting something far away.

"It just kept going and going incredibly fast. Fast forward at the speed of light these things just shot through my head." I could hear him crying while I laid absolutely motionless. He sucked in a deep breath and went on.

"Parties. Dancing. A blue dress whirling as candles flickered in a corner. And always over it all, over everything else the sound of crows circling circling always circling, those birds so loud and terrible as they picked clean a silent battlefield. A voice crying my name, a name I knew was mine but couldn't understand it, couldn't comprehend it, can't remember. I can't remember what you were calling me but it was you. It was you, Max. It was your heart breaking while I laid there bleeding at your feet…"

Holding me so tightly I couldn't breathe, Ian sobbed in agony as tears gushed down the sides of our faces.

"I looked at your face standing there next to Andy and wanted to kill him. I loved him but still wanted him dead. I could hardly keep my hands from wrapping around his neck and squeezing the breath from his body. I wanted him gone, Max. He was like my brother and I was feeling these things for no reason. I wondered if I'd lost my mind as my heart said at last, at last, feeling like a long journey was finally over while my mouth told you it was nice to finally meet you.

"I've heard so much about you my lips whispered as you pulled back and let go of my hand."

ONE HUNDRED TWENTY-SIX

He cried for a long time clutching me to his chest as his heart broke over and over. I wanted to make it stop, to help, to help him but I didn't know how. Didn't want to tell him about those things I'd seen on those long rides home after steak dinners, felt in the deep night my head pounding as I threw up in the boat shower wondering if maybe those security doors should never have reopened.

I knew this was about him and not me and wanted to tell him how I felt but couldn't find the words. Words that felt small drifting frail and weak from great heights while inside a deep hole was opening sending up giant stalks of yellow blooms searching desperately for the sun I hoped was hidden above those gray skies.

Turning toward him I did the only thing that felt right. Because he felt right. He felt like home to me. Whispering softly, my tears mixed with his as I laid our cheeks together holding him tightly to my heart our fingers together, pressed together so perfectly matched together as I said, "I'm just Max now. And you're just Ian now. And there's time, this time, we have this time." As his mouth hovered over mine he finished the words he'd started long ago in that cold river, "You're the most precious, my most precious commodity and I need you, Max. I need you desperately."

I realized all the times before that he'd made the first move, those fingers lightly running up my spine in a shower thousands of miles away. I leaned forward gently pulling down on his jawline kissing him pushing into him breathing his sighs down into my lungs because we'd been here before. Long ago we'd been together and together and together as over and over we'd lost each other yet found our way back even though it made no sense.

There's no logic here. No numbers to crunch as I said *fuck it* inside my head and kicked the doubts out the door because I knew he was right. Because I'd heard those birds too, that horrible howling as they spun up for battle as I stood watching those scald crows shooting on blue flames into the distance crying with relief that it wasn't him, hadn't been him snapped up by that Alaskan forest.

When it was him coming home from Shanghai not hating myself at all when he sauntered in saying *what's cooking, good looking* as I took what he would give me and clung tightly to it deep in the night as I cried for us. Always him in my dreams, clutching that comforter to my face seeing a long aisle, a priest waiting in a cold dark chapel as I knelt on thick beds of soft reeds wishing I were dead like he was dead in a plain wooden box. In that box alone he laid while I said nothing, my forehead resting silently on white silk emblazoned with a strange crest keeping him company all night before the long walk in the rain toward another dark hole. A hole where my name would be carved under his on a stone marker when I couldn't stand to go on and took a short flight from a tall tower whispering to the wind streaming past my face *I'm going home* feeling not the slightest bit sad when I shattered against the stones.

Reaching forward, my hands pulled his beautiful face toward my mouth whispering *I've always loved you* his lips answering *I know* those long fingers slipping up my thigh.

He slid his hand higher and suddenly realized there hadn't been anything under the t-shirt I'd taken off because I liked the way it felt when our skin touched. I sent my fingers to his waistband pushing those cotton boxers down toward his feet until his long arms finished the job. Moving closer I shoved him over onto his back and held his face between my hands kissing him deeply, our mouths in perfect timing as his hands wrapped around my waist before sliding firmly over my ass down in between my legs. Sitting up, I moved forward until I was looking down at his face resting between my thighs clenching the headboard with whitened knuckles as he did what he'd done forever, done before, done all the other times before this time until I cried out his name into the darkness.

He was over me now, inside me now in perfect synchronicity as we moved silently under the covers his face pressed into the side of my neck his hand clutching my upper back as he pushed into me knowing how it was done, how it was supposed to happen because we'd done this a million ways in a hundred lifetimes. Gasping, I arched back as he slowed, laughing quietly. I begged him not to stop telling him he'd be in big trouble if he didn't finish the job.

He complained that he only got one and wanted to save it up as long as possible. I reminded him there were twenty-four hours in a day and I'd be more than happy to throw out my schedule in order to accommodate his particular needs. He pulled me forward into his lap and I slid upward while he breathed in my ears calling me the devil, telling me I was the devil, that he'd sold his soul and gotten the better end of the bargain.

I licked up the side of his neck starting at the collarbone drifting toward his ear and whispered things that made him grin that wicked smile I recognized and welcomed as he stood up pushing my back against the wall lifting my legs with his strong hands. Thrusting, he gasped that the sight of us reflected in shining closet door was driving him mad as I sank down on my knees and took him into my mouth. Looking up I told him I wanted him to watch as his hands came down onto the back of my head pushing firmly, staring down with narrowed eyes while I sucked rhythmically, stroking him with a firm grasp.

I caught him watching me as he stepped away grasping me under the arms as up I went down onto the edge of the bed as he jerked up my hips upwards driving into me slowly from behind as I clenched the fur throw to my mouth muffling my screams. He ripped it away saying he wanted to hear me, needed to hear me, to come for him, with him as he leaned forward pushing down on the back of my neck throbbing deep inside me as we exploded with a blinding brilliance.

ONE HUNDRED TWENTY-SEVEN

It was a long time later as we huddled in the darkness wrapped up with all our skin touching that his voice whispered "…there's a reason I don't hate him, you know. I thought I would, that he would be Andy all over again but he's not. It's not. I don't hate him." I knew he was talking about Alain.

"It's like I know him but don't know him. Because I think he was always there, too, in the background. Taking my place by your side when I fell. Me holding you as earth dropped from our hands into his hole. I think we've always been this way. Planets orbiting past each other over and over coming so close during eclipse that it seems as if we're one although there's millions of miles separating us. Departing. Forever departing."

I saw a small tear leak from the corner of his eye and reached up a finger to brush it away. He leaned over me, "I don't know why, but it makes me happy to think that you're happy with him when you're not with me. That you make him happy, too. Does he make you happy, Just Max?"

I nodded saying he did make me happy as I choked back tears but told him Alain didn't need me. He didn't need me at all and I didn't need him either and would be perfectly fine if I never picked up that phone again. That I would sell Abraxis or burn him to ash. Erase Montreal from every map if he asked. "Just ask and I'll do it. I only need you," I pulled his face closer.

"But you want him. And he wants you back even if he doesn't need you." Great rivers of water ran from my eyes as I admitted it was true. It was true. There in the arms of the person I loved the most I gave voice to the silent sin that I also craved the touch of another. "He doesn't need you, Max," Ian whispered, "I need you. There's a difference."

He sighed. "And it's killing me, this needing you desperately. It's all consuming. I can't think when you're next to me, can't sleep. Can't barely eat. It's too much." "Is that why you left on all those trips," I asked as his hand stroked down the side of my face. "Yes," his lips touched mine, "because I start to lose myself in you. I lose who I am inside. But I always come back. No matter how far, Max, you know that."

Then he reminded me that it was good that he was in charge of navigating this ridiculous potential time warp karma crazy juju business because my Magellan skills were terrible and neither one of us could count on any of my future lives improving my dismal ability to determine north or south. "Well, I'm sorry my nose doesn't have very much iron in it," I said in a huff and smiled when he gently poked my nose ring, telling him "that's platinum."

"If we depended on you to find each other on this merry-go-round we'd all be married to notebook paper salesmen and miserable as shit," he said.

"Or a cheese seller." I sighed with delight while he made grumpy noises into the pillow next to my ear.

"Or Rihanna," he winked, "she's in my top five, you know." I smiled and slipped a hand beneath him stroking, squeezing as I leaned in closely toward his face and whispered *mine too*. He quivered with joy, a giant smile leaping across his face. His hands clenched around my throat just a little and he announced that our next lives should start right this second so as to improve our chances with that super hot piece of ass.

"You're unbelievable," I patted his face and we rolled over onto our backs. "Seriously, I thought you had a problem with this sharing business," I looked over at the side of his face. "Well, I'm never going to hop in the sack with the two of you and pretty-please no details on all of that, thank you very much, but I'd rather you be with him when you're not with me than be with someone else. I don't feel as homicidal when I think of you and him."

"What about Andy?"

He was quiet for a long time before saying Andy never smelled right. "He never smelled right for you. There were too many sharp points. It always seemed like he was dinging you around the edges. Accidentally, of course. Little pieces would be missing or dented when you'd visit up here. They'd grow back, you'd patch them, but you two just never seemed to look smooth and even." He winked. "Guess he should have used more emulsified carrots," he instructed me to complement him again on his youthful visage.

"But you were best friends," I was confused. Ian shrugged, "Loved him like he was family but I'd have stolen you in a millisecond if I thought I could have gotten away with it. Guess I wasn't that good of a friend, huh." He looked sad and guilty. I told him Andy had loved him back more than anyone else even himself, which is saying a lot, so he shouldn't feel bad. "Everyone's human," I reminded him he was not unique, that all men coveted someone as fabulous as me. "And so humble," Ian muttered condescendingly and he flipped me over onto my stomach. "You know what they say about pride…," he shoved me off the bed onto the comforter piled up on the floor.

I started to sit up when he landed flat on my chest. "Ok, you don't weigh less, you tool," I squeezed out a tiny gasp as he rolled us across the floor inside the comforter over and over until it was a giant ball of satin with us tucked inside.

"This is really nice fabric," I whispered and licked the inside rim of his ear. "It was a gift," Ian took my earlobe between his teeth and tugged as his hands rested on the sides of my face, "from a guy who has a shitload of money so I don't feel the least bit sorry if we wreck it." He rubbed his nose alongside mine and kissed me deeply as he whispered, "I know a guy who knows a guy who makes really nice comforters so…"

"So you're connected, is what you're saying," I joked as his hands slid down over my breasts pinching me slightly as he skimmed over the nipples. "I'm fixin' to be," he snickered, his arm slid under my hips pulling me upward so he could slide inside me with a deep sigh.

"There's not much room for movement wrapped up tight like this," his voice whispered softly in my ear. I helpfully recommended he take this opportunity to exercise his fine motor skills and slung a leg over the back of his thighs before I slowly began to move. We managed to press every square inch of skin together while delicious friction built higher and higher until the sweat from his face dripped down onto my cheek and slid slowly into my hairline. I tilted upward pushing my hips forward one foot on the ground slinging the other calf across his back. He begged me to come for him and laid his forehead against my shoulder feeling me rippling inside over and over as he filled me completely. "Jesus Christ, Max," he gasped. I squeezed him tightly, his weight pinning me against the floor. I cried out a last time and fully clenched hard around him as he came over and over until finally collapsing across me barely breathing.

ONE HUNDRED TWENTY-EIGHT

"I can't breathe," I squeaked and he confirmed the occurrence had been awesome. "No, really, I can't breathe," his weight was squashing the air from my lungs. He grabbed my waist and unrolled us across the floor until finally I could suck in some fresh air. *Ahhhhhh…* I let my arms fall flat on the carpet.

He laid next to me and stared at the ceiling as his fingers rubbed the back of my hand. "Time for a shower, cow lady," he said after a few minutes and warned me that this time I was not allowed to pee down the drain no matter how tempting. He hauled me up with one hand and threw me across a shoulder.

"Just as long as I get to use the last of the Relaxation Elixir," my voice told his back as his hand smacked my ass. "It's peppermint for you," he told me he'd used the rest of the sandalwood that evening before commencing our sixth grade communications. "But the charcoal soap's all yours," he saucily warned me not to drop it.

We stood under the hot water for a long time until he graciously offered to wash my hair if I'd reciprocate by taking care of his most important parts. "Not the same level of effort but I'll take one for the team," his fingers massaged my scalp and I made happy noises.

"Your shoulder looks good, baby," he lightly touched the tiny scars where the surgeon had sewn up the broken parts. "Feels good, too," I said and proved it by using both arms to perform my end of our cleansing bargain.

"Will you stay with me tonight?" My hands gripped his shoulders as he demonstrated various uses of the built in shower bench. "Every night," he looked up at my face, "as long as we sleep in my bed."

"And why is that?"

"Because I'm old and need my orthopedic pillow, that's why."

"Good god, are you eighty?" I bent over laughing when he informed me that he was a good half inch shorter from pulling G's for eighteen years and quite enjoyed the overnight cervical adjustment his fancy pillow provided. He reached over my head and turned off the water.

"So I get the shitty pillow, is that what you're saying?"

"No, I'll share," he dropped a towel across the top of my head and stuck a toothbrush in his mouth. "But only half. You can only have half."

"This is pretty nice," I admitted as we spooned under his sheets a short time later. "Just stay on your side," he warned, bumping me when I encroached slightly over the arbitrary orthopedic property line. I yawned, whispered *love you* and slowly backed up into his arms. He replied, "My consent negates the adverse possession pillow claim you're plotting," and I cursed myself for leaving my real property textbook laying open on the coffee table.

"I think you should consider going to Montreal," Ian said as he performed the Magic Egg Maneuver the following morning. Slowly I put down my crust-with-toast. Did he not want me here anymore? "I know I've been here for a while," I started to say before he jumped in.

"No, no it's not that. It's not that."

"Although I must admit you and me together is exhausting," he sighed dramatically and flipped an egg over his shoulder across the kitchen which I tried to catch with my plate but naturally missed. He picked it up off the floor, wiped the refrigerator off with a sleeve and tossed the egg out the back door onto the lawn. "Something will eat it," he turned back to the stove as birds zoomed in to snatch up the unexpected bonus and told me it was a miracle either of us were able to walk.

"I am pretty sore," I admitted sheepishly that maybe the shower adventures had put me over the edge. He smiled and pumped his arm in the air victoriously as he declared his work here was done.

"And, we even made to breakfast this time," modestly he congratulated himself for being incredibly efficient while still delivering quality product. "So why should I go to Montreal," I asked slowly and considered the possible answers.

He looked over his shoulder and told me his unit was deploying to Hawaii for ninety days and he'd rather like to accompany. "Little bit of sunshine, some sand," he informed me there would only be government-sized piles of cash, "but likely many many dancing ladies."

He gave me a huge wink before saying, "No, really. I'd like to go. Give me a chance to get out of the Alaska winter and do some middle age rage of my own. And some fishing." I asked him innocently if he was planning on taking the orthopedic pillow and he confided he had a travel version he hid in the bottom of his mobility bag in a duffle with his running shoes. "Ladies man or not, the guys would never let me live it down if they caught me sleeping on that thing," he shuddered.

"Maybe I can borrow the big one when I go to Montreal," I fiddled with the orange juice glass. He firmly informed me that damn pillow was staying right where it was but he would give me the manufacturer and model number, that the unicorn had piles of cash and would be happy to buy me one. "Massive cash and probably also many dancing ladies," he said and ducked when I threw some crust at his face.

"I guess my recovery is to the point that I could go to Alain's as long as I keep up on my exercises," I thought about the logistics if I had to schedule a visit with my doctor for a check-up whilst in Canada. Nanook declared imperiously that he'd speak with the surgeon and Alain jointly so that my recovery plan would be clearly established.

I informed him he'd contracted a phrasing infection from our favorite unicorn, "Jesus, it's like you guys are in some sort of mind meld or something."

He paused, "I'd be ok with that as long as there's an accompanying wallet meld." "Any other meld you might be interested in?" My shoulders shook in silent laughter. "Mr. Mitts needs to check himself if he thinks a transfer of anything other than money is going to occur," he walked over very deliberately and slowly slid another egg onto my plate.

I thanked him for the egg noting it wasn't Wednesday Cheat Day but I appreciated the slight impingement of the diet rules in light of our smashingly excellent reconciliation. "Oh, there was definitely some smashing going on," Nanook laughed and we decided that perhaps after breakfast we'd review the state of our various personages and make a game time decision on potential horseplay. "I'm down with that," he said with a leer when I meekly informed him it might be the only option for a day or two.

"Be that as it may, cow lady," he tossed me an exercise band, "your mercy egg does not eliminate the daily PT." I groaned that my butt hurt, my head hurt, my everything hurt and I should get a pass but he still hauled me to my feet.

"Chop chop, whiny pants," and down to the torture chamber we went.

ONE HUNDRED THIRTY

"So you'd like to come here and grace me with your presence," the unicorn said gleefully over the phone the next day. "Very much so," I informed him not only would I be traversing the wilds of Canada but would also be bringing a large collection of exercise bands and assorted physical therapy implements. "The bands are stretchy. Very very stretchy." Alain laughed and grudgingly acknowledged that while FaceTime PT was somewhat amusing, hands-on assistance was likely needed in order to ensure I reached optimal recovery.

"I can send you the plane," he offered but I declined. "No, I insist," the unicorn firmly told me, "You can be independent and fly commercial when you go back to Alaska if you like but when you come here I will send the jet."

"I won't have anything but a small suitcase though," I told him it was ridiculous to spend all that money to shuffle me, my exercise bands and a motley collection of Old Navy sweaters in a fancy jet across to Montreal. "Silence," he ordered, "In this regard I will phrase as I want. Get on the jet and enjoy it." There was a pause before he sealed the deal, "There will be a cheese plate in it for you, butterfly."

Two days after my departure date had been agreed upon a calamitous clanging arose from the garage at the ungodly hour of six in the morning. I rolled over in bed and scraped my eyeshade up from my face flailing a hand around on Ian's empty pillow. What the hell was all this business and where were the earplugs. Ten minutes later the banging and slamming still hadn't subsided so I grudgingly slothed my way out of the bed down the hallway to the garage door which I discovered was flung wide open in a clear display of disrespect for my sleeping preferences.

"Oh," Ian turned and grinned up at me from where he was bent over his worktable, "how nice. You're awake." I pointed at the hammer in his hand, "Is this the cause of the noise? Because it looks to me like this racket might be purposeful."

"Since you're up, lazy bones," he bounded up the steps and grabbed me in a giant bear hug, "I thought I'd take my best girl bar hopping." I froze for a minute then let out a shriek of joy. "I'll get my clothes," I darted back up the steps. Ian yelled out behind me to dress warm and bring a hat, "and gloves! Bring those fingerless gloves for your bird hands." I waved my arms in the air in frantic acknowledgment and disappeared into the house.

Twenty minutes later I'd brushed my teeth, put on a pair of wind pants, a sweater, my new hiking boots and a thick jacket and was waiting anxiously by the car with a piece of toast in one hand and a travel coffee mug in the other. "Go go go," I jumped up and down circling my arm and encouraged Ian to pick up the pace. "Relax, cow lady," he sauntered past and face palmed me before opening my door, "plenty of daylight left. Moose aren't going anywhere, I promise."

We eventually skedaddled down the road to base and over to the aero club at what I felt was a reasonably spritely pace. In the parking lot I ran laps around the car trying to burn off excitement while Ian cranked open the huge bay doors revealing a tidy row small airplanes. I made a beeline for a bright yellow Supercub.

"Open sesame!" I scrabbled around with the door handle trying to flip the latch open so I could hop in the back seat. Ian politely moved me aside. "Let's get her out of the hanger first, Just Max," he laughed. I reluctantly raced back outside and chugged the rest of my coffee while I waited for him to pull the plane out and conduct his preflight walkaround.

"I can help you with this stuff, you know," I peeked over his shoulder at the checklist. He politely declined and said we would both die if I were left in charge, "Cow lady, you think north is whichever way your face is looking. No way am I ever putting you in charge of anything related to my airplane. Except if it needs engine work." He leaned back and gave me a loud kiss, "A line blows or something makes a funny clanking noise, you're my girl. Other than that, hands off my baby, please."

I tried to be patient and not fidget while he went through the stand-ard safety briefing and mashed a life jacket over my head. "Remember, headset connects like this," he reached over and pointed at the small wire, "and the harness buckles right over left. Like shoelaces." I slowly leaned in, pressed my forehead to his and crossed my eyes, "Information download complete. Can we go now please."

He smacked my butt.

"Up you go and remember not to grab anything but these bars," Ian pointed his finger at the ceiling and shoveled me up into the backseat, "Most of this is like gingerbread and comes right off if you pull on it." I grunted in acknowledgment and he shot putted me face first into the opposite side window.

I rummaged around my seat and connected all the various pieces of webbing and wires and put the helmet on over my hat buckling it tightly under my chin. Ian grinned at me fidgeting and patted me on the knee once or twice after I gave him an enthusiastic double thumbs up. I watched as he stepped back and around vaulting smoothly up into the cockpit's front seat. He looked like the Incredible Hulk. "You look like the Incredible Hulk," I said into the mic once he had his headset plugged in. "What?" he tilted his head to the side.

"You're gigantic inside this tiny plane. How do you even fit? I can't even see out the windshield you're taking up so much space!" I started laughing. He gave me the finger but I could hear him snickering through the headset. "Are you saying I'm fat, Just Max, because I'd like to remind you that this whole side of the plane is a door that can open during flight." He waved his right hand toward the wing and dug through his flight bag with the left. I clarified that he was not fat, he was gigantic. But in a good way. "Some guys have a girl in every city," Nanook of the North said and spun up the propeller, "I have a gym."

I listened to him talking to the tower, that tower's soft voice falling through the air slipping quietly through the headset that fit snugly over my ears. We sat for a while on the taxiway while a giant C-17 transport plane came in for a landing. It lumbered slower slower slower so slow it almost seemed like it would fall from the sky before landing at an incredible speed shooting past us down the runway its brakes billowing clouds of white smoke.

"Finally," Ian sounded exasperated, "could that have taken any longer? Jesus Christ." I told him to relax and he shushed me because the tower was talking now, giving us permission to drift into the wilderness to rage.

"Ready, Just Max?"

"Punch it, big daddy."

And he did. The propeller spun up with a giant buzz and we sprinted down the runway into the sunlight popping up off the ground within seconds. He tipped the Supercub in a tight left turn over the base angling away toward Six Mile Lake. "Gotta get some gas and then we'll be good to go," his voice said into my ear. I watched the tiny lake approach off my right side listening with one ear to the tower giving us clearance to land on the tiny dirt strip running down alongside the water. I gasped when he stomped on the brakes a little too hard on touchdown and heard him softly laugh through the headset.

"Oops. My bad, cow lady."

I unhooked all my wires and took a stroll down the docks while he put gas into the wing tanks. "Hey, where do you put the floats when you're not using them?" I yelled. He shrugged and said, "Storage." Made sense. I guess that's where the big fat bush tires were kept when the floats were on.

"When did you take the floats off?"

"Last week when you were at the doctor's office getting your final checkout," Ian glanced up and pulled the gas line around to the other side of the plane, "I didn't tell you because I wanted to surprise you. Maybe take you on a picnic. Feed you a sandwich and take your clothes off. Do adult things to you in broad daylight right out in the open where all the moose could watch. You know, the usual." He grinned.

I glanced down at a mamma duck with eight fluffy ducklings gaggled together in a raucous bunch next to his empty floatplane slip. There was a single baby stuck behind a floating barrier meant to keep oil and fuel spills from getting out into the lake. It was thrashing itself out of the water trying desperately to get over the plastic to its family who were all yelling loud words of encouragement. "Go tiny baby go," I waved my hands in the air and made shoving motions trying to move the duckling with the force of my giant brain, "go go go."

"Just lift the barrier, cow lady," Nanook of the North said as he walked by on his way back to the fuel shed. I laid down on my stomach and pulled the barrier up an inch or two and watched as the fluffball zipped under with a screech of relief and darted into the safety of its little herd.

"Happens all the time," he held out a hand to help me up, "I think the mother does it to make them stronger. Makes 'em go over the barrier like clockwork." I stared up at his face smiling down at me with the sunshine creating a golden halo around his head.

"You're a softie, I knew it," I grasped his hand tightly and he pulled me to my feet. He held a finger to his lips and leaned in closely, "Shhhhh, don't tell anyone but sometimes I bring my toast crust out and feed the babies." I tucked my face into the crook of his neck and took a deep breath. He smelled like home.

"Let's go," his palm stroked lightly down the back of my head before he turned toward the plane. I scrambled to follow and managed to climb in without assistance. A few minutes later we were airborne again and zipping over great swaths of open Alaska marshland.

"This is so different from when it's on floats," I said, my hands on my harness and my face pressed up against the window. "I thought you might like it," he tilted his face to the side and angled the plane down in a steep dive, "Let's see what's down there."

One hundred feet, seventy feet, fifty feet above the ground we went at eighty miles an hour zipping over the trees going to and fro and fro here and there swinging those small wings wide in tight turns.

"Look! A moose!" I pointed a finger out the left side of the plane down at a brown shape eating grass in the middle of a muddy plane. "Baby, moose aren't white," Ian laughed, looking out the right side down at two swans and their three progeny floating in a nearby pond. "The moose was on the left," I said in exasperation, "I know what a moose looks like."

"Sure thing, cow lady. Let's see if we can find you some more albino moose over here. I don't want to stress out the baby swans." He pitched the nose up with a smooth motion and we sailed skyward over a long shining stretch of river far above the white sandbars dotting the gray silty water.

"This looks like a good one," Ian said and put the plane into a gradual descent, "Let's see what's down there." We floated over a long sandbar close enough to get a good look at the ground. I said it was long enough to land on so he gave the plane a bit of power and tipped it up and around in a sharp turn. The force of the plane pivoting around that tight point pushed me back into my seat and I let out a small squeal of excitement. I could see him smiling as he tipped his head over toward the window and stared at the approaching ground.

"Ok. Hold on, cow lady." I gripped the harness and took a deep breath. He laid the plane down lightly on the sand and we rolled across the surface till the end where he put the Supercub into a steep climbing turn again.

"This is the best day ever," I crowed. I could feel happiness leaking off his edges as we came in for another run. "Let's land and get out for a minute," Ian whispered and gently put the plane down on the sand pulling it swiftly to a stop.

He hopped out first and I hustled to make sure I was ready when he came around to the back seat. I turned and put out a foot but paused when I heard him say softly, "No no, sweetheart, don't step there." I looked down when I felt his fingers lightly brush the top of my shoe and saw I'd almost stepped on the wing connection where it clearly said Do Not Step.

I felt horrible. I yanked my foot back, glanced over at his face, whispered a quiet apology and felt my face burn a deep red. He smiled up at me and stepped back so I could get out. "It's ok, baby," he ran a finger down the side of my face once I was safely on the ground, "No harm done." I stared at his mouth and put my hand over his, pressing his palm against my face. "Thanks for bringing me out here," I said, "that was really nice of you." He stepped closer into the shadow of the wing above our heads.

"I can think of some ways you can properly thank me," he stared down at his hand on my cheek. I grinned and shifted backward. He moved in to take up the free space. A second later my shoulders hit the plane but he kept gliding closer until we were pressed up against each other, his right hand on the fuselage, the other around my waist. Very gently he leaned down and touched his lips to my cheek with a soft sigh before cupping my face in his hands angling his mouth over mine. We just stood there, our foreheads pressed together for a few minutes before he stepped back.

"I saw another sandbar down the river and I'm feeling lucky. Let's give it a shot."

"That looks super tiny," I stared down at a sandbar the size of a chopstick. He assured me that he was an excellent pilot and could make the landing. "I can stick it, cow lady," he sniffed snootily. I asked if he could turn the plane around and take off again.

"I said I could stick it, not that I'd be able to unstick it." He spun the plane around in tight descending circles looking at all the angles before leveling out for another exploratory run. "You count for me, Just Max," he asked. I agreed and laid out the numbers in my head as we rolled through.

"What'd you get?" he cranked up the power and came back around, "I had seven." I confirmed that I'd had six and one half seconds from one end to the other but the margin of error allowed for a count of seven. "Seven is good," Nanook of the North declared and committed himself to Chopstick Island.

We touched down just past one end and he quickly spun the plane down into an abrupt stop.

"Nailed it!" he shouted and pumped his fist in the air.

"Holy shit, I can't even see the sand on either side of the plane," I stared down at the river flowing by. He gave himself many congratulatory high fives and then slowly taxied the plane toward a slightly wider area at the end of the sandbar.

The plane seemed to rotate around a center axis right at the edge of the sand although I felt the wing on one side start to slip slightly downward before he pulled the nose swiftly around. He paused for a brief moment staring at the end of the sandbar seven seconds away. I cleared my throat.

"You ready," he rested his hands gently on the dashboard. I confirmed I was tightly buckled in and everything was secured. He took a deep breath and ran the propeller up to full speed before popping sharply off the brakes. We took off down that chopstick like a whore out of church and shot into the sky just as the sand turned into river.

"Let's do it again!" I bounced around in my chair with glee. He turned his head slightly, "Let's not and say we did, safety girl." I laughed. We flew in silence for a few minutes and I heard him say we should head back because the weather looked a little iffy over Anchorage. I sighed in disappointment.

"I'll bring you back out, Just Max," he said, "any time you want. Any time you want a ride you just let me know, baby." I made kissy noises into the headset and he snickered. We flew in silence for a few minutes before his voice asked if I wanted to give flying a go.

"See those screws," he pointed his hand toward the side of the windshield, "can you see the horizon line in between any of them?" I told him I could see a centimeter of horizon between his massive frame and the side of the windshield. "The horizon is between the second and third screws," I said. He told me to keep the horizon right in between those two screws and make little adjustments with the stick that was poking up between my knees.

I took a deep breath. "Just Max, you got this," he said softly, "just give it a try." I took the stick in my hands and he confirmed he'd let go up front. I confirmed I had control in the back. It was terrifying I was terrified. The plane suddenly turned into an untamable capricious beast swerving in oblique angles without warning. It seemed so smooth when he was flying it but now it was a disaster.

"You're doing great," Ian encourage from the front, "really good. Really awesome, cow lady. Nice small adjustments." I could see his hand on the dash and his knuckles didn't look white so I assumed he was telling me the truth. This was not fun. I did not enjoy this. "I'm not enjoying this can you take it back now please," I asked desperately. He put his hands on the stick up front and I confirmed I'd released control.

"I have the stick," he said and the plane immediately leveled out. I leaned back and took a deep breath. Flying and espionage, two career fields I could empirically cross off my list. A few minutes later I asked if there were books that would teach me how to fly. He said there were and would get me some.

"I think if I understood the systems and the physics of all this that I'd enjoy flying it myself more."

"This does not surprise me," Ian laughed, "I'll find you some books. And when you're ready I'll take you up and you can try it again." I nodded quietly and let out a contented sigh.

We flew toward Anchorage in companionable silence for a while. "What's the range on this thing," I asked quietly. He shifted in his seat. "Some place you want to go, Just Max?" I leaned back in my seat, "I guess it's too far for the Supercub, huh."

There was a moment of silence. "Yeah, it is," Ian replied softly. I wrinkled up my nose, "When you're out, do you ever—"

"Yeah, I do."

I closed my eyes. "What does it look like?"

"It's green now. There's small trees there, looks like. It's out in the middle of nowhere and the area is pretty rocky but you can still see it if you know what you're looking for." He cleared his throat. "The guys usually fly over when we're out. We'll just take a two ship across nice and slow. Just to check things out. You know, say hi and all that."

"That's nice," I whispered, "that's really nice. Andy'd really appreciate that, I bet." I saw him nod slowly. I thought for a few minutes, "What do you think when you go over? If you don't mind me asking."

He was quiet for a while then cleared his throat a few times. "I just tell him that we're all ok. That you're ok. We're all ok." He paused, "Are you ok, Just Max?"

I thought about it for a while. "I'm ok," I finally said, "I'm great, actually. I'm doing really well. Are you ok?" He shrugged his shoulders a little, "I think I'm as ok as I'll ever be. I'm good, we're good. It's all good." Ian pushed a few buttons on the dashboard. I heard the tower's voice as he flipped frequencies and asked for landing clearance at the base.

We came in for a nice quick landing and he stomped hard on the brakes when we touched down. "Tail winds," he explained when I made a squeaking noise, "we came in kinda fast." We puttered over toward the hangar and repeated the original process in reverse: Me offering to help and being shunned, him moving the plane into the hangar, then us back in the car out the gate driving toward home. It was a quiet ride. When he pulled the car into the garage I reached over and grabbed his hand, "Did I make you unhappy? By asking about it? I'm sorry."

"It's ok," Ian turned his head and lifted my hand to his mouth, "Don't worry about it, cow lady. You and me—we're ok, right?" I nodded.

"Let's get some lunch," he suggested and hopped out of the car racing around to open my door for me, "Burgers on the grill. How does that sound?" I smiled up at him and he grinned back.

"Also, I'm going to need a blow job to fully de-stress from our afternoon adventures," he smacked his palm down on the top of my hat, "So warm up your jaw on that beef, toots, you're gonna need it."

ONE HUNDRED THIRTY-TWO

That evening we ate dinner in front of the television because it was Wednesday Cheesy Horror Movie night. "I think maybe I like pizza better for movie night," Ian said through a mouthful of Moose's Tooth. I nodded and shoved another piece of pepperoni in my facehole, "Burgers twice in one day is a bit much. Maybe we can switch between burgers and pizza in the future. And next time let's get extra cheese." I licked sauce off my finger then stuck it in his ear.

He jerked his head away and reminded me that I was still on cheese restriction. I grumbled a little bit but snuggled into his side under the blankets anyway. We sat there for a while watching Hitchcock and eventually I saw his head start to nod. "Let's go to bed," I whispered and gently shook his arm. He tilted sideways and fell over squashing me into the couch, "I think I'll just sleep out here. It's so comfy." I tried to get up but he kept moving his arms blocking my attempts to extricate myself until finally I ended up spread eagled on my stomach with him sprawled across my back.

"I like you like this," he said conversationally to the back of my head, "So quiet and docile. It's a new you. An improved you." I let out a strangled grunt. He continued, "I'll let you up on one condition." I laid very still and modulated my next grunt into an affirmative noise.

"You have to tuck me into bed. And bring me a glass of water. And read me a story. Maybe two stories. Also I might need a foot massage because I've had a long day."

I agreed primarily because I couldn't breathe and also I was planning on spiking that water with strychnine. He rolled off the couch with a thud. I sat up and stared at his smirking face. Two could play this little game. "You'd like a story? Ok. Hmmm…," I tapped my finger on my chin and thought about my options. I suggested Harry Potter which he vetoed. "That's lame," Ian crossed his arms and looked petulant, "And you have to tuck me in and then tell me the story. After you verify that I brushed my teeth."

I sighed deeply and rubbed my face with my hands, "Ok, how about I tell you the story of the day I met you." Nanook of the North raised a skeptical eyebrow and reminded me that last time I told that story it ended with a broken iPhone and an international crisis level of personal embarrassment on my part. "And also a very rude insult to my sexual functions which you still haven't apologized for," he jabbed a finger at my face.

"No, this is a different story about the day I met you," I said with a blank look. He stared at me for a minute before reluctantly saying I could continue. I held out my hand for him to grab and he swung me up off the couch into his arms in a giant bear hug. "There's advantages to you being bird sized and me being the Incredible Hulk, huh," he squeezed and squeezed until I could feel my face getting hot. He put me down after I started making choking noises. I sucked in a deep breath and hauled him by his arm down the hallway to the bathroom where I jammed toothpaste on a brush and stuck it in his mouth. "Brush your chompers," I ordered, "and take your clothes off. I'll be back in a minute."

He opened his mouth to protest but I had already vacated the premises on my way to the spare bedroom where all my clothes were kept. I dug swiftly through the bottom drawer of the dresser until I found what I was looking for then changed in the attached bathroom. I examined my face in the mirror, dabbed on a little eye cream and curled my eyelashes. I looked damn good for my age even though my face was slightly wind burned.

I could hear Ian bellowing from the bedroom that he was done brushing his teeth and needed a story right this second or he was going to start crying and keep all the adults awake for at least an hour. I zipped back down the hall just in time to catch him taking his shirt off.

"Just the shirt. Leave the pants on," I said breathlessly. He threw his shirt in the laundry bin and turned back toward the bed. "And shut the closet door," I pointed a finger toward the wall. "Just Max this is not how story time works," he explained patiently, "I'm the one that calls the shots during story time. You can have story time tomorrow."

"Do you want me to tell you a story or not?" I put my hands on my hips. He wrinkled up his face a little and sniffed a few times before stomping over and shutting the closet door. When he turned around I was right there in front of him and he jerked back, startled.

"Shit! Is a heart attack part of this story?"

I smiled and leaned forward. "You have two options so listen careful-ly. I can tell…or I can show and tell. Your choice." He pondered that for a minute then asked if a presentation involving a rodent or dried macaroni was included in the show and tell. I promised him that no hamsters or noodle products would make an appearance. He made a few *hmmm* and *well* noises before grudgingly admitting that show and tell was probably better than just plain tell.

"I'm so glad to hear you say that," I ran a finger lightly down his collarbone over his ribs and hooked it in the waistband of his pants. He sucked in a sharp breath and said he was beginning to like where this show and tell was headed. He also asked if this story had adult themes. "It does have adult themes that are not suitable for persons under the age of twenty-one," I leaned forward and went up on my tiptoes whispering in his ear that a driver's license might be required to prove he was old enough to participate. It was obvious at this point that Nanook of the North was fully on board with nightly story time.

"Let's begin," I tilted back and looked into his face. "You already know most of the story of the day I met you but you don't know all of it. When you held out your hand and I touched you…you weren't the only person who saw things." He made a questioning noise. I asked him if he wanted to know what I saw that day, the pictures that flooded my mind the first time our skin touched. Ian whispered that he did want to know.

I pulled him gently toward the bed. "I saw us in a room like this one. There was a bed like this one. And a mirror…like this one." I turned him around to face the closet door, stepped back a foot or two and slowly stepped out of my jeans kicking them to the side. Ian paused, "Are you wearing my work shirt?" I looked down at the white button up dress shirt that hung almost all the way to my knees, "Yes, I am wearing your work shirt. Is that a problem?" He swiftly said there was no problem and then politely ordered me to continue.

I tilted my head to the side and said I'd seen us in a room with a bed in front of a mirror and while I talked I slowly unbuttoned that dress shirt inch by inch until it was completely open down the front. "Holy shit," Ian stared at the black lace bodysuit peeking through the white cotton. I confirmed the lingerie was new and gently pushed the shirt back off my shoulders until it fell in a pile on the floor.

"Where did you get that?"

"Do you really want to discuss my shopping habits right now?" I stepped closer. He swiftly reassured me that he didn't give a rat's ass where it came from but that he was super happy that I'd bought it. I reached forward and unzipped his pants, "I saw me and you and a mirror and I realized something."

He waited for me to continue. I pulled his pants and boxers slowly down to his ankles. "I realized that sometimes the best part of show and tell isn't the showing or the telling. It's the watching." I slid down to my knees and grabbed his hands and slapped them on the back of my head. "Now watch in the mirror as I suck you off. It's important that you finish. You have to finish or else you'll be too distracted when I start the good part of the story."

He pulled my face toward him and I licked wetly up his inner thigh. "This isn't the good part?" he said in a slightly strangled voice. I wrapped my mouth around him and used one hand to stroke the full length of his cock while I grabbed his ass with the other. "No," I shook my head, "this is just to take the edge off."

"I do have a lot of hard edges," he gasped and put both hands on the back of my head. I asked him if he was watching and he replied, "Fuck yeah I'm watching." I smiled, my hands keeping pace with my mouth and him hard as a rock against my tongue. "You sure I can't take care of you, baby," he threw his head back, eyes closed, "cause I can wait." My only response was to take as much of him in my mouth as I could. I could feel his breathing pick up and his hands pulling me in quicker and quicker until finally he gasped once or twice and came down my throat. "Fuck," he put a hand on the top of my head and pushed down propping himself up, "this is not at all what show and tell was like at my elementary schools."

I started laughing and pulled my head back slightly. He looked down at me and let out a deep breath. I asked him if he felt better and he confirmed that his edges had been temporarily dulled. He closed his eyes a little and squinted down at me, "Am I allowed to sit down for part two of this adult story? Because I'm feeling a little light headed." I shoved him toward the edge of the bed and told him to sit down facing the mirror.

I crawled on my hands and knees toward him staring at his face the whole time. I could see him watching my ass in the mirror and snickered silently to myself. Typical man. I sat back on my heels and ran my hands up the outside of his calves up toward his knees, "I hear you're a good student." I tilted forward and pushed myself up to whisper in his ear.

"I'm told you're a fast learner, is that true?"

He nodded and swallowed a little before clearing his throat, "I do ok, I guess."

"Graduated top of your class, I was told." I ran my tongue around the rim of his ear. He shivered a little before reluctantly admitting he was a total brainiac. I replied it was good that he was an excellent student because I was about to impart a lot of knowledge and wanted to make sure he was intellectually up to the challenge.

He grinned and told me he was up for a lot of things.

I slid forward and put my mouth closer to his ear, "Do you want me to teach you?"

"Teach me what?" He rubbed his cheek against mine and ran a finger up my thigh past my ribs across the bottom of one breast. I leaned back and put both hands on his shoulders and whispered, "Do you want me to teach you how to touch me?" Ian stared up at my face half hidden in the shadows and said he was more than willing to attend this particular refresher course even though he felt he'd been doing pretty good with only on-the-job training. I sniffed and said he might actually need remedial lessons and some extensive after school tutoring but I was more than willing to make an investment in his education. Pro bono.

I raised a questioning eyebrow and he held his arms out to his sides, "I'm all ears, cow lady." I swung around and sat in his lap, leaned back against his chest pushing my face into the crook of his neck before pulling his left arm under mine up over my breast. "I saw us like this," I said, "and one hand was here—" He ran his thumb over my nipple and made a questioning noise. "And your other hand was here…" I reached over and grabbed his right hand in mine and slid it across the lace covering my stomach down lower and lower between my legs until his fingers were against me with my hand over his. I sighed. He shifted slightly and reached down with his other hand running both palms over the top of my thighs before pulling my legs apart pinning them open with his knees.

"It's about the watching," he said, one glittering green eye peeking out from behind my neck, "right, Just Max?" I smiled and rubbed my face against his and stared at our dim reflections in the closet mirror. He ran his hands over my stomach gently. I reached down and took his right hand in mine and pulled it up toward my face. Slowly I sucked his thumb into my mouth and bit down lightly on the tip. Ian's jaw tightened a little and I could see the muscles in his neck getting stiff. I took his hand in both of mine and ran my tongue up between his index and middle fingers. I heard him whisper *Jesus Christ* when I pulled his hand down back between my legs.

Slowly I arched my back and showed him how I touched myself. "Like this," I pushed my back against his chest, "from the left and then down. Like this." I pulled his hand where I wanted it to go and watched his reflection close its eyes, his breathing heavy.

"I think we have a problem," Ian bit my shoulder gently a minute later. I leaned forward and stood up, "We do. We have a serious problem. In my mind, the day you shook my hand, I saw us like this but one crucial thing was different." He smiled and ran the tips of his fingers over my shoulder straps pulling them off down my arms inch by inch along my body until I was completely naked.

I stepped forward again and slid back into his lap. I saw us again in the mirror but now I was totally exposed and it felt suddenly super awkward. Thank god the room was dimly lit or it'd be damn near gynecological.

"This is so fucking hot," he said into my shoulder blade. I immediately felt better and stopped resisting when he pulled my legs open again. I must admit, I felt like a porn star. In a good way. I put my hand over his and slowly stroked myself as he watched in the mirror. He slipped his other hand over my leg and I felt his fingers slide up inside me while his other hand slowly rubbed me with his thumb and forefinger. I closed my eyes. Clearly no tutoring was required.

"We're going to have to spend a lot of time outside of class working on your technique," I gasped when he hit a sensitive spot. "Am I really that bad," Nanook of the North said with a predatory glance at my face, "tell me, cow lady, am I terrible? I can stop if you want me to." I ignored him, my chest heaving as I sucked in deep breaths. I knew he wouldn't stop because he could feel me tensing up as his thumb rubbed over and over, sweat beading up at my hairline.

I let out a swift cry and jerked slightly as I started to come. Ian wrapped an arm around my chest smashing me up against his chest pinning me motionless against him. I felt his face turn and watched him run his tongue up the side of my neck taking my earlobe into his mouth biting it firmly. "Is this what you saw," he said, pushing his palm down across me, "when you shook my hand? Is this what you saw in your mind? Tell me, baby. Tell me what you saw."

I threw my head back and pushed against his hand. I could barely hear him over the rushing sound in my head, the memory flooding back from that day, from the first time he'd touched me. "Everyone else in my life I've loved by choice," I held my fingers up to the side of his face, "but you, loving you is like gravity. It's like gravity."

Ian wrapped his arms around me and tucked his face into my shoulder. "You're like gravity," he whispered, "you're the middle of everything. You're the center of my everything, Just Max." He stood up and bent over pushing me down onto the rug on my hands and knees.

"Now it's your turn to watch," he said and pushed into me from behind with a single stroke. His hand gripped the back of my neck tightly with the other wrapped around my upper thigh as he pounded into me over and over. I watched his face in the mirror as he fucked me, his face with eyes closed turned up toward the ceiling. Suddenly he sat back and pulled me up into his lap and stuck his fingers in my mouth before stroking me swiftly. I arched my back in surprise as I came hard and felt him shivering against my skin before he let out a loud gasp.

We sat there in silence breathing hard for a few minutes. I felt him slowly tilting to the side and us slipping down to the carpet where he ended up flat on his back with me snuggled up under his arm. He ran his hand down the side of my face and pressed a kiss on the top of my head. We laid there for a minute before he got up and powerlifted me into the bed pulling the covers up tightly over us sucking me close to his skin in our standard spooning position.

"Can't fight gravity," he whispered and we drifted off into sleep.

ONE HUNDRED THIRTY-THREE

A week later Nanook brought me and my physical therapy implements to the airport and helped me up the magical steps. "Robert, my man. How goes it," he shook the pilot's hand. I swiped a slice of Brie off the galley counter on my way to the couch. Robert winked and said it was a shame Nanook was not traveling with Madame Butter Cow back to Montreal. "I brought you a list of properties with which you can bargain away your occurrences," Robert confided. I eavesdropped with half an ear and rearranged the cashmere blankets the unicorn had helpfully provided.

"Madame Butter Cow?" I raised an eyebrow at him and Robert informed me the staff had been informed of my surgical pronouncements and seen the iPhone photo of my medical chart. Nanook winked at me before giving me a last thorough smooch making me promise to be good *but not that good* he whispered. He patted my cheek and turned to leave. "Call you when I get there," I said, leaning out the door watching him walk down the steps toward his SUV. He blew me a kiss and shouted, "Love you, cow lady!", got in the car and drove away as I waved and waved and waved.

After we reached cruising altitude I began to settle in for a long nap. I gathered some cheese for the road on a china plate, meandered back toward the bedroom and opened the door to find a large black box sitting on the bed tied up with a blue satin bow. Cheese and mystery gifts? This fancy jet was a hit on my list. I set the plate on the side table and perused the box from all angles and saw there was a shiny black envelope tucked under the hand-tied bow.

Fancy schmancy indeed. I tapped a finger on my chin and pondered the contents of the box. Too small for a pony…too big for a puppy. Oh god I hope he didn't put a puppy in here. I jiggled it slightly and listened for the sound of movement within.

I heard nothing so I slid the satiny envelope from under the blue ribbon and opened it to find a creamy white card with the unicorn's initials embossed across the top in tiny black type. Jesus Christ, even the card was seriously legit. I shook my head in amusement and read the handwritten message.

Butterfly: Don't change for anyone. But if you feel like trying on a new pair of wings…enjoy.

In jubilation that it might be clothes I ripped open the box and found nothing. Nada. Zip. Zilch. I let out a loud groan of disappointment, flung open the door of the bedroom and found Robert standing there dangling a key from one finger. "Mr. Fourchette couldn't help himself, Madame Butter Cow," he laughed when I snatched it from his hand. I gave him a questioning look when he motioned to one of the walls along the side of the bedroom. "Still not getting it, Robert," I replied when he rolled his eyes. "I've heard about your lack of Magellan skills," he said over his shoulder. I remarked that the unicorn sure had saucy staff. He leaned down, put the key in a small hole drilled into the far side of the wall and slid open a huge door revealing behind it the Holy Grail of Awesomeness—an entire closet full of things in my exact size.

Joy joy joy! I gave Robert a huge hug and leaned out of the bedroom yelling for Andrea to get in the bedroom and tell me what looks good and bring that cheese plate. "Have zero fashion sense myself," I told the impeccably attired attendant as she sat on the side of the bed, "but I'm sure you'll tell me what goes with what."

By the time we landed in Montreal I'd discarded, among other things, a red leather skirt that squeezed me like a python, "I can't walk in this, it's inherently unsafe." Andrea assured me that anywhere I'd be wearing that outfit wouldn't require walking. "Maybe from the car to the door and back again but not much more than that," she confided. I agreed to put it in the Maybe Pile but firmly vetoed the stiletto heels that were set below the skirt's hanger. I saw her looking at the size and told her I'd turn a blind eye if her travel bag appeared suspiciously larger when we deplaned.

"Mum's the word, girlfriend," I slipped on a buttery soft pair of black leather thigh high wedge boots, "Oh my god these are fabulous." Andrea begged me to hate them, "They look horrible on you. Like a big fat whale. They should be discarded immediately."

"Har har, over my dead body," I checked myself out in the floor-to-ceiling mirror. "And they're wedges!" I informed her with glee that not only was I keeping them but that they were acceptable attire in large crowds because I felt reasonably certain I could move at a rapid pace toward an exit should disaster ensue. Andrea fell backward on the bed in disappointment that the buttery boots were not her destiny.

"Let's pick something out for me to wear when I get off the plane." We flung clothing all over the room like madwomen finally settling on a stretchy thick wool long sleeved boatneck black dress that barely reached my knees. "Very Jackie-O," Andrea whispered as she zipped it up over the slutty underwear that had been helpfully provided in another black box stacked in the corner of the closet. *To help you judge the fit of the clothing appropriately* the tiny card had innocently suggested. "And now the boots, now the boots," I jumped in the air with glee, "as long as you or Robert walk down the stairs in front of me in case I need stabilization." Andrea promised she'd protect me from myself and instructed me in proper walking techniques up and down the jet's center aisle.

We began final approach into Montreal around dinner time and when I began to tidy up the closet Andrea assured me she would take care of everything. I muttered under my breath that the reject pile was in the back left corner of the room and I hoped all those hideous designer clothes and shoes would go to a deservingly needy family. I saw her smiling and rubbing her hands together as I sailed out the door yelling over my shoulder that I'd photographed everything in the Definitely Keep Pile and called her a klepto.

"Ok, Robert, let's be gentle with the busted wing." I held out my arms.

He carefully helped me put on a dark crimson cashmere coat over the dress. "You look really nice," he confided as he adjusted the collar and brushed off the shoulders before slightly tugging down on the cuffs. He finally stepped back and declared I was fit for duty. "I appreciate the personal attention, kind sir," I replied with a curtsey. He leaned forward, kissed me on the cheek and whispered, "He's never smiled so much in his entire life and it's been our pleasure to have you aboard."

The steps flew open and down Robert went at a slow pace with me behind so I didn't fall on my face in front of the unicorn who was pacing anxiously at the bottom for my arrival. "Butterfly, you look amazing," he announced grandly, sweeping me into his arms and twirling us around. I thanked Robert for the flight, waved goodbye to Andrea who was peeking through one of the windows and took Alain's hand.

"Seriously? This is like Pretty Woman or something," I slipped down into a super fancy black Bugatti. "Except you're not a hooker," Alain said and snickered when I told him I'd be whatever he wanted if he'd let me drive this bitch. He snapped the glovebox shut when I started to rummage for the driver's manual and told me I could check out the specs tomorrow when he'd give me the keys and sit second fiddle playing tour guide around Montreal.

"I've missed you," he leaned over to kiss me before firing up the Formula One. "I've missed you too," I admitted to myself that his face did indeed make me very very happy. I whipped out my phone and loftily informed Alain I'd paid for a Canadian sim card so I didn't incur massive international charges during my visit. This was quickly followed by a loud *dammit* as I realized my text to Nanook in the USA would be on roaming.

Safely arrived. Zooming quickly to The Residence in a fancy spaceship. Text you later, love love I sent Nanook and disregarded the cost telling myself the exchange rate made the fee somewhat reasonable. Alain smiled in amusement and told me time and distance had not fixed my numbers problem before reaching over and lacing his fingers through mine. "I'm so glad you're here," he looked over at me and I saw it was true. I lifted his hand and kissed the back of it. "I'm glad I'm here too, with you," I replied with my face in full agreement.

Half an hour later we were in the middle of a rousing discussion of current trends in textile chemistry with the unicorn waxing poetic about some sort of revolutionary cotton treatment that made things feel like velvet *like velvet* he said, and waved his hands in the air until I politely pointed out we were about to run off the road. He apologized as he slowed and turned up a long driveway. On either side I saw a tall stone wall with giant carved ravens atop each post, a large iron gate swung back on either side of the entrance. Each raven sat wings folded with beaks turned down glaring intently at the pavement.

"Your pets are a little creepy," I whispered when we passed into the darkness of the heavily wooded drive. "The birds? They came with the house," Alain said and explained his mother's family had owned the property for years and named it Ravenswood. "Her maiden name was Corbeau, which means *raven* in French," he explained. I spotted a glow emanating over the top of an upcoming hill.

"Holy shit," I leaned forward in amazement when a fucking castle popped up out of nowhere sitting serenely in the middle of a rolling emerald lawn, "There's some seriously Faustian bargaining going on here." Alain laughed. "No, just serious business," he shrugged. "My father and my uncle run the company and, as you can see, they're quite good at it."

I glanced over and asked if he did anything at this enterprise besides turn cotton into velvet and he modestly admitted his mother had left him all her shares when she died, "So, added to the shares I got by virtue of being born, technically I'm the majority shareholder in ANF even though I never do shit." He pulled to a stop in front of the palace and hopped out as a serene gentleman levitated down the marble steps toward the car.

"Maxine, this is Henri," Alain opened my door before Henri could grasp the handle. Henri managed to rearrange his irritated face back into tranquility, offered me an arm and genteelly welcomed me to Ravenswood.

"Heard a lot about you, Henri," I smacked him on the arm and he looked rather startled. "Gonna have to get the whole story of this joint out of you sometime over a burger."

"I'm sure that can be arranged, Miss Maxine," he said faintly, glancing over his shoulder at Alain who shouted forward that he'd already informed Henri of my food restrictions.

"Goddamn it," I muttered to myself. Henri patted my hand and assured me in a whisper that all rules could be stretched for guests, "Perhaps during Mr. Fourchette's business hours there may arise an occasion requiring a tour of the kitchen." I told him we were going to be great friends. "I can feel it, Henri," I strode up the stairs, "kindred spirits, I tell you."

With Alain trailing behind and Henri at my side I entered a room that would have made Jesus Christ declare himself right at home. Soaring white walls arched up to meet a ceiling painted a brilliant shade of blue firmly holding up flowing chandeliers dripping glittering crystal. Small groupings of cream leather couches and upholstered chairs were carefully arranged on bright carpets thrown over a burnished wood floor. I saw what I was sure was a fucking Monet on a far wall strategically hung a safe and reasonable distance above a burning fireplace. This was just beyond ridiculous.

Henri silently disappeared through a doorway. "Your face is talking, butterfly," Alain whispered as two people stood up from a corner table. I cleared my throat and remembered you talking about flying, what it felt like to shoot through the air like a bullet before drifting through the clouds toward the ground. *Like touching the face of God* you'd told me with a distant look in your eye. I glanced up at Alain's perfectly symmetrical features. I suppose it didn't really matter if this was heaven or not since I'd already touched a hell of a lot more than this particular god's face.

The unicorn smiled down at me and bent toward my ear, "Ten minutes of introductions and then I'll need to confirm whether or not you found the other box I left in the closet." I assured him that I had but would appreciate the double check.

I tried desperately to look calm and collected and plastered a neutral smile on my face as the unicorn introduced me to his family. It was instantly clear where Alain got his fantastic genes when he waved a hand toward two incredibly gorgeous men wearing impeccably tailored business suits and said, "My father, Armand Fourchette, and my uncle, Michel Corbeau. Gentlemen, this is Maxine."

"It's so nice to meet you," my voice said brightly as I glanced away from the face of God, stuck out my arm and enthusiastically shook the hand of Satan.

ACKNOWLEDGMENTS

I'd like to thank my mommy for reading my book even though I know it probably made her feel dirty. And to my other mother who found great delight in the naughty parts. Kudos also to the rest of my friends and family who sighed inwardly with resignation when I said I wrote a book but quite convincingly told me they'd love to read it. To the rest of my acquaintances who don't know me all that well but read the book anyway—thanks for attempting to hide your embarrassment at knowing someone who writes smutty bodice rippers when I pass you on the docks.

And always always to M, who never once made me feel like my writing was a lark or treated reading it as a chore. Last but absolutely not least, to S, whose opinion I greatly respect even though he is a Republican.

9 780099 940 5833